Praise for Falguni Kothari

Author Falguni Kothari's exquisitely complex story of marriage, friendships, and unconventional choices reminds us that real love requires great courage."

—Jamie Beck, bestselling author of *When You Knew*

"A profound and deeply emotional twist on the classic love triangle…. Poignant and satisfying, *My Last Love Story* is ultimately the type of celebration of love and life that reminds us why we read in the first place."

—Jamie Brenner, *USA TODAY* bestselling author of *The Forever Summer*

"Kothari's well-written love story is a tearjerker with a twist. For fans of Cecelia Ahern's *PS, I Love You* and Jojo Moyes's *Me Before You*."

—*Library Journal* on *My Last Love Story*

"At once heartbreaking, delightful, and completely unexpected. A must-read!"

—Sonali Dev, award-winning author of *The Bollywood Bride*, on *My Last Love Story*

"Kothari's willingness to push boundaries and delve into the nature of love, her ability to explore emotion without letting it slide into mawkishness, and her resolute focus on staying true to the individual make this a book well worth reading."

—*Booklist* on *My Last Love Story*

"This culturally rich, emotionally wrenching novel takes everything typical about a love triangle and turns it upside down."

—*RT Book Reviews* on *My Last Love Story*

**Also available from Falguni Kothari
and Graydon House Books**

My Last Love Story

the
object
of your
affections

FALGUNI KOTHARI

GRAYDON
HOUSE

GRAYDON
HOUSE

Recycling programs
for this product may
not exist in your area.

ISBN-13: 978-1-525-82353-4

The Object of Your Affections

Copyright © 2019 by Phalguni Kothari

GraydonHouseBooks.com
BookClubbish.com

Printed in U.S.A.

In memory of my father,
for whom joy and life were synonyms.

the
object
of your
affections

"I'm selfish, impatient and a little insecure. I make mistakes, I am out of control and at times hard to handle. But if you can't handle me at my worst, then you sure as hell don't deserve me at my best."

~ MARILYN MONROE

PART ONE

From Concept
to
Conception

CHAPTER ONE

Paris

The things we did for love.

"Did you know that the global wedding industry is worth three hundred billion dollars? The US stake alone is fifty-five billion?" I waved my phone displaying the appalling data in front of my husband's face.

The stats—horror of horrors—had gotten worse in the two and a half years since our own wedding.

Neal, as usual, didn't share my outrage at mankind's follies, so he shrugged as if the matter was of no consequence to him—which it wasn't—and with infinite patience he brushed my hovering hand away from his face and continued to do unspeakable things to my mouth.

We were attending our fourth wedding of the year. Fourth! And, I'd been invited to half a dozen baby showers over the past ten months—two of which I hadn't been able to avoid. As if squealing over fake fluffy bunnies wasn't bad enough, such events were filled with busybodies who wanted to know when I was going to deliver some "good news" of my own. Seriously, the next person who asked me that question was going to end up in the city morgue. On an autopsy table. Exactly what was the correlation between pregnancy and "good" news, I had no clue. As if *not* being pregnant was "bad" news? *Aargh!* I could scream.

I'd bet that when Neal and I gave them our special news, they wouldn't care for it, either. Our families were going to go ballistic when they heard that we were considering gestational surrogacy when I was perfectly capable of bearing children.

Well, physically capable. Mentally and emotionally? The jury was still out.

Since Neal had more faith in our mothers than I did, he was welcome to explain it to them when it was time.

"Homo sapiens. Bat-shit crazy lot," I mumbled from the corner of my mouth, trying to keep my lips from moving as Neal worked on them, while going nearly cross-eyed as I recounted the zeroes that were peppered across the wedding industry article in *Reuters*. "And never satisfied with their lot in life." Maybe it wasn't *billions* but *millions*.

Nope. Eleven zeroes tacked behind the cardinal number three. My hope for humanity plummeted to earth. If that didn't prove beyond reasonable doubt that Man itself was the natural disaster devastating the world, I didn't know what did. What kind of senseless, overbred animal spends that kind of money on a fantasy ceremony solely created to propagate an even bigger fantasy, that of a perfect union and its glory-ever-after?

Don't get me wrong, I wasn't against the institution of marriage. I fully approved when compatible people tied the proverbial knot or cohabitated in a mutually beneficial fashion. Like my adoptive parents—the second set, as opposed to the first abominable pair—who'd been an excellent example of a square peg in a square hole kind of couple. Mr. and Mrs. Samuel and Lily Kahn had been harmoniously well matched on all fronts until the Judge's death separated them four years ago.

A second great example was my own marriage, which, though not of the square-peg-square-hole variety, was nothing short of marvelous—on most days. I'd married an amazing man who stroked my brain as vigorously as he stroked my emotions…and other interesting carbon-based assets. I'd absolutely hit the jackpot in the supportive husband sweepstakes. So, it behooved me not to screw things up and tread carefully with the surrogacy plans. *Do not dictate. Discuss.*

Neal and I had narrowed our list of potential surrogates down to two women and then reached a stalemate. Neal preferred Martha who came highly recommended by his close friends in California. I liked her too—our interviews had gone well—but she lived simply too far away. I couldn't even begin to imagine the scheduling and travel nightmare for both Neal and I every time we had to make it to a doctor's appointment. If it were up to me, I'd Skype in for the ultrasounds. But my husband wanted to actively experience the entire gestation since it would be the only one he'd—we'd—have. The other candidate was from Connecticut, just two hours away by car. We could see her every weekend if we wished. However, we hadn't clicked quite so well with her as we'd done with Martha. *Le sigh.* It would be so much easier if our surrogate lived in or around New York City, but compensated surrogacy was illegal in New York State thus not an option.

Well, no point in stressing over it right now as we weren't making any decisions this weekend. Better to put everything away and bask in my husband's masterful strokes instead.

Neal's touch was liquid cool on my face, arousing even when he didn't mean to stimulate, as it moved across my eyes and cheeks, brushed over my chin and throat. Though he didn't look it, the dear lad was dead on his feet—who wouldn't be after a sixteen-hour flight?—hence the one-word responses, grunts and shrugs at my attempts at marital repartee. Or, was he still brooding over our impasse about the surrogates?

Time-out, Counselor. Repetitive.

Either way, my husband was simply too sweet for not succumbing to a jet-lagged stupor after his whirlwind business trip to Asia. Instead, he'd rushed home from JFK, dumped his travel suiter, taken a hasty wake-up shower, loaded our wedding weekend bags in our metallic blue Tesla, picked me up from the courthouse only to dodge traffic for the next two hours on the I-87 North until we reached the vineyard in time for my college friend Lavinia's wedding rehearsal dinner. After all that dashing around, he was still on his feet taking care of my needs. Mind you, I had asked nicely for his help in putting on my war paint. Neal was just so much better at makeup than I was. So, yes, I would recommend the state of wedded bliss—or even unwedded togetherness—to anyone who'd had the good fortune to find herself (or himself) a Neal Singh Fraser.

In summation, I wasn't against marriage. What I objected to was the hoopla surrounding the ceremony. The wanton waste of time, money and resources in the planning and execution of said hoopla. How could anyone with an ounce of empathy justify spending such garish sums of money on a frivolous party when there were children starving in the world? When scribbling names in front of a marriage registrar in city hall—or the like—worked just as well as an elaborate exchange of vows in front of a priest or officiator? What difference did it make if two souls merged into one entity in front of four people or four hundred? The object of the exercise was to legalize a couple's commitment to each other, wasn't it? But no, some people weren't satisfied until a three-ring circus supplemented their nuptials, even when they knew, deep in their hearts, that sooner or later another even bigger circus would herald their uncoupling. Point in fact were the hundreds of embittered divorces and child custody battles filling up the dockets in family court. I'd been six when I was dragged into one such despicable battle between my first set of adoptive parents, so I knew firsthand what happened when love died and marriages fell apart. It was *that* kind of wanton waste I objected to. Not that I expected Lavinia and Juan's upstate New York lovefest to end in divorce. Or my own marriage. I didn't.

Oy vey. Did I?

Neal sidestepped to the vanity and abruptly I was nose-to-wall with the embossed yellow leaves on the maple-colored tiles. We were inelegantly squashed inside a bathroom that was tinier than my office at One Hogan Place—a space the formerly taciturn Lily Kahn had pronounced to be the size of a matchbox. As the crusaders of justice and the wielders of morality, assistant district attorneys deserved nicer offices, Lily had once emailed Manhattan's District Attorney, my boss, and cc'd me on it. My adoptive mother had morphed into one opinionated *meshugenah* since the Judge's death. It was another thing driving me batty these days—Lily's battiness.

Her growing obsession with horoscopes, incomprehensible at best, was getting to me. Last week, it had portended a change in my personal and professional life according to Lily. And today, I'd been asked to join a task force that was being set up between the DA's office and the United States Attorney's Office, jointly, to look into a human rights violation case. That took care of the professional change. The personal shift could either mean a bairn or a divorce trying to procure said bairn. Double *oy vey*.

After a lightning exchange of brushes, Neal repositioned himself before me. He settled one hand on top of my head to hold it steady, and with his right hand, he began to trace my full, shapeless lips into a discernible form. My mouth molded into a natural goldfish moue that needed special care. Indeed, my mouth and what came out of it warranted close attention. *Consider the offer carefully, laddie. Your freedom depends on it*, was my daily counsel to the perpetrators of crime. I'd do well to heed my own advice for the decisions I—oops, Neal and I— had to make.

"Quit fidgeting, hen. Nearly done. Close yer mouth. And no, don't frown so. And don't press yer lips together just yet," Neal instructed in his lilting Scottish brogue that never failed to capture my attention. More, the deep commanding baritone demanded immediate compliance.

I froze on the closed toilet seat and tilted my face up to look into my husband's loch-blue eyes. Fringed with thick sooty lashes, those eyes combined with his voice produced goose-flesh all over my skin even though he didn't mean to stimulate me. Was it any wonder then that I'd given in to Neal's mad vision of our own wedding? I still felt ill whenever I recalled—fondly, mostly fondly—the sheer wantonness of our three-day festivities. The truth was that I found it impossible to say no to this man when he was in the mood to charm.

"Now press."

I pressed my lips together and tasted strawberries as Neal plied his expertise on shaping them. God! But I loved him—all six feet two inches and one eighty-eight pounds of Scottish-Indian stubbornness. I loved being married to him. And yes, I'd loved getting married to him, exchanging vows and rings and kisses under the ballroom chandelier of his family's residential castle in Scotland. Our wedding might have been a self-indulgent waste of resources but it had come from a place of love and pride, and no one was in debt because of it. We'd made promises to each other in front of all the people who'd mattered to us—correction, everyone except the two people I'd loved and counted on the most in the world back then had blessed our union. My perfect day of joy would be forever tainted due to their absence.

At least the Judge had had a legitimate excuse for missing my wedding, being dead and all. But my best friend and maid of honor, Naira, had bowed out at the last minute. Her husband's business had been in trouble. Kaivan the Criminal had gotten his comeuppance the Indian media had claimed, and still Naira had stuck by him like a good little wife. Her choice had broken us for a while—I was a prosecutor, for God's sake, I couldn't stand by criminals. And then he'd died.

Things were slightly better between us now. We messaged each other off and on, and I mostly understood her stance, her choices—especially now that I knew just how much I would do or endure for Neal. But I still felt acid well up inside me when I remembered just how awful I'd felt on my wedding day. How desperately alone.

Neal cocked an eyebrow at me, divining my mood dips as expertly as he was reshaping my lips. "Are ye practicing your apology to her in your mind, then? Is that why yer nervous?"

My back and shoulders went taut. "Why should I apologize? She's the one who got all bent out of shape because I pointed out the truth."

"And I suppose ye would let people get away with bad-mouthing me to yer face, aye?"

"If it was the truth," I began but stopped when Neal's second brow joined its twin high on his forehead. Another stalemate. I let my shoulders droop. "Fine. I'll be...nice." I didn't do apologies. Mainly because I didn't make mistakes or speak out of turn.

Neal was right though. I *was* nervous about meeting Naira. It had been four years since we'd seen each other in person. Two days ago, I'd received a message from her after weeks of iMessage silence: Hopping on a plane to NY. See you at Lavinia's wedding.

What the hell kind of message was that?

"Stupid weddings." I pressed my phone to my stomach, willing the awfulness to abate. I was a mess at weddings— about weddings. I was better at marriage.

Because it served no purpose to get upset about the past or the state of the world, I made a concerted effort to shut a mental door on all my current grievances pertaining to weddings, best friends, starving children—any children, for that matter—and the task force. All that could wait until Monday. This wedding would not.

Sexy times with my amazing man should not.

Said amazing man skimmed a long finger down my nose and tapped its slightly upturned tip—yup, I'd been born disdaining the world—as he scrutinized my face.

"Ye look bonny. Now get dressed so I can start on yer hands." He'd offered to paint henna designs on my hands.

Neal was a globally coveted jewelry designer, a metal artiste and an honest-to-goodness lord—he was fourth in line to a Scottish baronage—and as such an expert on beautiful things and luxury lifestyle. He pulled me to my feet and nudged me out of the miniscule bathroom to get on with getting dressed. I stopped in the doorway to thank him with a kiss but he'd already turned to face the mirrored vanity and was putting my makeup bag to rights.

My pout swelled into a laugh as I watched my husband recap bottles of glitter and gold, click-shut eye shadow palettes, wipe faux-hair brushes with tissue and pack each one of the items into their designated pockets in my cosmetic bag with ferocious care. For a man who dabbled in paint, pencil shavings and liquid metals for a living, Neal did not handle mess well. He tolerated my slovenliness without batting an eye though, and it was one of the million things I loved about him. One of the zillion things I hoped would never change between us.

I hugged him from behind, pressing a kiss on the nape of his neck, careful not to mess up the fashion-plate paint job he'd done on my face, complete with intricate swirls of a *bindi* design in the middle of my forehead. It shone like a piece of jewelry embedded into my skin. The women at Lavinia's three-ring circus were going to hate me—they always did when Neal did my makeup.

My thank-you left a perfect bow-shaped pink kiss on his bare sandalwood-and-verbena-scented skin.

"There now, my gorgeous-ship. You've been branded as mine like the Fraser sheep on your family's farms." I wasn't a possessive person by nature, but with Neal all bets were off. I continuously did things against my better judgment with Neal, for Neal.

We were going to have a bairn together! If that didn't explain how weird my life had become with him, I didn't know what did.

Amused, his gorgeous-ship twisted around to shoot me a smug grin. Shirtless and barefoot, he still managed to look sophisticated and sexy. He was turning me on, probably why his smugness didn't irritate me. And gauging from the height of the tent in his pants, my lingerie-clad state was affecting him too.

Neal had been away at the Hong Kong gem and jewelry trade fair for the past week and we hadn't even hugged properly when he'd picked me up from work this afternoon, much less ravaged each other like we usually did after one of his business trips. And, today was our third engagement anniversary. It was our marital duty to put everything aside and celebrate with monkey sex.

"Fuck henna hands and wedding rehearsals. Let's fuck." I slid my hands up his hair-roughened chest to his shoulders, my intent as clear as the day was bright.

Third engagement anniversary. We'd been together for more than three years already. It baffled me that we'd lasted this long, considering we'd come together in an explosion of instinct and not intellect. After a mere six weeks of dating, Neal had impulsively suggested we get hitched on the night I'd taken the bar and in my post-exam fugue state I'd grunted, "Why not?"

I'd changed my mind the next morning, after guzzling down a gallon of coffee and sense. And lost them marbles again, a couple of months later, when I'd been giddy with excitement that I'd passed the bar on my first try. We were married within a head-spinning six months of my reproposal. Best impulsive decision of our lives.

Neal's hands came to rest on my hips. "Didn't ye say this weekend is dedicated to yer college friends?"

"Doesn't mean I need to be joined at the hip with them. However, you and I can be." I nudged his hips with mine. "We'll claim that you were jet-lagged and I was exhausted. Unless, you have your heart set on spending the night flirting with my friends?" I tweaked his ear playfully, confident of his answer.

"Dally with strangers or shag my wife? Now that's an impossible choice." Neal's lips kicked up in a sexy grin as he took the phone from my hand and set it aside. He freed my hair from the clip holding it up and out of my face. My bra was next, unhooked and tossed over his shoulder. Released from their lacy cage, my boobs thanked him by perking right up.

I giggled when he swung me up in his arms, and tension drained from my body as he carried me into the barn-style bedroom only slightly larger than the bathroom. It felt roomier though, as evening light poured in through the casement windows that showcased the lovely Hudson Valley and its river. The vegetation was slowly turning to gold outside. Unlike Manhattan, where the trees had only just begun to blush. Fall in New York was breathtaking. The vivid, fiery colors; the perfect weather—bright and crisp and spicy with the taste of pumpkin lattes and sangrias on your tongue. How could I have resisted falling for Neal in New York in the fall?

Careful not to jostle the outfit and accessories I'd laid out in one corner, Neal lowered me to the double bed. The coverlet was cool but its textured roughness felt surprisingly good against my skin. I sighed as pleasure spiked and washed away the last of my anxiety and irritation.

I pushed down my panties and kicked them off as Neal divested himself of his dress pants. We were naked in seconds, and then he was on top of me, crushing me with his large, warm body, my mouth with his. I bowed up and moaned as he slid into me, flesh to flesh, stretching me. Every nerve inside my body snapped like an electric charge. We'd starved for each other for a week, been separate entities for seven fricking days. We didn't need priming. We needed to devastate. Quick. Desperate. Now! Climax came quickly for both of us.

Spent, we lay there, breathing hard in the aftermath, hugging, laughing, still joined and shuddering with aftershocks. Perhaps a little disappointed that it was over so quickly.

Neal pushed up on one arm, but he didn't get off me. I didn't want him to. Not yet. He began to rain kisses on my face, nipping my jaw, teasing my ear, licking my collarbone.

"Better?" he asked, his voice gruff with satisfaction, his face ruddy with love. The scar on his chin, the one he'd gotten in a ski accident years ago, before I knew him, was stark white against the dark red skin where I'd sucked. The rest of him glistened and I felt my pores open too. His blue-blue eyes watched me with humor and a good dose of fatigue. *He* was the one tired and he was asking whether *I* was feeling better. Because he knew Naira's text had upset me.

Love gushed through me, quicker and stronger than my climax. I was glad I'd taken the time to be with my man, to take care of him. I ran a hand through the jet-black thickness of his hair, which tended to curl just above his shoulder. In three and a half years, he'd become as familiar to me as my own face. Every freckle, every scar, every hair follicle, so very dear. I'd missed him so much this past week, especially with everything that was happening at work. With Naira. With the surrogacy. He was always so encouraging and supportive. He loved me. It was such a wonder that he loved me at all, much less when I was a witch to him.

"I lo… ACK!" I began in a whisper and ended up shrieking as the room phone screeched into existence. My heart, beeping with affection a second ago, slammed against my chest with the impact of a judge's gavel. Wildly, my eyes sought out the culprit—a quirky 1980s-style phone on the nightstand that ought to be in a museum, certainly not for use anymore.

"That is possibly— No! That sound is several decibels worse than the FDNY sirens. *Gah!* It's the sound the hounds of hell would make if they'd been forced to skip dinner."

Neal stretched out an arm to reach the nightstand—he didn't have to stretch far—and answered the phone with a brisk "Hullo!" that belied the laughter rippling through his body. Obviously, he didn't think anyone had deprived Satan's hounds of their kibble. With a wink and an "Och, aye. Here she is," he pressed the phone's receiver to my ear.

It was Karen, Lavinia's pregnant maid of honor. It figured.

"Paris! Is your cell phone on silent? I've called and called and left a dozen messages. Are you okay? Not about to pass out for the night, are you? Because Lavinia will kill you if you do. Are you ready to partay? We're all already here."

Yup. I was in hell. In college, I'd run myself ragged trying to graduate summa cum laude in journalism and philosophy with a minor in Latin while making it my personal mission not to miss a single night of partying. Every month like clock-work, I'd collapsed from sheer exhaustion, sometimes passing out right in the middle of whatever I was doing, and would sleep for two days straight. What did it say about me that my friends didn't think I'd matured since then?

"We'll be down in fifteen minutes," I said coolly. Karen disconnected the phone without another word, apparently satisfied that I was awake and lucid.

I passed the receiver back to Neal. "I should've said I had work to finish tonight. Or, you could have brought back a dis-ease from Asia. Yes! We could both be infected by something sinister and avian right now. Something nasty and contagious. Damn it! I've been trained to think on my feet. Why didn't I think of it?" I wondered if it was too late to try the excuse.

Neal laughed heartily—I often amused him with hyperbole—sending our joined bodies aquiver again. Now, I was truly sorry I hadn't thought of an excuse. I needed more than that quickie with him. But I also wanted this night with my friends. It had taken seven years for us—all of us, includ-ing Naira—to come together since graduation. It was like a homecoming.

I also couldn't let Lavinia down. Not for her wedding.

"Ye can't ditch the lass. She came to our wedding and clocked in full attendance."

If I'd ever been in doubt that my husband could read my mind, those words cleared it up. But I wasn't programmed to give in without a fight—the reason I was a damned good prosecutor.

"The only reason Lavinia came to our wedding was because you paid the air and hotel fare for my friends and family. And arranged for corporate discounts at various hotels for those interested in a Scottish holiday *after* the wedding. Why wouldn't she have come?"

He'd offered Naira the same red-carpet arrangement and she'd still not come. *Ugh. Don't rehash the past. It's done. Finished.*

"Paris." My name didn't sound nice as an admonishment. Sometimes, I disappointed him with my quick criticisms and judgments.

"I didn't mean it negatively. But fine. I take it back." Arguing simply for the sake of having the last word never served any purpose. "I love you to the moon and back. You know that, right?" I took his face between my hands and kissed his mouth, quick and wet. An apology. I kissed him again and again worth several apologies. "Your eyes are red. If you're tired, I can go by myself."

The nonred part of his eyeballs twinkled green and blue and purple in the slanted sunlight. What did I tell you? Wicked charmer. "I slept on the plane. I'm fine for a bit. But, I'll probably need to crash after meeting yer esteemed friend."

He planted a soft kiss on my shoulder, then taking care not to hurt me, he rolled off and sat up on the bed. Even so, my body curved in response to his movement and I gasped as grief welled up inside me. No matter how many times we came together and drew apart, or how, in anticipation of the disengagement, I readied my body for separation, clenching it tight, or scolded my heart to behave itself, I still felt hollow when he left me. Like he'd abandoned me. Cast me out. Rejected me. Have I mentioned I have issues? Obviously, we couldn't stay joined together like a pair of incestuous conjoined twins forever, but my body didn't seem to understand it. Knowing this, knowing me, loving me, Neal never withdrew without a heads-up like that kiss on my shoulder.

We resumed our dress-up dance then, swirling around the room like a pair of professional ballroom dancers. Mid-October temperatures had cooled the room even without air-conditioning and the sweat dried off our bodies quickly. Deodorant took care of the rest. I rice-papered my face, and it was enough to repair my makeup. Last, I slipped a pair of emerald-cut diamond earrings onto my earlobes while checking my appearance in the mirror above the TV unit.

Neal stood behind me, adjusting his tie. His dark suit complemented my copper-and-blue brocade jacket that I wore over a pale blue summer dress.

We were always a study in contrasts, whether in or out of clothes. I was tan to his fair, voluptuous to his lean; a frugal vote to his extravagance. His mixed-race heritage and my evidently South Asian DNA had blessed us with bold looks and hardy genes. I liked how we fit—not totally in sync but complementary like the set of decorative vases on the console table by the TV. I adored who we were, together and separately. I valued the person I'd become from loving him.

"Here, let me help." Neal took the two-inch thick smaragdine diamond bracelet from my hand. It wasn't hard to clasp shut, even one-handed, but my mind had been elsewhere and I'd missed the clasp's opening twice now.

"The henna would've flattered it, but I enjoyed these hands

on me better," he said gruffly, closing the bracelet around my wrist. Then he kissed the back of my hand.

The bracelet was a Sotheby's certified Neal Singh Fraser classic. He'd given it to me on our first wedding anniversary. I'd accepted it reluctantly, not wishing to hurt his feelings. Make no mistake, I loved my bracelet. Took delight in it more because Neal had made it himself. Not just designed it or hunted the planet for the perfect stones to set in it, but also fashioned it with his own hands like an old-fashioned goldsmith and not with the help of machines or hired artisans. I couldn't imagine how he'd done it or how long it had taken him to cast and shape and finesse the train of interlinked pink-gold rings. Each ring in turn was alternatively pavé set in smaragdine—Neal's brand's signature emerald green color—and white diamonds. I marveled at his talent. I did. But owning expensive pieces of jewelry did not sit well with me no matter the sentiment attached to it. It was a frivolous indulgence just like a circus wedding. And I disapproved of it.

It wasn't the first piece of jewelry Neal had given me but it had become the last. Maybe that was why I was partial to it. A few weeks after our anniversary, I'd told him that such presents made me feel uncomfortable instead of happy, and I couldn't enjoy them as he meant me to. He'd stopped giving me expensive trinkets after that. Instead, he planned special things for us to do on our special days in addition to donating large sums of money to Right is Might—our NGO of choice and the reason we were together.

Neal understood my soul. He cared about the betterment of humanity. He might not be as politically driven as I was, but he cared. And that was another one of the zillion things that made him amazing.

"Henna my hands tomorrow," I said by way of compromise. My husband liked to pretty me up, and I indulged him when I could. It was what marriage was about, wasn't it? Knowing each other's peccadilloes and loving that person anyway? Working out a compromise where one could? Like I'd compromised my stance about not ever having children, and he had compromised his by having only one, and with a surrogate.

Then, before I got too analytical or anxious again, and before Karen sent out a search party for us, I took my husband's hand and dragged him down to the wedding rehearsal dinner, where unsurprisingly Naira didn't show. My best friend had become adept at breaking her word.

"No amount of rehearsing prepares you for marriage," I told Lavinia later that night as part of my bridesmaid's duties. "You have to wing it just like you do everything else in life."

How I was going to wing being a mother though, I had no fucking idea.

CHAPTER TWO

Naira

Hope glittered like morning dew across the lawn of Lavinia's wedding venue. Crisp and cool, it soaked into my shoes, tugged at the hem of my peach-and-gold tissue sari as I jettisoned out of the taxi on a patch of green at the edge of a full parking lot. Hope was the only emotion I clung to these days. Hope, and the desperate desire not to quit.

I was late for Lavinia's wedding. Not the fashionable make-an-entrance sort of late, but Indian Standard Time–late— meaning monstrously late. I'd be lucky to catch the tail end of the wedding ceremony.

I'd overslept. In fact, I'd slept for thirty-six hours straight, and that was after zoning out for most of my sixteen-hour Mumbai to New York direct flight. I felt wonderfully rested. The grogginess in my bones, the listlessness of mind that had debilitated me of late was gone. The fruits of a deep, dreamless sleep—or of not being under my family's watchful thumb?

I started forward, the world sparkling before me. Bright white tents rose along the length of a converted barn to the right, and fields of grapevines dotted with trees strung with mirrored balls and fairy lights rolled for miles to the back and the left. The sun burned above it all, saturating the land with its golden joy. There was a paddock on top of a rolling hill beyond the parking lot and a group of dapper wedding guests were gathered there, clicking selfies and groupies with a pair of tuxedoed cowboys on horseback. Rather adventurous guests, I thought. Also, I'd missed the ceremony if people were spreading out and taking photographs. Or, maybe not. These days clicking the perfect selfie was more important than watching the main event itself.

I increased my pace, meandering through a garden-like area toward an enormous tent from which a sizable number of guests poured out, some with heaped plates and some without. More guests were clustered around the garden, nibbling on hors d'oeuvres or sipping bubbly or cappuccinos. Everyone was chattering animatedly as if discussing something magical. Yup. I'd definitely missed the ceremony.

I couldn't believe I'd gone to sleep on Thursday night— I'd landed at JFK only that afternoon—and woken up straight on Saturday morning, completely missing Lavinia's rehearsal dinner. I hadn't slept through the night in more than three years, let alone through two nights and a day. I hadn't even woken up for food, and only once to use the bathroom. I hadn't heard my phone vibrate at all. Shocking, when every sound it had made for three years had affected me on a visceral level. I'd finally woken up this morning to a gazillion missed calls and texts, mainly from my mother and mother-in-law—everything from "Are you ill?" to "Have you been kidnapped?" I'd replied that I was fine and getting ready for the wedding. But I hadn't called them back. I didn't want to speak to them. Not yet. I didn't want to get sucked back into the quicksand of my problems. I didn't want to think about my life. I needed a break. I wanted one month to myself. One week. Just one day. To be free. And I wanted to spend that time salvaging my college friendships and my sanity.

Trepidation knotted in my belly along with hope and desperation. I didn't know what kind of reception was in store for me. It would be awkward, of course. I'd disconnected with most of my college friends after graduation some seven-odd years ago. Not Lavinia and Paris, but the rest. In my defense, it was difficult to stay in touch when you lived half a world away. *Difficult but not impossible*, my conscience pointed out evilly. I ignored it.

The truth was my life in Mumbai had consumed me, kept me busy with work and domesticity, with travel, the social scene and, eventually, the problems. And my friends had grown busy in their own lives in the US and wherever else they'd settled after college. But I needed my friends now. I needed some positive connection to this world.

Stop beating around the bush, Naira. Admit that you need Paris Jaya Kahn's unique brand of tough love to help you sort out the mess you've made of your life.

Paris would call a spade a spade and wouldn't allow me to do any less. I didn't need to be mollycoddled or petted or protected or lied to. I needed someone to tell me to stand up and take control of my life, choose my own path and destiny, as no doubt Paris would. The reunion depended entirely on her though, and whether or not she still considered us friends. The last time we'd met in person was nearly four years ago when she'd been sitting shivah for her father. The last time we'd spoken on the phone was the week of her wedding two and a half years ago. We'd fought. Brutally. Since then, we'd communicated strictly via texts and emails, coldly exchanging no more than a birthday greeting or condolence message, and recently through likes, LOLs and applicable emojis on each other's social media.

I'd sent her a brief text just before boarding the plane, so she knew I was coming, was prepared. Perhaps I should have called? But my plan had been so last-minute. And I'd thought it would be easier to meet her with everyone in one fell swoop amid the happy buffer of a wedding celebration. Then, depending on the vibe, I'd meet my friends one-on-one and reestablish rapport. But now, I wasn't so sure. I'd chosen to ignore Paris's black-or-white nature. You were either loyal or you weren't a friend. You were either good or bad, nothing in between. She'd always had strong opinions and a rigid moral compass. She'd never approve of the choices I'd made in the past three years. She hadn't approved of the ones I'd made before, either. My twanging nerves weren't unjustified.

Pieces of gravel began to slip into my open-toed pumps, making me wince, and I hobbled toward a nearby bench to sit and take them out lest the sharp edges tear into my skin. I didn't have time for medical emergencies. I had an agenda in New York and only a limited amount of time to fulfill it before suspicions arose.

Some of the other women were having similar trouble with the gravel, and were either leaning on their partners, shaking out their shoes, or had found a place to tidy up like me. I exchanged smiles with the salt-and-pepper-haired lady sharing my bench.

"It was a beautiful ceremony, wasn't it? Everyone is wearing such lovely clothes." She roved an appreciative eye over my bedecked self. "Are you family or one of the bridesmaids?"

Given my unmistakable South Asian appearance and attire,

complete with bangles and *bindi*, the lady's assumptions were entirely logical. Lavinia had asked me to be her bridesmaid and to wear something peach today. She'd invited me to be a part of the ceremony and I'd let her down.

Speaking of logic, it struck me that I shouldn't presume things about Paris. If I'd changed in the last few years, she would have too. Maybe she'd softened her stance on life the way I'd hardened mine. After all, Paris had gone and done the unthinkable. She'd allowed herself to be domesticated.

"Bridesmaid. Lavinia and I were in NYU together," I explained to my bench partner, swallowing the laugh that always bubbled up whenever I thought of Paris as a wife. Sloppy, stubborn, commitment-averse Paris—a socialist to boot—had married a Scottish-Indian gemstone baron. She'd married one of the high-flying Singh Frasers. I couldn't get over it.

Regret chased my amusement at the thought of Paris's nuptials. I hadn't been able to go.

My stomach tightened. I didn't have time for regrets, either.

Not to be rude, I exchanged a trickle of small talk with the lady—Penny—as we resumed our walk up the path. Penny, it seemed, was Juan's cousin from his mother's side, older by two decades so more like an aunt. She gushed over the lively nontraditional and nondenominational ceremony and the venue and how, unlike her initial apprehensions, the two-hour train ride in from New York City hadn't been all that taxing.

I agreed that the commute to the vineyard was easy. Several times during my years at NYU, I'd ridden up hereabouts with friends to go apple picking or hiking or skiing, traveling via different and invariably the cheapest modes of transportation available to students. Taking the Metro-North from Grand Central to Poughkeepsie was so much easier than having to endure the bumpy five-hour plus bus ride from Times Square or Penn Station.

I hadn't taken the train this time, but a private taxi. I'd been so late, and I couldn't have managed running through the station and hopping on and off a train in a sari.

Penny and I parted ways inside the largest tent where she made her way to one of the buffet lines in the corners. People were scattered across a thick array of lilac-bowed chairs that swept around a staged arbor decorated with blush pink-and-peach peonies. The groom was on the stage, laughing and taking photos with his mates. I didn't see Lavinia or any of our mutual friends there.

Lavinia's parents stood just off the stage surrounded by well-wishers. I began to make my way to them, to offer my congratulations and ask where Lavinia was. I took two steps and abruptly stopped as a couple of things occurred to me. If I asked about Lavinia's whereabouts, they'd know I'd only just arrived. They'd crack a joke or two about the tardiness of Indians from India. Worse, what if they snubbed me?

Lavinia's parents were from Mumbai. They knew about my circumstances. The whole bloody country knew.

Heat shot through my belly as I imagined their looks of sympathy and censure. The shaking heads. The downturned mouths. The disgust. The sneers. Damn it. I shouldn't have come. I wasn't ready to show my face in public.

Why had I come? What was I trying to prove and to whom? Had I seriously thought being a spectacle in New York would be less ugly than it had been in Mumbai? That I'd magically wrap New York's give-a-damn veneer around me like six yards of courage in a single day?

I turned on my heel, blindly seeking an exit. When was the next train to Grand Central? I fumbled with my clutch, pulled out my phone and brought up the train schedule. I needed to call the taxi back or find another one. Right this minute, I'd even settle for a bareback gallop to the station on one of those horses in the paddock.

In my rush to flee, I nearly sent a gigantic urn filled with calla lilies and lilacs flying into a group of elderly aunties waiting in the food line. They looked at me as if I'd lost my mind. They weren't entirely wrong.

"Are you all right, honey? You look a little peaked. Put some food in your belly," one of them said helpfully. "Or are you one of those who only lives on cheese?"

"Not cheese, Mina. Grapes. My granddaughter only eats ten grapes a meal."

I backed away, thanking them and apologizing profusely, while they continued to jabber among themselves about the idiocies of the very young. Then, I simply sagged against the first wall I came across. It took everything I had not to slide to the floor and curl up like a petrified worm.

Be strong. You've taken the first step. You're in New York. Don't panic now.

I fixed a glare at a hanging wooden arrow sign pointing the way to the bar and the bathroom. I breathed in, debated my next move, breathed out and scolded myself. Once again, I had choices to make: imbibe a shot of Dutch courage or throw up? Stay or go? Now or never? As my panic ebbed, I began to notice other things. The rough wooden wall against my back. The scarcity of people around me. Good. No one had witnessed my idiotic behavior except the aunties. I headed for the bathroom before I got splinters in my clothes or skin. I'd freshen up and try this again—being around people.

The tent transitioned into the barn hotel through a long rustic hallway. Stag heads with oversize antlers leaped out of the walls, and thick leathery furniture had been placed in strategic alcoves along the corridor. The space was a stark contrast from the fairy-tale-like wonderland of the tent or the earthiness of the valley outside. Thick pillars of candles burned all over the vaulted room—rooms, plural, as the corridor led to a narrower lounging area, which opened to a furnished great room decked out in more lavender-scented candles, flowery decorations and an enormous antler-style chandelier swinging from the open-beamed rafters. A fire roared inside a huge hearth, the flames leaping high enough to lick the bear head on the wall above it.

My panic attack had completely faded from the sheer shock and growing anger I felt on behalf of the deer and bear heads looking down on me. Those poor animals. To be hunted, exposed, victimized like that. I knew exactly how they'd felt before their heads had been lopped off.

So many people had wanted Kaivan's head on a spike for what he'd done to them—correction, what their greed had allowed him to do to them. Now those same people had turned their spiteful eyes on my head.

I wondered, yet again, if it was my brother-in-law, Vinay Singhal, poisoning everyone's minds and leading the hunt. Either way, if I didn't want to end up as a taxidermy metaphor, then I had to convince Paris to help me. I had to get over my bad, her mad and everything in between and patch us up. And to do that, I had to stay and see Lavinia's reception through. Cowardice was a luxury I couldn't afford. Neither was pride.

The restrooms were burrowed beneath the grand staircase in the great room. I joined the queue of women waiting to use the facilities. I would not flee. I would stand and face the music—even the ghastly techno music Paris listened to—without cringing or crying. I was going to tell her my pathetic story—well, most of it—and she was going to listen.

Through some lovely ladies inside the restrooms, I found out that the bride was taking pictures in the tent at the back of the barn. So, there I went, pumped up with renewed determination.

I found them immediately. It was impossible to miss the fourteen or so swirls of peach gliding and twirling across the dance floor with *diyas* in their hennaed hands. They weren't only taking bridal photos for posterity; Lavinia and her bridesmaids were doing a last-minute dance practice before the reception. It warmed my heart that Lavinia had asked me to wear peach today. It made me weepy. I had one good friend in this city still.

Paris had been the maid of honor at my wedding even though traditional Indian weddings didn't require one. But Paris had declined to be Lavinia's MoH, citing crazy work hours as an excuse. Now that I could believe as Paris's work ethic was as immovable as Mount Everest.

My first glimpse of Paris confirmed my suspicions that she'd changed since our last meeting. It was a shock to see her even though I'd seen photos and videos of her life on Facebook. Gone was the unkempt Paris with the cropped hairdo and aggressively black wardrobe. The woman across the room wasn't just beautiful—Paris could never be something as benign as *beautiful*—she was stunning in peach silk *sharara*-style pants and a halter-neck blouse made of a frothy gauzy fabric that had been stitched together in clean lines. No doubt her fashionable yet frill-free outfit had been designed by Helen Pal, Paris's fashion designer sister-in-law. Well-groomed, her hair shimmered halfway down her back in a long straight line. Her face glowed with happiness, her makeup was subtle and highlighted her best features. And, would wonders never cease, was that a hand-painted *bindi* on her forehead? Like the ones models painted on for fashion shows?

Hadn't I known it? I felt like clicking my heels and yodeling. I'd assured Paris she'd stop traffic if she just bothered to groom herself. She hadn't been interested before. Or rather, she hadn't cared about outward beauty, always rebuffing my attempts to lure her into an afternoon of shopping and salon treatments. She'd dissed my battles with beautification as frivolous nonsense and a complete waste of valuable time.

My heart lifted when she smiled at Lavinia and said something that was no doubt smart and sarcastic. This was Paris. Sarcasm was a given. Years rolled away and my cheeks began to hurt from grinning. They hurt also from trying not to cry.

I'd missed her. Unbearably. Why had I stayed away for so long? I started toward her. There were so many things I had to tell her. So many gaps we needed to fill. Then someone screamed my name and I jolted to a stop. I was only a dozen feet away from my bestest friend.

Paris whirled, her eyes darting across the tent, zeroing in on my face. Her mouth formed an O of surprise before she snapped it shut. Her hands, red and gold with faux henna designs, were cupped in front of her body as if she was begging for alms. A tiny flame shook inside the *diya* she held, lighting up her face in a soft, golden glow.

The *diya* brought another tidal wave of NYU memories to mind. We'd used *diyas* as props in our intercollegiate dance-offs. Only those *diyas* had been made of battery-operated plastic, not the real deal like these ones.

Before I could take another step, I was surrounded by our friends. Lavinia launched herself at me after setting her *diya* down on a table, the flame dancing madly as though sensing our excitement. I hugged her tight and wished her all the happiness in the world, abjectly apologizing for my tardiness. I was a bad friend.

"It doesn't matter. You're here now," she said, happy tears filling her eyes.

Nothing could mar a bride's happiness on her wedding day. Not ill-timed friends or even absent ones.

God, Paris, I'm sorry. I'm so very sorry for not being there for you on your wedding day.

I hugged Aria and Olga and Stacey and Karen, who was huge and pregnant and looking very much like a fertility goddess in a one-shouldered blush pink Grecian-style gown. I hadn't known—hadn't expected that one of my friends could be pregnant. I should have though, as we were all crossing into our thirties on our next birthdays.

I couldn't quite control the dash of envy I felt at Karen's fecundity even while I drowned in sheer joy. We all jostled for space, bouncing madly, uncaring of the spectacle we made of ourselves. I even embraced a couple of women I didn't know and was introduced to between the hugs and screams. We were attracting attention with our hysteria; people were staring at us. But, for once, I was beyond embarrassment. I had nothing to feel ashamed about here, nothing to be careful about. Everyone was shouting and laughing and hurling questions at me. I felt welcomed and wanted. I felt as if I'd come home.

I looked for Paris in the mayhem. She stood stiffly only a dozen feet away. Shock had melted from her face, coolness taking its place like ice sheets glazing over stone. Maybe there was even a sliver of disgust in her eyes.

Stop being a fucking doormat. You're better than that, she'd hurled at me over the phone when I'd called to tell her I wasn't coming to her wedding. She hadn't believed me when I'd said the decision was mine.

I swallowed the hurt that had taken up residence in my throat since that conversation. I wanted us to—*needed* us to forgive each other for our unkind words. Tears wet my lashes but I didn't blink. I wouldn't look away. Couldn't.

"Hi," I whispered, hoping she wouldn't make a scene. Yet, I braced for attack.

Paris broke eye contact and shot a wry look at Lavinia whose face shone with an *I told you so* expression. Nothing should mar a bride's happiness on her wedding day.

I really hoped we wouldn't have our showdown here. Our friends grew quiet around us, waiting for the inevitable explosion. Paris had a volatile temperament and I was no meek mouse—or I hadn't been before.

I took a step forward, then another. Paris didn't move. My rib cage hurt when I released the breath I'd been holding. She wasn't leaving. That was…good. I wanted to run to her. Hug her, hard. Apologize to her and yell at her at the same time for…everything.

Then suddenly out of nowhere, a bunch of girls ran between us, giggling and shouting. I stepped back automatically. One of them had a man's shoe in her hands. The groom's shoe.

I grinned, recognizing the *joota chupai*—a custom in which the bride's sisters hid the groom's shoes, then made him buy them back. Ostensibly, to teach the groom the art of marital negotiation before he left the *mandap* or wedding site. Kaivan had taken my older sister, Sarika, and her family to the Maldives as his shoe-release remuneration. Sarika's husband, Vinay, had given me money and that too only after I'd reminded him, several times, that he owed me. My smile died. Like how he repeatedly reminded me of what Kaivan and I owed him now.

A gang of boys thundered past us to catch the girls and snatch the shoe back. It seemed Juan's family had been apprised of this fun but mercenary little Indian wedding custom.

I looked back at Paris, wondering what fun customs had been part of her Jewish-Scottish-Indian wedding, again feeling awful that I hadn't been there to see it.

Everything happened in slo-mo next. Paris did a double take as a boy headed straight for her. He was looking over his shoulder, grinning with the impudence of youth. She dodged a head-on collision by swirling out of his way as he dashed past her. As she turned, her stole slid off her shoulder, falling to the floor in a graceful heap. She reached for it in reflex. The flaming *diya* in her other hand tilted as she bent low. Oil spilled from the earthen cup, splashing the hem of her beautiful *lehenga* pant. Oops. It was impossible to get oil stains out of embroidered silk. Then Paris flinched as if hurt.

The oil was that hot that it had burned her?

"Paris! Your hand. The *diya*!" I yelled, rushing forward.

But my warning came a second too late. Paris slipped on the spilled oil on the floor, her arms flailing for purchase. She righted herself promptly, but in doing so, lost her hold on the *diya*. It smashed to the floor, its contents flying willy-nilly. The flame went out and I whooshed out a breath. Disaster averted. Then suddenly, the silken hem of her *lehenga* began to blaze.

Holy shit. I wondered if Paris would ever forgive me now.

CHAPTER THREE

Paris

I hobbled into my hotel room, feeling like the world's clumsiest klutz. A goddamned *shlemiel*. For crying out loud, hard-core criminals pissed in their pants when I marched into a courtroom, or so much as looked at them sideways.

Okay, slight exaggeration there. Though I thanked God that this wasn't a courtroom and that no one from work had witnessed my graceless tumble. As it was, I was never going to live it down with my friends. Or hear the end of Neal's lectures on safety and fire hazards. Or Lily's on the inauspiciousness of using fire as a dance prop. Wait! Maybe Lily no longer considered fire as holy or symbolic after her divorce from Judaism, maturity and sanity.

Letting go of Naira's shoulder, I collapsed on the bed, irritated beyond belief at the tween who'd triggered my fall, and even more at myself. How could I have been so distracted as to forget—*forget!*—that damn *diya* in my hand? Hadn't I warned Lavinia that the *diya* dance was a lawsuit in waiting if the tent was accidentally set on fire? Forget accidentally setting a human being on fire. But Lavinia in her absurd nothing-will-go-wrong-at-my-wedding mood had chucked my advice out the window for the sake of authenticity, ambience and tradition. The *diya* dance had been performed at every wedding in her family since the dawn of civilization, apparently. "After all, we're all adults and know how to be careful," Lavinia had said in her nauseating bridal daze.

Well, she'd miscalculated that one because I definitely wasn't adulting today. And this mishap was exactly why I was against weddings that tried to compete with the Cirque du Soleil, especially when kids were involved. I shuddered at the thought of getting involved with kids on a daily basis.

Pandemonium followed me inside the room in the guise of my shrieking friends who were making too much noise to make any sense, if they were indeed trying to help. Naira, who seemed dumbstruck with panic, wasn't adulting today, either. Usually, she was the one we'd relied on in a crisis back in college. She'd known all the Zen answers to life, and a bunch of home remedies for life's ailments.

I pressed my fingers into my ears and yelled loudly enough to drown everyone else out. "Thank you all for your well-meaning prattle, but I'm fine. My foot is fine." I stuck the appendage in question a foot off the floor as irrefutable evidence. Half my toes were red and part of my skin on the top of the foot was on the hotter side of the temperature gauge. It was probably going to blister, but I wasn't screaming in pain so it must be okay. Really, I felt more stupid than hurt anyway. "I'll survive a bit of peeled skin. Now get out. This room is too small for all of us to congregate in. And for the love of eardrums everywhere, stop screaming, Aria. You'd think I'd been burned alive."

Downstairs, Naira had helped me remove my block heels and a quick side peek confirmed that she still clutched them between her hands like loaded weapons. My brain sputtered to a stop again at the sight of her.

Naira was really here. In the flesh. She'd come for Lavinia's wedding and not mine? Oh, she'd tried her best to come—*blah blah blah*—she'd explained then. *But she hadn't tried hard enough, had she*, I thought in resentment.

I frowned at my foot—it was still stinging—wondering why Naira was here. It couldn't just be the wedding. I was certain of it. I frowned harder, wiggling my toes, then hissed when it hurt. I needed to do something about the stinging. I'd deal with Naira later. I had to sort out my foot before it got infected. For that, I needed my room back, and some peace and quiet.

"Look, guys, the reception's already started. I suggest you quickly run Naira through the dance choreography so she can fill in for me. We all know she's a way better dancer than I am," I said on a stroke of genius. They could all get out of my hair and let me breathe. Think too. *What was she doing in New York now? What had happened?*

"What? No!" Naira exclaimed, coming out of her stupor. "I'll ruin the dance if I join in out of the blue. I'll stay and help you. Lavinia? We'll come down once she's better. Okay?" She raised her eyebrows first at Lavinia, who nodded joyously, then at me.

I wasn't ready to let go of my mad. "You don't need to stay. I can manage by myself. You've come to enjoy the wedding. Don't let me keep you from it."

"I'm staying," she said, shooting me a look that read: *don't be an ass.*

My back stiffened, but Lavinia interjected before I could open my mouth and trigger an all-out war of words. "Thanks, darling. We appreciate it."

Lavinia didn't even try to disguise her meddlesome glee. She'd been trying to get Naira and me to make peace for a while and I imagined she was going to take full credit if we did so at her wedding. My nostrils flared but Lavinia was already herding our excitable group of friends out of my room.

"Can one of you find my husband and tell him what happened and that I'm fine? Or, never mind. I'll tell him myself," I shouted at their retreating backsides.

I didn't want him to hear an embellished, screechy version of the fiasco. He was going to be a pain in the tuches about it as it was. I frowned at my foot again. I couldn't bear to look at Naira. And because the room was seriously tiny, and she stood way too close, I couldn't not look at her size six-and-a-half golden mules peeking out from under her peach-and-gold sari.

I couldn't wrap my head around her sudden appearance in New York. And looking like Little Orphan Annie. Naira had always been on the petite and dainty side, but goodness, she looked like a wraith right now. As if Death had kissed her and sucked the life out of her.

Was she still grieving for the criminal? I peeked at her from beneath my lashes. Nearly three years as an ADA had honed my people-reading skills, and I hoped to get a solid read. Tiredness, nerves and maybe a dash of guilt were painted on her face.

Good. She *should* feel guilty for standing me up at my wedding. I'd also tack on the charge of disturbing the peace. If I hadn't been gaping at her in the tent, I'd have seen that child coming right at me and spared myself some humiliation.

"You can set my shoes down." I gestured toward the closet by the door.

Naira did so, then came back to me. She bent over my foot, worrying her bottom lip. She seemed just as averse to making eye contact as I was.

"Do you have Neosporin in your travel kit? Let's at least get it under cold water to cool the skin," Naira, the queen of home remedies, suggested when I shook my head about the Neosporin.

"Good idea." I stood up, but as I began shuffling toward the bathroom, the heavily embroidered and slightly charred hem of my *lehenga*—which was also soaking wet thanks to the quick-witted Samaritan who'd thrown a pitcher of water at me when I'd set myself on fire—scratched against my skin, making me gasp in pain.

"Close the door. I have to take off the pants." I reached for the side zipper and tugged.

As I balanced on one leg and stripped, Naira hovered behind me, arms at the ready to catch me if I toppled over. The thought of her trying to break my fall sent a flutter of amusement through me. I still had half a foot on her and, at a minimum, an extra thirty pounds of curves and muscle. If I fell on her, she'd be squashed like a gnat against a flyswatter.

The zipper got stuck halfway down my hip and I had to rezip and unzip twice before getting it right. Our friendship had also been stuck like my zipper for two and a half years, and neither of us had dared to force it closed or open it up again. Until now.

When I finally stepped out of my pants, tears blurred my vision.

Naira's eyes widened into circles of panic. "Is it painful? Paris, you need to see a doctor. We have to go to a hospital. I'm going to text Lavinia and check if there's a doctor among the guests. Odds are there should be. Tell me what to do! What do you need me to do?"

"That's not why I'm…" I gestured to my face, sounding as choked up as I felt.

I hated putting my emotions on display. I hated her. So much. I would never forgive her for the two years of silence. But I was absurdly happy to see her. I still couldn't believe she was standing right in front of me.

"Why did you shut me out?" I sniffled, so embarrassed by the quaver in my voice.

"Why didn't you force me to talk?" she countered, her face pale and stark. "I waited for you to call. I waited for you to come. I expected you to barge into my house after the… funeral. After you'd finished your case. I waited every single day. But you never came."

A tear rolled down my face as I gaped at her. "You told me you wanted to be left alone. That you needed time and space to grieve. You told me to respect your wishes."

The week following the funeral, she'd told me she needed to be with Kaivan's family, that his parents, his sister were inconsolable. They were her responsibility now and she had to take care of them. A month later, she'd said she was busy sorting out the will, the finances, settling the debts. That her family was helping her and things were a bit hectic and urgent in her life. She'd implied that she didn't have time to spare for me.

Had she been lying? I hadn't pushed because I'd genuinely believed that she needed to be with her family. Naira was super close to her family, especially her mother. Also, I'd never liked Kaivan the Criminal, so it had seemed a little hypocritical to show up and mourn him. But now, in retrospect, I realized I should've gone to Mumbai. Neal had even bought our tickets and I'd made him cancel. I should have forced Naira to talk to me, to pour her heart out, confront her grief. But I'd been so angry with her after my wedding that I'd let my anger blind me.

"I never thought you'd listen," she said, confirming my suspicions. "You never ever listen to other people. You always do what you wish. Ordinarily."

"God, Naira. If you wanted me to come, why the fuck didn't you just say so? Why play games?" I frowned at her. My head was beginning to hurt too.

"Because I was punishing myself, okay?" she shouted in frustration.

"What?" Now I was completely dumbfounded.

She threw up her hands. "I didn't come for your wedding. I wasn't there to support you when I knew... I knew how hard it must have been for you to trust him...to commit to marriage. Doubly hard with your father gone and I still didn't... couldn't come. So I thought I didn't deserve your support in my time of need. So it's quits, okay? We both have one tally mark each in the terrible friend department." She ended the declaration on a half moan, half hysterical giggle, reminding me how we'd kept score of who was a better friend back in college.

We stared at each other for the next several heartbeats, thoughts whirling. Mine certainly were. She was right. Everything she said was true. We'd been punishing each other and ourselves for our crimes. It was past time to stop.

I nudged her hand, tapped it with a finger, really. That's all it took. One tap and we were in each other's arms, crying and laughing and cursing at one another. Bouncing—well, I hopped.

The door swung open amid this drama and Neal, my husband, my lover, my mate, stood there, key card in hand and his tuxedo jacket folded over an arm, looking understandably bewildered. But so gorgeous.

I drew back from Naira, gurgling with happiness. I flapped a hand between them and tried to introduce them to each other. My wonderful self-flagellating bestie and my amazing man—the two people on this planet who knew the core of me down to the last misshapen pinkie-toe.

Neal sauntered deeper into the room, his gaze zeroing in on my red foot. Not the one with the bad pinkie-toe.

"I'm fine. It's nothing," I blurted out, co-opting his lecture.

"*Hmm*. Read this." He clicked his phone on and showed me the screen, never taking his frown off my foot. It was a text from Karen: Paris on fire! Needs u in bedroom now!

Oh, good lord! That Karen was such a ninny.

"I will say this, hen. After such a provocative message, the last thing I expected to find in my room was my wife...erm, half-naked with another lassie in her arms. Warn a lad next time, aye?" Finally, his blue-blue eyes lighted on mine. They were brimming with unholy humor.

I was done. Slain. As I was slain the night we'd met. Neal's deadly combination of wit and Scots and the absurdity of the situation had me sliding to the carpeted floor howling with laughter, my burned appendage all but forgotten. Naira tried to maintain decorum—on account of Neal, I supposed—but my giggles were too contagious and soon her body was also shuddering in mirth on the floor beside me.

We laughed for a long time, Naira and I, even after Neal's amusement changed into exasperation. "It wasn't that funny," he said, standing over us with his hands on his hips.

Nope, it wasn't. But I knew why we laughed even if he didn't. We laughed because there was no longer any reason to cry.

Our friendship was back on track. *Mazel tov!*

Some friendships were toxic. They made you bitch or turned you into a raging bitch. They made you hate and be loathed in return. They brought on migraines instead of inner harmony. You couldn't laugh like a loon with that friend. You might let out a witchy cackle or two, but genuine mirth? Heaven forbid if you dared to be genuinely amused on a toxic friend's watch.

The same was true of toxic relationships. I'd seen firsthand the destruction such relationships unleashed on marriages, families, friendships, children. It was ugly what humans did to one another in the name of right, might and possession. Even before I'd thought about being a lawyer or fighting for people's rights and justice, before I'd ever imagined that I might have a future that didn't involve tears and harsh words, I'd experienced relationship toxicity. My birth mother had given me away on the very day I was born. Just ejected me from her womb and her life, and like a cuckoo had tricked random suckers into caring for me.

The first couple who'd adopted me as a three-month-old infant had eventually turned toxic too. Perhaps they hadn't planned to harm me or each other. I'm quite certain they'd dreamed of being the perfect parents, once. I sometimes had flashbacks—or was it only wishful thinking—that I'd laughed a lot as a toddler. But by the time I was six, Jared and Sandra had hated each other's guts and they'd channeled their mutual hatred through me. They divorced, obviously. And they divorced me too. I was meant to be a joint project and not a sole responsibility. Once Social Services had taken me off their hands, neither one had ever checked up on me—not even out of guilt or duty or simple humanity. Maybe they'd realized I was a cuckoo—wrong bird, wrong nest.

And then there were friendships and relationships that were effortless. Not that you didn't have to put some effort in maintaining them, but they were easier to navigate, solid as stone and, most important, forgiving.

My relationships with Neal, Naira and the Judge had always been solid.

And there I went, thinking weird, maudlin thoughts in the middle of a happy occasion. I simply wasn't capable of sitting still *and* being Zen in mind, which, due to my own klutziness I was relegated to this evening. I'd been advised to stay off my feet—Lavinia had managed to tag a wedding guest who was also an ER doctor, and had dispatched her to my room for emergency foot care. The doctor had applied ice and aloe vera to the blister and proclaimed me as good as new again. As long as I stayed off my feet, she'd seen no reason for me to hide out in my room, nursing the burn. Except, I'd then realized that my *lehenga* lay in a puddle on the bathroom floor and I hadn't packed any spare clothes. Naira had come to the rescue, quickly fashioning a sarong-style skirt out of my chiffon and gauze *dupatta* and my outfit was decent once more.

(Sidebar: I loved the ease of the makeshift skirt so much that I made a mental note to tell Neal's sister, Helen, to incorporate the style into whatever outfits she designed for me henceforth.)

We'd made it to the reception in time for the *diya* dance, which went amazingly well despite the confusion my absence created in the choreography. Now, almost every guest and their mothers were wiggling their tuches off on the dance floor as the DJ brought the tent down with eardrum-busting music.

I shifted, easing my outstretched leg off the footstool Neal had found for me, and gingerly placed my burned foot on the floor. I hated the feeling of pins and needles in my appendages—especially when it happened during a particularly long and drawn out deposition or trial—thus I kept shifting positions.

"Okay?" Naira shouted into my right ear.

I nodded, smiling. I'd tried— We'd all tried to get Naira to dance but she was determined to demur. Jet lag had fatigued her, apparently. I didn't believe her.

"Go. Dance!" I poked her again.

"I'd rather keep you company," she said, her lips curving in a dreamy smile.

She wasn't jet-lagged. She was tipsy, I decided in amusement.

We'd been guzzling the infamous Girlfriend Cocktails since dinner. The GFC had been invented by our very own Naira in sophomore year, if you could believe it. The jalapeño-spiked-cocktail recipe had been liberally shared with all the bartenders working within a six-block radius of NYU. The bartender at Lavinia's wedding was the latest recipe recipient.

"Are you heading straight back to Mumbai after the wedding?" I simply had to know if she'd come just for the wedding.

The dreaminess in her eyes dimmed. She shook her head. "I have things to take care of in New York. I'm going to be around for a month. Probably longer if all goes well." She brightened again. "Fun, right? We can catch up."

"Of course, we'll catch up. What things?" Probably something to do with the criminal.

She flapped her hand at the speakers blaring out remixed Bollywood songs. "It's too long a conversation to get into tonight. Or shout out."

I nodded. True. A wedding wasn't the place to hold an interrogation. If Naira was going to be in town for a while, we'd have plenty of opportunities for confessions and cross-examinations. Still, questions and thoughts kept hammering inside my skull. And I was dying to tell her about Neal and the surrogacy. She was going to be gobsmacked. Happy gobsmacked. Naira was as baby mad as my husband.

Speaking of my husband, Neal was headed for our table, a

whisky in his hand. He'd been schmoozing with some men-folk at the bar ever since the dancing had started. But every once in a while, he'd come by to check on my foot. He stopped behind my chair, bent to give me a sweet, whisky-laced, inverted kiss.

"Need anything?" He straightened with a final press of his lips on my forehead. His question included Naira, but she'd turned her gaze away from us. To give us privacy.

My amusement spiked. She was still a prude.

"You guys don't need to babysit me. Go and dance. Have fun," I said, making eyes at my husband, hoping he'd take the hint and ask Naira to dance. This business of Naira not wanting to dance like some tragic widow was rubbish, and I was having none of it.

"But I'm having so much fun babysitting you," Naira teased.

Neal tossed his whisky back, set the tumbler down and gallantly held his hand out to Naira. *Attaboy!* "Come on, lass. I may not be anywhere near yer world champion status, but I promise ye, I'm not a bad dancer."

"Oh, no. That's not even… You don't have to… I don't want to dance. Really." She looked at me pleadingly to rescue her.

I made a shooing motion with my hand. "Just go. It's high time you both get to know each other. And what better way to do it than dancing together? That's how we became friends with Lavinia and the gang, remember? Go. Let loose. It's silly for all of us to sit around and growl at the world."

Then, my husband turned on his full Scottish charm and within two minutes flat, he was leading my best friend onto the dance floor.

There was another reason I wanted Naira to dance with Neal. During the family performances, instead of watching the dances, Neal unsurprisingly had been more interested in seducing a set of fat twin bairns into fits of giggles as they bounced in their parents' laps at the table next to us. Neal was a natural-born baby magnet, and I was used to seeing teeny tots turn into putty in his hands.

Naira was as crazy about babies as my husband—or, she had been. Back in college, she'd worked in the NYU crèche three mornings a week, and would eagerly volunteer to baby-sit professor's kids in the evenings and on weekends. Yet, she hadn't joined the game of baby peekaboo an hour ago. She'd sat between Neal and Stacey's boyfriend, Matt, and looked on wistfully at the drool dripping down two shapeless chins as the twins blew raspberries at my husband. Something about the sadness of her posture had struck a nerve even in my toxified heart. She'd looked afraid to move, as if by twitching even an eyebrow she'd wake up from her dream—her dream of family.

Drat it. Naira should've been playing with her own children by now, not babysitting her dead husband's family and debts. Just one more thing to hold against Kaivan the Criminal. And that was when the brilliant idea had popped into my head.

Both Neal and Naira were Super Parent material.

I wasn't.

Both Neal and Naira came from happy, healthy, normal families. They *understood* family.

I didn't. Family was something other people had. Not me.

I got the shakes just thinking about holding a miniature human in my arms. Naira didn't. *It's my life's purpose to be a mother,* she'd said to me often enough. While my life's purpose was to simply stay ahead of whatever catastrophe chased me.

I'd never wanted kids. Never imagined I'd fall for a man who did. But I had, and now here we were, short-listing surrogates and making Neal's dream come true.

I didn't want to be a mother. But Naira did. Hell, she'd be

more of a mother, all the way from Mumbai, than I'd ever be in person.

So why not just ask her to?

Holy shit. Could I?

Should I?

Would she?

Would *he*? I wondered, my mind and heart racing a mile a minute.

I stared at my husband and my bestie whirling about the dance floor in a fast Viennese waltz. They were out of sync with the music as it was a samba booming out of the speakers. Still, they looked amazing together. Neal was leading, dipping Naira or simply lifting her off her feet when she stumbled on the unfamiliar footwork. She was tiny enough for him to lift up bodily without straining a back muscle, as in my case. My husband could ballroom dance like the lord he was—or would be. However, with any other kind of dance, he was a complete moron.

Naira, on the other hand, was a trained Kathak dancer and possessed an innate grace. And she had Neal's number right from the first twirl. She'd started off as stiff and as reluctantly as a Victorian heroine in his arms, but now her expressions ran the gamut, a different one on display every time they swung past. Her eyes sought mine as they whirled past again, begging me to refute the obvious. I shrugged in answer. *It is what it is.* Yes, my tall, talented and disgustingly romantic husband had no rhythm in his bones whatsoever. Hey! No one ever got the full package, did they? Everyone had to compromise somewhere. And I'd rather be married to a dance moron than a crook any day.

Oy gevalt. I had to cease comparing our husbands even inside my own head. And my tongue seriously needed to be slapped with restraints. I was going to keep my opinions to myself this time. I had no right to judge Naira or Kaivan or their life together. I should never have said what I'd said to her when we'd last spoken.

A marriage was an understanding between two people and only two. I knew that now, after falling in love with Neal, after I'd caught myself willingly compromising my viewpoints just to make him happy or to keep the peace between us.

Sometimes, we managed to keep the peace. Other times, not even a compromise sufficed.

It seemed nontoxic relationships weren't any easier to fathom or navigate than toxic ones. They hurt just as badly if one misstepped. And yet, a good relationship demanded the best of you. It forced you to become better than you'd ever imagined yourself to be. The hurt was there, of course it was, but it was a sweet pain that built character and not the horrible pain that stripped you of your humanity. A good friend might cause you to panic and burn yourself, but she stuck around to make sure you didn't blister…much. She made you a skirt out of a scarf, and maybe even agreed—gladly—to mother your baby. However, what a good friend didn't do was flash her boobs at your husband.

My eyes widened at the tableau before me. Pants on fire wasn't enough, Neal wanted to create an even bigger scandal at Lavinia's wedding. For one bizarre moment, I was impressed that he'd again read my mind and so was checking out the feasibility of Naira's mammary glands.

Why in hell was he peering at Naira's cleavage so intently? Was there a food stain on her blouse or sari? Neal was a maniac about stains. He carried Tide to Go everywhere.

They abandoned the waltz altogether as Neal leaned in to— Ah! He was fascinated by Naira's necklace. I blew out an exasperated breath. I should've known a bauble was involved. Admittedly, Naira owned some beautiful pieces of jewelry. I'd seen her trousseau when I'd gone to Mumbai for her wedding the winter after we'd graduated, while I'd been cramming for the LSATs and working as a paralegal at Smith, Stone and Smith.

Neal reached for the pendant while it was still nestled between Naira's boobs. He really had a one-track mind about baubles. Aghast, Naira jumped back and crashed into a group of lively young dancers, who simply hooted at her and twerked even harder. Her face and neck was the same ruby red as her pendant when she spun on her heels and made a beeline for our table, an elated Neal dogging her footsteps.

While the unfolding drama was entertaining, I rebuked my husband with a stern shake of my head. Neal's bauble obsession was a running joke in the family. Ordinarily, Neal was a thorough gentleman with his to-the-manor-born mannerisms and gently bred inside voice that he even used outdoors. But when it came to his passions—which often revolved around stones and metals and inventive combinations of the two—he lost all sense of propriety.

They both reached the table together, with Neal's eyes still riveted on the pendant. Naira took it off and dropped it in his hands like it was a hot potato.

"It's one of mine," he said, smiling slowly.

"It was a gift from my husband."

Naira's defensive tone gave me pause. Did she think Neal was accusing her? But before I could reassure her, Neal shot her a grin. "He has excellent taste, lass."

Bless his charming heart for trying to put my friend at ease.

"Thank you." She returned his smile hesitantly. "Your jewelry is spellbinding. You're so talented. Kaivan and I loved coming for your shows. Yours and your sister's."

A spell-breaking discomfort spread through me as Naira laid it on thick, as if buttering up a professor for a better grade.

When I'd first started dating Neal, she'd been less than encouraging of him, mostly unflattering. She'd gossiped about his wild reputation and his wastrel appetites, warning me to be careful. I'd brushed off her concerns because his reputation had only augmented my plans of temporarily fucking his brains out and moving on. After all, I hadn't been looking for love or any of its accompanying agendas. Then, when things had become serious, I'd stopped discussing Neal with her. And soon after that, we'd fallen out.

Neal and Naira started talking about the fashion shows: Which ones had she come for? Had the Delhi one been better than the Dubai one? Which Bollywood star would be their next brand ambassador?

It was easy to forget that the Singh Frasers not only knew celebrities themselves but were celebrities of the fashion world. They were such regular people with me.

The conversation didn't interest me, so a part of my attention went back to examining my idea from different angles, and the more I thought about it, the more convinced I became that I was on the right track.

"I remember this piece," said Neal after fondling his creation for a few minutes. Rubbing those long, blunt-nailed fingers over the smooth-faced stones, circling the edges, the ridges and peaks of metal with the pad of his thumb, testing the angles of the prongs by raising them to eye level, and whatnot. "It was part of the first collection I designed. Everyone was surprised when most of the pieces sold on the very day of the showing. Ye were one of the clients?" He laughed, clearly delighted by Naira's good taste in baubles.

I refrained from pointing out that she might have good taste in jewelry, but I had better taste in husbands.

"My husband. He'd been in Delhi on business and had accompanied his cousin to your jewelry show. Kaivan—" she paused when her voice wobbled, took a deep breath and went on "—refused to buy anyone else's designs after that. We have invested in several of your pieces but...this one's my favorite."

It boggled my mind that Naira was still mourning the bastard after everything he'd put her through. And she'd been worried about Neal's wastrel appetites?

I'd also had it with the apple-polishing going on before me. Fine, Naira loved and invested in fine jewelry, but the way she was sucking up to Neal was just...weird.

I stood up and tucked my arm through my husband's elbow. "Honey, I need to stretch my legs. I'm done communing with my chair and my ass hurts."

"Look at this!" Neal took that as an invitation to shove the rose in my face instead of teasing me with butt jokes.

I rolled my eyes, but looked at the necklace nonetheless. Dozens of fine strands of gold had been braided together to form a long chain from which a rose-shaped pendant with a center stone the size of a robin's egg and the color of a pink rose dangled. Layers of paper-thin diamond-encrusted petals had been arranged around the stone to make the rose head.

"It's very pretty," I said, impressed. You couldn't be anything else with Neal's designs.

"That's not all," said Naira, removing her earrings from her ears.

She took the rose from Neal, turned it around and fitted the earrings into some hidden slots and locked them in place. Suddenly, the budding rose was in full bloom and as big as my palm.

"The pendant can be worn as a whole, like so, or as a set— earrings and necklace. I wear the braided rope chain daily. The pendant can also be worn as a brooch. And..." Naira began to unclasp the petals, and not just the ones that were earrings.

The beauty of a Neal Singh Fraser design was that the piece

could be worn in more than one way. It was why his pieces were often touted as *functional luxury* in fashion magazines.

Neal was beside himself with excitement, but he didn't try to hurry Naira along. One by one, she removed twenty-four petals in all, setting each one on the table, until only the rose-colored teardrop remained looped on the chain, big and brilliant. I'd seen the assembling and dissembling magic of Neal's jewelry before—my smaragdine bracelet also came apart as three bracelets and came together as a long necklace—and yet, I couldn't help but be enchanted.

"This was the stone that started it all," Neal burst out as soon as Naira handed the pendant to me. "My first successful experiment with lab-grown diamonds, and because the stone sold as quickly as it did, Nanu agreed to let me design an entire collection using CVDs—solo. This was the piece that started my brand, Paris."

Whoa. This was monumental. It'd taken Neal six years to convince his nanu—his late maternal grandfather—a conventional and traditional jeweler in India, to use lab-grown diamonds for a trendier line of jewelry. Traditional jewelers disliked mixing natural or "real" diamonds with CVDs, which were diamonds manufactured in a lab through a process called chemical vapor deposition, even though CVDs were the more eco-friendly and humanitarian diamond-buying option since they weren't drilled out of the earth or controlled by a syndicate. It seemed that this pendant and by associative action, Kaivan Dalmia, had been instrumental in my husband's success as an innovative and relatively green jewelry designer. Which was just awful because I did not want to be indebted to that man even by association.

I sat, pulling Neal down to sit on the chair next to me. I didn't look at Naira because… One thing at a time. I set the stone down on the table between us. There was always an interesting story behind each of Neal's baubles.

"Okay, babe. Tell me how and where you grew this fat little diamond, and why is it posh pink in color?"

CHAPTER FOUR

Naira

Call me.

Sometimes, the simple ping of a text could destroy your peace of mind. Forget peace of mind, it had the power to destroy your life.

I'd never forget the text I received from Kaivan the day he got arrested. I'd been in the middle of uncrating a new shipment from Bali at An Atelier in Mumbai, my high-end home goods store I'd built, owned and nurtured until two years ago. I'd pulled out a pair of candle stands from the popcorn packaging—samples from a new artisan—when my phone had pinged an incoming message. I'd ignored the message for a full two minutes. I'd been so pleased with my find and had already been imagining how the carved wood would look against a red backdrop and two small silver elephants at their base for the Instagram photos. Distracted, I'd picked up the phone and had to read the message three times for it to sink into my head.

Arrested. You know what to do. I love you.

Nine words. That's all it had taken for my entire world to go black. My husband *had* prepared me for his eventual arrest, and I had known what to do. I'd called our lawyer, and along with my father and brother-in-law, I'd marched into the police station and demanded Kaivan's release. But that was then.

Now? I'd made a mess of everything Kaivan had worked so hard to save. I thought... I was quite positive that we had both trusted the wrong people, including his lawyer, Naresh Rawal, and my older sister's husband, Vinay Singhal.

My phone pinged for a second time, jerking my attention back to the present. Two texts in as many minutes. That man had zero patience, I thought as I stepped out of the shiny midtown office building that housed the Weinberg Law Firm handling the life insurance trust Kaivan had set up for me. Only then did I read Vinay's newest message.

What did the lawyer say? CALL ME!

I ignored the order. Vinay was in a tizzy to know if we could access the funds all at once. It was always "we" whenever he spoke about my money. He hadn't been able to glean the answers himself on his last trip to New York. And no wonder as James Weinberg, the lawyer handling the trust, was a fiftysomething-year-old powerhouse of a man who wouldn't have cared to be bullied. No wonder too, I'd been able to finagle this trip alone. It seemed that James Weinberg had told Vinay—via email, he hadn't even answered Vinay's phone calls, much less agreed to meet with him—that if "we" wanted to dissolve the trust, then "I" the beneficiary had to meet with him in person. Even today, James had let me go only after I'd promised to think about what it would mean for me to dissolve it.

I was coming to realize that the longer I stayed away from my family, the clearer my vision got. And the less I confided in them or relied on them, the better off I was.

I was tempted to power off my phone, completely disconnect with the world. But I wasn't that brave. Besides, Paris would be reaching out if she was going to be super late.

I slung my crossbody bag over my peacoat and began walking toward the Times Square station to take the subway down to Houston Street. Paris and I were meeting for drinks and then dinner at a new vegan restaurant in Greenwich Village. This would be our second meet-up since Lavinia's wedding, and the first one alone. We'd gotten together on Wednesday night with the NYU gang—everyone except Lavinia who was on her honeymoon in Argentina—at a speakeasy-style pub in the Meatpacking District, and as usual we'd gotten rowdy and shouty and Paris and I hadn't had a chance to catch up. I couldn't…wouldn't explain my situation over the phone. So, tonight's dinner was important, and perfect since it was Friday night and we'd be able to stay out till late with impunity— unless her husband wanted her home early.

I didn't know how my friends still did it—the late nights, the drinking and that too after a full day of work. And then manage to get to work on time the next morning. I'd felt haggard all of yesterday after the pub night. I was too old to binge on Girlfriend Cocktails. Too old, tired and gauche at twenty-nine. I wasn't hip anymore. Had I ever been?

A dog walker hurried past me as I strode down the Avenue

of the Americas, herding a pack of nine lapdogs of all shapes and colors. Maybe I could get a dog. A small one. Or a cat. Maybe then I wouldn't feel so unloved.

If I was being honest, I wasn't quite prepared for a heart-to-heart with Paris. A simple reunion with an estranged friend would've been tricky enough without blubbering neediness all over it. Also, Paris was going to kick my ass for letting things get this bad. And if she agreed to help me, I'd be—I'd certainly feel—indebted to her. Before, I'd been the rock and she the emotional mess. It would cause a tectonic shift in our friendship, never mind that I hated taking favors from anybody. But I didn't have a choice anymore. My family had left me no choices.

I cut off the phone as soon as it began vibrating and flashing Vinay's name on the screen. Damn him. Just damn him and his grubby, greedy soul.

Was he being greedy or was he simply looking out for me? Just like my father. They'd both been there for Kaivan and me from the moment he'd gotten in trouble. Of course, they'd recovered their own losses first—Kaivan would've done the same if he'd been in their shoes. I shouldn't be doubting them, second-guessing their motives. I had no proof that Vinay was doing anything wrong. But I couldn't seem to shake the feeling that something *was* wrong.

"Stop overthinking. Talk to Paris and figure this out," I told myself out loud.

The sooner, the better. I'd fallen apart at the lawyer's office because of one kindly look from James Weinberg and an assurance that he was in my corner. I hadn't cried in months, so it was understandable, expected, even a welcome relief. Though, I don't think James had thought so. The poor man hadn't known what to do with me and had called his assistant inside the conference room to mop me up. I'd already wasted so much of his time today, beginning with arriving late for our meeting. I'd miscalculated how much time it took to walk from SoHo to midtown. I was turning into one of those annoying late-*lateefs* who had no respect for anyone's time or schedules.

At least, my meetings with the directors of the three art galleries in SoHo had been less emotional. All three had agreed to carry a few of the pieces of my art collection on consignment. The pieces would be arriving from India any day now. It wouldn't be money up front, but the sticker price we'd settled on had been higher—much higher than what I'd been quoted in India. Vinay had brought that art dealer to me, and again, I wasn't sure if the quote had been correct or they'd conspired to con me out of some prized art very cheaply.

The phone rang again and this time it sparked my anger. Though it banked quickly as I checked the display and accepted the call from the worldwide shipping service I'd used.

"Mrs. Naira Dalmia? This is Randy from At Your Doorstep."

"This is Naira. Is something wrong with the shipment?" I asked, expecting the worst.

But nothing was wrong. In fact, my shipment had arrived earlier than expected, and Randy would be delivering the six crates and twelve boxes full of artwork to my doorstep. Which meant parts of the collection would be proudly on display in the SoHo galleries within a few days and hopefully would sell soon after that. Perfect. I should get a move on the auction houses too for the collector's pieces.

"We'll be there in half an hour," said Randy.

"Now? Tonight? Oh, but…I'm not at home." I stopped in my tracks right outside the Olive Garden at Times Square. Luckily no one was walking behind me or I'd have gotten an angry earful.

"Is there someone to accept the shipment? If not, we can take it to the warehouse, and set up a delivery date for next week. Storage will cost you though."

That did it. "I'll be home in half an hour."

I wasn't about to let a Husain, a Warhol and three bronze artifacts from Ancient India sit in some warehouse somewhere. The whole point in getting this shipment to New York was so it wouldn't be sitting in a Mumbai warehouse. I needed to sell most of it ASAP. I was strapped for cash and also, it was getting too expensive to care for and insure. I refused to sell the collection to Vinay who couldn't tell a Raja Ravi Varma work from a Raza. This art collection had been Kaivan's and my passion: I wanted another passionate art lover to enjoy it.

I double-checked ETA and my address with Randy and hung up the phone. Then I pressed my hands to my chest and tried to absorb everything I'd accomplished in a week and would accomplish in the coming weeks. My friendships were on the mend. And maybe, just maybe my finances too. But at what cost?

Once again, I felt like an object in a time-lapse video, frozen in the center, with bright, colorful New York racing all around. I'd been living inside a time-lapse since the day Kaivan was arrested. So many things had happened that were beyond my control and understanding that I didn't know how to respond to the world anymore, so I'd stopped responding. Everything triggered a panic attack, so I'd disengaged from everything and everyone, even myself. And now I wondered if I'd be able to reconnect with myself, with life, again.

"Stop being melodramatic," I said to myself and resumed marching down the street.

I didn't have time for wishy-washy thoughts. I had to inform Paris about the change in plans. I scrolled through the starred contacts on my phone and clicked on Paris's name. She picked up on the sixth ring.

"Naira! I was about to leave a message. I'm running late," she huffed into the phone as if she was actually running. "Are you at the restaurant already?"

"No," I said, then quickly added, "Look, something's come up. I'm sorry for doing this again, but can we take a rain check on tonight?"

Silence followed my request. And stillness, as if Paris had suddenly stopped running or even breathing. I'd canceled on her yesterday too. I ran my tongue over my lower lip. I couldn't just cancel on her for a second time without some explanation.

"I have to go back to the apartment. There's a shipment coming in and I have to be there to receive it."

"I see." Another long silence filled the connection. "Your place on Central Park West?"

It wasn't my place, per se. Kaivan had bought the apartment as an investment, then transferred the deed to me only months before his arrest. The only reason I was still in possession of it was because it had been rented out, fully furnished, and the tenants had moved out only last month.

"Temporarily my place. The Realtor has scheduled an open house on Sunday and expects the apartment to sell quickly." I scrunched up my face. "Can we reschedule for tomorrow? I know it's the weekend and you might have plans with Neal."

I started down the steps to the subway. If I didn't hurry, I'd be late.

"Nah…" Paris's voice trailed off behind a gust of sirens blasting down the road on her end.

"What?" I stopped halfway down the steps of a remodeled subway station, pressing the phone to my ear, which made a bunch of New Yorkers hiss at me in annoyance. "Sorry.

Sorry." I lurched out of their path only to get blasted by the ones coming up the stairs. Subway steps were not the ideal place to stop and chat. "You're breaking up, Paris. Can you repeat what you said?"

"…not cancel. Need to talk…I'll come…grab dinner…"

I tried to fill in the blanks. "You'll come to the apartment and we'll grab dinner after and talk, is that what you mean?"

"Yes, I want to run something by you. Unless you rather wait until tomorrow?" she said, clear as crystal, finally.

A stupid smile bloomed on my face. But since she couldn't see it, I said, "Flat number 16B," to demonstrate my glee at her offer.

"Great. Just getting out of the office. Shouldn't take me long to get there. Same place we dropped you off on Sunday, right?"

"Yup. See you soon." I disconnected, thinking the day just kept on improving. At this rate, I'd be floating free in a week.

Famous last words, as pessimists would say.

By the time Paris arrived at the apartment, I was in full panic mode. I was devastated. No, I was angry beyond compare. I couldn't believe how gullible I'd been. Again.

I waved her in and we hugged and air-kissed like uppity socialites connecting at a party. No high fives, backslaps or palms pressed to the chest namastes between us now. The namastes had been done in jest mostly—after Paris had wised up to the fact that the greeting wasn't customary at all. But, for a hot minute back in freshman year, I'd made her believe that all Indians went around bowing and touching each other's feet.

I checked my phone. No missed calls or messages. This time I was waiting for Vinay's response, and he was avoiding me. I wanted to hear his explanation for my missing masterpiece. Couldn't I have one day—just one day when I didn't have to deal with a new calamity?

"What's wrong?"

What was right? I wanted to moan. I didn't know how to tell her that my art collection was missing four items—the Husain and three sixteenth-century bronze sculptures of the Buddha. The eighteen crates and boxes had been packed, sealed and taken away by the shipping guys before my very eyes two weeks ago in Mumbai. They'd been delivered still sealed. But, when Randy had opened the largest crate containing three paintings, just twenty minutes ago, the Husain hadn't been in it.

I knew in my gut that when asked Vinay would place the blame on At Your Doorstep for either messing up the shipment or stealing from it outright. I knew as well that it would be a lie. But how could I call him out on it without starting an all-out war with my family? Or another scandal? Besides, who would believe me over him? The world saw him as an upstanding businessman while I was the widow of a man the media had labeled a criminal.

"You know, if I'd passed by you on the street, I wouldn't have recognized you," I deflected Paris's question, hoping—praying—Vinay had a plausible explanation for the missing art.

It wasn't just diversion or flattery, Paris did look amazing in a plum-colored tailored suit and her runway-worthy office bag was to die for. Handbags were my weakness. I hadn't shopped for one in forever. And gone were the days when I could stroll down Madison or Fifth, pop into any store and buy anything I wanted without checking the price tag.

"Balenciaga." I ran my fingers over the supple gray skin, loving the texture and the thickness of the Italian leather. The only two places I couldn't give up the use of animal products were handbags and shoes. "It matches your outfit. Remember how annoyed you'd get when I'd match my shoes to my handbag or accessories? How the mighty have fallen," I teased.

Paris *tsk-tsk*ed on cue. "And you haven't changed at all. Still into glam shams."

Oh, but I had changed. Change was inevitable, wasn't it?

"Why mess with perfection?" I retorted cheekily, trying in vain to dig out the woman I'd once been. "Besides I'm not the only one in designer clothes right now."

Paris rolled her eyes, stepping over and around the packing materials strewn on the living room floor. Randy and his crew were still opening the last of the crates and boxes in the shipment. There was no place to sit anywhere because the sofas and chairs, even the coffee tables and dining table were piled high with things. Later, I'd sort everything into piles: sell or store.

I felt awfully self-conscious. "Sorry about the mess. I was supposed to declutter the apartment for the showing, but now that the shipment came in, it's impossible. These paintings and collectibles are for the art galleries. I'll send them off tomorrow. Those antiques are for an auction house and a private collector." Minus the artwork Vinay stole. "I'll have to make it all look like part of the decor."

Paris took stock of the living room, then her eyes traveled back to me and she took stock of me until tiny folds appeared between her brows. "How bad is it?"

How bad was it that I'd been reduced to sell an eight-by-ten photo frame because it was made of silver? I swallowed hard and it hurt. "Bad. I'll tell you once they leave."

One of the guys from Randy's crew came out of the guest room. He smiled, picked up a couple of the water bottles I'd set out for them on the kitchen countertop and strolled away.

"Do you want something to drink?" Paris had come straight from work. The least I could do was be a good hostess.

She shook her head. "No thanks. Need to pee though."

I directed her to the powder room by the foyer, took her

bag and jacket and draped it over the circular marble table that I'd pushed into a corner so I could parade boxes in and out of the apartment without tripping.

"Nice place," she said. "You shouldn't have an issue selling it."

I suppressed a smile. Paris had learned the art of small talk. "That's what I was told."

The Realtor, Crystal Lang, was confident the apartment would sell right away. Thank heavens—one less thing to worry about. The first showing was on Sunday, hence the attempted decluttering.

She hesitated at the bathroom door, clearly wanting to say something, but thought the better of it and closed the door.

I guess we were both feeling odd around each other. The old vibe was there, especially when we brought up the past, and yet, there was this new awareness that we didn't really know each other anymore. I hoped it was temporary.

I retraced my steps, looking around the apartment. It *was* a nice place—two bedrooms, two and a half bathrooms, a den, a kitchen, a separate dining room and a maid's room. For Manhattan standards, it was a good-sized space, but compared to my twenty-thousand-square-foot penthouse in Mumbai, which had spanned three full floors with two terraces, it was tiny. That flat was no longer my home, either. I'd sold it to pay the banks, and to settle Kaivan's parents into a small town house northwest of London, close to their daughter in Golders Green. They expected me to join them once I'd settled our affairs here, while my parents expected me to go back to Mumbai and get married again. I wasn't interested in either of those options.

I poked my head into the guest room and answered Randy's questions about where the pieces from box number twelve should go. Which room, which pile. I passed by the Warhol on my way to the other bedroom to run a brush through my shoulder-length blunt. It was a blessing Vinay didn't know art or he'd have taken it too. When would he call? I was ready to jump out of my skin.

The master bedroom was a hodgepodge of personalities. It seemed every tenant had left their mark on it. I couldn't understand what Kaivan was thinking, renting this lovely apartment to strangers when it was loaded with expensive art and antiques.

Had thought. My hand froze while applying gloss to my lips. Past tense. Kaivan was past tense now.

I turned away from the mirror, suddenly aching for my husband. How could I miss him even more every day? Shouldn't I miss him less after two years? Think of him less?

At least living in this apartment didn't feel as tragic as living in the Mumbai one had. Probably because we'd never lived here together. There were no memories to battle here, no echoes to run from. There were no traces of him to miss or get angry over here. I treated the apartment like a hotel suite, a temporary place to sleep and shower in. I wouldn't allow myself to look out of the windows, at the sweeping views of Central Park that you could see from almost every room. I wouldn't let myself get attached to a place like I had my Mumbai home and An Atelier ever again. Or for that matter another person. Attachments only led to suffering.

Paris had known that even as a child. Which made me very curious about how she was managing the art of detachment within her marriage. She hadn't looked detached at the wedding. In fact, she'd—

The phone buzzed inside my jeans' pocket. I fished it out and saw it was Sarika calling, not Vinay. The bloody coward was hiding behind his wife's skirts as usual.

I'd been trained in the *Art of Living*, and meditated every day. I knew how to influence my mind into calm, focus on my kundalini and find my Zen space. But all my training flew out the window the minute I heard Sarika's explanation about why her husband had pilfered four pieces from my husband's—now *my*—art collection without so much as a by-your-leave.

A red haze flared around the fringes of my vision and shot down to my kundalini. This time I didn't wait for Sarika's cawing and bitching to cease, I simply let loose my wrath.

"Now then, *desi* girl. What the fuck is going on between you and your sister?"

I wondered if that was Paris's prosecutorial voice—cajoling, yet firm. Minus the expletive. I wanted to see her interrogating a witness on the stand. I'd bet she was a sight to behold. Or, no, I didn't ever want to see the inside of a courtroom again. Not even for Paris. Everything I'd done over the past two years had been to avoid involving lawyers and judgments, and maybe that was why it had been so easy for Vinay to manipulate me.

"Ftharth ftheaking," Paris ordered after she'd sucked the last two olives of her Girlfriend Cocktail into her mouth.

Carrie Bradshaw and her gang had had their Cosmos and Manhattans. We had our Girlfriend Cocktails—a Grey Goose martini, shaken, with a dash of passion fruit concentrate, a button-sized chunk of jalapeño and a drop of vermouth.

I drained my glass in three gulps, hoping my face didn't match the scream waiting to typhoon out of me as chilled, spicy vodka lit a fuse from my throat to my belly. That. Felt. Ghastly. But, tasted good.

One night, after a particularly hard-won dance trophy, I'd concocted the GFC with the assistance of an incredibly cute Armenian American bartender. It had instantly become a raging hit, especially among our troupe of twenty-odd dancers whose palates tended toward the spicy, and had eventually become a staple drink at the Lexington Avenue Dosa Bar.

Being at the Dosa Bar tonight was strange. I felt chronologically displaced, like a character in *The Time Traveler's Wife*. Like the last seven years hadn't really happened and Paris and I were still students, celebrating our triumphs with vodka and our disappointments with even more vodka. The Dosa Bar had been our go-to place for all of life's events. At street level, it boasted an Indian fusion restaurant serving specialty—wait for it—dosas. But one flight up—usually where students wound up on most weekends—was a cozy, crowded, insanely noisy bar lounge. We used to bookend our dinners at the lounge, consuming half a dozen martinis between us by the end of the night. I remembered several nights when the count had gone up to half a dozen drinks each. Bad nights, those.

I wondered if tonight qualified as a bad night. Or was it worse than bad?

My brother-in-law had stolen four pieces from my husband's carefully curated art collection and his wife—my own elder sister—didn't think he'd done anything wrong.

"He's helping you with everything, isn't he? Running around sorting out the mess Kaivan created. So what if Vinay took a few pieces he liked? Consider it a fitting compensation for his time," she'd said.

Why was I surprised by this? Hadn't she done the same thing with my jewelry under the guise of "keeping it all safe for me"? I hadn't let her take everything. I'd fought to keep the jewelry Kaivan and his parents had given me. And, at least, Sarika had intimated that I could have my jewelry back once my troubles were over. Her husband hadn't even bothered with pretense. I was supposed to simply gift whatever remaining assets I had to him now?

Did my parents know that my sister and her husband were

taking advantage of my bad luck and robbing me blind? Did they care?

How had it come to this? To a place where I couldn't trust my own family? To the point where I didn't know whom to trust at all.

My tummy churned like the blades of a food processor, mincing anger, despair and helplessness into an unpalatable pulp. The taste of hope, so tender and sweet, had been all but eroded from my tongue.

I dropped my head on the edge of the bar and closed my eyes. I didn't care that the leather-edged granite counter was sticky and gross. I just wanted to sleep forever. And when I woke up, I wanted it all to go away. I wanted Kaivan to be alive.

"Goodness, Naira. What is the matter with you? Talk to me. Please." Paris grabbed my arm and shook me when I didn't respond, her nails digging into the flesh of my upper arm.

"You quit biting your nails." Nothing made sense anymore. Not even Paris's nails. I shifted, peering at the French-manicured hand wrapped around my arm. A thick princess-cut eternity band and a sizable emerald cut solitaire framed with smaller diamonds adorned her ring finger. No classic round for Paris. Or hearts or pears or anything cute. Just four solid lines telling the world that she was taken. Her eyebrows were arched when I met her eyes.

"They're fake," she admitted, and signaled the bartender—who wasn't an Armenian American cutie or a man—to get us refills by tapping her nails on her empty martini glass.

For a confused second, I thought she meant her rings, not her nails. My mind felt completely jumbled. I couldn't even recall how we'd gotten here—to the Dosa Bar. Or, I could, hazily. I remembered shouting at Sarika until my throat felt raw. Paris and Randy had come running into the room and tried to calm me down. Paris had wrestled the phone from my hands while Randy had run back out to fetch a bottle of water. I'd begged for something stronger—way stronger. And now here we were drinking GFC martinis. I suddenly wondered what had happened to Randy and his crew?

"Did you tip Randy when he left? Did he take all the garbage out?"

"Yes," Paris said. "He cleaned up while you cleaned up in the bathroom. Tipped him too. Now talk. What's going on?"

"Why don't you go first? You wanted to run something by me, didn't you?" Glum. I felt glum. Completely in discord with the peppy lounge music trying to pound my eardrums into dust.

"Quit stalling, Naira. Spill it."

Paris and I had discussed worse things, washed far dirtier linen in front of each other. Why was I embarrassed to tell her of my failures? "How long do you have before you have to go home?"

"However long you need, girlfriend." Her expression softened. She'd learned how to enhance her eyes with tasteful applications of eyeliner and mascara instead of butchering them with overuse—all on her own. I was so proud of her. Not just for her glamorous transformation, but for everything she'd accomplished despite her rough childhood. And I'd fallen apart at the first sign of trouble.

Paris was my hero. She was who I wanted to be when I grew up.

"Neal is in LA. He won't be back until tomorrow afternoon. Not that it makes a difference. I do my thing when I want to," she assured me.

Unlike Kaivan and me. She hadn't said it but I knew she was thinking it, comparing our marriages as I'd often done. Kaivan had been a possessive husband. He hadn't liked anything or anyone stealing my attention away from him. Paris had thought he was a bully. To some he was, but never to me. She'd never understood that what he demanded of me, he gave equally in return. And that I'd loved it—his attention, his possession. Everything.

I stared at my nails, untidy from a hasty home manicure. Cuts lined my fingers from packing. Kaivan and Paris had never seen eye to eye. I'd never understood why he'd taken such a dislike to her from their very first introduction. He'd never told me. And now he never would. Paris hadn't helped matters by being...exactly who she was. Neither one had tried to hide their mutual aversion, not even for my sake. Which was why I was determined to get along with Neal no matter how uncomfortable he made me. Whatever I knew about him was hearsay at best and was in his past. He'd seemed like a great guy at Lavinia's wedding, not at all the brash drunkard the media made him out to be. If I'd learned one thing since my troubles began three years ago, it was that the media sensationalized everything. Also, as proved by the example sitting in front of me, people changed.

I pushed my hair out of my face and sat up straighter on the bar stool. I could do this. I had to make amends. "It's a M. F. Husain, one of the art pieces my brother-in-law...borrowed."

Her eyes narrowed. "Borrowed? Really? That's why you were shouting 'thief' at the top of your lungs?"

"Borrowed," I repeated firmly, embarrassed that I'd lost control like that.

I would get the Husain and the other pieces and all my jewelry back. Eventually. I refused to believe Vinay was a thief. I shouldn't have said what I'd said. He was family. Sarika was right. He was only trying to help. I was like his kid sister. Of course, he'd take care of me. And I was fond of him too. Sometimes. Well, I would be when all of this was sorted. I shouldn't have jumped to conclusions. My mind had become the devil's workshop. He wasn't turning my father against me. Everything would be fine once I got busy again.

"In her defense…" I began and Paris snorted, cutting me off.

"In her defense? Are you serious?"

"Can you stop echoing my words?" I cried, then took a deep calming breath and continued, "In her defense, she believes they've only taken back in kind the money I owe them."

"You owe them or Kaivan?" Paris asked pointedly.

"Does it matter?"

The distinction sure didn't matter to the people who'd lost their money, including my own family. Kaivan owed them, therefore, as his widow and beneficiary, I owed them. And I would pay them back. All of them. All of it. I would pay back every paisa we owed even if it took me the rest of my life to balance the scales. Only, I hoped it wouldn't take that long. I hoped with the sale of the Manhattan place and the art portfolio most of the debt would be paid.

The problem was—and this was why I'd become suspicious—the debt pool seemed bottomless. I didn't know if Kaivan really owed all those people such tremendous sums of money or whether the figures had been fudged now that he wasn't there to confirm them. And if the figures had been fudged, who'd fudged them? Vinay or the others? I couldn't separate fact from fiction anymore as there was no way to corroborate, as, apparently, such deals took place by word of mouth—or so Vinay explained. The people who'd come to me with burden of proof, I'd already paid back in full with interest where applicable.

Paris opened her mouth to argue no doubt. I shook my head, silently begging her to leave it alone. "I'm handling them. Okay?"

Badly. And I'd more or less run away from Mumbai. But that was okay. It was…easier.

I didn't want to discuss my family tonight. I didn't even want to talk about Kaivan. I was done explaining his business to people. The world had judged him and found him guilty and nothing I said would change anyone's mind. Even the people who'd liked and respected him before spoke horribly about him now, forget the sycophants who'd hounded him and begged him to invest their money. Paris had never liked Kaivan to begin with. And if she ever came to know just what my husband had done to try and get us out of this mess, it would be the end of our friendship.

I took a sip from my replenished cocktail. "He was jealous of you. Kaivan. Of our friendship. He didn't like that I told you things I wouldn't share with him. That's why he behaved badly around you. I think."

My lousy attempt to brush my husband's flaws under an imaginary carpet was interrupted when the maître d' from the restaurant came to get us. Our table was ready, and by the time we'd been seated, our GFCs replenished and our orders scribbled down—again, we paid homage to our college days by ordering the spicy hummus crepe and the chilies and cheese dosa special to share between us—I'd regained some of my poise.

I reminded Paris that she'd been the pot to Kaivan's kettle. "I'm not yet forgiving either one of you. Your attitude wasn't any better around him. You both should have forced yourselves to get along for my sake. But neither of you showed the slightest respect for me or my feelings. Did you even once consider the position you put me in? To choose between you? And I didn't, you know. I didn't choose him over you. *You* made that choice for me."

Paris had fought with me, then she stopped talking to me

when I didn't make it to her wedding. She'd cut me off like she did with anyone who disappointed her. It couldn't have been any other way. I didn't know how to explain that to her without bringing up events I'd rather forget.

She had the grace to look abashed. Neal's influence perhaps? "You're right. But, God, he made it difficult for me to like him. And I stand by my opinion that he wasn't good for you. Especially now, after everything he's put you through. I swear, Naira, if he were alive, I'd shoot him. Clean head shot."

"Me too," I agreed, squashing the awful roiling in my gut. "Through the heart."

"He hurt you."

"Yes." I couldn't look at her, or expand on that. Oh, but I wanted to. He shouldn't have died. My chest was tight with memories and it hurt to breathe. Kaivan had died just before his thirty-fifth birthday. How was I supposed to get over it?

Paris touched my hand and the air between us thickened in wordless apology.

"It's okay," I said, squeezing her hand in return.

She opened her mouth, paused, then shut it. Then opened it again and cleared her throat, and still didn't say anything. I raised my eyebrows in encouragement, curious because Paris wasn't the hesitant type. She bulldozed over conversations.

"Did he abuse you? I have to know," she said in a rush.

For a second the question didn't register and I stared at her blankly. Then I yelped, "What! Are you out of your mind?"

"That's a no…right? I thought…when you… Shit, never mind what I thought. I was wrong, obviously." She grimaced, looking both vaguely relieved and tortured.

Now, my mouth opened and closed a few times before I found my voice. "I cannot believe you thought that about him…about me! Do you know me at all? You think I'd stay with a man who hit me? You think I'd marry a man who disrespected women in any way? Kaivan would have died before harming one hair on my head. He loved me."

The shock of Paris's insinuations scattered my other worries to the four winds. I stood up, stiff with outrage.

"Calm down. It was just a question." Paris tugged at my hand, urging me to sit. But I was too distraught.

If I could only tell her what Kaivan had done for me it would prove his love. *Oh, God!* She'd thought he'd abused me?

"It was surreal seeing you at Lavinia's wedding. Even now, you look...wounded. Shattered. I don't know. I never thought any such thing before, never got that sense. And you might be petite, girlfriend, but you've always been fit because of the dancing. But you don't look well right now. So I wondered."

I looked wounded and shattered? I felt an absurd urge to giggle. That had to be an improvement from the marble statue that my mother had said I'd become. No, I hadn't been abused. Ever. Not even the harsh rules we'd had to abide by in my father's house could be called abuse.

"Naira, please." Paris tugged on my hand again. I sat because I had no other choice. I needed us to forgive and forget. She gave my hand one last squeeze and let me go.

"It's been on my mind this whole week so I had to make sure. It drove me crazy to think that I might've missed the signals. Or that I'd failed you, failed our friendship," she added, softly.

"You are so not the Green Arrow. And I don't need saving." Not in that way.

My droll superhero reference had us both snorting out in giggles. We'd been obsessed with the TV show back in college. We'd even stood in a five-hour queue just to get a picture with the lead actor of the show at Comic Con.

The welcome distraction of fangirling over our shared object of lust, Stephen Amell, who only seemed to be improving with age, went some ways in smoothing my ruffled feathers. From there it was a natural regression into the past. Paris updated me on our mutual acquaintances. It was silly to snigger over the boys we'd crushed on and the girls we'd barely tolerated. But we did it anyway, at least until my bruised heart ached a little less.

Our dosas arrived, and between swallowing chilies so hot that my eyes watered, I began to tell her my tale.

Obviously, Kaivan wasn't a buffoon, I clarified at the outset. He'd been a shrewd businessman. But luck hadn't favored his last investment and to recoup the loss he borrowed heavily and reinvested. It was the only mistake he'd ever made. Well, two. But the other one had nothing to do with business.

"He planned for contingencies." I ignored Paris's skeptical eye-roll. "He never took his success for granted. Understood that businesses can fail, empires can topple. He invested in property, art, stocks—I've liquidated most of it. I've come to sell the last bit of our assets in New York. The Realtor assures me the Manhattan apartment will move fast. And you're right, I don't have to sell the apartment, which is in my name, to pay off Kaivan's remaining debts. I can declare bankruptcy, but I don't want to. I want to get our goodwill back and start with a clean slate." I took a gulp of my GFC and forced myself to go slow, think before I spoke. I didn't want to accuse someone falsely. I didn't want Paris to know the whole truth.

"I have money. I'm the sole beneficiary of a life insurance trust Kaivan set up, and I'll receive a yearly stipend for the rest of my life no matter where I live. I don't need to work, but I can't fathom being idle forever. I want to open a lifestyle store here like the ones I had in India. An online atelier, to begin with. And that's where you come in."

I wanted Paris to go into partnership with me.

"I'll put in the money and manage the whole business, but

I need your name on the front of everything. I can't start anything in my name in India, not with all the legal hassles attached to it. Besides, I signed a noncompete when I sold An Atelier in Mumbai to Vinay. And until I have my immigration status sorted, I can't legally start anything in New York."

I also couldn't trust that the courts or Vinay wouldn't try to usurp or shut down any business I started in my name. I hadn't gone to my father with this plan because one, he wouldn't defy Vinay. And two, Papa was old-school. He'd never understood my need to be self-sufficient. Kaivan had and he'd been so proud of An Atelier in Mumbai.

"Wait. You're moving here?" Paris blinked in surprise, then grinned, then screamed in excitement.

"I'm trying to." I probably had the same goofy grin on my face.

Immigrating to New York was a complicated and expensive undertaking, but it was the best option I had. I'd always loved New York. I'd spent some of my happiest years here, mainly because of Paris. I needed to find a cheaper place to move into—much cheaper than the Central Park West apartment. I'd already promised to transfer the bulk of the money from its sale to India to pay off the debts. But the money I'd make from selling the artwork was mine. And then there was the trust—which I didn't need to dip into if I didn't want to. Not yet. If I lived sensibly, I could build up another atelier, albeit slowly. The best part about moving here was that I wouldn't have to deal with my family.

"It would solve some of my problems, not the least of which is my mother. She wants me to get married again and keeps sending me these weird photos of potential suitors and their stats." I shuddered.

Paris smirked. "Unsuitable suitors?"

"I feel like we've had this conversation before. Wait. We

have had this conversation before. Remember how my mother would send me dossiers full of 'suitable boys' during junior year?" Seven years had gone by—how was I still standing in the same spot? "Oh, they're all suitable. My mother is an excellent matchmaker. She found Kaivan for me, didn't she?" I sighed, smiling bitterly at the thought of my husband. "But I'm not in the market for remarriage." Once was enough.

Paris nodded as though she totally understood. "For now, you mean."

"Forever. I'm not ever getting married again." When Paris gaped at me, I elaborated. "You saw what was going on in the apartment…with my sister. That's just the tip of the iceberg. I'm responsible for Kaivan's old parents now. His sister too, to a lesser extent. I'm never going to be free of the legal hassles in India. There are three hundred and eighty-five cases against Kaivan, and now me as his wife and partner. Do you know how disorganized, not to mention corrupt, India's legal system is? I'm paying legal fees through my nose just so that I don't have to go to court every day. Which suitor is going to put up with all that baggage?" And that was only the visible baggage.

Paris looked shocked. "Why didn't you tell me how bad it was?"

"And what good would it have done? What could you have done?" I shrugged. There was nothing anyone could do. This was my life now.

"What about your life goals? Your dreams of love, marriage and baby carriage?"

My dreams had died along with my husband.

"Not all dreams come true. Most don't. Didn't you tell me that? Besides, I've already ticked off love and marriage so that's two-thirds of my life goals accomplished. Not bad, right? And the new atelier can be my baby. Without the poop and diapers," I joked bravely.

Paris stared at me, eyes narrowed, as if she didn't believe the veracity of my words. But I meant them. Every single one.

"Honey, you do know that you don't need a man to have a child these days. Or raise one, if that's what you want."

Even through the ache in my chest, I felt laughter bubble up. Of course, Paris would suggest something so outrageous with such earnestness.

"Do I need to remind you that I'm old-fashioned? And even if I wasn't, I *can't*, Paris. I have too many financial burdens as it is. I can't afford another one no matter how much I want it. Please, can we stop talking about babies? It was...*hard* seeing Karen—I mean I'm super happy for her, but—" I shook my head and put a stone over my heart. "Can we focus on what I need to get done to stay in New York?"

I went over everything again. Then I paid attention to my dinner for a bit, giving Paris time to digest my plan.

"I know I'm asking a lot. I know we haven't exactly been in touch these two years. I realize that we don't know each other as well anymore. But I have no one else, Paris. And you won't have to risk any money." *Just your name*, I added silently.

I let her see my desperation. I didn't know what I'd do if she refused to help. Unlike Kaivan, I didn't have a contingency plan. I couldn't bear the thought of going back to India. Which left London and living with my in-laws as my only other option.

"Let me think about it," she said after several beats. "When do you need an answer? And I will have questions."

"Ask me anything," I said immediately, my heart lifting. She hadn't said no. "Regarding timing...um...the sooner the better? I have a month before I'll have to...explain things back home." I was so not looking forward to that confrontation.

Paris returned my tentative smile with one of her own. "I hope you don't mind, but I'll discuss this with Neal because— Ha!" she exclaimed suddenly, and sat up straight in her seat. "You know what? You should talk to Neal directly. Yes, that's what you should do. He's the perfect person to go to for business advice. Him or his brother, Deven. They know all the ins and outs, the laws and the red tape, on a global scale. And Dev's a wily bastard and intimidating as fuck. He'll probably know how to sort out your legal hassles. Maybe you won't even need a partner."

"Oh." I hadn't been expecting that. "I don't want to bother your husband."

Not only that, if Vinay found out that Neal Singh Fraser was helping me, it would trigger a nuclear war. I'd never told Paris that Neal's ex-fiancée was Vinay's brother's wife's sister. Oh, yes, we lived in a very tiny world. The Singhals still held an insane grudge against Neal because of the way he'd treated and ditched Simran, practically at the altar, even though she'd moved on and married someone else too.

Also, I didn't want to take advice from another man ever again. Men tended to complicate the simplest of decisions with their arrogance and chauvinism—my husband included.

"Don't look so terrified. Neal doesn't bite. Not unless I ask him to." Paris winked at me, then looked impressed when I didn't go all hysterical at her sexual innuendo. Though, I was sure my cheeks were on fire. "Jokes apart. Neal is your best bet, honey. Trust me."

I didn't really have a choice, did I?

CHAPTER FIVE

Paris

A dense fog settled over Manhattan on Monday morning, cloaking my bird's-eye view of the city from our sixty-second-floor aerie. Only the very tops of the Brooklyn Bridge and select high-rises poked through the blanket of gray velvet like ghostly turrets on some ancient Scottish moor. The view was more sinister than romantic, though my own Scotsman would disagree.

Neal was due home any minute—an entire weekend later than scheduled. His work—if hobnobbing with the who's who in Beverly Hills could be called work—had kept him in LA until late Sunday, and weather conditions had further delayed him at the airport. He'd ended up taking the red-eye to Newark via Detroit at the last minute.

My head spun just thinking about the various disruptions

traveling for work caused—traveling in general caused. I was glad that my job was restricted to one city, one general half-square-mile area, and on most days to one single chair. This travel upheaval was one of the reasons I wanted our surrogate to be within driving range. If all the back and forth from California was going to upset my work schedule, I was going to get cranky.

Where was he? I had to leave for work soon, but I had plans for us before that. I Snapchatted a sexy selfie to him, in case he needed an incentive to hurry the hell up. He replied with a picture with his eyes agape and his tongue hanging out like a dog's. Then we kind of sexted for a bit.

Neal: You have too many clothes on.

Me: If you don't get here fast, I'll start and finish without you.

Neal: Don't you dare! Damn Holland Tunnel traffic.

As we bantered, a weather channel helicopter flew past the Brooklyn Bridge, heading straight for the nebulous jaws of the dark gray smog. I clicked the atmospheric photo and posted it on Instagram, hashtagging a whole slew of related terms to it.

I'd barely finished uploading when Naira's text popped up on my screen.

You're awake?

Clearly, she was too. I called her and she picked up on the first ring.

"Still jet-lagged? How was the showing?" I asked, putting her on speaker. Then I sank down on the sofa to finish the rest of my coffee.

The showing had gone very well according to Naira. Seven potential buyers had shown up and the Realtor believed the place might go into a bidding war. Which was all good news.

Our Friday night chat had derailed my own plans of asking Naira to help me with the surrogacy business and what came after. But I'd had the weekend to regroup, and now I was on a mission to get my bestie's life in order first so she could help me deal with mine. Neal's travel upheaval had upended my plan of hashing out Naira's start-up issues and I was determined to get it done tonight even though late nights on a weekday sucked. But with Diwali coming up in just a week and its accompanying celebrations and parties, closely followed by Thanksgiving, and the unpredictability of Neal's travel schedule—he was always jet-setting off to different parts of the world to meet with clients or check on some product or attend some jewelry fair or host an event—it was better to get this meeting off the agenda. I also couldn't keep both the potential surrogates in limbo for much longer. I needed to give them an answer, one way or another.

I'd given Neal a heads-up about Naira's partnership proposal. He'd agreed to talk to her, understand her requirements and then advise us both regarding next steps.

"What time will you come?" I squinted at an incoming message, then huffed out a breath. My daily horoscope, a forward from Lily.

"What time do you want me to come? I have meetings with an art dealer and an art appraiser at Rothman's Auction House."

"How about six? I should be home by then," I answered absently, reading the state of my fate today.

You might pick up some rather disturbing thoughts from a friend, neighbor or relative, Taurus. This person could be upset over something and not communicating his or her feelings. It isn't appropriate to try to coax this person into sharing with you now. They aren't upset with you, but they might be if you push! Back off and let this person come to terms with the problem. Your friend will talk once the time is right.

I frowned. What in hell did that mean? And why was I wasting time on nonsense?

As if prophetic texts weren't enough, suddenly Lily was calling me. I ignored her. If we spoke now, we'd fight. She sent another message. A normal one.

You read your horoscope. I can tell. Please call. I have something urgent to discuss.

Oh. My. God. Lily had figured out what *Delivered* meant on iMessage.

"Er, Naira? Let me call you back." I hung up and called Lily and she began to discuss her birthday trip. And I used the term "discuss" loosely. It wasn't a discussion. It was barely a conversation. All I had to do was make some noise every other sentence to indicate I was listening.

Sighing, I stood up and walked away from the floor-to-ceiling windows that ran the length of the living room, three sides displaying outrageous views of the city. I set my coffee mug on a coaster on top of the stainless steel breakfast bar in the open kitchen while Lily jabbered on. If I got a headache, it would be Neal's fault. He'd created this birthday monster.

This whole marriage business confounded me sometimes. The constant back-and-forth. The consultations about everything—from a bathroom mirror to what gift to give Lily for her seventieth birthday, which was the cause of my current dilemma. Shouldn't Lily's birthday gift be my choice since she was my mother? But no, Neal didn't think tickets to the runaway Broadway hit *Hamilton* were enough. He wanted to throw Lily and her twin sister, Rachel, a grand birthday party and sponsor a weekend trip to the Bahamas for them and a few of their friends. Lily had other ideas.

"Do you really think it's okay if I tell him we'd rather not have a party and would like the birthday trip to be an Antarctica cruise? It's much more expensive. Are you sure he won't feel offended?"

I assured her he wouldn't. "Neal lives to make people's dreams come true." I said it sarcastically, although it was nothing but the truth.

"He's such a sweet boy. Is he home yet?"

"Not yet. He was delayed in LA, I told you this."

"Yes, yes. *Bubbala*, I hope you have breakfast ready for him. He works so hard."

"Uh-huh." I bit my tongue instead of pointing out that I worked equally hard.

"Men need pampering. Especially the good ones."

"Neal just walked in, Lily. Let me get to the pampering. I'll talk you later," I lied and clicked off my phone.

According to Lily, my energies would be better spent lavishing attention on my sweet husband instead of fulfilling my own ambitions, and making sure he had nothing to complain about. Workaholic wives needed to be extra vigilant on the home front or else the marriage suffered. She believed that when men were left to their own devices, the devil took over their groins. Also, their brains and souls, but mostly their groins. Whereas housewives—the true *balabustas*—whose sole purpose in life was to wait on and wait for their workaholic husbands didn't get up to as much mischief. Idle women, apparently, had more fortitude.

As much as my intellect, feminism and several web-based

statistics to the contrary wanted to collectively roll their eyes at Lily's sexist, nonsensical theory, my gut seemed to agree with her. I'd switched into wife mode last night and tidied up the apartment just as the man-of-this-house liked it. Breakfast warmed in the oven. The coffee machine was stocked. The master bath was ready too. The Jacuzzi bubbled with scented water and I'd lit a cluster of candles around it. Everything was ready and simmering for the master's return.

Neal had three choices: a long, sensual bath with me playing *rajah's handmaiden;* a leisurely breakfast with fresh scones from his favorite bakery; or, simply me—naked and horny beneath my short cream silk robe. I grinned. I was always horny for Neal and workaholic wife or not, my husband didn't seem to be bored of me, yet.

Seriously, how bad was the traffic this morning? Restless, I went to the door to wait.

There were four apartments on our floor, all evenly spaced from one another; two each on either side of the suite of elevators in the middle. Ours was at the end of the north side of the building, and the decorator—we'd rented a partially furnished apartment and had filled in the missing pieces ourselves—had placed a lover's bench in the nook outside the door, complemented by a real-looking silk-leaved ficus tree in a large brown pot and a matching umbrella stand.

The bench was an unnecessary accessory in my opinion, mostly used for holding packages or the boxed laundry that the building concierge delivered to our doorstep. I made use of it today to wait for Neal.

It was another ten minutes before the elevator pinged open. I jumped to my feet as his gorgeous-ship rumbled out, slick in dark jeans and a stone-gray sweater, carrying an extra large suiter on one shoulder. I added a shoulder massage to my mental couples-therapy session.

My heart pinged too as he ambled closer and closer, a sexy smile lighting up his face. Sometimes my feelings for my husband devastated me, terrified me.

"Cabbie was a numpty. Took us all over the fookin' highway before we took the tunnel. And what's with the Scottish weather, eh?"

Neal stopped right in front of me, under the lintel of our home. I stretched up and twined my arms around his neck, pulling his head down for a hungry kiss.

He smelled like a stranger. I hated the sweet smell of airplanes on his clothes, so I nuzzled along his jaw where the scent of his aftershave lingered until he became familiar again. Sandalwood, and a hint of verbena.

"I missed ye, bonny lass." He nipped my lips.

"I missed you more." I clutched at him, needing to annihilate the space between us, the strangeness. He opened his mouth wide over mine in perfect understanding and took over.

We twirled inside. He kicked the door shut as our tongues relearned the textures and the taste of us. He dropped the suiter, and free of its weight, free of the tribulations of travel and job, he pushed me flat against the wall next to the door and went to work on me.

Our reunion options dwindled down to me. Just me. And only him.

Blood rushed from my head to my feet, and I would have slid to the floor if I wasn't pinned to the wall by hard, tensile muscles. My breathing fractured. When we came up for air, his electric-blue eyes smiled into mine, then narrowed. He sniffed the air between us like a dog who'd caught the scent of his prey. Ah. He liked the new scent on me. Smiling, I prepared to be devoured. But instead of yanking me closer, Neal stuck his nose in the air, his nostrils aflutter, and sniffed strongly. I burst out laughing when his stomach rumbled in tandem with the inhalations. Alas, it wasn't my perfume that he found irresistible but breakfast.

"Do I smell tattie scones?" he asked, happily.

"You do. The bath's ready too. The new essential oils you brought from Hong Kong smell divine." It was our ritual. A welcome-home ritual. A day of leisure ritual if this were Sunday. The Kahn-Singh-Fraser ritual. I was confident we'd cross out all three choices on my to-do list within the hour. The only question was in which order?

Hunger took precedence over horniness.

No, that didn't sound right. Hunger dragged horniness into the open kitchen, ordered her to strip off her lovely robe and sit on the bar stool—naked—while he served up a full Scottish breakfast after he too had stripped down to his eager natural state. Hunger also filled the coffee mugs to the brim, and the scent of fresh-ground coffee intoxicated the air. Hunger was a very thoughtful human being.

We ate from the same plate. He fed me eggs and pieces of buttered scone, and I fed him sausage and bacon and most of the tattie. My conscience wouldn't allow me to eat meat any-more, not since our sophomore year when Naira had shown me a video of a cattle slaughterhouse. I was okay with fish though as my conscience wasn't above my health.

We used our hands to feed each other, and while we ate and kissed and caressed, we made love to one another with our eyes.

Halfway through breakfast the sun came out, unsettling the blanket of fog outside and the haze inside us. A different, calculated kind of hunger overtook us then.

Neal took me right there on the breakfast bar. Usually, be-cause of the extra height of the bar, he'd turn me around and take me from behind as I braced against the steel countertop. But today, we needed to make love face-to-face. We needed to reassure ourselves that we were still there, still together, that nothing had changed between us in the time we'd spent apart. He stepped between my legs, dragging me to the edge of the bar stool. It was atrociously uncomfortable. The bar stools were shaped to cup our full asses and not for hanky-panky.

"Wait. I've an idea," he said when I winced and let out a loud, "Ouch!"

He reached for the kitchen towels and told me to lift my legs. He stuffed the towels between my bottom and the stool, so the stiff edge wouldn't bite into my skin. "Better?"

I nodded, shifting my ass to get comfortable on top of the kitchen towel. I wasn't the one with a hygiene fetish. Right then, neither was he.

He touched me then. Everywhere. He knew what I liked and what I loved. He spent a delicious eternity rubbing, teasing, suckling my boobs. I was so incredibly sensitive there that I was panting in no time. He could make me come just by licking my breasts, but he didn't. He knew exactly how to make me sigh and what would make me tremble. When I reached for him, desperate and moaning, he knew to step back as it would drive me crazy not to touch him, and he knew when to lean into my touch and make me shudder with love. Make us both gasp for breath.

He knew I was far from perfect in body, mind and spirit. And I knew he wasn't a superhero. But we were glorious together. Perfectly magnificent.

After, I wrapped my arms and legs around my husband and held him close. I couldn't let him go. Not yet. Sometimes, this need I had for him embarrassed me, so I buried my face in the crook of his neck until our hearts beat less erratically and my limbs were ready to comply again.

★ ★ ★

We discussed Naira's proposal while we got dressed for the day.

"I spoke to your sister too, for some perspective on the whole thing," I commented as I sprayed moisturizer onto my skin and rubbed it in. Wanting to help my bestie out didn't mean I wouldn't do my due diligence.

"Which one?"

"Helen. Who else?" I shot a quick frown at him as he snatched a pair of bright green sports socks out of a drawer.

Our marriage had another ritual where my husband walked me to my office in the morning. We were apart so much that the days we were together, we tried to make up for lost time. The walk served as a warm-up for his daily run. Sometimes, he ran across the Brooklyn Bridge and back. Other times, his route took him to his uncle Liam's place on Howard Street, just off Canal, where he'd end up taking a pint of Guinness or tea with his uncle with a dash of family gossip. When he felt inspired, he'd remain there for the rest of the day and worked on his metal murals as he'd set up a makeshift studio in one of the rental apartments his uncle Liam owned.

Apparently, today was going to be no different.

"You've been flying from city to city for nearly three weeks. How are you not exhausted?"

"Because I'm Superman?" Neal smirked, puffing his chest out like Henry Cavill.

"Narcissism is so unattractive. Although, if you dress up as Superman at my office Halloween party next Friday, I'll have to reconsider that comment. There's something about manly muscles covered in red-and-blue spandex that makes me...*umm*." I closed my eyes and shivered as my imagination went a little wild. "Do you think they ever did it while flying? Superman and Lois?"

"We could add it to our bucket list. I've heard of couples attempting a shag while skydiving."

"You're kidding me!" What did I say? Humans were bat-shit crazy.

"Want me to look into it?"

"No thanks." I shuddered. I hated flying. I barely survived plane rides where I was sitting as still as possible and buckled up. I was not going to jump out of one voluntarily.

Neal laughed, kissing me back to solid ground.

"By the way, your number one fan wishes to go on an Antarctica cruise for her birthday. That sounds as bad as sky-diving."

"Does she, now?" His grin widened. "Now there's a woman after my own heart."

I rolled my eyes because obviously the adoration went both ways. "You started this. You sort it out." I poked him in the chest, partly to drive home my point and partly to make him stop crowding my space so I could finish getting dressed. "About Naira…"

Neal stepped back, switched on the flat-screen TV and sank down on the bed to pull on his socks, dividing his attention between the news channel and ogling me. "Aye, what did Helen say about her? And why is it obvious that ye spoke to Helen? Ye could've spoken to Flora."

Technically, Flora was Neal's cousin, his father's younger brother's daughter. She'd been orphaned as a child and had been raised by Neal's parents, though not formally adopted. Neal and his siblings thought of her as part of their brood, but I didn't think Flora saw it that way. Neither did I.

"Because Helen lives in India and schmoozes with the media there. Because she knew Kaivan Dalmia peripherally and knows whom to tap for information about him, and not

Flora, who is studying to be a veterinarian in Edinburgh. Aye?"

Two years older than Neal's thirty-three, Helen, though a little ditzy—scary thought considering she was the mother of three tiny humans—was a savvy judge of character.

Neal pinched my butt for imitating him. "Fair enough. What did she tell ye?"

I revisited my entire conversation with Helen as I applied my makeup. "Nothing the internet didn't. Kaivan invested in gold options because he was tipped off about…something. But he lost a whole lot of money when gold rose instead of fell. So, he borrowed more money and tried to recoup his losses. Then the Indian government demonetized some Indian currency, and that was the straw that broke him." I placed my hands on my hips. "I don't understand. Isn't that insider trading? But Helen didn't seem to think so. She said that he played the market and lost. And that his information was solid and if luck had been on his side, his investments would have made him and his investors an obscene amount of money. But since the opposite happened, his rivals took advantage of his misfortune and made him a scapegoat, instigating the banks to foreclose on his loans."

"Sounds right," Neal mumbled, scouring the stock market footers on MSNBC.

I took the TV control from his hand and shut the screen off. I wanted his undivided attention. "I don't get it. If Kaivan used a tip to bid on options, that's a crime." I'd been an ADA for two and a half years. I knew how that game was played.

"Not exactly, lass." Neal sighed when I crossed my arms across my chest, meaning business. "You really want me to explain it all to ye right now?"

"Please. But do it on the move. I'd rather not be late for work." I shrugged on a dark blue suit jacket over black slacks and a mauve shirt. I had a couple of courtroom stints this morning, and then grunt work for the task force for the rest of the day. We'd be examining and verifying a truckload of documents and statements from over three hundred female employees. What had been a civil suit against the factory for violating the basic rights of its employees, in terms of minimum wage and number of bankable hours, had turned into a criminal offense. The factory owners—it was a damned syndicate—had been additionally charged with money laundering, immigration violations and human trafficking. That was why both the US Attorney's Office and the Manhattan DA's office were involved. It was going to be a crazy busy day. Hell, year.

"The way options work is that X is the price of a stock today but tomorrow it might go up or down. You gamble on that price going up or down. If you think it's going down, ye buy the future option of the low price while selling at the higher price of today. Or, if ye think it's going up, then you buy today and when it goes up tomorrow, ye make money."

"That doesn't sound shady."

Neal tapped my upturned nose, clearly amused by my disappointment that nothing nefarious had gone on. "It's not. When a person gambles on options in the kinds of money Dalmia played in, ye better be certain of the outcome. You could hedge the risk with insurance…which if he had done, it might've saved part of his arse. But, most of the time in deals such as these, yer assured of the outcome beforehand. Why would anyone risk that kind of money otherwise, aye?"

What he'd described was essentially the plot of *Billions*. "So, he was sure the gold price would go one way, put all this money on that surety and lost it all when it went the other way."

"That sums it up nicely, my wee lamb." Neal beamed at

me like a proud papa while he put on his running shoes in the foyer.

I leaned against the shoe closet, sliding my feet into a pair of sturdy beige pumps. Or, I'd been about to when I remembered that I'd left my office phone charging by my bedside. I hurried back into the bedroom to retrieve it.

I had a bad habit of forgetting the BlackBerry at home, then begging Neal to bring it down to my office or to the courthouse. It was so convenient to have your home and office within a ten-minute walking distance of each other, and to have a husband who mostly worked from home and was at your beck and call—when he wasn't traveling.

I walked back to the foyer. It was weird that while I often forgot the BlackBerry all over the place, I never forgot my personal cell anywhere. Handling two phones was a bother, but, as a rule and for full transparency, I had to use the Black-Berry for all work-related calls and emails. The DA's office had its own private server that could be accessed from anywhere and tracked.

"But he must have done something dreadful to be arrested and have so many allegations against him? He can't be innocent." All three hundred and something cases couldn't be fabricated no matter how corrupt the legal system was in India.

Neal followed me into the elevator and we rode it down.

"I've explained this before, hen. Things aren't so black-and-white in India. They aren't anywhere in the world. People with money and power rarely do things by the book. Dalmia may not be completely innocent, but I doubt he's as culpable as they made him out to be, either."

The explanation didn't ease my confusion, in fact I was more troubled by it than ever. My daily horoscope was right. I'd picked up some rather disturbing thoughts from a friend.

"What about you? How by the book are you?" I leveled a

look at him. Even if Deven, the sharkiest of all business sharks ever, kept the Fraser books, Neal had to be aware of…things.

Neal pleaded the fifth as usual. I stalked out of the elevator as doors swept open. I never knew what to feel about Neal's businesses. And now I didn't know what to do about Naira's. Ugh. Why was everything about humanity so shady?

The doorman greeted us jovially, a finger to his hat, as we whirled through the revolving doors of the building and out into the streets of New York. At once, childish screams accosted my ears. Our apartment building was on a block that boasted a preschool on one side, a college on the other and a playground right around the corner. The shortest route to my office was past the playground that was always burgeoning with kids at any point in the day, any day of the year, rain or shine or blizzard. The littlest snot-filled ones made my husband go all soft and playful, while I tried to school my "ick" face as we walked by. Kids, as advertised, weren't my thing.

I kicked up my pace, preempting Neal's habit of pausing to watch the toddlers shriek and slither down the tomato-red slide, or cheer at the children as they raced around the child-proof playground. Sometimes, he joined them in a quick game of tag. He was adorable when he did that, and it made me feel like Maleficent, casting a nasty spell on him when I stood there tapping my foot at the scene. I didn't know how to be around kids—I couldn't bullshit and claim there was a Santa when there clearly wasn't. I especially didn't know how to be around Neal when he was around kids. Which was going to make the next decade of our lives pretty darned interesting.

I didn't like children—what? Wasn't I allowed to even think it? Wasn't it enough that I'd stopped saying it out loud? I didn't want children. I truly felt no overwhelming desire to grow one and pop it out from between my legs, even one who might look and laugh like Neal. I'd been completely honest about my stance as soon as our relationship got serious three summers ago. After he'd gotten over the shock of my disclosure, he'd tried to understand my thought process, and only once had he attempted to reason my issues away. I'd set him straight on the score. I'd told him if not having kids was a deal breaker for him, then we should end it right then.

It still shocked me that he'd given in. Neal adored children. He was a terrific playmate to Helen's brood, and to an assortment of pint-size cousins and godchildren. But he'd chosen me over fatherhood—chosen us. I'd never forget what he'd told me on a crisp October morning such as this, just as the shimmer of predawn had brightened the sky. We were practically living together in my tiny flat between the bridges by then. I was trying to scare him into leaving me, to go back to his large, prolific Scottish clan-dom.

"That is your idea of a family, isn't it? A manor house, a dozen dogs sleeping by the hearth, half a dozen children playing in the back garden. That is your reality, your natural state."

What were we doing with each other? I'd wondered. How desperately I'd tried to protect my heart but he'd smashed through all of my defenses.

"We'll fashion our own family, lass. If it must be just the two of us, then that's what our natural state will be."

With those words, he'd robbed me of the strength to resist him. I'd risen to my knees on the bed we'd made good use of all summer and half of fall, I'd taken his solemn face between my hands and kissed him a promise in return.

A promise that had weighed heavier and heavier on my heart until I'd caved and come up with a way to have my cake and eat it too. I'd presented him with a well-outlined surrogacy plan this past February on his birthday.

We walked in silence for several minutes, basking in the sounds and smells of the city, ignoring the slight tension that shivered between us since the playground. We needed to discuss the surrogates, choose one of them, but neither of us had brought it up since Lavinia's wedding. I wanted to tell him about Naira, but I'd decided to keep my own counsel until I'd spoken to her. There was no point in stirring up a hornet's nest if she wasn't interested.

We crossed Park Row and headed toward Centre Street, past the classic white-stone structure of city hall.

"How was the party at Roman and Jamie's on Saturday? Meet any interesting Hollywood celebrities?" I broke the silence when I couldn't stand it any longer.

More than his clients, Roman and Jamie were Neal's friends. Roman Wilson and Neal had been in university together in Edinburgh. Roman had moved to Beverly Hills a decade ago to dabble in the movie industry first as the talent, now as the bank. He'd met Jamie, an award-winning set designer in her own right, soon after. Neal had reconnected with Roman since our marriage, and because he and Jamie had so much in common, both being artists, they got along fabulously too. Jamie had suffered several miscarriages before they'd had their first child through surrogacy. They'd introduced us to Martha, the California surrogate.

"It wasn't that kind of party," Neal said softly. "I didn't tell ye before, but Roman and Jamie have adopted a wee bairn from Nepal. It was her welcome party on Saturday that they asked me to stay back for." Abruptly, he pulled me to a stop, his blue eyes roving all over my frozen face. "They said the orphanages in Kathmandu are bursting at the seams. If you're unsure about the surrogacy, then we could consider... There are so many bairns that need a home, lass."

His silence *had* been thicker than usual at the playground. The Wilsons had been the reason why I'd even considered surrogacy. And now they'd adopted a baby. Fuck.

No! Just no. I could not—would not adopt a child. Even though I was adopted myself—not once but twice—I was not a proponent of the system. Who knew better than me how quickly adoptive families could shatter? Or that even when everything seemed perfect, it was still a sham? I would never put a child in the untenable position of being at someone else's mercy, someone else's whim. I'd been shuttled between seven different foster homes while the family courts had decided whether the Judge could adopt me or not. It had taken several years after the adoption for me to begin trusting my situation, trusting him, and even longer for Lily and me to reach an understanding and a mutual tolerance of each other. She hadn't wanted me and had made it clear in her neglect of me. Even now, we only got along because we'd both made a promise to Samuel Kahn on his deathbed that we'd take care of each other. And because Neal put family first.

So, if it were up to me, I'd eradicate adoptions and foster care systems from the face of the earth. I'd pour money and resources into building state-of-the-art orphanages and childcare centers that functioned like boarding schools. Then there would be no need to distribute less fortunate children to random families like day-old bread. I'd rather give them knowledge and skills and fashion them into self-sufficient adults who forged their own paths. Adults who wouldn't be scarred by well-meaning adults and their constant seesaw of indecision. It took a village to raise a child, didn't it? So create the damned village, don't settle for a hut. Hire the right professionals, the right teachers and mentors, and not parents who were as screwed up as the children they were supposed to raise. For God's sake, the adoption laws in this country were as slack as its gun laws. At least with surrogacy, we had to have mandatory medical and psyche evaluations for all involved parties, and the IVF process could weed out bad chromosomes from the zygote.

I didn't know my medical history because no one had a clue who my biological parents were, much less had any information on them. All I knew was that I was the product of a classic high school movie cliché. My birth mother got knocked up by her math tutor when she was fifteen. To save her reputation and her future, her parents sent her many states away to an ashram in Pondicherry, a city in southern India, to have her baby among strangers and subsequently leave it—leave me at the ashram's orphanage. After one of their vicious fights over who would get responsibility for me, Sandra, my first adoptive mother, had screamed that Jared was welcome to me as it had been his bright idea to rescue me from my fate. Both Jared, an eye surgeon, and Sandra, a dental surgeon, had been in India with *Médecins Sans Frontières* offering free health clinics and humanitarian help to the less fortunate. They'd met in Paris to train for the clinic. They'd begun slipping into love there, then fallen hard for each other that summer in Pondicherry. They'd fallen in love with me too. Until they'd come back home to the US, to real life, and fallen out of love. *C'est la vie, oui?*

The Judge had called Sandra a schlub, a tasteless oaf of a woman not only in attire but also in comportment. The Judge passing judgment on Sandra never ceased to amuse me. He'd been a man of principle and integrity. A man of his word. A man who didn't mince words. He'd presided over Sandra and Jared's divorce, and appalled at what they'd done to me by "un-adopting" me, he'd petitioned the courts for my guardianship without consulting his wife.

I put on a brave face even though I wanted to wrench free of Neal's grasp and scream at him for even asking me this again. "I thought we'd decided on surrogacy, a biological bairn. But it's up to you. Whatever you want, babe. The whole baby project is for you."

Neal sighed. "I just want to make this easier for ye."

Nothing about having a child was going to be easy for me. The only thing that was easy was loving Neal.

"Let's go. I'll get late," I said, hoping he'd take the hint and drop the discussion. We walked briskly, cutting across Foley Square, and drew closer to the courts.

"So, we have a guest for dinner, aye? I can throw something together or are we ordering in? I'll be stopping by the market for the meat. I can pick up things for a pasta and a salad too." Neal slanted a smile in my direction. His blue eyes were full of hurt for me, and filled with patience once again. He wouldn't push. Not about this.

Was it possible for a heart to burst from love?

"Don't worry about dinner. Oh, you're in for such a treat. Naira's cooking tonight, she'll get the groceries. Just pick up some cheese when you're getting your meat. Something to pair with the wine you brought back from LA. And, get some rest, honey. Unless you have a busy day today."

Neal brought the back of my hand to his lips. "I've a meeting up at the Diamond District later this morning. That's about it."

Neal's work took him into midtown several times a week. "Who are you meeting?"

"A watchmaker. Jamie introduced me to a friend of hers…a potential client if I can deliver what the lass wants and soon. I'm to design a pocket watch for her father's ninety-fifth birthday. Don't—" He raised his hand, ostensibly to stop me from passing judgment.

Too late. My back was already stiff, and I'd already been ripe to gripe. "Seriously? Now we're giving ninety-five-year-olds bespoke jewelry? Is he going to tote the thing about at his next hip replacement?"

Exasperation clouded Neal's long sigh. "People have a right to live as they wish and use their resources as they see fit. Ye can't hold the whole world up to yer standards. It's unfair. Anyway, I'd like a consult with the watchmaker as I don't want the mechanics to affect the design I have in mind for the watch face. I need it figured out, and the costing, before I head back to LA with a couple of samples later this week."

"You're off again?" My stomach flipped over at the thought of him leaving me so soon. I hated when he traveled even though I loved welcoming him back home, and even though I looked forward to having the apartment all to myself, messy and hot.

"What about Diwali?" The five-day festival of lights began on Sunday, and we'd already committed to attending two parties over the weekend.

"One-day trip, hen. You won't even miss me." He kissed my nose, a quick goodbye. And he was off, jogging toward Chinatown.

I pushed the heavy brass-framed entrance of One Hogan Place and went inside, grumbling under my breath. This was exactly why I needed Naira through the baby ordeal. I refused to be stuck monitoring the kid alone. What if I broke it?

You won't even miss me. What a joke. It was dreadful how much I missed my husband already.

CHAPTER SIX

Naira

"I understand yer the reason my wife gave up meat, and why she thinks '*draamebaaz*' is an insult?"

"Guilty as charged." I grinned, remembering how I'd tricked Paris into believing *draamebaaz* was a Hindi curse word when it simply meant a melodramatic person. "Or not guilty for saving the animals that might've otherwise become martyrs to her meals and her anger."

With my attention divided between cutting tempeh into bite-size pieces and sautéing onions for the rogan josh curry, it took me a few seconds to notice the wry look on Neal's face. Oops. Had I inadvertently insulted his own carnivorous lifestyle?

"I didn't mean that you shouldn't eat what you want. I'm not some card-carrying member of the Indian Vegetarian Congress…although my grandfather was and…oh, lord! I didn't mean to… I have no quarrel with…" I shut up as I was only making it worse.

Neal looked more amused than offended. "Relax, lass. Nothing I haven't heard before as my younger sister is vegan."

He bent his head over the frying pan and inhaled so deeply that his chest cavity expanded, stretching his full-sleeved Henley taut. He'd pushed the sleeves up to his elbows, displaying some lovely lean muscles, and I wondered bizarrely if he did yoga and not weights.

"I've only ever had my grandmother's lamb rogan josh. But if yer curry tastes as incredible as it smells, I just might convert."

"Really?" Delight shot through me, but it was a temporary high.

"Nope. I love my meat, lass. No offense to the animals." He winked, making me laugh.

Though animal slaughter wasn't a remotely funny subject, I couldn't help but be charmed by Paris's husband. His lovely manners had put me at ease from the moment I'd arrived. I'd been a little freaked that I'd been late—damn Vinay and his obnoxious messages that bordered on insults.

What's going on with the trust?

Why is it taking so long to get the money out?

Are you sure you know what you're doing?

And the last one from this morning: I WANT ANSWERS!

Who did he think he was demanding answers from me? I fumed. With every passing day, I was even more determined to make a life in New York. And for that I needed to impress Neal and Paris with my business plan.

I'd already got off on the wrong foot about making an impression due to my lateness because I'd had to stop at three grocery stores to gather all the ingredients I needed for the rogan josh. I'd still been missing two key ingredients when I'd arrived. Neal had handed me a pair of nonskid house socks from the shoe closet—their apartment was a no-shoes zone like my parents' place in Mumbai—although here it had more to do with hygiene than offending a higher power residing inside the temple built inside the house. As I began the prep for dinner, Neal had run down to the closest bodega for the poppy seeds and dry bay leaves that I simply could not make the curry without.

If I'd felt weird puttering around Paris's kitchen in her absence, or ordering her husband about as if he were my sous-chef, the feeling was long gone. It had been my idea to cook my infamous tempeh rogan josh that Paris loved as a thank-you for Friday and…whatever happened tonight. Only, I hadn't expected to be cooking it *in* her home. I'd suggested making dinner. Paris had accepted. Then somehow the offer had been refurbished, and now, here I was, stirring the curry pot in her kitchen.

Making tonight's dinner wasn't only about gratitude. Cooking was as much of a relaxing exercise for me as yoga or dancing was. And boy, had I needed to relax after such a stressful weekend. Damn Vinay. I wouldn't let him spoil my evening. *Stop thinking about him, then!* I blew out a breath. Also, cooking for three people was so much more fun than cooking for one.

When Kaivan and I had entertained, I'd preferred hanging—hiding?—out in the kitchen with our master chef rather than making small talk with guests I had nothing in common with, guests like Vinay. My passive-aggressive stance had given Kaivan no small amount of amusement. *You can tell when Naira likes someone or simply tolerates them by the amount of time she spends in the kitchen.* He'd once teased me about it in front of my parents who'd not been amused that I'd snubbed my wifely duties and our elitist guests in favor of befriending the hired help. My father had scolded me as if I were still a schoolgirl and living under his thumb, demanding that I make them and my husband proud. Kaivan had respectfully asked Papa to butt out of our lives. He'd said my behavior was no longer their concern.

Everything had been overturned in the last two years, including my father granting me the respect of knowing what was best for me.

"Refill?"

I glanced at Neal as he gave the wine decanter a swirl. They were both blurry. I didn't know if my eyes stung because I'd been staring at the curry for so long, lost in memories, or the memories themselves. I had sense enough not to rub my eyes with onion-stained fingers, and I blinked rapidly until my vision cleared. There were only a couple of sips of the Malbec left in my glass but I shook my head. "Not yet. I need to pace the reds or the tannins will give me a headache."

He set the decanter down, took a quick sip of his scotch and resumed dicing some vegetables for me. Neal had volunteered to be my kitchen helper/sous-chef, since I didn't know where the colanders, sieves and nonstick pans were in this beautiful open-style, pristine white contemporary kitchen. He'd also proved to be an entertaining companion and had kept up a steady stream of conversation that didn't feel forced or awkward. Probably because we had so many things in common to talk about like the latest Bollywood movies and appreciating the *ghazals* wafting out of the Bose wall speakers. His endless playlist shuffled between Indian and Scottish ballads.

Kaivan had been partial to *ghazals* too when I'd forced him to relax every once in a while and enjoy some music. On rare Sundays, we'd give the house staff a surprise day off and I'd cook his favorite meal from scratch. We'd shed our responsibilities for the day and focus on each other, making each other happy, making each other laugh. My husband, the boss of thousands, would eagerly transform into my sous-chef, my cabana boy—whatever I wished him to be that Sunday. And we'd—

I burst out laughing as Neal began crooning the *ghazal* in an accented nasal falsetto—the singer was female. It completely destroyed the gravitas of the song, which was about graves and wishes, but it kept the mood in the kitchen from getting maudlin.

"I'm shocked the curry didn't curdle with that rendition," I felt bold enough to tease, which only made him warble louder. I shook my head when he urged me to sing. I was a dancer, not a singer.

I hadn't expected to like Neal so much. He wasn't the person I'd imagined him to be—his nature, I meant, and not his looks. The good impression he'd created at Lavinia's wedding was only getting crisper and clearer every time I met him.

Section by section, I slid the tempeh into the simmering sauce. It wasn't that I'd expected him to be an asshole. Why would Paris marry an asshole? But I'd worried we wouldn't get along because Paris and Kaivan hadn't, which was why I'd worn the rose pendant at Lavinia's wedding, hoping it would serve as an icebreaker and we'd have a nice story to exchange.

I realized I'd arrived from India with preconceptions planted in my head about him. Fashion magazines labeled him and his sister as temperamental divas. There was more than one piece of footage of him on YouTube, knuckle-deep in a drunken brawl or parading about with skimpily clad supermodels. Granted, some were old videos mixed with the latest fashion show footage that had likely been doctored by the media for maximum effect. Then there was the whole drama of his broken engagement. My family just didn't think well of him—though at this point I couldn't care less what my family thought about anything. I'd told Paris all the gossip when she'd first started dating him, but she'd laughed it off. "No wonder I'm attracted to him. Swoony McDreamy blue eyes, notwithstanding, he's a baaad boy. Let's see if I can make him worse," she'd said gleefully, as if accepting a challenge.

Clearly, Neal wasn't worse off with Paris, nor she with him. They made a perfect couple. I was so happy Paris had found her mate despite her hard resistance to love and codependency. She hadn't mangled the relationship at the first sign of trouble like she'd done with her other boyfriends. Not only that, her relationship with Lily had also changed. For the better. I was so proud of her.

I ceased stirring the curry, which was simmering nicely, and tapped the wooden spoon against the pot in lieu of knocking on wood. Our lives had taken such sharp turns since college. Neither one of us were where we'd planned to be. And it was okay, I told myself. What didn't kill me would only make me stronger.

"And that's that." I vowed under my breath, settling a splash protector on the curry pot. If only life came with a splash protector to keep the hurt and taint away.

"It's done? That dinna take long," Neal asked in surprise.

Would Kaivan have entertained a friend of mine if I was late from work? I'd like to believe he would have though I couldn't imagine it. Then I remembered that even while I was around he and Paris had found it impossible to be civil to each other.

"Nearly done. We'll let it stew for twenty minutes." I turned the heat down low, then swept my eyes over the organized chaos on the countertop. I set the timer on the rice cooker and switched it on. "The wild rice will be ready in twenty too. Paris is on her way, right?"

"It's what her text says. She'd better get here before that timer goes off, aye? Because I'm no' waitin' a minute longer to eat that scrumptious-smelling curry." He smacked his lips and groaned as if he was only a step away from reaching the Pearly Gates.

The heat from the cooking range transferred onto my cheeks. His accent. *Uff.* No wonder Paris had melted like butter for him.

I washed my hands in the sink, trying not to think about how similar "scrumptious" had sounded from Kaivan's mouth. He'd had a British accent because of the decade or so he'd spent in London for university and then his first job at a hedge fund.

Gah. Don't think about him. Concentrate on making dinner.

The salad had to be nice and chilled by now. I should toss it with the mango dressing and parmesan flakes. Maybe even plate it, since Paris was on her way.

I grabbed the salad bowl from the fridge. I'd never been clumsy. Not in the kitchen—not anywhere. But I was then. One minute I had the bowl in my hands and the next my hands were empty. My heart rate rocketed into the strato-sphere as I watched the large cling-wrapped ceramic bowl crash to the floor, and the carefully shredded leaves of kale, baby spinach and thinly sliced green apples explode from it.

I stared in horror at the carnage around my feet, hands shak-ing. That was my life right there. Something scrumptious that had slipped from my fingers. A sob rose to my throat. Then I shattered too.

At some point, I realized that my face was buried in Neal's chest and he was rubbing my back in soothing circles, mur-

muring things to me in a mishmash of Hindi and English. "It's all right, lass. *Hota hai*. Shit happens. We didn't need that salad. Who eats leaves and fruit besides coos anyway?"

I wanted to laugh when he said "coos." He was being so nice.

What was wrong with me? Why couldn't I find my footing? How was I going to make any of this work if I kept falling apart?

"Come on. Come away from here." With a hand on my back, he guided me around the dozens of pieces of fired clay and destroyed food to the living room area. He settled me on a lush white leather sofa and set a box of tissues within reach on a glass-topped coffee table. He dashed into the kitchen, came back with my wineglass topped off. After I'd taken a couple of sips and I was breathing somewhat normally, he went back into the kitchen and began cleaning up my mess.

Kaivan wouldn't have been so nice, would he? Had Kaivan been a nice man? God. I didn't know anymore. I didn't know anything anymore. Why was I fighting with Vinay? What was the point?

I guzzled the wine down like it was water. Anything to get rid of the soup of nerves in my stomach. I was so embarrassed by my behavior that I couldn't even bring myself to get up and help Neal. If my legs ever stopped shaking, I'd run out of the apartment and never come back.

How had Paris done this? How had she found the strength to go on, to live on, when life had knocked her down over and over? I wasn't that brave. But I wanted to be.

When the kitchen floor was spick-and-span again, Neal brought the wine decanter and his own replenished whisky glass to the coffee table. He went back into the kitchen once more and brought back a platter of cheese, nuts and fruits that we'd munched on while cooking. Then he took the sofa opposite mine and smiled at me.

"I'm so sorry. I think my hands were wet and the bowl slipped." My blood still raced around my nervous system like a horse at the derby. "Thank you." I gestured toward the kitchen with my empty glass. Then realizing it was empty, I set it down on a coaster. "I didn't even help you." So much for trying to impress him and Paris with my unparalleled lifestyle skills.

"Och. No trouble, lass." His kind blue eyes lowered from my face to my fidgety legs. "Let's make sure ye didn't step on anything. Ceramic may not be as sharp as glass, but it can cut."

I looked down at my jeans, and one by one at the soles of the thick socks covering my feet. Apart from a few pieces of salad stuck on my jeans and socks, I was none the worse for wear. Still, I should've thought of it. I removed the leaves, wrapped them in a used tissue and tucked it away in my pocket to dispose of later.

"Now then, are ye up to talking shop?" he said in a brisk, businesslike manner.

I wasn't. But I would. It was why I was here.

"Shouldn't we wait for Paris?"

I knew I'd overstepped the boundaries of friendship when I'd asked Paris to become my business partner. I wasn't going to sugarcoat it. Money muddied all relationships, and I wanted full transparency. It would be her name on the paperwork—on the lease, on the bank loans if we needed them, and hopefully we would when we expanded—but in the beginning, it would be her name, her reputation, even if it was my money at risk. Business was about reputation and goodwill, if I'd learned anything in the last three years, it was that. If I missed a rent payment or absconded from this country or failed to pay off a bank loan or died, Paris would be liable for my debts. For that reason, I had to leave embarrassment and shyness aside and treat this evening like a business meeting—shattered bowl notwithstanding.

I winced mentally. Was broken pottery an auspicious thing like broken glass, or was it bad luck? Whatever it was, I would amaze Neal with my knowledge and savvy.

"She'll catch up. And let's spare her eyes from glazing over, aye?" Neal grinned.

Smiling back, I began to tell him about An Atelier in Mumbai, which of course he'd heard of, and to my delight, he'd patronized a few times. He'd bought housewarming gifts for friends from the Delhi shop. He'd been directed there by the Hyatt concierge where he'd been staying.

"How fantastic! We push marketing and publicity hard through hotels."

I explained how An Atelier in Mumbai had come about.

"I'd wanted to launch it as an online store first, but Kaivan thought a physical store would make a bigger impact. He loaned me the capital and I opened my first shop on Linking Road, in the hub of Mumbai shopping. I never imagined that in just a few years I would be able to pay back Kaivan's loan in full, and open another three stores across Mumbai, plus one each in Delhi and Hyderabad. When I sold it to… uh, sold An Atelier, we'd been ready to launch another three stores in India, and I'd been in talks to set up a franchise outfit in The Dubai Mall."

Then Kaivan got arrested. Our joint accounts, business accounts, even my personal accounts were frozen. Most of our assets were seized. We'd been strapped for cash, and I'd used An Atelier as collateral to borrow money from Vinay Singhal to pay for Kaivan's legal fees, and eventually, I'd been forced to sell it to him. A few months ago, when I'd finally surfaced from my grief, or let go of it enough to salvage one tiny bit of my life, I'd focused on getting An Atelier back. But Vinay had refused to negotiate a buy back for anything less than several pounds of my flesh and every last drop of my blood. Business was business, and it had nothing to do with family, he'd said.

Fair enough. Which was why I hadn't bothered to tell him that I was no longer interested in buying back An Atelier in Mumbai.

I didn't tell Neal any of that. Instead, like a proud mama, I showed him An Atelier in Mumbai's website on my phone. Vinay hadn't changed a thing about it. Why would he? It was perfect.

I pressed my lips together as they wobbled. I would *not* cry again.

"This is the model I will mirror for An Atelier in New York. I...um...can't use that name obviously because of branding. I signed a noncompete agreement when I sold it—which is also why it's better if Paris's name is on everything for the new store and not mine. I'll have to come up with something catchy like An Atelier...but that's for later. Can you see how easy it is to navigate, click and buy?"

"This is...interesting. Let's put it up on a bigger screen. I want to take a closer look. The computer's in my office," he said, standing up and giving me a hand.

I got a belated tour of the spacious apartment as we meandered toward Neal's office. A long thick gallery led from the main door straight down to the living room with passages or doors branching off to bedrooms on either side of it. A gorgeous terrace with a high glass railing skirted all along the outer perimeter of the apartment. While the views and the space was awe-inspiring, the decor itself was colorless. There was lots of glass and white and leather everywhere. No personal photos or artwork on the walls. There were some odd pieces of furniture that looked as if Neal or Paris had picked them out, like an ocher-colored chaise that graced a glass-walled alcove just off the living room. The space was very likely Paris's den as the floor-to-ceiling shelves behind the chaise held full sections of law books.

Just as I was beginning to get used to all the morbid white, Neal ushered me into his office, and I gasped in utter delight. Tartan tapestry, metals and sparkly things glittered out of the walls and furniture. Bursts of color were everywhere. A room fit for an artist, I thought.

A wave of windows occupied one entire wall of the room from floor to ceiling, framing the boroughs of Manhattan and Brooklyn by moonlight. I could only imagine the sunlight pouring in during the day, bringing the flamboyant and eclectic room into bright focus. A long, clear glass desk ran perpendicular to the windows. It was equipped with all sorts of fascinating thingamajigs and light fixtures that I wanted to look at closely, that I wanted to touch. But later. Behind it, against the wall, was a workstation. Above that, riveted into the wall, was a beaten-metal artwork of seven horses racing against the tide. It was too big for such a small space, and yet it was perfect. It reminded me of the painting Vinay had stolen. Husain did horses best, but these horses could give Husain a run for his money.

I spun around, taking in everything. This room was all character, and none of it easy. Were Neal's easygoing mannerisms a farce, then?

"This room is so different than the rest of the place. You changed this room. You had it decorated, designed it." Why hadn't they bothered with the rest of the apartment?

"Aye. I need this equipment to fit just so. I had the firm that handles the rentals in the building remove the furniture from this room to fit that in." He patted his hand on the extralong, extrawide glass table.

Ah. Now it all made sense. They were renting this apartment. It wasn't theirs.

The custom-made jewelry-designing table came with backlight options, USB ports and dozens of sleek drawers of different sizes running along its belly on two sides. One side of it was hinged: the glass top could be raised like an architect's drafting table, Neal explained. I really wanted to try all the gadgets, but I wasn't here to play.

The computer screen sat on the workstation behind the designing table, sharing counter space with trays full of stencils, rulers, tiny bottles of paint, fine-tipped brushes and weird-looking quills in clear plastic holders, and sheets and sheets of paper—all of it arranged with regimented neatness.

No, Neal couldn't be an easy man to live with. Not for a woman like Paris who thrived in chaos.

"Don't you use a computer program to design?" I bent to admire a hand-drawn sketch of a clock…or, no. It was a detailed design of a pocket watch on his desk.

"Sometimes. I prefer to draw the preliminaries by hand."

I tried and failed to imagine him drawing my rose pendant with its dozens of delicate diamond-studded petals by hand.

"Wow. How long does it take to draw something so detailed and intricate? Doesn't your hand hurt?"

"Work hazard." Smiling, he picked up a stress ball from the designing table and squeezed it. "Time depends on several factors. I start designing on paper, then transfer it to the computer once I'm happy with it. The CAD/CAM program converts it to a 3-D image, so I can check it from all angles. I used to do that by hand too. All the angles and perspectives. But aye, it hurts like the devil and gives me a migraine, so I don't do it that way often now."

I preferred to use my hands too, wherever possible. It was the man against machine conundrum.

"I went on a diamond and jewelry factory tour in Amsterdam some years ago. The designer used a drafting table like yours, only it had a computer screen built into it. He drew right on the screen with a stylus, using special software." I ran my fingers over the fine lines of the rudimentary design of the watch face. "He designed a ring for me within minutes by picking and choosing different shanks and stones. A machine created a wax model of the design, and then the mold was cast into metal, and finally, the goldsmith set the stones and polished the gold to a finish by the end of the two-hour tour."

"That sounds about right for a standard ring."

Since my face probably broadcasted my absolute fascination with the process, Neal offered to show me how and where he had his molds cast, and how his pieces, which were the opposite of standard, came about.

I accepted happily. "Thank you! I work with potters and glassblowers and fabric designers—I'd love to add jewelry makers to my contact list."

I loved visiting workshops and factories, watching people or machines—didn't matter which—build things. I'd been the kid who'd taken the family electronics apart to see what was inside them, how they worked. I'd been the one to fix things around the house when I was too impatient to wait for a plumber or a handyman. Another thing I'd learned since my life had turned upside down: not everything could be fixed.

I swallowed hard, thinking of my family again. *No. No! They didn't deserve to be missed.*

I pasted on a bright, bright smile and turned to Neal. "Let me show you the website. It does so much more on a desktop screen."

Switching on the computer screen, he pulled up An Atelier in Mumbai's website in a couple of clicks. "Attractive. Dynamic. Aye, I see what ye mean by easy to navigate."

He scrolled through page after page, clicking on random items, asking me what I had in mind regarding pricing, import duties, delivery options—everything I'd worked out for the US.

I told him the truth. "I don't have the details. I didn't know...this wasn't even an idea when I sat on the plane. But it is now, and I'll have numbers and projections ready for you by the end of the week."

"I don't need the details, lass. Just throw some numbers at me so I have an idea. The India ones will do for now."

Those I knew like the back of my hand and he seemed... pleased...by the stats. He asked about the merchandise and my sources. Would they be the same ones I'd used in India or new ones for a US market and consumer base? Did I plan to buy the inventory or would it be on consignment? What would make up my inventory for the US market?

I answered all his questions. The more we discussed, the more ideas came to me. There was nothing I didn't know about opening a lifestyle store.

"I want to start small here, smaller than Mumbai. That—" I pointed to the website "—is what An Atelier in Mumbai became after three years of blood and sweat. I'll work out a five-year plan for here." I hoped it wouldn't take that long to lift off. If it did... I'd cross that bridge when I got to it.

He didn't ask me anything else, so I assumed that I'd managed to convey my vision. He continued to scroll through the website, scrutinizing each page for long minutes. Pondering my fate, he seemed less like an artist and more like the CEO of an A-list company even in his casual attire of dark jeans and a collarless shirt. Right then the similarities between Kaivan and Neal were too stark to ignore, too obvious for me not to compare them.

My legs turned to rubber in a combination of fear and anticipation and grief, and I grabbed at the back of a jewel-green office chair for purchase.

Then Paris walked into the room, and the relief I felt upon seeing her was so immense that I literally ran across the room and threw my arms around her. But even her snarky response to my weird behavior couldn't save me from making an utter fool of myself in front of her husband for the second time that evening.

I hid in the bathroom until hiding in it began to upset me even more than my complete loss of composure in Neal's office. I took stock of my face. There was nothing I could do about its puffiness or its blotchiness, so I ran my fingers through my hair until the ends of my blunt flipped out. It would have to do.

I forced myself to step out of the bathroom sanctuary. Paris and Neal were in the kitchen, talking softly and making gooey eyes at each other over the trays I'd prepped with empty serving bowls. Their cozy bond shot a poker straight through my heart. Kaivan and I used to be like that. Like we simply had to touch each other, open our souls to each other every night.

Snap out of it. I couldn't start crying again.

"Chef's back," I said extra loudly when it looked like they'd start kissing any second. "Please move aside so I can serve dinner."

Keep your hands and mind busy and you won't have time for hysteria, I told myself sternly.

As soon as I stepped into the kitchen, Paris blocked me with her body. "Nope. I got this. You and Neal did your share. Now you get to relax. Babe, pour Naira some vino."

I stared blankly at Paris. She'd removed her jacket—the one I'd sobbed on and stained with my snot—and had rolled up the sleeves of her work shirt. She brandished the wooden stirrer in the air like a baton. She was serious!

I swallowed a manic giggle and accepted a fresh wineglass from Neal, then I hovered right outside the kitchen, just in case. Paris was no kitchen queen or helper or even a kitchen ghost.

"Don't stir the curry fast, you'll crumble the tempeh. Get the condiments out from the fridge. The fried *papadums* are in that box on the counter."

"Exactly how incompetent do you think I am in the kitchen?" She rolled her eyes, but followed my instructions to the letter, adding a snarky comment or two about the stress of serving spicy condiments at the right temperature. And the woes we'd suffer the morning after eating said condiments.

The giggle now tickled my tummy, but I was still too shaky to give in to it. It wouldn't do to start cackling like a lunatic on top of sobbing like a hyena in front of prospective business partners.

I got out of Paris's way and helped Neal set the table. Inspired by the thick pillars of candles stored inside the side buffet, I even got fancy and arranged half a dozen pillars on a mirrored tray and placed the whole thing in the middle of the thick oak wood dining table. The fresh sea breeze aroma of the candles would dispel the smells of masalas and fried onions from the air. A major drawback to cooking in an open kitchen was the odors it spread through the space, even with a powerful hood exhaust. It took over the room, sank its oils into the furnishings, until you aired out the space. Or lit scented candles. Or tucked cinnamon sticks into the rolled up serviettes. The sticks would also absorb the smells. I had Neal slide open the doors to the terrace too, and a rush of air brought with it a fresh coolness.

"Honey, where have you stashed the salad?" Paris called out as we aired the apartment. She had her head stuck in the fridge.

I froze, my cheeks burning, and no amount of cold air blowing in from the open terrace could cool them down. My eyes darted to Neal's instead of just confessing to the catastrophe.

"The dug et it," Neal said, winking at me.

What? I frowned, wondering if I'd misheard. His accent was so thick just then and the *whirr* of the helicopter outside had distorted his words even more.

"What dog? You got us a dog without discussing it with me? What the hell, Neal?"

Ah. He'd meant *dog* not *Doug*. Neal was such a dear, but I couldn't let him cover for me.

"I dropped it. I've probably damaged your gorgeous parquet floor. I'm sorry." I would replace the bowl. And if there was a dent in the kitchen floor, I'd replace it too. It was only fair.

Paris whipped her eyes from me to the floor, then back to her husband. "Why would you say a dog ate it? What is wrong with you?"

I started giggling then. Who would have guessed that Paris and Neal were a twenty-first century version of *I Love Lucy*? As for what was wrong with Neal? From where I stood, nothing whatsoever. My best friend's husband truly was the sweetest man on earth. I'd been worried about him for nothing.

CHAPTER SEVEN

Paris

I lost my patience halfway through dinner.

Naira was laughing again, largely due to my husband's incessant jocularity. She'd even lost the deer-in-the-headlights look she'd sported back in Neal's office. It was the perfect time to steer the conversation to Naira's business quandary, but Neal was taking his own sweet time getting to the point.

I suppose he was just being cautious. Her breakdown had shocked me too. I'd asked Neal if he'd been too critical of her idea, overtly harsh in his evaluation of her goals. Neal wasn't one to beat around the bush or lead anyone down the primrose path with false praise or promises. If he'd found fault in her business plan, he'd have told her. Gently perhaps, but he'd have let his opinion be known.

He'd assured me that wasn't the case. Which meant Naira

was simply overwhelmed. She'd been dealing with a lot and was still fragile, I got that. But all sympathy aside, I was past ready to call it a night and to strip down to my bra and panties—it's how I ate dinner on most nights. I'd had a long day and I needed a bath, some de-stressor sex and at least six hours of sleep so I could tackle tomorrow without falling on my face. But my husband and bestie wouldn't quit nattering about Michelin-star restaurants and the latest trends in time-pieces. I wondered if they'd notice if I left, showered, napped and came back while they discussed world cuisines and gos-siped about mutual acquaintances. I stifled a yawn.

Vicious. It had been a vicious day. Unusually so. I wanted to cleanse it off my body.

Sensing my *ugh*, Neal leaned in to kiss the side of my neck. On cue, Naira blushed and got all flustered and uncomfort-able again. I both smirked and sighed. The woman was still violently shy of PDAs. Crazy. The first time I'd brought my fuck buddy to our dorm room, Naira had run from us as if we'd give her rabies. In her family, even married couples didn't kiss or hold hands openly, much less indicate in any way that they shagged. She'd never seen her father show any kind of af-fection to her mother. Well, the Judge and Lily hadn't exactly flirted up a storm in front of me either, but I had been in no doubt of their love for each other or the respect they had for one another. Or, that they'd been quite active in the bedroom right until the week he'd been hospitalized.

I was rather surprised that Naira hadn't changed at all even after marriage. Come to think of it, I hadn't seen her kiss her husband. Like, ever. Indian weddings, despite being massive colorful circuses, didn't have the final you-may-kiss-the-bride act. I'd seen them hold hands though, and flirt. Kaivan had been an intense, even sexy, man. He'd sure known how to make a woman blush.

And, ick. Why was I imagining them being cutesy together? And why did I know just how active the Judge and Lily had been in the bedroom? Now I really needed that shower.

I rolled my neck from side to side, watching Neal take a third helping of the rogan josh and gobble it up. Probably why he didn't want to talk business yet. His mouth was too full.

Prudery and shyness aside, Naira's Michelin-star cooking was always a hit with the guys.

My scrambled brain tried to recall the last time I'd seduced Neal through his stomach. Like actually cooking a meal from scratch and not just heating up bakery-bought scones or throwing a bag of salad together or a pasta quick-fix.

Oh, crap. It had been over a year ago at Thanksgiving. And, I'd only cooked that day because we'd been hosting. In fact, it was the last party we'd hosted at home. I'd rebuffed all of Neal's attempts to entertain since then, claiming it was too much of a hassle or I was too busy with work or lazy or whatever.

Now I felt like a complete ogre. I needed to get my shit together and practice a holistic work-life balance.

I thought that for about half a second. Then, I got pissed off for feeling guilty about not optimally fulfilling my wifely duties. I was giving him a freaking bairn. How's that for satiating the ultimate wifely duty?

"Oh, wow, how do you know Chandra *didi*?" Naira's excitable question pulled me back into their conversation.

Great. One more person they'd found in common to gossip about, and this one apparently deserved the respectful suffix of *didi*—older sister. I'd heard both Neal and Naira use the term periodically while addressing their sisters.

"I know her from Chandigarh. My family used to spend every summer there at my grandparents' house while growing up, and so did hers. By the way, your rogan josh is on par with my nanima's."

Wow. If Neal was comparing Naira's cooking to his maternal grandmother's, she'd truly impressed him.

Neal had adored his maternal grandparents. He'd lost his nanima just months before we'd met at the Right is Might fund-raiser. Sadly, both his grandparents had died within a few weeks of each other. Neal had been extremely close to them and had been devastated by their deaths, especially because he'd missed being by his grandfather and mentor's deathbed and funeral as he'd been busy getting high at a weeklong rave with his ex and a group of toxic friends in Ibiza. It had been a life-altering moment for him, an epiphany, and he'd cut himself loose from all that toxicity.

We'd both been grieving and lost when we'd first met. It had been only six months since the Judge's passing for me.

"All summer, we slept on the terrace, under the stars, with our bellies stuffed with food and mischief. Dozens of mattresses would be rolled out as all our neighborhood friends would sleep over. We played cards all night, did daft things, anything to keep from sleeping. Who wants to sleep when there was so much life to live, aye? We'd stuff our faces all day and gorge on tubs of fresh biscuits and fruit and sweets at night."

My husband could mesmerize you with words. He strung them together like diamonds on a gold chain, shiny and eye-catching.

"One summer, I pestered Nanima to teach me how to cook." He shot me a thoroughly cheeky grin then, and said, "Because that summer, a bonny wee lass had moved into the house right next to ours."

Neal laughed, his blue-blue eyes traveling far away from me, to a time and a place beyond my reach. I took his hand, anchoring him to me.

"Ye should have seen what happened to us then, to the lads.

We were ten of us—ten boys counting me and Dev, and we went berserk after Pudgy."

"Wait!" I had to interrupt him. "Pudgy?" I didn't even know this girl, this phantom rival of my husband's affections, and yet I was offended on her behalf.

Neal squeezed my hand. "Nothing to do with her weight, hen. Dinna get yer panties in a twist. She was as skinny as a scarecrow. I've no idea why her family called her that, but they did. And I never bothered to find out her real name. Not then."

"Of course not. One Pudgy is the same as another, right?" I said pointedly.

Neal didn't even try to argue down to a misdemeanor. He proceeded to give us a ridiculous account of his first foray into the matters of the heart. He'd wanted to impress the lass by baking her a cake in the shape of a heart. Love's labor, if you please. I rolled my eyes, not at all taken in by the charlatan I'd married. But I could see Naira was fooled. She was hanging on to his every word. He had her eating out of his hands and he hadn't even cooked!

Neal toiled day and night in Nanima's kitchen until he mastered the art of cake making. Then, late one night, after his siblings and mates were deep in their slumber, he jumped from his terrace to hers with his heart and his heart-shaped chocolate cake in his hands. It seemed the houses were built close enough together that he could leap from terrace to terrace easily. He crept into his wee love's home—into her room like some creepy stalker dude, I corrected, but he ignored me—only to find Tommy, one of the neighborhood lads, already there and with his hand down Pudgy's pajama top, no less.

We were wiping tears from our eyes by then.

"It taught me a valuable lesson, aye?"

I snorted with laughter. "Enlighten us, please."

"I spent half the summer trying to impress the lass with a cake. If I'd just told her of my interest from the start, it might have changed the outcome, maybe?" He shrugged grandly, not in the least bit upset about his epic fail. Not now. His gorgeous blue eyes fixed on mine, shining with promises that would last a million years. "Now, I go after what I want from the start."

I wondered what my wily husband intended with his story or if he intended anything by it at all.

"Cute. Did we make enough small talk? Can we get down to business now?" I asked.

We got down to business. Just not the one either Naira or I were expecting.

"How set are ye on a solo operation?" Neal asked.

"What do you mean? Paris will be a sleeping partner. And I can't afford to hire anyone else. Not at first," said Naira.

"Nay, lass. What I mean is do ye want to open yer own shop at all? Because my company has plans underway to launch its first concept store—Fraser Bespoke. Fashion, art, home design, luxury goods, all of it consolidated under one brand, but individualized to the client's tastes and requirements. We launch in Edinburgh at Christmas and in Dubai by spring of next year. Eventually, London, Paris, New York and…we'll see where else. The website is being designed, but we've run into snafus already. Yer website and your understanding of social media, of lifestyle is impressive, Naira. I'd like ye to consider working for Fraser Bespoke."

"What was that?" I was still disoriented by the surprise proposal Neal had thrown at dinner.

A stunned Naira had gone home after promising to sleep on the tentative job offer, and a second promise to cook a full Marwari meal for us the next time. Naira was a Marwari, which was a community of people who hailed from several regions in the northwest of India. Their special cuisine and their language was also called Marwari.

And though Neal was only half Sikh, he'd gone full *desi* man on me tonight, lording it over the dinner table while his belly was being catered to.

I brought his lordship down to size by making him load the dishwasher while I put the kitchen to rights. If I'd been alone, I'd have left the entire mess for the cleaning service to deal with; they were due to come on Wednesday. But Neal wouldn't be able to sleep until everything was spotless again. And if he woke to a dirty kitchen, he'd be moody for the rest of the day.

And good luck to him when we had to deal with the *fakakta* baby bottles, baby toys and baby poop every day.

"The bonny, clever lass is exactly who Dev's been looking for. And she dropped right into my lap." Neal pressed a rough, happy kiss on my lips. "Thanks to my brilliant wife."

I didn't feel particularly brilliant just then. What I felt was blindsided. This was not how I'd expected this dinner to end.

"Back up a bit, hon. How did we go from advising Naira on *her* business plan to offering her a job?"

"Wasn't that a stroke of genius? When she comes on board with Fraser Bespoke, the rest will fall into place. We take care of our clan, aye?" He shut the loaded dishwasher and started it.

When, not *if*. Sir Galahad had retired to bed without me. Neal, the bloody business shark, had come out to play as soon as he'd smelled fresh blood. God help us all.

I left the kitchen towel flat on the countertop so it would dry, and went into the bedroom. I needed to think this through.

"I didn't know Fraser Global was branching out into concept stores." I opened a drawer, took out a sleep shirt.

Neal raised his eyebrows meaningfully as he stepped into

the walk-in closet behind me. "Since when are ye interested in Fraser business?"

Ouch. That certainly put me in my place.

It was true that I wasn't interested. Didn't mean I was ignorant. On his father's side, Neal descended from a line of soldiers and sheep farmers. His great-great-great-grandfather had branched out and become a tailor in Inverness. His son had expanded the home tailoring shop into a clothing store. Every generation had added something to the enterprise until Fraser Global now comprised of several department stores in Scotland, massive amounts of farmland and a whisky distillery or two. Then there was Neal's maternal family, the Singhs, who'd once been jewelers to kings.

"What does this expansion mean for you, Neal? More travel? More events? What?" I addressed the biggest part that was bothering me about this new development.

Here, I'd been worrying about what an awful wife I was, and there he was planning on being an absentee husband. I couldn't deal with a baby if he wasn't going to shoulder the bulk of the responsibility. It just wasn't happening.

"No more than usual." He stripped out of his shirt. Paused after he'd flicked open the first button on his jeans as if he'd realized how brisk he sounded. "Do ye wish to know about it?"

I didn't. Not really. I was tired. I didn't even have the energy to stand under a shower anymore. But I still said, "Yes, if you don't mind."

I had to understand what was going on before I either went ahead with the surrogacy or scrapped it.

The concept store would be a one-stop shop for a certain category of clients. Helen's fashions, Neal's jewelry, stylized home decor, art, maybe even cars and boats and planes—any luxury one could possibly want in life tailored to them. This was a huge leap from the department stores that mainly sold woolens, tartans and things made in sterling silver.

"Dev's been planning it for two years. He beta tested the website a while ago, but we ran into a few snags. We canna figure out what's not working, and that's where Naira comes in, hopefully."

"What are you doing?" My eyes widened as Neal plucked his phone out of his back pocket.

"Calling Dev. He's in Mumbai. It's midmorning there so he should be awake. He'll want to interview Naira as soon as possible."

Wait. Just wait. This was moving way too fast.

Deven was head of operations for the Fraser businesses since he was the Fraser with a business degree. Sometimes, when he and Neal talked shop, it sounded like gibberish. As my husband said, I wasn't interested in Fraser Global, and understood SEO and such terms even less. All I knew was that Neal's money allowed me to do what I loved because I didn't have to worry about paying bills. I didn't have to contribute to our home fund, Neal took care of it all. He even encouraged me to invest my money or use it as I pleased. While an ADA's salary wasn't fantastic—I'd made way more at Smith, Stone and Smith as a paralegal—and though my little office often felt claustrophobic, the perks and benefits I received as a civil servant boosted my paycheck nicely. But Neal's financial clout allowed me to be more than an avenger in a courtroom. It let me be magnanimous beyond my wildest dreams. I wasn't a gold digger, but Neal's background had factored into my decision to marry him. And yes, I did take advantage of his money and his nature to ease my conscience.

"All I asked you to do was give her some advice. You should have consulted with me before offering her a job."

Neal pressed the phone to his ear. "And why would I do that? Ye asked me to fix her problem. So I did."

Aargh. He'd just un-fixed everything! "This is stupid. I asked you to offer her a solution."

"Ye said—" he began but I cut him off.

"She's barely landed in New York and you're already planning to ship her off. I need her here, Neal. Don't you get it?"

He stilled, his focus suddenly arrowing right at me. His phone crackled and I could hear Dev's "Hello" even from several feet away.

"I'll call ye back," Neal said and dropped his hand to his side. "What's this about, then?"

I think he knew, deep down. But he wanted me to say it out loud.

"I was going to ask her to be our surrogate. Once you'd helped her open her shop, Atelier...whatever the fuck it's called, in New York."

"Are ye daft, woman?" he growled out in a half shout when it finally sank in that I wasn't joking about Naira being our surrogate.

"Woman, is it? Not love or hen?" I raised my voice too. "And you are daft if you think I'd rather trust a complete stranger over my best friend to have our kid."

"The lass is troubled. Anyone can see that. Ye canna impose on her like that."

I set my hands on my hips. "If she's so troubled why did you offer her a job?"

"That's different." He scowled.

"Really." I raised my eyebrows. "How? This is the second time you've met her, and already you trust her enough to offer her a job at Fraser Bespoke? Your gut knows what kind of a woman she is—unless you're confessing that your gut was seduced by her cooking skills."

"Her résumé speaks for itself."

I stopped him right there. "Our friendship speaks even more loudly. I've known Naira for ten years, Neal. She knows me. I know her. I trust her…with my life. With yours. With the child's." I knew this was the right thing to do. I knew it in my gut.

But Neal didn't sway. "She's emotionally unstable. Ye saw it."

"That's just bullshit. Just because she cried? If you think she's messed up, then what the fuck am I?" I stepped closer to him and touched his chest, felt his heart thump solidly against my palm. "She's one of the strongest, smartest women I know. She comes from a very conservative family, Neal. You know that type of situation much better than me. You know how much she's had to fight to get here. She's not messed up. She's just lost and frightened and grieving."

I told him how sweet and full of hope Naira used to be. How simple her dreams had been.

"She's dreamed of having children for as long as I've known her. She's a baby magnet just like you. Now she believes she can't ever be a mother because of her circumstances—of someone else's making, mind you—and it's not fair, is it? She's hurting, Neal. You and I, we can fix that," I pleaded softly.

Neal didn't respond for a long, long time. We stood there, staring broodily into each other's eyes until finally, he took a gargantuan breath and whooshed it out.

"Jesus, Paris. You dinna make things easy, do ye?"

But I was. I was giving all three of us our heart's desires.

"By the way, I haven't asked her yet. So it's quite possible this whole discussion was pointless. And it'll be back to fighting between California and Connecticut for us, mate." Then I gave him a sweet thank-you kiss on the lips and went into the bathroom to brush my teeth.

★ ★ ★

Over the buzz of my electric toothbrush, I heard the faint rumble of Neal's baritone as he chatted with his brother about Naira. Now that the Big Idea was out of the bag, I didn't feel any pressing need to micromanage the conversation. Neal knew what I was about, and I trusted him not to jeopardize our best surrogacy option by handing Naira over to Deven, the slave driver. We'd never see her during daylight office hours ever again if Deven got his hands on her.

I couldn't wait to ask Naira now, and began devising a plan as to how to go about it. I had to present the idea in such a way that the possibility of her saying no diminished to nil.

I was no longer tired. I was wired, and decided a shower was just the thing to help me decompress. A quick one, as I did need to sleep. I had a long, vile day ahead of me tomorrow, starting with a special victims case that had been on the docket for months. Then the task force. Always the task force these days.

I stripped off my clothes and stepped under the shower. The gush and throb of water sluicing down my body felt instantly amazing. The fatigued nerve endings on my skin were soothed. It took my brain slightly longer to wash itself clean of thought, but it did. Finally, when I was on the verge of catatonic happiness, I cupped my hands beneath the automatic wall-mounted soap dispenser, and caught the pool of foam it spat out. I began to lather my body, then hummed when an extra pair of hands joined my endeavors. I turned, raised my face up to my husband's. We kissed beneath the rain. We helped each other get squeaky-clean.

"I'm sorry," he said once we were. He bit my ear, ran his tongue along my wet shoulder and back to my lips. "Forgive me?"

For what? I wondered. For putting up with me? For being

nice to my friend? Or was he apologizing for thinking badly of me?

I'd seen it on his face, the judgment, the confusion, the distaste he hadn't quite been able to hide when I'd told him the Big Idea. He thought I was a coward, deep down. I knew Neal didn't really understand why I didn't want children. He was a product of his environment, and his environment was a Norman Rockwell family.

While my world was full of vile things and hateful people and I didn't know how to explain that to him. I never talked to him about any of my cases, I refused to taint him like that. The Judge had never brought work home either, for the same reasons. But what I did and what I saw every day at work was the worst of humanity. It left a terrible stain on my soul.

But I didn't want to focus on our differences tonight. So, I kissed Neal deeper, sliding my tongue into his mouth, making him groan. I wrapped my hand around his throbbing penis, squeezed until he cursed. Until he gripped my wrist and forced my hand away. The shower area was large, and there was a bamboo bench fitted to one wall. He sat, pulling me to stand between his legs. I wrapped my arms around his head, kissed him again. His hands roved all over my body, circling, rubbing, tweaking, pushing in until I was squirming for breath.

"Are ye with me now?" The intensity of his gaze, so sexy, so blue, unnerved me.

He'd known I was upset all along. Distracted. He'd known I needed space to clear my head so he'd taken my friend off my hands and entertained her on my behalf. He knew, without being told, when my heart was heavy and my soul felt raw. How? *How?* When I took such care to hide it.

My head had cleared and I didn't want a speck of space between us. I pressed into his hands, tugged parts of him in recompense, and had both of us panting for release in minutes. I set my right foot on the bench by his thigh, bracing a hand on his shoulder, another on the wall behind his head. I touched my forehead to his and began to lower my body onto his lap. I stared into his teal blue eyes, wet with lust, drowning under the rain shower as he pressed up and into me. His hands gripped my hips, helping me move, controlling my movements. Ah God! I closed my eyes, let my head fall on his shoulder. I had no breath left even to groan.

This was how we communicated best. Where our minds were in total sync and our souls sang a benediction to our love. It was when we were apart that we floundered, where our differences were highlighted.

That was why I'd agreed to have a bairn with him. So that we'd have one thing in common, at least.

CHAPTER EIGHT

Naira

Crystal Lang sold the Central Park West apartment within days of the showing, as promised, and for more than the listed price. I was both giddy and stunned by the warp-speed velocity of the whole process—poles apart from the shameful auction of the Mumbai flat that had dragged on for months because no one had wanted to buy a place that had brought ill luck to its owners, certainly not for a fair price. In New York, not only had the sale been quick, the new owners wanted to move in by mid-November, which gave me about three weeks to find a new place, sort out the paperwork and move lock, stock, and barrel into it. Talk about pressure cooker stress.

I'd narrowed down a list of potential rentals off the Realtor's website, but the two flats I'd seen so far had been blah at best. I needed light in my house, and air circulation—that was not negotiable. I'd also love a positive energy flow, and I wouldn't say no to a fluid layout, one that didn't have abrupt walls rising out of nowhere or no walls at all to demarcate spaces. In my mind, those weren't unreasonable demands, but it had been pointed out to me that for Manhattan and my budget, I was asking for the moon. I couldn't get over how pathetic some of the apartments had been on the website.

"Don't settle for something you hate. Just move in with us," said Paris from her perch across the room. "You can have the guest room. No one except Neal's mother stays with us, and she isn't planning to come anytime soon—or at least I hope not."

Paris had come over to help me pack up my life—it was my sixth move in ten years—since she was free as a bird for the evening as Neal was in LA tending to his watch fob client. She'd come straight from work, craving a bitching session. Paris was in some sort of battle-to-the-death competition with a coworker, whom she had a touchy work history with, while they worked on some major case together. She'd been sidelined because of him before, and just today he'd tried to make her look stupid by giving her only half the message and then claiming she'd misheard him. Paris had looked ready to punch someone when she'd walked into the flat an hour ago. Pizza, wine and a vigorous vent had put a dent in her mad. I'd put her to work, hoping the physical labor would further calm her down. Paris was a problem solver, not a problem handler.

"I'm sure it won't come to that, but thank you for the offer," I said in answer to her question. My heart warmed at the unconditional support she and Neal were giving me. "I mean, it's Manhattan, concrete jungle. How hard can it be to find a rental here?"

Paris looked at me like I was crazy. "Is that a trick question? It's a buyer's market, Naira. You might want to consider buying rather than renting."

Crystal had told me the same thing, and that I'd have a better selection of apartments to choose from if I were to buy. But buying was out of the question. I couldn't lock down that kind of money. However, if I accepted Neal's job offer with Fraser Bespoke, I would possibly be able to make mortgage payments without breaking out in sweat. But, did I want to put down roots in New York so fast? What if things didn't work out?

I made a face. "I don't know. The thought of being homeless is surprisingly freeing. Metaphorically speaking." No obligations. No shackles.

I'd been rooted all my life. Been Naira Dalmia née Manral forever. It would be good to just be Naira for a while, unattached and maybe a tad irresponsible. I imagined myself flitting from rental to rental, free as a bird, without tethers binding my flight or baggage weighing me down. What if I shrugged off the debts placed on my shoulders? What if I reneged on my promises? What would it feel like to cruise along life's highway in a top-down convertible, my hair blowing in the breeze?

I crash-landed back to reality because I *had* baggage and boxes and responsibilities and I couldn't shrug them off. And if I was going to start up the online atelier, I needed a place—even a semipermanent one. Permanent would be even better. I was so tired of packing and unpacking my life, I thought, in a one-eighty-degree switch from my earlier convertible pipe dream. But maybe the first choice I had to make wasn't about buying or leasing an apartment, it was about my own shop versus Fraser Bespoke.

I was still reeling from the shock of Neal's offer, even though we'd discussed it again in more detail over the phone. I still couldn't believe he'd made me the offer. He barely knew me. Not that I couldn't be trusted with such responsibility. Still.

We'd also discussed the best way to start a business in this country, change my visa status, start immigration paperwork. Neal had been super helpful with his suggestions, his advice and his time. So, either way, I owed him and Paris big-time. "A thousand home-cooked meals, is what ye owe me," Neal had said when I'd asked how I could ever repay his kindness. He was such a sweet man.

I raised my arms above my head and bowed back into a shallow backward bend, groaning as my vertebrae popped and stretched into a seamless line again. I was knee-deep in bubble paper and boxes and I was only halfway done. When had I accumulated so many things, so many burdens? When had Kaivan?

I'd hired movers for the heavier tasks. They would come over on the weekend, box things up and take everything away to a storage facility. But they'd cautioned me to handle the things I didn't want manhandled or broken myself.

Paris had shucked her shoes and her jacket by the sofa as soon as she'd arrived, tackling her frustrations from work by popping Bubble Wrap until I'd screamed at her and put her to work. She was sitting cross-legged on the carpet now, her forest green pencil skirt hiked up to her panties, and was carefully wrapping a jade Buddha in cotton first, followed by two rounds of Bubble Wrap. Exactly as I'd shown her.

"I don't know how to thank you and Neal," I said softly, trying not to feel embarrassed or needy or weepy. I'd turned into such a crybaby. I had to start my daily exercise routine and power up my endorphin levels.

"You put him up to it, didn't you? The Fraser Bespoke offer? I can't accept it if that's the case." I had to know the truth.

"Have you lost your mind? I'd never interfere in his business even if he let me—which he doesn't. He means it, honey. He is super impressed by your atelier in Mumbai. And so is his brother," she said while ripping off short pieces of sticky tape and tacking them on her forearm.

Relief made my spine hurt a little less. "Really? God, Paris. He's the sweetest man. You know that, right?"

Paris snorted, smiling wryly. "Yeah, yeah. But fair warning. He's not all that sweet when it comes to Fraser business. If you screw up, you'll face the entire Fraser firing squad and God help you then. That's the board of directors made up of the whole extended Fraser clan. Uncles, aunts, cousins, everyone except Flora, Neal's younger sister. She's sort of a free spirit and wants nothing to do with business—family or otherwise."

"They sound lovely," I said wistfully. They sounded exactly like my family—or how we'd been before the shit hit the fan.

"Does that mean you're on board?" Paris asked, her head cocked to one side.

"I don't know." I blew out a breath. I needed to talk to someone about these life-altering decisions. No. Not just *someone*, I needed to talk to Kaivan. He'd have known what to do. He'd have known how to finesse the offer or demand better terms or understand the fine print in the contract. He'd have known how not to get screwed over. I had no delusions about the role I'd play in Fraser Bespoke no matter how well Neal presented the package. I'd be working *for* them, not *with* them. I'd have no autonomy, no decision-making powers. I'd simply be an employee. Expendable.

If I opened my own store, I'd have the power to do whatever I wanted, however I wanted—like with An Atelier. But, as Neal had pointed out, it would be a solo enterprise and I'd bear all the risks. Could I afford that? However, I'd also reap the profits.

"Do you see the dilemma?" I asked after explaining it all to Paris.

"That is a tough decision," she agreed with some sympathy. "I have no idea what to tell you. What are you going to do?" She set the Bubble-Wrapped Buddha in the carton by her side, then crawled through the mess to hug me. "Don't look so miserable."

I wanted to cling to her. But I forced myself to behave.

"Have you talked to Neal?" She sat back on her haunches. "You should, you know. He's great to bounce ideas off and to streamline knotty thoughts. He'll help clear some of your doubts, which may make your decision a little easier. And he won't pressure you one way or another. I know that for a fact. Do you want me to talk to him?" she offered when I continued to look unsure.

"Absolutely not!" My hand shot out and grabbed her arm as if she might call him right then. "I'll sort it out. I've taken up enough of his time. He's been very helpful. As have you. He's gone above and beyond for me and... Seriously, Paris, your husband is the dearest man. Please don't bother him with this. Promise me."

Paris rolled her eyes. "He's not that sweet. Not all the time. Catch him in one of his moods and you'll see just how anal and obstinate he is. Ha! No wonder you bonded so well. You both are two peas in a pod."

"I'm not moody or anal," I said defensively. I never used to be, at least.

Paris grinned. "I see you didn't dispute obstinate."

"Like you're not any of those adjectives? You're a nightmare to deal with. How we ever became friends remains a mystery to me," I said dramatically.

"Spoken like a true Bollywood aficionado." Paris scooped

up her phone from the carpet when it began to vibrate. I prepared to grab her again in case it was Neal and she told on me.

"It's Lily," she said after checking the caller ID, then groaned. "Shit. I ditched our weekly dinner and came here instead, and now... Drat it. I should take this. She's called me six times already." She stood up and walked to the windows. "Lily! What's going on?"

It had been time to take a break anyway, I thought, standing up and stretching too. Then I went into the kitchen and reheated the leftover extra large pizza pie we'd ordered for dinner. I poured us two fresh glasses of the rosé I'd opened earlier and started on the dishes in the sink while Paris finished her call.

"I can't believe you actually return your mother's calls now," I commented when she came in ten minutes later, after I'd heard her discuss what sounded suspiciously like Hollywood gossip. "I can't believe you even know who Jude Law is much less whom he's sleeping with."

Paris grimaced, picked up a slice of jalapeño and pineapple pizza straight from the oven and bit into it. I did the same. I was too tired to lay out fresh plates or do the hostess dance. And as both of us had warmed our bums long enough, we ate standing up at the kitchen counter.

"Can you believe it?" Paris muttered around a mouthful of pizza. "She calls me twice a day, morning and evening. If I miss her calls, she messages incessantly until I call her back. I'm so grateful she's not comfortable yet with video chat or I'd be screwed. Add to that, we have weekly dinner plans and a standing Sunday brunch date with my handsome young man." Paris batted her eyelashes, imitating her mother, I suspected. "*Feh.* She's like my parole officer that I have to report to every week. She's become clingy after the Judge."

Did all widows become clingy? I wondered, acknowledging

my own need to do so. These days it was Paris, but I'd clung to my mother after Kaivan had died—no, from even before that, since his arrest. It was another reason I'd left Mumbai. I'd needed to cut the cord so my father or Vinay couldn't use her to manipulate me.

"It's nice that you're bonding," I said, meaning it.

Back in college, Paris had had a tenuous relationship with her adoptive mother. She'd professed to hate Lily, and I'd stared at her stunned that she'd dared to say such a thing, to even think it, and mean it. What kind of person hates their mother? I'd been naive and sheltered all my life and I hadn't been able to fathom that families could hate each other—not outside of books and movies. I was no longer that innocent.

"It's nice. Mostly." Paris chucked the calorie-laden pizza crust into the garbage.

"What?" I was fascinated by this Paris who bonded with her mother.

"It's like I'm taking care of a teenager. I think…she's going senile," said Paris, wincing.

I knew exactly where she was coming from and that was why I didn't dismiss her worries with meaningless platitudes. The same thing was happening to my father-in-law. His brain's deterioration wasn't pronounced, but it would be in a few years, the doctor had said. When that happened, I'd have to move closer to them and take care of them. Kaivan would've expected it. I wanted to do it. But I had a few years until that eventuality.

"She's growing old. It's inevitable." God. It was never ending, life's suffering.

"She used to be sensible, biddable. She's just bizarre now. There's no other word for it."

"What are her doctors saying? Have they diagnosed her

with…" I coughed into my fist, wondering which sounded less horrific: dementia or Alzheimer's. "Anything?"

"Not yet. Her reports show she's healthy as a horse both in body and mind. But I don't trust them. My therapist says…"

I'd picked up the champagne flute to take a sip of my rosé, but I set it back down hard enough to chip the thin glass base against the stone countertop. I was really having bad luck with crockery this week. Or was it good luck?

"Wait!" I did a double take. "You have a therapist? Why?"

"Hello? I'm head to toe a morass of issues. Of course I have a therapist. I've had one since I was six." Paris frowned. "Don't you?"

When I shook my head, she gaped at me and I couldn't stop gaping at her. How did I not know this about her?

"You didn't get therapy or grief counseling after Kaivan died?"

My chest suddenly felt tight and I struggled to breathe.

"That's not how it's done in India. And before you ask, it's not like in the movies either, where the wailing widow breaks her colored bangles against the walls and wears white all the time. As you see, I'm as colorfully dressed as I used to be."

The joke fell flat because Paris looked at me in confusion. So, I told her what the customs for widows had been in India until as recently as my grandmother's generation, and probably still were in some rural areas. Widows had to live in seclusion, only wear white saris with no ornaments, nothing that could attract another man's eye, and spend their days at the temple, praying.

"I didn't have to do that. I was cocooned by my family and Kaivan's family. They took care of me, grieved with me. They were all the support I needed." Maybe I should have sought other forms of therapy and not relied on my family so much.

It occurred to me too late that I'd been in a perfect position to advocate change for some of the more archaic and unfair customs related to widows that might still be prevalent in India. It shamed me to realize that I'd never given it any thought. If I had, I might have helped others, and maybe I might have found some peace.

Paris would have thought of it, and would have fought for change while I'd simply wallowed.

She gave me a long, hard look, but left it alone. "I was made to understand that it was Lily's way of grieving and coming to terms with the Judge's absence from her life. Apparently, she feels alone and lost in her widowhood. What utter crap. Lily's never been alone in her life. She's a twin, isn't she? And she and Rachel have always been close. Rachel was already widowed and practically living with them when the Judge died."

Paris couldn't understand that kind of grief because—how could she? And I prayed she never would. Losing a husband transformed you. I was unrecognizable even to myself. I was hard and bitter, clingy and weepy. Needy. Weak. I'd given in to things I shouldn't have. But then, I'd given in even when Kaivan was alive. The choices I'd made would appall Paris. Somedays, I couldn't even look at myself in the mirror.

The only place I'd felt the slightest bit at peace in the last two years was when I'd visited Guru*ji*, my family's spiritual teacher. He'd assured me I'd heal, in my own way and at my own pace. He'd said that the echoes of loss may never stop ringing, but my heart would get used to the noise. I guess in India spiritual teachers took the place of therapists.

I'd asked him how one might redeem a compromised soul, and he'd said, "Pray."

I guzzled down the glass of rosé and poured myself more. I topped off Paris's glass too. She hadn't stopped yammering, adding sweeping hand gestures to her tirade. She seemed hyper tonight. More so than usual.

"Am I right or wrong?" She glared at me, clearly expecting an answer.

"*Umm.* About?" I asked sheepishly. "I zoned out."

"Naira! I'm spilling my guts here, telling you that my marriage is on the brink of disaster and you can't be bothered to listen?"

It took me a second to process that statement. "*Whaaat?* What the hell are you talking about? I thought we were discussing your mother. What the hell is wrong with your marriage?" I caught her arm before she flung it out again. "Tell me."

Paris had my undivided attention now. But for one teensy selfish second, I wondered what would happen to my job offer if Paris and Neal got divorced.

"Tell me what's wrong." I modulated my voice so it wouldn't come out as a shout. Though, I wanted to shout at her. Scream. Less than three years married and she'd already screwed things up with that sweet man. I wasn't even surprised.

"We're having a bairn." She made it sound like a death sentence.

"A barn? What does that mean? You're buying a barn?" That's all? That didn't sound horrid. It was strange though. "And what does it have to do with your marriage not working?"

Paris's mouth fell open, then she burst out laughing. I mentally reviewed what we'd both said and failed to understand the joke.

"Not…not…*barn*. Though, I suppose that's next. *Bairn.* B-a-i-r-n." She spelled it out, between wheezing and snorting with laughter. "As in baby. We're having a baby."

She was pregnant. My eyes dropped to her flat stomach, and my heart…oh, God. I felt as if she'd stabbed a spike into it.

"Barn and bairn. That is insane. You are insane, *desi* girl." Paris was still laughing.

My hands started to shake. My body shut down as if someone had pulled the plug on my life support. My brain wanted to shut down too. Desperately. I knew what was coming, but I didn't want to hear it. I didn't want her to explain, to complain like she used to about marriage, babies, men or mice. I didn't want to discuss anything about babies.

"Congratulations. I need to finish packing." I turned around blindly and walked away. I knew I should've gushed over it. Laughed with her. Been happy for her. But I couldn't. I couldn't breathe. I couldn't help but think she had the life I was supposed to have. Oh, God. I was a horrible friend.

I yanked open a closet door in my bedroom and began pulling my clothes off their hangers. At the back of my mind, it registered that I didn't need to pack my clothes. The movers would deal with them. It was part of their job. But I couldn't stop myself. I needed to do something to stop my hands from shaking. To stop myself from bawling.

"Hey. Honey, what's wrong? What did I say?" She'd followed me into the room, but she wasn't laughing now.

I bent my head, squeezed my eyes shut, blocking my tear ducts. I would NOT cry.

"Naira. Oh, honey."

The pity in her voice demolished my meager cache of strength. I collapsed onto the bed, buried my face in a bunch of clothes and cried my heart out. I sat up when every drop of wretchedness had been wrung out. Paris was kneeling by the bed, her hands clasped to her chest as if she was praying.

"When?" she whispered, her face pasty, colorless, her eyes knowing and glassy from unshed tears.

Paris rarely cried. She wasn't weak like me. Or unhealthily emotional.

I wiped my face with the edge of a silk cocktail dress. It was Kaivan's favorite dress. I blew my nose on it. What did it matter if I ruined it? Where was I going to wear it? What did any of it matter anymore?

If not for Kaivan's parents whose well-being was my responsibility, I'd give away everything, sign away the trust fund. I'd renounce the world like a Jain monk and live in an ashram for the rest of my life. But my husband had meant for me to take care of his parents as he'd meant to keep me safe, and I couldn't let him down by throwing my life away.

"A month before your wedding. Six weeks after Kaivan's arrest." I curled my hands into fists over my clothes to keep from reaching for the framed photo of Kaivan and me and smashing it to bits. I didn't know why I'd brought it to New York with me. "I started spotting on the day the CBI took him in for questioning. I was under three months pregnant. We hadn't told anyone yet, except for our parents. My mother wanted to wait until I'd completed the first trimester to announce the good news—it's a custom in my family. Also, it's done because the chances of miscarrying in the first trimester are greater—as proved.

"The gynecologist prescribed a mild bed rest, advised me to keep off my feet as much as possible. But with Kaivan detained and then arrested, rest just wasn't an option. I had to arrange for bail. It took five...nearly six weeks to arrange everything. Our accounts had been frozen and I had to...sell stuff, take personal loans to collect enough money. I couldn't think about the baby or my health. Getting Kaivan out was my priority."

My heartbeat was fast and strong. How could my heart still beat when I'd lost her? My perfect little princess.

Paris covered my hands with hers. "Of course, you had to get him out."

Fresh tears leaked from my eyes and dripped down my face. I couldn't wipe them. Paris was squeezing my hands. She hugged me then, hard, and let me cry on her shoulder.

"I'm so sorry, honey. So very, very sorry," she murmured over and over.

Sorrow always felt never ending, everlasting. But it did in fact end. And I did eventually stop crying. The iceberg on my chest thawed. It would be back, and I'd fall apart again. But for now, I locked myself in the bathroom and splashed water on my face, unclogged my nose. It had become a daily ritual, like bathing.

When I walked back out, Paris had hung my clothes back in the closet, everything except the snot-riddled cocktail dress. She'd left it in a corner. I'd have to get it laundered.

"Thank you," I began, but Paris cut me off.

"God. Don't thank me. I wasn't there for you. I wasn't there when you were going through hell. I pouted when you said you weren't coming for my wedding. I pouted and bitched about you for weeks—years. I didn't even try to find out why you'd bowed out."

The self-disgust in her eyes stung me.

"You didn't know. And I didn't want you to know. I didn't want you to cancel your wedding or postpone it or not enjoy it. I didn't want you to worry about me. I wanted you to love every glorious second of your ceremony."

We both knew she would have flown to Mumbai if she'd known. We also knew it would have been a disaster if she had. Paris and Kaivan would have fought even through the bars of his jail cell. She would have blamed him for my miscarriage, for our misfortune. She would have begged me to divorce him or leave him to rot in jail and reap the fruits of the seeds he'd sown. And when I would have refused to listen, she would have called me a coward, a doormat or worse. We would have fought. We would have broken each other with words.

That was why I'd pretended to be fine and lied about what was really going on. I'd pissed off Paris for a short time, but I'd saved our friendship in the bargain.

"I always believed that when you found the right man, you'd want his baby. Sorry, bairn."

I shivered as we walked along the western length of Central Park. The bite of cold slapping my face was refreshing, even enjoyable. It kept me in the present. Soon, I'd need gloves and a hat to subdue the effects of inclement weather. But not yet. A loose scarf around my neck, spritzed with Coco Chanel, was enough for now.

We'd decided—or Paris had—that I'd been boxed in— pun intended, *ha ha*—in my *godown* of an apartment for long enough, and I—both of us—could use some fresh air.

The walk had been just what I'd needed. Being out and about, surrounded by the hyper energy of New York, even at night, I was beginning to feel optimistic again. Hopeful.

"Are you sure you want to talk about this?" Paris cast a dubious frown my way.

I nodded. "I'm mostly fine with it. Well, not fine, but I've learned to cope." I flapped my hand in dismissal. "Seriously. I'm good. I was barely pregnant. I don't despair at the sight of babies or anything. In Mumbai, I even babysat my nephews on weekends." I smiled to show her I wasn't simply being brave. Time had lessened the trauma. It still pinched like a fiend, but it wasn't a debilitating hurt anymore. "I'll babysit your bairns too, for however many hours you need. For free." I chuckled. I was getting rather fond of that word. *Bairns.*

"Uh-huh. Cute." She stuck her tongue out at me.

We were strolling at a snail's pace, and it took her another half a block to open her heart.

"About that. I'm not pregnant, so the congrats is premature. However we are in the process of deciding how to get pregnant."

"If that's a euphemism for your sex life, thank you for not getting graphic."

She grinned. "It's not. It means we're negotiating."

"And what does that mean?"

I'd been curious about Paris's marriage forever, wondered how it could function with all her rules and goals. If Paris was negotiating having children, already it boded well for Neal. The Paris I'd known had rarely compromised and had been dead set against banal social customs. That Paris wouldn't have talked to her mother on the phone even once a month, let alone several times a day. So wasn't this an interesting twist?

"Let me give some context." With that, Paris launched into the tale of her and Neal's sudden and short-lived first engagement. "We met at the RiM—Right is Might—summer fundraiser, if you recall. Neal was there as a sponsor. He'd donated his artwork for the live auction and he ended up raising half a million dollars in one night. I was there with Toby. Remember him? My fuck buddy all through law school?"

I smiled as a horse-drawn carriage clip-clopped past us, relishing the sight of a Manhattan classic, and the fact that Paris was as frank as ever.

I knew parts of the engagement story. Paris had been abnormally moony about Neal from the start. She and I were still chatting on the phone daily then. It was insta-lust between them. They'd spent a good chunk of the night flirting with each other, but they'd each left with the dates they'd brought to the event—which was considerate of them. Paris reached home—alone and animated—and texted Neal. Sexted, more likely, because when Paris wanted something, she went after it. Neal had been equally in thrall. Several flirty texts later, they decided they couldn't wait a second longer to be together. And how fortunate for them that their lodgings seemed to be within walking distance of each other.

Neal took over Paris's life from then on. She finished law school, received her Juris Doctor. She spent the summer volunteering at RiM, working at Smith, Stone and Smith, and studying for the bar exam, all the while marinating in a sweet romantic haze. Paris had become lost in an exciting new life that summer while I had been trying to hold on to mine.

Kaivan's businesses had begun to implode. He'd made a bad call on an investment, and had been up to his ears trying to reverse the loss. He didn't tell me anything at first. He pretended everything was fine in our life. We holidayed in Europe as usual. He didn't want me worried because I was on a mission to get pregnant.

Paris and I had been absorbed in our own little universes that summer. We'd started to drift apart and we hadn't even realized.

"It happened so fast. Meeting him, falling for him, getting engaged, then breaking it off. Then the second proposal—well, it was more of a mutual proposition that time. He said and did all the right things. I told him I didn't want children. I didn't mince words and still he stayed. He understood—understands me." Paris laughed and sighed and shrugged on the same breath. "It would have been foolish not to marry him."

Our shoulders were touching and I felt her happiness, her wonder, roll into me. "I wish I'd been there to see it. See you fall. Stumble. Be a fool in love." But I did see it, could see it even now when she looked at her husband. And it made me so happy…and so envious.

She sniffed, shooting me a sideways glance. "Do you miss him?"

My heart, blooming with happiness a question ago, wanted to shrivel up and die. But I wouldn't let it. "I don't want to talk about him. Can we talk about you? About happy things?"

We came to a stop at the edge of Central Park West and Columbus. We'd planned to part ways there and go back or forward to our respective domiciles. But we weren't done talking. I didn't want the night to end. I pointed to a bench on the sidewalk and we sat, facing each other.

Paris ran her fingers through her long hair, then twisted it over one shoulder. "Where was I? Oh, ha! The whirlwind affair. I honestly thought it would break off." The streetlamp cast a yellowish light on her amazement.

"The affair?" I nodded in complete understanding. I'd also thought the gemstone baron would be just another notch in Paris's revolving door of affairs. A rich novelty. I'd thought how could he be serious, either? He'd just broken his engagement to Simran after going out with her for five years and being engaged to her for one. So, I hadn't paid attention when Paris had spoken of Neal that summer. I should've realized he was an aberration simply by the number of times she'd brought his name up in conversation.

"All of it. Every stage of it. When we started sleeping together, I thought—oh, we are so going to burn ourselves out in one week. Then one week became two months and I thought—that's it. I'll get bored now. But I didn't get bored, and neither did he. And now here we are, halfway through our third year of marriage." She shrugged helplessly. "Everything happened so fast. We didn't give ourselves room to change our minds. What if...once the dust settles, once our marriage becomes routine and stale, we realize that it isn't all that amazing? What if we change our minds about stuff we've agreed upon? It happens. People change their minds. They start resenting each other. And, let's be honest, Neal and I have nothing in common besides sex."

And there she was. Overthinking, pessimistic Paris.

I wagged my finger in her face. "I knew it. I knew you were going to self-sabotage your marriage." God. I wanted to smack her. Hard.

Her back went ruler stiff. "What? Rubbish. I'm telling you what I think. What I feel. What if Kaivan didn't want kids and you—?" She slapped a hand over her mouth, eyes stricken.

I pulled her hand away. "It's okay. Really."

"No, it's not. God. I'm sorry for bringing this up. Just forget the whole thing. Okay?"

I sighed. Yes, thinking of my miscarriage was painful, and knowing I'd never have children of my own pinched my soul. But the wonder of sharing personal agonies and worries with my bestie overshadowed the pain.

"Do you know how long it's been since I've talked to someone without a filter? Without weighing my words or gauging their reactions to my words? I've not bared my soul for a long, long time." My eyes filled up, but this time my heart didn't weigh heavy. I needed this talk as much as she did. "Nothing you say will upset me, Paris. What'll hurt is if you don't."

CHAPTER NINE

Paris

There was a terrible, horrible reason why Naira had turned her back on our friendship.

Yes, she'd been torn up about her husband's arrest, and maybe she wouldn't have come for my wedding even if she hadn't miscarried, but I should've realized—I should have sensed she was hiding something. I, who prided myself on reading people right, had read my own best friend wrong. I wanted to kick myself for being completely selfish and self-absorbed.

Bravely, Naira exposed her wounds. Some had scabbed over but some were still bleeding. I couldn't imagine—didn't have the tools to imagine what it felt like to lose a husband and a child within months. I'd lost the Judge, the only father I'd ever known, but it wasn't the same thing. I'd hurt terribly for the Judge—no, that was a lie. I'd blocked it. I'd blocked his death, what it made me feel. I'd blocked it all. I'd found distractions instead—mentors, lovers, taken up projects he would have approved of and been proud of, like working for the DNC and volunteering at RiM. I'd wished to honor his life by following in his footsteps and not sit around being devastated by his loss. I hadn't cried for the Judge until I met Neal. Not that the release of emotion had filled the hollowness he'd left inside me. It remained within me, murky as a bottomless loch even now.

My therapist said that the hollowness was an expression of my grief, my defense mechanism to deal with loss. I wasn't ready to feel the pain, so I hid it or hid from it. Different people expressed sorrow differently, he said. Some cried. Some didn't. There wasn't a right or wrong way to feel, to grieve, or even one way. There was no right or wrong or the only way to do anything—not even life. Every person and situation was unique and flourished or withered within its own ecosphere.

Naira had cried when she lost her baby, I was sure. She would've absorbed the pain, let it consume her soul. Naira didn't shy away from feeling feelings.

My respect for her rose, not that it hadn't been high already. She had been through hell and yet, here she was, fighting. Smiling. Hadn't I told Neal that Naira was strong beyond measure? She deserved a standing ovation, IMO. I settled for a bone-crushing hug.

"In a way, it's good that it happened because how would I have coped with a baby on top of everything else?" She pushed back and pressed her fingers over her eyelids, clearly still emotional, then gave me a watery smile. "I'm okay. It's okay, really. Now get a move on your baby fast so I can become a doting aunt."

Oh, the plan was for Naira to become so much more than

an aunt. However, I needed to make some sort of an opening statement before jumping to the plea.

"It's complicated. Being married." Was that an understatement or what?

"No shit, Sherlock." Naira grinned as she blew her nose on a used tissue she'd dug out of her jacket.

"I don't know how I got myself into this situation. I'm a planner. Daily goals, weekly goals, yearly goals. You've seen my Life Goals spreadsheet from college. Nowhere in it was a baby. Nowhere in it was marriage. Neal derailed my entire life in one season." Cool air ruffled the fine hairs on the nape of my neck and I suddenly shivered. "We're both alphas. This should not be working. Yet, here we are. Jungle mates for life."

"You love each other," Naira said simply.

That didn't mean shit. "I still wake up every day and wonder if today is the day we'll break up. If today is the day we'll say or do something irrevocable, unforgivable." I looked up at the starry sky full of random rotating objects. How often did planets align just right?

"Every day I fall more and more in love with him but there are always doubts. But then there is also this conviction that I am right where I'm supposed to be. And that he and I are meant for each other. We're solid. We are not Jared and Sandra. It isn't just impulse or sheer stubbornness keeping us together but something bigger. Do you—" I broke off, feeling ridiculous. I could never put it into words exactly what I felt for Neal. "Did you feel the same?"

"Doubts *and* certainty?" Naira's eyes were glittering with unshed tears again. "Yes."

I'd wondered if she'd had doubts. She hadn't expressed any—not before her marriage, not after. Not even after Kaivan became a criminal.

"He has this magic touch..."

"Ack! DO NOT describe your sex life to me," she yelped, plugging her ears with her index fingers for good measure.

I hadn't been about to but...

"No? But the bawdy tales of The Baron and His Bitch are so invigorating." I couldn't resist teasing her like I'd done in college. Discussions about penises—size, shape, skill—and my advanced ability to suck cock had made saintly Naira squirm and pray for my irreverent soul. Nothing had been sacred then. Nothing had been a secret.

She didn't know I was no longer so flippant, that it was different with Neal. *I* was different. I didn't know if it was out of respect for him—for us—or out of fear of jinxing us, but I shied away from boasting about how great we were in bed. *Kein ayin hara*, as the Judge would say after counting his blessings to divert the evil eye.

I burst out laughing when Naira broke into song, no doubt to drown out any sexcapades I felt inclined to share. I yanked her hands down. "I can't believe you're still a prude after being married to a man like that."

"Like what? For the last time, Kaivan wasn't a criminal. He was ruthless in business, but he was a good man, Paris."

She'd missed the point totally. "And a sexy one."

Naira's mouth dropped open. "You found Kaivan sexy? *You?*"

I rolled my eyes. "Honey, you don't need to like someone to want to burn up the sheets with them. So the prosecutor in me was always wary of the...uh, ruthless fiend in him. Didn't mean I was blind to his appeal."

Tall—not as tall as Neal though—fit, not muscular, thick beard, piercing brown eyes. Oh, yeah, Kaivan had had sex appeal.

It struck me then that unless Ms. Prude had flipped her scruples one eighty degrees, she hadn't had sex since she cremated her husband over two years ago. Maybe even before that, since her miscarriage. And if marriage wasn't anywhere on her horizon, I had my doubts the situation would improve anytime soon. The thought appalled me enough that I was momentarily speechless.

"Our bodies are machines, you know? If you don't use all your parts regularly they'll shrivel up and die. Want me to tag someone for a booty call?"

Naira looked as if I'd just bought her a membership to a sex club. "Oh, my God! This is not open to discussion."

"All you have to do is ask." But I let it go and steered the conversation back on track. "Every marriage functions on compromise, right? And sex." I glanced at her again, shaking my head. "I still can't believe you haven't—"

"Paris, stop it!" she screeched, bouncing up from the bench.

"Okay. Okay! I'll stop." I stood up too. I'd heard that pregnant women got horny. Another tick mark against the Big Idea if it was true. "Where were we? Ah, yes. Compromise. I do stuff for Neal, and he does stuff for me. Or it's supposed to work like that. He moved to New York because my work and Lily are here, despite his own family being two oceans away. He accepted we wouldn't have children, even though he adores kids. It was insane that he even agreed. It was such an unfair thing to ask of him." I didn't deserve him, his compassion, his support.

"You feel pressured into having kids?" Her frown was barely visible in the moonlight, but her tone was sympathetic.

"On the contrary, I'm still not going to have the kid. Doesn't mean he shouldn't, right?"

"What does that mean? Oh." Realization dawned. "You want him to have a child with someone else? Like a surrogate?"

I smiled. This was why we were best friends. Naira totally got me. "Yup, exactly like a surrogate. I will cut off his penis if he tries it in any other way. Anyway, choosing the right surrogate is a mind-boggling endeavor. Everybody needs to be on the same page at the same time. Trust has to be implicit. There are steps, tests, procedures. Legally, surrogacy is an even bigger clusterfuck than adoption—which was the other option, but we decided on surrogacy and biological children."

I briefly explained everything I'd learned about surrogacy in the past six months. Most of it wasn't pretty. When I finished, Naira stared at me as if I was a fascinating yet repellent specimen on a slide under a microscope.

"The way your mind works is simply...stunning. Only you could come up with such an unusual solution."

That pinched. "We're nearly two decades into the twenty-first century, honey. Conventionality is dead, or should be. Tell me, why should I do something I don't want? And why should Neal give up his dreams if there is an alternative which can make us both happy? Where all three of us can be happy?"

In for a penny, in for a pound, I thought, and made my request. "The reason I'm telling you all this is because I want *you* to consider being our surrogate."

Of course, she was shocked. Horrified. Gobsmacked. She began shaking her head.

Terrified she'd veto the idea in reflex, I blurted out, "Or, if not...if that's too much, just be the kid's guardian. The mother figure. God in heaven, Naira, I'm asking you—I'm begging you to take the kid off my hands!"

The next morning, I dashed off to work after spending a harrowing night in bed alone, suffering from the worst case of regret ever to burn a hole in my stomach.

I couldn't get the last few minutes of last night out of my head. The awful silence following my verbal vomit. Naira backing away from me as if I was Serena Joy from *The Hand-*

maid's Tale all set to throw her into a pregnancy dungeon. Then pivoting and running home with a hasty goodbye wave.

I'd wanted to follow her, but I'd restrained myself. I had to give her time to stew on it.

I should've waited for Neal to ask her. We should have asked Naira together. He wouldn't have let me botch it up. I wouldn't have said what I'd said at the end if he'd been there.

"Couldn't ye wait another day?" he'd scolded over the phone last night. I'd called him right after the fiasco and demanded that he fix it. "*We* haven't discussed this sufficiently yet. I sure as hell am no' a hundred percent sure this is the best option. No' with her. I asked ye to wait until I got back. But no. Why mind me? At the very least, ye should've waited until she'd come to a decision about Fraser Bespoke. This muddies the waters, can't ye see? What in hell was your hurry, lass?"

I wanted it all locked down before our perfect alignment of planets changed. But if I told him that, he'd laugh at me.

I stepped out of the north entrance of the Criminal Court Building where a bunch of hard-hat workers were repairing the sidewalk for the second time in two years. The noise of their drills left no room in my head for noisy thoughts. Perfect. The butterflies inside my belly had fled too, partly because I'd won the case and exhilaration was sweeping through me. I'd caught a break when the perp on trial had unexpectedly implicated himself on the witness stand, making everyone except the defense attorney dance with glee. Justice had been meted out in less than an hour without fuss or folly.

I crossed the street and walked to Foley Square. I wasn't expected at the Department of Justice—the task force's HQ—for another hour. As it was nearly noon and I had time to kill, I decided to grab an early lunch. I bought a veggie gyro from a food truck, then walked a little away and sat down on a bench to have myself a little congratulatory picnic.

The weather was brilliant, high seventies and not at all like the end of October, and went a long way in improving my mood. I checked my messages and emails, saw that I'd missed two calls from Lily, but none from Naira.

Of course, she'd call. She just needed space to think.

I returned Lily's call via video chat. That way I could count it as having lunch together since I'd ditched her for dinner last night and breakfast this morning.

"Hey, you two." I waved when the Merry Widows of White Plains, aka Lily and Rachel, appeared on screen. They weren't identical twins, but similar enough to be thought of as identical. "Big dates?"

They were clearly getting spruced up in front of the bathroom vanity. Lily's Audrey Hepburn–like hair was in curlers, and Rachel was dabbing makeup on her face.

"Hello, *bubbala*!" they greeted in unison.

"What a lovely surprise in the middle of the day." Lily's face crinkled into a smile. "We are meeting the beaus for lunch and then we're catching a movie at the IMAX. A romantic comedy."

"How nice."

The beaus were a couple of widowers the Merry Widows had met at Scrabble Night at a community center a few months ago. I'd felt compelled to run background checks on the gentlemen, especially when the four of them started double dating and taking weekend trips to the Jersey Shore. I still couldn't believe Lily wanted to go on a three-week-long cruise to the South Pole with them. She'd hated to travel before. Who was this Lily who dressed in trendy clothes and went on cruises and to the movies? Why did she do things with Charlie she'd never done with the Judge? It seemed unbelievable that she wouldn't be around for Thanksgiving. We'd never not celebrated the holiday together since I'd come to live with the Kahns.

"And how is that sweet girl? Did you help her move?"

Lily and Naira used to get along like a house on fire, probably still would. They were both Sagittarians and had similar housewifery philosophies.

"She's fine. We were packing, Lily. She won't be moving for another couple of weeks."

I took another bite of my gyro as Lily pulled the curlers out of her short white bob and patted her hair into place. She looked really good for her age, as spiffy in her sleek red pants and checkered blouse as the Aston Martin parked on my right by the curb.

Why had I decided to video chat with her?

Oh, yeah. Guilt. And a promise given to a dead man on his deathbed to take care of his wife who didn't seem to need any taking care of.

Also, I didn't want to accidentally call Naira and seem desperate. The ball was in her court.

"I always liked that girl. So soft-spoken and helpful. She was a positive influence on you, teaching you all about India."

"Hmm" was my reply since my mouth was stuffed with hummus and salad.

It was the truth though. Naira had taught me everything I knew about India, from Bollywood to the diversity of Indian cuisines, culture, attire—and bhangra. I'd shunned that part of me until college, deciding my roots ought to be Jewish and American like the Judge's. I'd wanted to please him. I'd wanted to be just like him.

I thought differently now. Naira had introduced me to my biological heritage, and Neal had immersed me in it. Because of them, I'd learned to be comfortable with my other self.

"What's wrong, young lady?" When I looked back at the

screen, Lily was giving me the death stare. "You look awful. Your eyes are sunken in and your face looks all pinched."

Here we go again. "Gee. Thanks for pointing out how bad I look. I haven't slept well, if you must know."

"Why not? Don't say you've fought with your young man again? You're too bossy with him. It's unbecoming. You should appreciate your man more."

"I appreciate him just fine." I wouldn't let her get under my skin. Not today.

Lily and I had never shared an easy relationship. She'd been a different person back then. A frumpy, timid housewife who hadn't so much as sneezed without her husband's permission. I'd had no respect for her. That Lily had disapproved of me too, and been jealous of my relationship with the Judge, who I'd hero-worshipped. I'd thought he walked on the moon. He'd been the bridge between us, our only connection, until his death had forced us to change. While I'd changed subtly, a whole new Lily had emerged from the ashes complete with sassy curls and effervescent clothes.

"It never hurts to put him first, Pari. Put relationships first and not ambition."

Pari. Pronounced as in gay Paree. Sometimes, people asked me whether my parents had named me after the French capital. Had I been born in Paris? Conceived there? Had my parents met in Paris? As a child, I'd wallowed in the fairy tale of being Paris, the symbol of desperate love and devastating passion between my adoptive parents. And it had been true for a while.

I'd been Pari before being Paris. My birth mother had called me Pari. In Hindi, *pari* meant angel or fairy, a nickname given to little girls who hadn't been named yet. Jared and Sandra had pounced on the symbolism of my name—I was their angel, the *pari* who'd brought them together. They'd met and connected first in Paris. They'd started to fall in love there. I was supposed to remind them of gay Paree forever.

It hadn't worked out like that. Life rarely did. So now my name meant nothing and symbolized failure more than anything else.

I didn't want to fail as a wife, but Lily was making it sound as if I was.

I dumped the half-eaten gyro into the trash, my appetite gone. I shouldn't have called. "He works all the time too. His ambitions are also huge."

"Yes, but he's a man."

"And a man can do nothing wrong?" A sour taste filled my mouth.

Lily's expression shuttered. "Must you always be so prickly?"

Yes, well, who'd made me that way? I didn't know whether the Judge and Lily had made a conscious decision not to have children or they simply hadn't been able to get pregnant. I'd asked the Judge about it once, but he'd dismissed the question. He'd told me never, ever to bring it up with Lily. Ever. When I came into their lives, they'd already been married for thirty years. Lily Kahn hadn't wanted to raise a belligerent brat, but the Judge had overruled her objections. She'd never let any of us forget that I'd been forced on her. That I'd been unwanted.

And that was my maternal history. I'd been abandoned by two mothers and been a thorn in the side of the third. Was it any wonder that I had no sparkly feelings toward motherhood?

"I have to get back to work, Lily. I'll see you on Sunday."

CHAPTER TEN

Naira

Bright and early one morning in November, I found my-self in Englewood, New Jersey, ringing the doorbell of a lavish ivy-ridden Tudor-style mansion. I had an appointment with the owner of the house, one of the largest private urn collectors in the world. We'd been introduced at Rothman's Auction House last week, and Gerald Cutler had indicated interest in the twelfth-century Buddhist monk urn and the limited edition colored-glass vase by Daum that I wanted to sell. Both the items lay at my feet, carefully wrapped in their individual boxes—the Daum in its original packaging.

I was ushered into a long museum-like drawing room that smelled strongly of orange furniture spray by a man about my age who introduced himself as, "Sam. Mr. Cutler's assistant."

We set the boxes down on a semicircular console table by

a large grilled window that overlooked a sprawling garden, a tennis court and a swimming pool with an attached clubhouse.

It seemed Mr. Cutler had been detained at the doctor's, and I was brought a pot of chamomile tea while I waited. I hoped he wouldn't be too long. I had about three hours before I had to meet Crystal Lang at 2:00 p.m. She was supposed to show me three more flats today.

The euphoria of a quick sale of the Central Park West flat had died a morose death in these past two weeks since I hadn't found a corresponding apartment to move into. Not one I liked anyway. Time was running out. I had barely a week left before I had to move out of the apartment, and if I didn't find something by then, I'd have to either move into a hotel or in with Paris, and each option had its pitfalls.

I wanted my own space. A place I could be blessedly alone and relatively Paris-free. I hated that I felt like I needed to avoid her, but she'd become relentless in her pursuit of the "Big Idea" as she put it. She'd given me a two-day grace period after her initial proposal before launching a full attack, starting with formally asking me to be a surrogate with Neal in tow.

The chamomile tea did nothing to calm my nerves. I was too…jittery. Of course, I'd been jittery ever since I'd landed in New York—even before that—but recent events had shot my anxiety up several levels.

I wasn't being fair. Paris wasn't attacking me, she was simply being Paris. And I got it completely—got her. Even if she and Neal hadn't individually explained their motivations, I knew Paris. I wasn't exactly appalled by the idea. Well, not anymore. As Paris had said we lived in the twenty-first century. Movie stars had surrogate babies all the time. So did alternative lifestyle couples and people who had difficulty conceiving. It wasn't the idea itself that was shocking, but what my role in it would be.

I couldn't get Paris's dramatic words out of my head. *"Naira, I'm asking you—I'm begging you to take the kid off my hands!"*

I hated that she felt that way about her own future child. I was beginning to feel some sympathy for Neal. Not to mention the child.

I'd researched surrogacy on the internet. It was a rapidly growing industry worldwide which—I sighed—was neither here nor there. I didn't have time to get muddled up in yet another project, whether personally or peripherally. My priority was to find a residence and decide about the new business. Everything else would have to wait.

Gerald Cutler came home just before noon—a tall, debonair man in his seventies who carried a gentleman's umbrella like a walking stick. It was drizzling outside. The weather had suddenly turned in the last hour. Shit. I hadn't checked the weather before leaving my house this morning, and I didn't have a coat or an umbrella with me.

"I'm so sorry, Naira. But it's my prostate, you see? Sam. Sam!" Gerald shouted after kissing me on both cheeks. Sam appeared at the drawing room door. "Bring us champagne, and tell the cook to set out brunch."

I protested, but not hard enough to offend Gerald. I couldn't afford to put off patrons, not when they were avid collectors and paid in cash. Cash was good for me right now. I didn't need to tell my father or Vinay about the cash transactions.

When our brunch ran into lunch and Gerald still showed no signs of winding down or letting me go, I excused myself and called Paris. "Can you meet Crystal at two? I don't think I can make it back before two thirty. I'm still in New Jersey."

"Done," Paris said brusquely and hung up, clearly busy at her own work.

I sighed and rejoined Gerald in the solarium. I hated taking favors. Especially ones I knew would come to bite me on my ass.

★ ★ ★

Three hours later, our business satisfactorily concluded, I sat ensconced beside Gerald in his chauffeur-driven SUV. He'd insisted on driving me back to the city, as he had errands to run there too. However, we were stuck in a tunnel traffic nightmare, and Gerald's nonstop commentary was giving me a migraine.

I winced at the uncharitable thought. He was just a lonely old man. I should have more sympathy for him as that would probably be me in forty years—alone and desperate for company.

I opened my eyes, lifting my head off the headrest when the SUV jerked, sputtered and jerked again. I looked out of the rain-splattered window at the rows of gloomy, blurry buildings. We'd barely moved in the past twenty minutes. I could still see the red canopy of the pizzeria a block away. We were about five, maybe six blocks from my destination—Neal's uncle's bar on Howard Street—and it looked like the rain had let up temporarily.

"I'll walk from here. Thank you so much, Gerald. I hope you enjoy the urns." I asked the driver to pull over to the curb, and before Gerald objected, I got out and dashed down Canal Street.

The day had grown even more dismal and cold. It had been incredibly sweet of Neal to check out the flats with Crystal Lang for me. Paris had sent him in her stead as she hadn't been able to go herself. I couldn't understand why he was being so nice to me. Was it the surrogacy? Was his wife forcing him to be nice?

Paris I understood. I knew what drove her. We were best friends. I could fight with her during the day and still enjoy partying with her at night. We simply shared that kind of friendship—the kind where she could ask me to be her surrogate without any awkwardness. The kind where I thought of her as the sister of my heart.

But Neal? Why was he going out of his way to help me even though I wasn't sure of Fraser Bespoke? About that, he'd asked me not to make any decisions until I'd spoken to his brother, who was coming down for Thanksgiving just to meet me. We'd hash it out then, he'd said.

Paris had warned me about Neal's brother. "If you think I'm stubborn, Deven's a freaking bulldozer. He'll just steamroll over all your objections. Good luck with that."

I wasn't worried about Deven Singh Fraser. I'd cut my baby teeth dealing with businessmen like him—my father, Kaivan. I knew what I wanted. I was used to being my own boss. I had a certain vision of my work. I wasn't sure Fraser Bespoke was for me. But being part of an exciting venture was tempting. It was also a huge opportunity on a global scale. And I'd be doing exactly what I loved without personal risk. If I was on their payroll, I wouldn't need to use the trust fund at all, and maybe the noose around my neck would loosen. If I promised to hand over my monthly stipend to Vinay, would he be satisfied?

About halfway down the third block, the heavens ripped open in a sudden rainbow-enhanced thunderstorm. Within seconds, I was soaked through my jeans and my pale blue cashmere sweater to my bones. Every time a gust of wind whooshed past—which was every ten seconds—my nipples turned into pebbles and my skin, my scalp included, puckered into a demoralized mass of frigid gooseflesh. The only saving grace were my waterproof Wellington boots and my handbag, which I used to shield my head. I arrived outside Liam's Bar breathless and utterly squelchy.

Howard Street was undergoing major construction. Some of the old brick buildings were getting a face-lift. Some already had. The architects or building designers had gone for the gentrified yet classic look, maintaining the signature style of the area.

I ran up a set of thick concrete steps to a stone-gray portico built on top of the pavement and took shelter under its striped blue-and-white awning. The portico led into a squat two-story building, its white brick facade marred with fire escapes. There were two doors at street level. A glass-paneled door on the left opened to Liam's Bar, and the blue door to the right into the main building that Neal's uncle owned where apparently Neal had his artist's studio. On either side of the building were construction barriers, blocking my view beyond them.

I was about to pull open the bar's door when my phone rang inside my handbag. It was my mother. I noticed then that she'd called seventeen times in the past two hours. Strange. I hadn't heard it ring or felt it vibrate even once. Maybe Gerald's house was in a dead zone. When I mentally calculated the time in Mumbai, I was shocked. Why was my mother calling me at one thirty in the morning? Worried, I called her back. I had to dial twice before getting through.

"Mummy. What's wro—"

"Why aren't you returning my calls?" Despite the unpleasant slurring in his words, Vinay's demand was clear.

My heart began to gallop harder than it had when I'd run. Why did Vinay have my mother's phone? Would I have to start screening her calls too?

Shit, shit, shit. I clenched the phone hard, wondering what would happen if I smashed it to bits against the wall.

"I've sent Papa an email detailing everything that has been sold. He'll receive the money by the end of next month. Other than that, I have nothing to say." *That's it. Stay calm.*

"But I have plenty to say to you." Alcohol sloshed in his

voice as he launched into a mildly abusive diatribe about how irresponsible and uncouth I'd become.

He asked about the trust fund again.

"I'm not breaking the trust, so stop harassing me about it. And I'm not coming back to India." Somehow I found the courage to blurt that out. New York, Paris, Neal—they were making me bold.

Vinay didn't like that at all. His rage crashed down harder than a thunderstorm.

It seemed surreal now but once upon a time I'd called this man *jiju*—an address reserved for a beloved brother-in-law. And I'd called my sister *didi* though we'd never really gotten along. We'd turned everything into a competition, vying for our parents' affections, for our teachers' praises. When I'd fought with Papa about college, Sarika had taken his side.

"Why are you wasting money on a degree you won't use?" She'd been perplexed that I'd aspired to be more than a wife and a mother. "What was the need to work?" she'd asked because in our family women didn't work. They shopped and traveled and hosted kitty parties. But when I got accepted into NYU Stern, Sarika had been proud of me for a brief spell. She'd already been engaged to one of Mumbai's eligible elites and had joined the Hostess with the Mostess sorority. She'd had no reason to be jealous of a nerdy younger sister.

Then four years later, when my "useless degree" landed me the affections of Kaivan Dalmia, who was an even bigger catch than Vinay Singhal, Sarika had been jealous. And that jealousy had slowly boiled over into viciousness when my hobby had turned into a thriving business, and because my husband had been better-looking, a better businessman and a better husband than hers was.

"Everything you do is my business. I tell you to stand, you

stand. I tell you to sit, you fucking sit," Vinay said in awful tones.

I told him to go fuck himself and hung up on him. I was bloody tired of his threats.

The next instant I froze, staring at my phone in shock. What had I done? He was going to punish me for this, surely. But how? He couldn't turn me into any more of a pariah in the family than I already was. And he wouldn't dare come after me legally in the US. Not if he wanted control of the trust fund. The policeman and the goons on his payroll in India had no clout in New York, did they?

Oh, God. *What had I done?* I sagged against the wall and pressed trembling hands to my head.

"Are ye okay, lass?" a soft voice asked above my head, a warm hand touched my arm.

I was startled enough to scream but it came out like a squeak. I should just give Vinay what he wanted and end this torture.

"Naira, what is the matter?" Neal asked sharply. Worriedly.

Everything, I wanted to shout. I was in a freaking *Game of Thrones*–style blood feud with my family. And right now I was Sansa Stark, in the clutches of the Lannisters.

I burst into hysterical laughter at my mental wittiness, making an ass of myself in front of Neal for the third time.

"There ye go. Not too hot, is it?"

Neal's eyes were a different hue today. Gray as the gloom outside, and my mood. I didn't trust my voice not to wobble yet, so I shook my head and took another cautious sip of the hot chocolate. Ian, the bartender, had somehow conjured it up just for me.

Liam's Bar was a typical sports bar with one long wet bar running along the length of the place that could seat twenty-odd patrons. Opposite the bar were eight booths. I was sitting in one of the booths, Neal sprawled on the seat opposite me.

I took another grateful gulp of the soothing hot chocolate, which in turn soothed my nerves. Or was it simply Neal's big, brawny presence? He was so tall and well built, who'd dare to threaten me in his presence? Certainly not short, ugly Vinay.

I measured the breadth of Neal's shoulders with my eyes, imagined the circumference of his biceps beneath the checked shirt that was rolled up to his elbows, gauged the knocking-power of his large fist, currently curled around the handle of a beer mug. He definitely exuded the right amount of menace to scare off any thugs Vinay might send after me. *Let them come*, I mentally shook my fist at the universe.

"Are ye going to tell me what that was all about?"

My brother-in-law was a psycho, that was what this was about. Had he hated Kaivan that much? What else could it be? Why else would Vinay behave in such a way? Why did he want me destitute and completely beholden to him? Worst of all, how could my father not see this?

"I overreacted to a family squabble." It was a version of the truth.

Neal leveled a knowing look on me, but didn't push. Instead, he started describing the apartments he'd seen that afternoon. As I'd suspected, none of them had been ideal. One flat had been too dim, the other closetless, and the one on Wooster Street was as "wee as a tree hoose."

"Twenty paces from wall to wall. That's not a hoose. That's a nest for a wee birdie, aye?"

I laughed. His descriptions were always so entertaining. Neal had a wonderful sense of humor. Wry, British wit. Like my husband's.

"I'm sorry I wasted your time. And thank you for meeting Crystal for me."

He waved away my gratitude. "Now, if ye've finished the drink, I need ye to come with me. I have something to show ye."

I took one last sip and scooted out of the booth. I wondered if he wanted to show me his studio. I'd been dying to see it, but he hadn't been working there of late.

We had a couple hours to kill before our dinner reservation at a new Indian fusion place in NoHo that I'd wanted to try out. Paris and I had planned to hang out in SoHo before and get in some window-shopping. Neal was supposed to have joined us straight at the restaurant. But, my trip to New Jersey had jumbled up the plans.

We chatted with Ian and some of the regular bar patrons as we made our way outside. It was barely drizzling now; still, I stepped under the awning.

"Dinner will be my treat tonight. Please don't argue."

Neal didn't argue. His expression eloquently indicated what I could do with my request. As in, stuff it. Neal didn't let me pay for anything when we went out on the town.

I sighed. "Fine. I'll cook all the home meals for the next decade."

"I'd be a fool to say no to that." He grinned, pulling open the blue door of the main building. "After ye."

We walked into a narrow T-shaped lobby with stairs but no elevator. Unspeakably curious, I followed him up the stairs. The building was old but well maintained. The walls were whitewashed and plain, but solid. The ground floor had two doors on opposite sides of the landing. As did the first; one was painted red and the other one was white. The next flight of stairs brought us to the top, where, again, there were two doors facing each other over the landing. They were metal brown. A matching set, with matching hardware. Neal opened the door on the right.

I peered inside. "Is this your studio?"

"That's my studio." He pointed at the door opposite. "This is Uncle Liam's place."

Grinning broadly, he nudged me into a horrendously cluttered entryway that yawned into a horrendously cluttered living room. The sprawling loft-style flat had double vaulted ceilings and several skylights currently being bombarded with fat sporadic raindrops. Though it was rainy and cold outside, it felt much colder in here. My eyes, hands, my face, everything refroze. I began shaking so badly I could barely hug myself and rub my arms.

"Jesus. Yer still frozen." Neal looked me up and down. "Och. Let's get ye dry first."

Dry sounded wonderful. I followed him into the flat. It looked very much lived-in and loved. Objects from all over the world filled it cheek by jowl. They hung from the walls, the ceiling. Colorful rugs and tartan throws littered the wooden floors and cozy sofas, and the sheer number of books lying around made the space a fire hazard.

If time had a smell, it would smell like this, I thought. Of books and leather and memories.

Neal pulled out fresh towels from a linen closet in the hallway, dry clothes from the bedroom, and handed the pile to me. "They'll probably be too big on ye, but they're warm."

"Th...th...tha...nk...you." Even my teeth were chattering.

Neal opened the door to the hall bathroom and pushed me inside. "Get dry. Then we'll talk."

I closed the door and started stripping as quickly as my stiff fingers allowed. The bathroom was spacious and quaint, with wainscoting and a claw-foot tub. The fixtures were ornate and fussy, but gleamed like they were well tended. I couldn't stop my envy. None of the bathrooms in the flats I'd seen so far had had even a quarter of this one's appeal. If only I could afford a place like this. It was perfect. SoHo location. Lots of light. Lots of room. I could almost picture the living room decluttered and artfully arranged with select things.

There I went again, mentally redecorating someone else's home. Occupational hazard because of An Atelier in Mumbai where clients had paid me to treat their homes and offices like my personal canvases. I'd splashed my signature on three hundred spaces so far.

I ignored my beeping cell phone. I didn't need that shit again.

I was still cold when I came out of the bathroom, dressed in a pair of rolled-up sweatpants, thick socks and a hoodie. But not for long. Neal had started a fire. He handed me a glass of wine as I crossed the room to stand by the hearth.

"I'll throw yer clothes in the dryer." He made to go but I flapped my hand to stop him.

"No need. I've hung them up in the bathroom. They weren't as wet as they felt. They should be dry soon enough."

"All right. So, this is Uncle Liam's flat." He swept the hand that held his wineglass across the room. "The whole building is his, aye? He's been away since summer, so I've kept an eye on things—the bar, the tenants."

Nodding, I took a sip of my wine—an excellent Italian merlot. Neal launched into a fascinating story about his uncle Liam, I suppose to kill time while my clothes dried. I wondered if Paris was meeting us here before dinner.

Uncle Liam was Neal's father's youngest uncle—so technically he was Neal's great-uncle. He had emigrated to America in his youth. He'd never married, though he'd briefly been engaged once—or so the family believed. Uncle Liam had never confirmed or denied it. He bought the building in the 1960s and the sports bar quickly became a local favorite. There were six apartments in total in the building—four of them tenanted. Uncle Liam did well for himself for a lad who was a nomad at heart. He spent half of every year traveling the world. Which accounted for the eclectic knickknacks strewn about the place, I deduced.

"He's off on one of his adventures, and has only just intimated that he won't be back until March. Might even be next fall as he plans to climb Mount Everest and is training for it."

It was obvious Neal was extremely fond of his uncle. He also sounded wistful as if he envied his uncle's adventurous life. But why should he feel envious? He and Paris had an amazing, unrestricted relationship.

I took a long swallow of my wine. I was projecting my own wish to be a free bird onto Neal.

"He sounds like an amazing man," I said sincerely.

"Aye, that he is. And, he'll be delighted if ye house-sit for him."

I blinked. Then blinked again. Was it suddenly too warm, too hot, too much? I lurched away from the fire and sat down on an armchair by the window. "What?"

Neal's face split into a foolish grin. "Ye need time to find the right home. It canna be rushed. Ye can stay here until ye do."

What was this? Why was he being so amazing? And what was his ulterior motive? Was it Fraser Bespoke? The surrogacy?

"It's too generous, Neal."

This was a huge favor he was doing for me. Massive. Bigger than the job offer. No, I didn't consider the job a favor. I had the credentials and the expertise and I'd work my ass off if I accepted it. So, it wasn't a favor, rather a mutually benefiting partnership. But this. I looked around the living room. How on earth would my things fit in here when it was already bulging at the seams? And I didn't even have much stuff. Just four large Briggs & Riley suitcases full of clothes and some boxes of artwork.

"There's literally no room here." I cringed. Where were my manners? Instead of thanking him I was nitpicking?

He cocked his head at the door. "My studio's right across and there's plenty of extra space in there. I only use the living room, so the rest is yours if ye need it. Or we can move some of Liam's stuff in there so ye have more room in here. Will that do, lass?"

It would more than do.

"I will pay rent," I said flatly. I wasn't a charity case.

"Fair enough," he replied as if he'd been expecting it, and quoted an amount so ridiculously small that I blushed, feeling like a charity case anyway. I tried to fight him on it but he wouldn't listen. He said it wasn't about money for Uncle Liam.

But it was for me. I wouldn't be in anyone's debt. Never again. Though I couldn't bring myself to refuse the offer because it was too good to be true.

"And, lass," said Neal, doing some blushing of his own. "Don't go thinking that this or Fraser Bespoke is contingent on you being our surrogate. One has nothing to do with the other, aye? Ye decide whether you want to do any of it, or not. Ye honor us either way by yer friendship."

And just like that, I began crushing hard on my best friend's husband.

CHAPTER ELEVEN

Paris

Being midweek and happy hour, Liam's Bar was packed. Three flat-screen TVs held court over three different sections of the bar for the sports enthusiasts. One showed a soccer game; the second was set to horse racing; and the third, and by far the most crowded section as it was centered above the bar itself, had a cricket match on.

I found my husband there, sitting on a bar stool with a half-empty glass of Guinness in front of him. He twisted about when Ian hailed me, yanking me into the V of his legs. He put his mouth on mine, triggering a chorus of cheers and ribaldry from the regular patrons sitting and standing around us.

"Howdy, lover." I played my part, ruffling Neal's thick, black hair in affection. He needed a haircut, but I liked also that I could grip handfuls of it.

I parked my tush on the chair he vacated, then simply leaned into his chest as his arms slid around me, pulling me close.

"Ye smell good," he murmured against my cheek, his intent to seduce clear.

"Charmer. I smell like bad deo trying to cover up ugly BO." But he had me smiling and trembling with nascent desire.

"Ye smell like my woman." He ran his hands up and down my back, kneading the tension from my shoulders until I purred.

"Where's Naira?" I asked, stifling another delicious moan.

"Hmm? Ah, she was tired and cold. She went on home."

Then, suddenly, Neal's hands were off my shoulders and clutching his own head as a player on the TV screen ran into position below a ball that seemed to be falling from the sky. Too bad the ball bounced out of his cupped hands.

Neal went ballistic. "Ye wee idiot. Can't ye catch a ball that's desperate to fall into yer hands?" He cursed at the screen, using ridiculously hilarious Scottish words. My favorite being: *bampot*.

I didn't bother to ask if we were going to dinner. If Naira had gone home, and the cricket match had just become exciting, then we weren't going anywhere.

Just as well. I could use a Guinness with my man and some regular fish and chips. Food we could recognize as opposed to weird fusion dishes. We could make it a date night. We hadn't had one of those in several weeks, so it would be nice.

England lost the one-day against Australia, making my husband pout moodily. While the beer and food and the company had worked wonders on mine.

We walked home, hand in hand. The rain had washed the city clean, suffusing the air in petrichor, except for the patches where garbage had been left at the curb for the morning collection. Neal was on the phone with a client in Japan, who'd called precisely as we'd left the bar. When you had businesses all over the world, you pretty much worked around-the-clock.

Neal was still on the phone when we stepped inside our apartment. He headed into his office and I went into the bathroom for a long shower. I was sitting on the edge of the bed in my sleep tank and shorts, rubbing cream into my skin, when he strolled into the room. He bussed an absentminded kiss on my forehead, set his phone to charge and then headed into the bathroom. I followed him, watched him strip and pee.

"Did you ask her to move in with us? She won't listen to me. Says she doesn't want to impose." I threw up my hands. "What does that even mean?"

"It means she values her privacy," he warbled from under the rain shower. Definitely moody tonight.

I positioned myself diagonally opposite the shower so he couldn't ignore me. "I don't think she should be alone. She's still grieving, you know."

He'd heard me, but Neal continued to soap himself. Then wash himself. Finally, from under the steaming jet spray, he shot me a beady blue stare. "I've set her up at Uncle Liam's."

His hot naked bod was an impressive distraction, so my brain took an extra minute to process his words. Then I exploded.

"You did what? Why would you do that? She practically lives here already. She's comfortable here." I scrambled around for a better reason. "Besides, Liam's place is too messy. It'll upset her chi or something. Naira's a bigger neat-freak than you are. She'll probably rearrange his whole house if she stays there. Liam will hate that."

Even here, at our cleverly decorated rental, Naira had moved a couple of pieces of furniture around for a better flow and feng shui energy. She'd bought orchids for the side tables and the bathroom vanities, and cared for them herself or made sure I did when she wasn't around. She was a born nurturer and homemaker, which made the Big Idea sublimely perfect.

Neal remained unconcerned. "So, she'll arrange it back when she moves out."

Drat it all. Didn't he get it that we needed to work on Naira 24/7 or her conservative upbringing would win. I wanted to strangle him for doing something so idiotic instead of what I'd told him.

"Let the poor lass breathe, hen. It's barely a fifteen-minute walk between our places, not the other side of the world. And, Paris, I'm fond of the lass. I am. And I do wish that she agrees to the surrogacy, but I want some bloody privacy too. I want our home to be ours again. For Christ's sake, a man should no' have to look over his shoulder every time he wants to fart!"

And that, ladies and gentlemen of the jury, was how one bitch-slapped the mad out of a dispute.

Speechless, I gaped at my husband, who glared back as if I'd been torturing him over hot coals for weeks.

Neal was definitely the clichéd moody artist. He needed lots of alone time, much more than I did. I'd neglected his needs for the past few weeks because my attention had been on Naira. On rekindling our friendship and the Big Idea. Why hadn't he said anything to me? He'd been nothing but courteous, charming and chivalrous in front of Naira—everything he'd been brought up to be. I'd forgotten that his manners wouldn't allow him to be a rude host, one who took his downtime even when there was a guest in the house. One who locked himself in his office or studio to sulk or brood for no reason at all. Appearances had to be maintained in front of people who weren't family.

Naira was the same. She'd give herself a migraine, catering to a houseful of demanding guests, rather than tell them to fend for themselves. No wonder she and Neal snapped when they reached their breaking points. I didn't have breaking points since I snapped all the time.

Was that what was going on with him tonight? Or was he having second thoughts?

Neal wasn't stupid. He was a jeweler—a *johri* from an exalted lineage of *johris*. Gauging the potential brilliance of a rough diamond was in his blood more than his training. One glance through his magnifying loupe at a dirty, lumpy stone, and he'd be able to tell its worth. He knew the worth of the Big Idea. No, this was just a mood. One easily flipped by lavishing attention on him—on us. We both needed it.

Later, in bed, Neal coiled his body around mine, spooning me from behind, and kissed my ear. "If ye really want her here, I willna argue."

Stars burst inside me as if I'd exploded in climax again. How had I even found this man? How was I so lucky?

"I love you." I squeezed our laced hands tightly and brought them to rest on my heart. "Thank you. But you're right. Liam's place is better."

For now.

I took Naira to a surrogacy and adoption law seminar the Saturday after she moved into Liam's apartment.

It wasn't harassment to bombard her with information, as Neal so indelicately put it. I was simply building a case for a favorable verdict. In order to make an informed decision, didn't one need to have all the information first? Besides, when the cat was away—Neal was traveling again—the mouse could do whatever she damn well pleased.

Naira was staring up at the sunlit facade of the courthouse when I walked up to her. She was bundled up for a Siberian adventure this morning and winter hadn't even officially begun.

"Gorgeous building, huh?" I stood next to her and we admired the seven-story Manhattan landmark with its Corinthian columns and statues of prominent historic figures looking out at the city.

Right about here yesterday, I'd literally stepped on a flyer advertising the seminar in a bold neon-green headline. Even Neal wouldn't have ignored such a sign.

"It's even more impressive inside." I strode through the triple-arched main entrance of the building into a spacious hall with an imposing opera-style double marble staircase. It was empty today, being the weekend. "Sometimes the DA's office holds press conferences here. Different departments have ceremonies, commemorations here too. It's also been featured in quite a few movies and TV series."

"Wow." Naira's kohl-lined eyes went as round as the buttons on her snow-white coat.

She looked good today. Definitely better than she had at Lavinia's wedding over a month ago. Her color was high, her stride purposeful. She no longer flinched or startled at unexpected sounds. No, I wasn't harassing or pressuring her. Naira wouldn't have come if she absolutely didn't want to.

We made our way up the stairs and I gave her a little history of the building. "It's constructed out of stone and is fireproof because it was built to house the city's paper records. Thus, it was called the Hall of Records at the time. The seminar is on the second floor, and the courtrooms are on the third."

Naira was looking every which way, taking it all in. "It's gorgeous. I noticed several books on New York City at Uncle Liam's. I'll look up this building, and other landmarks. They'll be good venues for photoshoots…for the shop."

"I'm sorry I couldn't come to help you unpack, but it's been crazy at work this week." And getting crazier by the minute.

Naira flapped her hand, grinning. "It's okay. Easier to just do it all myself than give you instructions and hear you moan. Besides, I feel like Alice who's tumbled down a rabbit hole. Uncle Liam has the most fascinating collection of things."

I nodded. "That he does. I love that creaky old place with its nooks and crannies and tchotchkes."

Neal had stayed with Liam the summer we met, and I had several fond memories of the place. Naturally, we'd fucked all over the apartment—all over mine too. We'd basically just fucked all summer long until our brains had turned to mush.

I shot Naira a sly grin. "Want to hear a funny story about when Liam walked in on us in the bathroom?"

"Eek. No, he didn't!"

"Oh, yes, he did. It was the single most embarrassing moment of my life. Neal had been wishing my boobs a good morning, and in our passionate haze, we forgot to lock the door. Liam walked in, saw us and just nodded politely as if he routinely came across such sights in his bathroom. Thank God I'd been propped against a wall with Neal's body covering 90 percent of mine. Imagine if I'd been on the vanity with a mirror against my—"

"TMI, Paris!" But she was giggling madly, so was I, and she hadn't blocked her ears in mortification.

We stopped halfway up the grand staircase, trying to get ourselves under control before climbing the rest of the way.

God, that had been an insane encounter. "I still can't make eye contact with Liam, and I stammer like a twit if I have to talk to him directly while he turns the shade of a beetroot. We make it so obvious that something is up with us that the whole Fraser clan is trying to guess what it could be. After that day, Liam took to stomping about the apartment whenever I was around, or booming out random questions or monologues so everyone knew where everyone else was at any given moment." As I said, fond memories.

We were still giggling as we reached the all-purpose room on the second floor where the seminar was being held. The panel introductions had begun when we entered. There were about eight people up on the dais. The room was fitted for an audience of maybe a hundred but it wasn't close to being full. Naira and I quietly poured ourselves some free coffee from the refreshment table and took our seats at the back of the room.

For the next hour, a host of surrogacy pundits, from agents to lawyers to social workers to medical experts, examined the industry from various angles. Surrogacy was a multibillion-dollar industry worldwide and everyone wanted in on it. Surrogates and intended mothers were called to the dais to share their stories. Most sounded happy and thrilled and fulfilled by their choices. They'd all had fairly positive experiences, much like the Wilsons, but most of the panelists agreed that it was rare for a surrogacy to go smoothly. Glitches were the norm, they said. Then the discussion took a downright horrific turn and I wondered if Naira and I should leave. I didn't want her freaking out about the bad stuff. That was my job.

"Family courts are inundated with surrogacy cases gone wrong. Blackmail, extortion, abuse, outright theft—you name it and it's happened. Legally, it's a veritable shit storm," said one of the panel lawyers.

Surrogacy laws were too loose-ended. Everything was an issue—the legality of the terms of the contracts, the morality of the agencies that charged money. There was no precedent for a penalty for reneging on the contract. The courts had to intervene and the decision relied on the goodness, understanding and personal beliefs of the judge. There were also cases where surrogates had refused to give up the baby after birth. Yet intended parents had to place their trust and their baby's health in the hands of a stranger, and vice versa. There were cases where intended parents had refused to accept the baby.

"Can they even do that?" Naira looked visibly shocked as we stood at a light to cross the road after the seminar.

We'd stayed until the end. We'd even spoken to some of the panelists, who'd been nothing but open and encouraging. They'd given us their cards and said to feel free to get in touch. One of the surrogates had advised Naira to join a potential-surrogate support group immediately. "You'll see what the process is like firsthand. And you'll get all the answers you need," she'd said.

Though it was a bright, sunny day, it was cold and we decided to head home, to the Spruce Street flat, and chill indoors for the rest of the day, and order takeout when we got hungry. Mostly, I didn't want to dress up and go anywhere. I was in sweatpants and a thick *Law & Order* promo sweatshirt and no one was getting me out of those today, except maybe Neal.

"Can they order up a kid like a milkshake from Shake Shack and then simply not show up to pick up their order? Apparently." I seethed on behalf of a child I didn't even know.

"It sounds awful. I can't believe someone would do that."

"Humans are awful beings, honey. We walk about the earth like we're the only creatures entitled to do so. We twist and manipulate everything to our advantage."

I was feeling particularly vicious about certain specimens of humanity these days. "At work, we're building a case against this family—well, it's now an organization, but it started off as a family garment business that employed only women. These women were taught to sew, tailor jeans and shirts and such. Be self-sufficient. Then in comes this bad relative from somewhere and decides there should be a bigger profit. So, the abuse starts. Stricter working hours. Inhumane penalties for missing a workday or messing up an order. Sex in the workplace. All good intentions out the window. And you know what's truly evil? That the women have been so brainwashed they don't even realize it's abuse." I shut my trap, exhaling noisily. I never spoke about work after-hours. "I'm sure you've heard and read about many such stories in India."

Naira caught my arm, forcing me to stop and turn to her in the middle of the sidewalk. "You amaze me, Paris. What you do. Who you are."

I shrugged it off. "It's my job. And the feeling is mutual." I gave her a quick hug. "There are very few humans I can tolerate. So, consider yourself one of the lucky ones," I added with a wink.

We walked in silence for several minutes before we had to detour from our straight path, as the street up ahead had been completely dug up. There was always something going on in Manhattan. A road getting repaved, a building coming up. A law being broken, I thought as a couple of cop cars zoomed past us, sirens blaring, closely followed by three howling FDNY trucks.

"Did you understand the legal issues the panelists talked about?"

"Mostly." Naira shot me a curious glance as we meandered through City Hall Park.

I raised my eyebrows in askance.

"I'm surprised you trust this process. It's not at all…what I imagined. I mean, anything and everything can go wrong. Even legally."

I snorted. "I don't trust it, honey. I trust you. Neal and I both trust you. And you trust us, right?" She rolled her eyes as if I'd asked a most ridiculous question. I gave her a faint smile. "I couldn't choose a surrogate for the longest time, even though the whole thing was my idea. And now I know why. I can't do this with a stranger."

"But why are you doing it at all?" she asked quietly.

Why indeed?

"I told you it's for Neal. I want to give him his dream." A bus hissed to a stop right next to us as if underlining my conviction. Or was it calling me out on a lie? "That's the primary reason. But it slowly dawned on me that it wasn't only a matter of giving him a child. If it were, I wouldn't have any issues choosing any random surrogate, would I? The thing is I don't only need someone to gestate and birth the kid—that's the least of it. What I want…hope for is a…uh…a coparent."

"A what?" Naira stopped in her tracks again. If her jaw tilted any lower, it would hit the pavement.

At this rate, we wouldn't get home till evening. I put my arm through hers and hauled her onward.

"I'm clearly ill-equipped to be a mother. If you didn't have your financial issues, you wouldn't even think twice about having kids. So, it's killing three birds with one stone, really."

"Please don't talk about killing birds, even figuratively. It's upsetting." Naira tried to tug her arm from mine, but I held on tightly.

"Fine, fine. Let's talk about fate, then. You coming to New York now is fate. Opportunity has come knocking on our doors. We cannot ignore it, can we?" I reasoned.

"Can I ask you something? And you have to tell me the absolute truth, okay?" Naira looked at me quite seriously.

I drew an imaginary X over my left boob. "Shoot."

"You seriously have no desire to get pregnant? You won't resent the bond between the surrogate and your baby?"

I felt like I'd already won with her question even though she'd tried to sound as impersonal as possible.

"I won't. I have no desire to get pregnant. There is no biological clock ticking away inside me. You know that. And legally, it will be my bairn—Neal's and mine—so what's to resent? Labor pains? No thanks. Believe me, I've thought long and hard about this and it is for the best. Imagine all my negative vibes and cynicism flowing into the kid via my umbilical cord. It will be born screwed up. No, this is for the best."

"It's not quite so clinical, Paris. You're failing to grasp how immense and instantaneous the connection between a mother and child can be. I know." Naira pressed her hand to her stomach. She was clearly flashing back to her pregnancy. Perhaps imagining feelings that hadn't really been there. Hindsight was always enhanced and tweaked by our brains. Another one of humanity's follies—believing there was more to our existence than biology.

When we passed the playground below my building, I decided to show Naira what I meant rather than tell. I detoured inside the playground full of kids and parents and au pairs even on a chilly Saturday morning.

"Paris? What are you doing?"

I held up a pointy finger, indicating that Naira wait and watch. I marched up to a chubby little baby gurgling happily at the world from inside his stroller, as his mother watched her older toddler play in the sandbox. I made small talk with the mother, exclaimed how cute her baby was, and then I began making cooing noises at him. The bairn promptly started wailing. His mother frowned, picked up the baby and buried his face in her neck.

I quirked a smug eyebrow at Naira, who continued to look confused.

"What?"

"Keep watching."

I sat on a bench where a father fed apples to his twin girls. They were around two years old, I estimated. I did nothing else. Just sat there, smiling at the children. Within minutes, the girls got fidgety, then one got cranky and she kept shifting away from me, sliding closer and closer to her sister until she was nearly sitting on her sister's lap.

I scanned the playground, my eyes settling on a grinning, toothless toddler on a swing. His mother stood behind him, pushing him gently. I played peekaboo like I'd watched Neal do a hundred times in the last three years. I didn't even go near the kid—I did it from fifteen feet away. Not in the least entertained by me, the kid burst out crying and his perplexed mother ran over to pluck him out of the swing.

I crossed my arms and looked at Naira, whose stunned face said it all.

"Now do you get it? They *know*—the kids. They know in their gut that I'm persona non grata."

Naira's jaw worked. "That's just..."

"Coincidence? More like a contagion. It happens all the time. It's like I'm covered in a natural kid repellent. So, getting you and Neal to coparent any bairn of mine is actually a coup."

CHAPTER TWELVE

Naira

I loved Liam's apartment. It was cozy and enchanting, stuffed with mismatched sofas and wall-to-wall shelves that groaned with books and strange, wonderful objects from faraway lands. The bedroom opened onto a concrete terrace with wrought-iron furniture that had been arranged between hundreds of potted plants. I had my morning chai there, weather permitting. Sure, it was a messy place, but there was a difference between messy and eclectic. Liam's home was a testament to a life well lived and traveled. An adventurous—fearless—life and I hoped some of it would rub off on me.

Not that I had time to run off on an adventure. I was busy as a bee these days, my routine chock-full of activity. I exercised daily to keep my endorphins on the up-and-up. Then there was the move and the settling in; the discussions with

Neal about ateliers and Fraser Bespoke; the discussions with Paris and Neal about surrogacy.

We went over it and over it from every angle and I still had doubts. So did Neal. But not Paris. She was so confident, so sure that everything would magically fall into place exactly as she planned. So I played devil's advocate and tried to shatter her delusions. What if I couldn't carry the baby to term? I had miscarried before, after all. What if our coparenting styles were poles apart? Who'd get the final say in it?

"We're talking about nature and biology. Neither can be controlled," I pointed out in exasperation as we huffed and puffed on neighboring ellipticals in the building's gym one Saturday afternoon. Neal had gone swimming in the heated indoor pool one floor above us.

"I know that." She rolled her eyes, her face dripping sweat. "We try. If it doesn't work…" She shrugged.

If it didn't work, it was up to me to try again or not, she added. If not, they'd go with Martha—if she was still available.

Could it really be as simple as she made it seem? Was I overthinking it?

"What if I get too attached? What happens then, Paris? What if I can't give up the baby? What if I turn into one of those psychos who kidnaps babies from their cradles?"

Paris laughed in my face. "Yeah, no. If you had some crazy-ass personality disorder, I'm pretty sure you'd have exhibited it by now. Besides, you're going to be a part of the kid's life so why would you?"

Paris truly didn't understand the bond between a mother and a child, did she? Maybe, just maybe, I could show her what it was about.

A week later, I was still at a crossroads about everything. Suddenly, there were too many directions I could take, and having all these choices and options after having none for so long was confusing.

Then Deven Fraser came to town, and life went from "hardly any time to think" to "no time to breathe or sleep."

Neal's younger brother was a swarthier, more serious version of him. With a *dastaar*—a turban wrapped around his head—he'd look as Sikh as his maternal forefathers, no question. His eyes were a deeper blue than his brother's, an intense midnight color. Nothing escaped his attention, and he weighed every word before uttering it. Frankly, I was a little terrified of him even though we were roughly the same age. He was just a few months older, having already turned thirty while my birthday was coming up next week around Thanksgiving. He was totally the shark Paris claimed he was.

In the days leading up to Thanksgiving, we talked shop during the day—Neal, the Shark and I—and once Paris came home from work, we went out on the town. Neither Neal nor Deven seemed to need any downtime between work and play or sleep. We went to the movies. We went clubbing. We ate out all the time. And every night, no matter how late it was, we always ended up at Liam's Bar for a nightcap.

Tonight was no different. Except, I felt different. I was drunk. No...*no*... I was pleasantly tipsy. Slightly uninhibited— no, no. A *lot* uninhibited. I hadn't a care in the world. New York was my shield, my sanctuary, my salvation.

I'd finally chosen my future path. I wanted to be a part of Fraser Bespoke. I wanted to spearhead the setup for the North American pop-up stores. It hadn't been decided if we'd launch in New York or LA first, but they wanted to start the process immediately with a target for a soft launch in late spring to early summer. We needed to start hiring people, building relationships with local and nonlocal vendors, getting a portfolio ready, merchandise samples, drawing up marketing plans, assisting in developing and overseeing the web presence. In short, I'd be doing everything I'd have done for the atelier, except invest my money. However, I had a caveat—no, no, a request before I accepted.

"What if they refuse to hear me out?" I stared at my reflection in the large mirror above a round metal sink. I looked a fright with my raccoon eyes and tired hair, like I hadn't slept well in days. Which was about right. But, the question was would I go into business with someone who looked like me right now?

Shit. I bent and splashed my face with ice-cold water until I felt a bit more alert.

"Just march out and spill it before you make yourself sick. Rip off the bandage. Do you want me to ask?" Paris said, refreshing her lipstick.

Paris and I had squeezed ourselves inside the single unisex bathroom for a tête-à-tête.

I patted my face dry with a paper towel and sighed. "Thanks. But, I have to fight my own battles." Stand up for myself like I'd done when I wanted to study. Like I should do with Vinay. Like I should have done with Kaivan.

I took the lipstick from her and swiped it over my own lips. Not that it made a difference. I still looked drunk. But, I had to do this now. In the bright sobriety of daylight, I'd accept whatever terms Deven boxed me into without a squeak and I'd be miserable.

I marched out to the bar—luckily it was mostly empty as it was close to one in the morning. The two Fraser sharks were hovering in front of the TV, their sharp teeth flashing, absorbed in the intense one-day international match being played between India and Pakistan in Mumbai. This was an important ODI because it was the first time in several years that the Pakistani team had been allowed to travel to India and play.

Tensions between the two countries were still high, I didn't think they'd ever lessen, but this was supposedly an iconic match to show both nations that even if we were on opposite sides of the political fence, we could still "play" together.

My grandmother had once compared Sarika and me to Pakistan and India. She'd said that though we were products of the same environment and gene pool, somewhere along the way, we'd split into two warring countries. My grandmother had been partial to me, but she'd also expected more of me. *You are smarter. More sensible. It is up to you to mend the rift*, she'd said.

I was bloody tired of being sensible and forgiving and sweet.

A triumphant roar rose from the TV as India scored four runs. For a second, I missed it—my city, my people, even my family. I stared at the screen as it panned out to the stands, trying to see if my family—cricket crazies, all of us—were in the audience, watching the match live. My family had year-round box seats at Mumbai's Wankhede Stadium.

"I want a partnership in Fraser Bespoke," I blurted out after Virat Kohli, the captain of the Indian cricket team, once again swung his bat and thwacked the incoming ball in the air.

This was it. I'd either hit a six like Kohli or I was out.

Deven's impatient eyes cut to my face, then back to the screen, then back on me as the ball landed in the crowd for a six. The whole stadium went mad with excitement. Neal turned to face me, sliding his hands into his pant pockets in a deceptively relaxed posture.

I flapped my hand, clarifying, "Not globally. I don't have that kind of money to invest, obviously. But I want a small… um, wee share in the US venture."

That was my condition. If they wanted me to set up and run a concept store, then I wanted a stake in it. I wasn't going to put myself in a position where they could fire me on a whim. I came from a business family. I knew how such things worked.

Kohli thwacked the ball again, three for three. It arced high in the air maybe for another six runs, but my gut didn't think so. The ball plummeted straight into the cupped hands of a Pakistani fielder. The crowd erupted again, this time booing and not cheering. Kohli had been caught out before his century. But, he'd played well at ninety-two runs. India still had a good chance to win.

Neal and Deven studied my face for what seemed like an eternity. They were trying to intimidate me, see if I caved. They looked at each other when I didn't back down—thank you GFC for the Dutch courage—and some mental communiqué passed between them. Deven flicked a glance at the TV screen, noticed he'd completely missed the catch and flared his nostrils looking rather peeved.

"Fine. We'll talk tomorrow."

I was so shocked that he'd actually agreed and so quickly that I gaped at him until he raised his eyebrows high. They wanted me that much? *Eek!*

Inanely, I stuck out my hand, which he took, smiling now, and I shook it, vigorously. I shook Neal's hand just as vigorously, making him laugh and my eyes prickle. Horrified that I'd get emotional in front of my brand-new business partners, I left them to the game and rushed outside. The icy night was a shock, enough to keep me from crying. I took several deep breaths of cold, cold air, hugging myself hard. They wanted me. They'd meant every word during our meetings. They weren't going to use me for my contacts and throw me aside.

Paris came out with my woolen cape draped over her arm, carrying two glasses of the GFC. Ian had become an expert in our bespoke brew. I swirled the cape about my shoulders, then took my glass.

"Wasn't so bad, was it?" Paris asked, clinking our glasses.

"It was awesome. They— You are awesome!" I broke into

a giddy smile even as a tear or two rolled down my cheeks. My throat felt swollen with all these crazy emotions. My heart was full—no, it overflowed with happiness tonight.

We sat on the stoop and finished our drinks under a bright, round moon. Was this Kaivan's doing? Was he looking out for me from up there? Was it why he'd set up the trust in New York? So I'd have to come here and reunite with my bestie?

I drew my attention from the stars to Paris's squiggly profile. This was all her doing. She and Neal had saved me. Their trust in me meant everything. It was a gift beyond measuring. I wanted to reciprocate. I had to.

"I'll do it."

"Huh?" Paris turned her head lazily to look at me and froze when my words sank in.

I froze too. Everything around us stopped. The air. My breath. The gushing in my veins. Maybe even the moon ceased to spin around the earth for a heartbeat. My brain erupted into images and ideas. My skin felt electrified as if a thousand billion atoms oozed happiness from my pores.

"The whole thing? The surrogacy, coparenting, everything?"

I nodded jerkily.

"Thank you," she said, her voice hoarse and soaked in gratitude.

I smiled then. Satisfied that she was every bit as emotional about it as I was. We finished our drinks in a silence flush with the promise of the future.

For the next few days, I was holed up with the Fraser brothers at the lawyer's. We went over everything we needed to address and include in the contract—the broad frame of my job description, filing for a change in my immigration status with USCIS. My salary would be less than what they'd initially offered because now my package included a 1.5 percent stake in Fraser Bespoke, not just US but worldwide. They wanted me to eventually oversee global communications once the US stores were launched. Broadly, my title would be Director of Communications. I realized, only when the lawyer mentioned it, that my stake had come from Deven and Neal personally. They'd each let me buy out a fraction of their personal stakes in the company.

"I won't let you down," I swore, still completely stunned and moved beyond belief by their faith in me. "I'll get your vision off the ground as quickly as possible."

"Yes, you will," said Deven gruffly even as Neal winked and said, "I've no doubt, lass."

We celebrated with champagne and laughter and dived right into the thick of things. But, even with all the business goings-on, the surrogacy stayed in my mind.

Paris and I decided not to tell anyone until all my medical reports came back clear. I'd miscarried before, and while my gynecologist had ruled it as, "Just one of those unfortunate things that happen without cause," I still wanted to make sure it hadn't been me—my womb.

After the tests, I would tell my family and in-laws before we took it further. I worried about my in-laws especially. It wasn't that I needed their blessing, but I was still their daughter-in-law and I didn't want them hearing about my decision from strangers. I didn't want them hurt by gossip. And there would be gossip, I had no illusions about that.

But even with all of these worries and uncertainties, and Vinay's obnoxiousness that knew no bounds, I had much to be thankful for during the holidays.

We'd been invited to Lavinia and Juan's for Thanksgiving dinner weeks ago, and I'd agreed to help Lavinia with the vegetarian part of the menu. So, by the time Thursday afternoon rolled around, I was physically and mentally drained, and was honestly fed up with socializing. I couldn't believe Paris was putting up with it all without even a little bit of snark. What had happened to my best friend since her marriage? She was unrecognizable, really.

"Honey, you look exhausted. Why don't you sit down? Put your feet up. I'll help Lavinia with...*umm.*" She looked around the boisterously packed living room, and the overflowing buffet table. "Whatever she needs help with."

I didn't wait for her to rethink the offer, and gleefully plonked down on a window seat that had magically remained vacant in the madhouse. From my vantage point, I saw Paris sashaying over to Lavinia in her pointy heels. She looked chic in a festive yellow A-line dress with an asymmetrical hemline. Who was this person? Seriously?

I took off my ballet flats and massaged my poor exhausted feet. Served me right for trying to please everyone. The past week with Deven had been insane and I'd spent yesterday going over my agenda and objectives for the next few months. Then I'd gone grocery shopping on the eve of Thanksgiving in New York City. I was nothing if not a masochist. I'd prepped and marinated foodstuff until midnight, and at five o'clock this morning, I'd staggered into the kitchen again to start the actual cooking to bring to Lavinia's. I'd hoped to leave right after dinner.

Yeah. That didn't work out. No one took pity on me even though I was practically falling asleep on my feet.

"Just one more game, and we'll all leave." My college friends chorused every time I looked in the direction of the front door. Or, just one more song and one more drink and one more story.

Only Deven seemed sympathetic to my plight, and only

after I'd amused him by yawning all through his…lecture? Anecdote? I had no idea what he'd been saying.

"Come on, let's get you home," he said, placing his hand to my back and propelling me toward the door. Which was a good thing, because I was seeing double of everything now.

"Thank you," I moaned, ready to genuflect and kiss his feet for helping me escape. Dimly, I noticed that no one dared to stop him from leaving. Scared little cats. No one said, "Just one more hour, Dev. Don't be such a wet blanket."

He dropped me home—uh, to Liam's flat—and I fell face-first into a dreamless, worry-free sleep.

I woke up after noon on Black Friday, my entire body achy and slow. I'd missed the doorbuster sales, which was…just as well as I was working at decluttering my life. I didn't need to purchase more things.

Still, I felt a twinge of FOMO. I adored a good buy. I felt the same about shopping malls what a child felt about Disney World. The energy inside An Atelier on sale days had been its own reward. Oh, how I loved haggling with vendors over prices and the quality of goods. I couldn't wait to start doing it again.

I made my daily calls to my mother and in-laws. Brief and cordial was the way to go. I used to chat with my mother for hours, but now our conversations were stilted because while she understood my need for independence, she didn't approve of my stand against my father and Vinay, or my desertion. My decision to be a surrogate might just be the final nail in the coffin of my relationship with my family.

Paris called while I was brewing a pot of masala chai to go with my chili cheese toasts in lieu of lunch.

"Be ready by seven. We are going to bring in your birthday with a bang. I've made dinner reservations at Eleven Madison Park. The chef is thrilled to experiment with the vegetarian tasting menu for us. And, we're going dancing after—the lads insist—so you better rest up as it'll be another late night."

"Yes, Mother," I said, and stuck my tongue out at her even though she couldn't see it.

I fell asleep on the sofa while air-drying the fresh coats of pumpkin-orange nail polish I'd applied on my hands and feet, and woke up with a start with drool on my face when I should've been heading out to commence my birthday celebrations.

Shit. Tardy again.

I messaged Paris that I'd meet them directly at the restaurant. I dashed into the shower and got ready in a record ten minutes. Then I went temporarily nuts when my strapless bra decided to star as Houdini's prop by disappearing from my lingerie drawer. I searched my whole closet and couldn't find it. What to do? What to do? I didn't have time to steam iron another dress that wouldn't need a strapless bra, even beneath a jacket.

Suddenly, I remembered I had an extra one and some stick-on cups in one of the suitcases I'd stashed in the studio. All my brand-new, never-worn-before clothes were there. I grabbed the keys to the studio and scampered across the landing, freezing from soles to scalp in a fluffy white towel. I cursed myself for overnapping. I was clearly living up to the Indian Stretched Time standard.

"Aha!" I exclaimed in triumph, fishing out the bra. Saved by my super organizational skills and faultless memory. I'd known exactly where it would be.

I dashed back and—

"Ack!" I stopped dead in the doorway of Liam's flat, staring at Deven staring at me in shock.

Oh, God. Oh, my effing God. Why in eff was he here?

His shock quickly dissolved into amusement when he saw just what I clutched between my breasts. His whole face, not just his eyes, lit up like the Christmas lights on the Rockefeller tree—I'm not exaggerating—while I felt as if I'd stepped into the path of one of Daenerys Targaryen's fire-breathing children.

I was absolutely, hideously mortified. I wanted to jump down from the landing and die. Thank God for the towel, teensy-weensy though it may be.

His eyes trailed down my body as if pulled against his will because he kept dragging them back to my face. The deep appreciation in their midnight blue depths went some ways to overshadowing my embarrassment. When had a man last looked at me like that?

Two years and three months ago.

"Sorry for barging in, but the door was open." His grin wasn't apologetic at all. It was wicked. Flirtatious.

I was surprised. Deven had been nothing but amazing and friendly this past week—just like his brother. But he'd never flirted with me, never crossed that line. He was going to be my boss—it wouldn't have been right. As if that wasn't enough of a deterrent, I was going to have his brother's child. The thought was like a bucket of cold water thrown at me.

I pointed in the general direction of the bedroom and simply ran there, very aware of the hot gaze burning my behind.

Just as I was about to slam the door, I heard him clear his throat. "Take yer time, lass. Dinner isn't until nine now. The lovebirds are busy too."

"Oh, God!" I kept repeating as I got dressed.

What was he doing here if dinner had been postponed? Had the lovebirds kicked him out to do lovebirdy things? For once, I hadn't been the *kabab mein haddi*—the third wheel—in Paris and Neal's love nest.

A picture of a love nest writhing with naked bodies popped into my head. *Gah.* Not helpful! Then, without permission, my imagination imagined what Deven would look like writhing and naked—thick muscles twisting, tan flesh turning, blue eyes smoldering, as his full, sensual lips curved into a wicked smile.

Oh, God.

And thus began my thirtieth, flirtiest and craziest year.

CHAPTER THIRTEEN

Paris

When I told Neal that all systems were a go with the surrogacy, he cried. He denied it, but he went all red in the face, his eyes turned glassy and his voice got thick with emotion. That's crying, in my opinion.

Naira had passed most of the medical and psychological screenings with flying colors. Neal and I had already done our evaluations months ago, so we were set. I'd forwarded all the records, labs and application papers to the nurse practitioner at the fertility clinic, who would review everything, then schedule us in for the first IVF consultation.

Neal took us to dinner that night at gastronomically brilliant but astronomically expensive Per Se with its stunning bird's-eye view of Columbus Circle and Central Park to celebrate our happy alliance.

"And just in time for Christmas. Let's surprise the clan with our news over the holidays, aye?" He grinned as we clinked our flutes together.

"I don't see why we have to tell anyone until Naira's actually pregnant," I pointed out practically. Why create a hullabaloo for no reason?

I was subjected to twin disapproving frowns between courses four and five. My vote was discounted and the Big Reveal was scheduled for the December holidays.

Christmas was a massive deal for the Frasers, even more so than Diwali. Neal and I usually spent the year-end holidays with his family in Scotland. Although, Christmas was still a working holiday in many parts of Scotland—quite an oxymoron, that—I wasn't allowed to bring my work along. Which was in parts frustrating and in parts completely relaxing.

Originally staunch Catholic farmers, the Frasers were traditionalists in the sense that Christmas was celebrated more in terms of a bountiful harvest (replace by profitable year) than anything remotely religious. It was a less important festival than Hogmanay or New Year's Eve, though they celebrated both with similar aplomb.

A good chunk of the extended family, most of whom worked for Fraser Global in various capacities, gathered in and around Inverness from Christmas Eve until after the turn of the year. Sometimes way after, like the third or fourth of January. In Scotland, not only the first day of the year but also January second was a national holiday, to allow people to recover from the never ending Hogmanay celebrations, usually involving the limitless consumption of whisky.

Neal's parents, Niall Fraser and Minnie Singh, presided over Riverhead Hall, a restored manor house roughly the size of a mini castle, on their twelve-thousand-acre Riverhead Estate located somewhere west of Inverness. The estate ran along the edge of the River Beauly and overlooked the Beauly Firth on its easternmost side. It was where my husband had been born, where he'd played as a little boy and where I'd been married, and so I was rather fond of the imposing old place with its oak-paneled walls and staggering chandeliers and zig-zagging corridors. The main house, painted a warm butter yellow on the outside, was the oldest structure, but annexes had been added to it during different eras and in varied styles. The hodgepodge architecture didn't take anything away from Riverhead's overall grandeur.

The buildings weren't overly decorated for Christmas, inside or outside, as the main party took place in a full-service hotel in Inverness to accommodate the entire clan—by clan, I mean the Frasers, their friends and extended families, and their employees from all across the world. Every single person connected to the family, personally and professionally, was invited to the annual Christmas ball and the extended brunch the next day on Bonus Day, which was a Fraser take on Boxing Day.

Traditionally, Boxing Day was when the clan chiefs or fief lords would hand out "boxes" full of rations, clothes, coin and/or whisky (or wine depending on country) to their tenants as Christmas gifts. Though, Neal's family didn't have any royal blood or a chiefdom in their ancestry—the baronage had been a recently bestowed honor, as recent as around a century ago. It had been awarded to Neal's great-great-great-grandfather for his exceptional service to his country during the British Raj in Chandigarh. It had been passed down through the male heirs and currently Neal's uncle James, his father's oldest brother, held the title. He had one heir who seemed to show no interest in marriage or the production of heirs, hence the title could possibly be passed on to Neal's father, and consequently to Neal. It was an unlikely scenario according to Neal, yet I'd been appalled when I'd first heard of it. The clever lad hadn't brought it up until I'd been well and truly hooked. Not that it would've changed anything. His wealth certainly hadn't changed my mind—in fact, it had been in the pros column of my Why-Should-I-Marry-Him list—a title wouldn't have made much difference.

Coming back to Bonus Day. Neal's family had adapted Boxing Day in their own way by giving their employees bonuses on that day. Years ago, someone had joked about it no longer being Boxing Day but Bonus Day, and since then the name had stuck.

It was fantastic what the Frasers did on Bonus Day. As the main board members of Fraser Global were already swimming in more money than they knew what to do with, none of them took a salary, but took, for form's sake, the smallest cut of the yearly profits. The rest of the money was distributed among the Fraser Global workforce as a big-ass bonus, and each employee's bonus depended on the number of years they'd been in service and their positions. This year had been my third Bonus Day and I was still awestruck by the sentiment and magnanimity behind the event.

And yet, that evening, for all their goodwill and generosity, when Neal and I finally broke our "good news," we faced undiluted disapproval.

We were back home at the mini castle after the festivities—Neal's immediate family, that is. All of us had gathered in the great room, around the fire roaring inside an ancient stone hearth, the walls and paneling festooned with tartan bows, and a ceiling-height Scotland pine spreading its woodsy scent all around. Neal had planned to tell his folks over whisky and leftover pudding.

I hadn't expected anyone to jump up and dance the hora

when we told them of Neal's imminent fatherhood, but I had expected something. Perhaps, a cautious, "Congratulations?" Maybe a good luck wish? Questions, certainly. Anything other than the utter, log-crackling silence that followed our pronouncement. Neal began to speak, not explain but just map out what our next few months would be like.

He didn't tell them about Naira. We'd decided to wait on that news until after his family got to know her a bit. Naira was in London right now, visiting with her in-laws, doing the same thing we were. Hopefully with better results. Tomorrow, she'd take the train to Edinburgh, and Deven would meet her there to show her the Fraser Global empire—the original flagship store, the new concept store, the wool factory, the headquarters and the farms as they headed back to Riverhead for Hogmanay. Deven was already on his way to Edinburgh—he'd left this afternoon. Too bad, Neal would've benefited from some backup.

Seriously, what had Neal expected from his mother and sister who'd popped out three kids each? Compassion? Understanding?

"I'm so sorry you can't have children," said Helen, her hands over her heart. "Shall I ask my doctor to refer you to a fertility doctor?"

I pressed my lips together and looked at Neal. He began fielding most of the questions with short and polite answers, but Minnie and Helen were nothing if not persistent. They simply could not wrap their heads around my decision not to have children.

"But why ever not?" Helen's blue eyes had ballooned to unnatural proportions during the explanation.

"Does there have to be a reason?" I countered.

Apparently, there did, and they tried hard to get to the bottom of it. Whose egg would it be? Mine. Then why couldn't

I simply have the child? If I had a mental block, I should get some therapy and get on with life.

I'd expected Helen's reactions. She didn't mean it in a bad way. In her mind, she was simply trying to find the best solution.

Minnie Singh however was another creature altogether. She went for the jugular.

"Are you going to tell the child the truth? That his own mother hadn't bothered to give birth to him?"

Neal had warned me that we'd be bombarded with questions, but even then I was appalled by how intrusive and insensitive they got. If this was what family bonding meant, I was glad of the nonbond Lily and I shared.

"It's our decision. It's our choice," I said bluntly, violently annoyed now.

But Neal's mother wouldn't let it go. "At the cost of my grandchild's well-being? I don't think so."

Minnie Singh wielded the same scary intimidation tactics as her younger son, the son that most favored her in looks and temperament. It worked well on other people, but she seemed to have forgotten that her older son knew her well. And that even though I didn't, I still wasn't the intimidated-by-her-mother-in-law type.

Minnie was the de facto head of the clan even though she wasn't a Fraser. The story was that when Minnie and Niall had met in college, the Frasers had been deep in debt. Their sheep farms were barely crossing the red line, all three stores—in Inverness, Glasgow and Edinburgh—were on the verge of being sold, as was the Riverhead Estate. They'd been in talks of filing for bankruptcy. Then Niall got married, and his wife brought with her a huge influx of capital and saved them by creating Fraser Global. It was why Niall and Minnie lived at Riverhead and not James Fraser, who was the heir apparent.

218 • THE OBJECT OF YOUR AFFECTIONS

Neal's uncle didn't live far though, just over in the next village, in a smaller manor house. In spite of it, there seemed to
be no animosity between the elder Fraser brothers. They were
all just happy that the business had been saved, and in the fact
that it now flourished.

I'd never been sure if Minnie approved of me, though she'd
never once made me feel unwelcome in her home. Which
wasn't to say that I didn't know that I'd been absorbed into
the clan with open arms only at her say. It just couldn't be
helped that Minnie and I rubbed each other the wrong way.
We were both strong, stubborn women.

I especially didn't like it when she'd just show up in New
York, unannounced, and then would expect us to change our
plans to suit her schedule. The first time it had happened, I'd
let it go. The second time, I'd asked Neal to tell his mother
that in the future she should let us know, in advance, of her
plans and not when she was boarding the flight or had landed
in New York. He'd given me a most offended look. "I don't
have a problem with my mother's visits. If you do, you tell
her that."

Neal had been very clear from the beginning that his family meant the world to him. I liked them too, and for the
most part we got along. Perhaps because we lived on different
continents. But Neal had also never stopped me from voicing
my views or having a difference of opinion with them. So,
I'd asked Minnie to kindly let us know of her travel plans.
To which she'd replied, "I don't plan anything. I simply do
what I want."

I'd learned to keep my mouth shut after that. This time
too I was keeping it shut. I'd said my piece to the effect
that I too shall do as I please and that was that. Besides, an-
nouncing our plans before Naira was even pregnant had been

Neal's idea. Let him deal with his family and I'd deal with Lily when the time came.

The Fraser men were largely silent. Except for Neal. I hoped that meant they were Switzerland in this—neither here nor there. Niall was a debonair, older version of Neal, with laugh lines radiating out from around his eyes and mouth, telling the world of his easy spirit. Not tonight though. Tonight, he was the grim reaper.

Helen's husband, Shyam Pal, had tried to leave the room when the arguments had heated up, but Minnie had arched an imperious eyebrow and made him sit back down.

Flora came to sit beside me as the drama between Neal and his mother intensified. And Helen's kids, who'd been prancing around the Christmas tree singing Scottish holiday ditties, thought they needed to shout rather than sing to be heard. All three classic attention-seekers.

I'd wanted Neal to lie about our reasons, but he'd refused. He wouldn't lie to his family. I'd begged him to wait to break the news, but he'd not agreed to that, either. He'd hoped to give them a Christmas surprise. Stupid man.

"In case yer looking for a surrogate, I'd like to volunteer," Neal's flame-haired, animal-crazy sister, Flora, whispered for my ears only. Her father had been Niall's youngest brother, who'd died along with his Irish wife in a boating accident when Flora was only seven.

I kissed her cheek, beyond grateful for her matter-of-fact support. No wonder we got along so well. "We have one. But, thank you for the offer."

When my Bonus Day good mood had been smashed to fucking smithereens, I stood up.

"Minnie, we informed everyone as a matter of courtesy. But it's our decision. Our life." Then I walked out of the room.

Neal had dug this hole. I'd let him scramble his way out of it.

★ ★ ★

I went back to Neal's bedroom to pout and pace. The spacious room had been fully renovated for our wedding—it had been my bridal suite—and the decorator had taken great pains to dig out my unique tastes and preferences over transatlantic phone calls and emails. Apparently, my tastes ran toward minimalistic, yet cozy, while Neal was an eclectic and eco-friendly kind of guy. So, the bedroom boasted the barest amount of furniture, but whatever pieces there were, from the massive bed with a padded, red headboard, the TV console, the nightstands, the bench at the foot of the bed and the desk were all massive pieces of natural wood, shaped into clean lines and polished to a shine. It was a modern room with its reds and taupes and Lalique light fixtures, and yet it managed to blend perfectly with the old-world charm of Riverhead. Just like the people who lived in it.

I didn't think of this room as ours, couldn't think of Riverhead as our home. But I knew, someday, Neal would inherit a part of it. And that day might come sooner than I'd imagined because Neal's parents had talked about retiring and letting their children manage the estate during their Bonus Day speeches. What would I do if Neal wanted us to move here? If he had to?

I collapsed on the bed, suddenly freakishly overwhelmed.

Neal came in half an hour later. He walked to the dresser, to the side where a maid had left a jug of water and two glasses for the night. He poured himself a tall glass of water, his throat convulsing as he chugged it down. He would be thirsty. The men had been tossing back whisky since last night, and would probably keep at it until the New Year.

He wiped his mouth with the back of his hand while his eyes—which seemed to be sparking off electricity—bored holes into mine.

Damn, but he was gorgeous when he got broody. I loved Neal in jeans and a T-shirt or dark, trendy shirts and formal pants. I loved him when he wasn't wearing anything at all, but Neal in a kilt took my breath away. And when he looked at me in a certain way with his blue-blue eyes, I became a puddle of goo.

He made a funny little sound at the back of his throat, then asked, "Are we doing the right thing?"

I'd been afraid of exactly this. "You wouldn't be asking this question if not for your mother."

"Aye, well. I'm asking it now."

"I love you. Enormously. I want to make all your dreams come true as you've made mine."

We reached for each other at the same time. He took my hands and pulled me up to sit on the bed. Then he sat beside me.

"That's no' what I asked."

Our hands were linked, palm to palm, but I felt a chasm widen between us. There was a part of me, a pathetic, lonely part, that feared I wasn't good enough for him. That I was keeping him from great things. From fatherhood. I was only trying to rectify it.

"Yes, I think it's the right thing to do. For all three of us."

"And she agreed to it…of her own free will, aye?"

I dropped his hands as if they'd burned mine. "What the fuck are you insinuating?" What the fuck had Minnie filled his ears with? "You think I manipulated Naira into something this important?"

"So, ye realize how serious this is? I wondered. She is beholden to us in a hundred different ways right now. Have ye considered that she might think she canna say no? Ye must have considered it as yer so thorough. So, I'll ask ye again, did ye set all of this up?" He wasn't giving me an inch.

"Set it up how? And set up what? You think I somehow arranged for her to land in New York? Or stuffed words into her mouth when she told me 'I'll do it!'" I shot up from the bed, royally pissed off now. To hell with his dreams and our marriage. He caught my arm before I stomped away, and with a flick of his wrist spun me back to face him. Nose to nose.

"Have ye also considered her future? What if she wants to remarry? From the little I've come to know her, she seems conservative. She'll marry within her community and I'm no' sure Indian men are accepting of...unconventional choices."

"You are." Even as I said it, I knew it wasn't true. Neal wasn't conservative but he wasn't all that liberal, either. He had lines he'd never cross. Some he'd crossed only because of me. If he'd fallen for and married someone like Naira, he would've been a different person. A happier man, I think. His family certainly would've been.

"She doesn't want to marry again." I believed Naira. But then, I'd also believed Neal when he'd said that he wanted me more than he wanted bairns.

"She says that now but what if she falls for someone? Have ye not noticed Dev looking at her? One nod from her and he'll be on her like butter on toast." Neal abruptly shut his mouth, perhaps realizing he'd gone too far.

I had noticed the flirting at Thanksgiving, but that didn't mean shit with Naira. "As you said, she's conservative. It's strictly flirt but no touch with her. And, even if she wants to take it further with Dev, so what? What does it have to do with her being our surrogate?"

Neal opened his mouth, then closed it. Then opened it again and ran his fingers through his hair while he stared at my face as if he'd never seen me before.

"Absolutely nothing," he said eventually.

"Then what is the problem? Frankly, a boss-employee flirtation is vastly more problematic than asking a friend to bear your bairn," I pointed out.

Neal heaved a sigh, and rubbed his tired eyes with his fingers. "I'm her boss and her friend too. Or did ye forget about that?"

I hadn't forgotten.

"Fine. I'll ask her again. I'll make sure that she's very sure," I said. That was all I could do.

CHAPTER FOURTEEN

Naira

"Mumbai is my soul, New York my sanctuary, but Scotland... Ah, Alba has taken my heart. It's like a fairy-tale setting," I said dreamily. Oh, I'd fallen in love with Scotland. Not just a city or town or wee village, but all of it.

Huddling to beat the cold, Paris and I walked arm in arm down the streets of a village with an incomprehensible name, behind a group of kilted first footers shouting *"Slàinte mhath!"* every other minute. Pronounced either as sanjhe-va or sanjhe-ma, I couldn't clearly tell yet. However it was pronounced, it sounded splendidly lovely.

I'd been to Edinburgh before, as a child with my parents and with Kaivan around five years ago. I'd loved visiting it then too. But, this time, being *involved* in local activities, experiencing Scotland like a native was simply out of this world.

"I love the cobblestoned wynds and closes in Edinburgh. I love the blustery firths, the winding white country roads leading into the highlands, the glorious wind-whipped lochs, the fairy-tale àrds... I hope I'm saying that right. The crags and glens and moors and...the Frasers." Of course, I was drunk. I held on to Paris for dear life or else I'd be weaving and tumbling, not walking.

"I get it. Sheesh! You love Scotland!" Paris groused, her nose and cheeks red with cold.

A flashlight passed over her face and mine right then—probably Neal—checking if we were okay. My face felt frozen stiff, even though both of us were bundled up like a pair of astronauts preparing to launch into space. I was wearing two woolen pullovers, fleece-lined pants, a heavy wind- and rainproof coat, fur-lined boots, and a woolen monkey cap and thick cashmere-lined leather gloves. And still, when the slightest wind stirred past me, my entire body shivered like the tracks on Scotland Rail.

We stopped by a house. "Hoose! A wee hoose," I yelled, pointing at it. Then I doubled up and laughed because Paris let out a startled "Yeep!" and shot me a dirty look.

Everything was so "wee" in Scotland. A wee dram, and a wee moment, and a wee lamb. God, I'd made such a fool of myself in front of Deven, blubbering over a sweet, wee lamb on our drive up from Edinburgh. The last five days had been... I had no words to describe what I was feeling other than magical.

My trip to London had been—not magical. I shook my head, at least I think I did. I didn't want to think about London. I only wanted to think about Scotland. And Scots. And splendid scotch.

I disengaged my arm from Paris, and walked, slowly, toward the group of Scotchmen now entering the hoose behind Neal. Deven was waiting outside, so I tapped his leather jacket. He was laughing at something when he looked down at me, and even through my tipsy eyes I saw his face soften. His proximity did things to me that I didn't want to feel, and yet adored feeling, so I snatched the bottle from his hands, waved my fingers at him and made my way back to Paris. I took a swig straight from the bottle like the men had been doing all night. Not to be gluttonous, I offered it to Paris too, who seemed highly entertained for some reason.

"You seem to be getting along well with Dev," she commented.

"Hmm." I sat down next to Paris, bum to bum, on a low stone wall bordering another wee hoose. I held up a hand, spreading my gloved fingers and indicating the number of days I'd just spent with Dev. Deven. Dev.

"I cried on his shoulder," I admitted shamefully.

Paris took a swig of scotch too. "Is that all you did?"

"Unfortunately. He's a gentleman." I flapped my hand to indicate nothing had happened. "All we did was work, work, work. He showed me the ropes, so to speak."

Their vision for Fraser Bespoke was so much clearer now that I'd seen it with my own eyes. He'd introduced me to so many people at the head offices, and many of them had just returned from Inverness and the annual Christmas ball, still basking in a joyous esprit de corps—to use one of Paris's fancy phrases. Two days ago, we'd started driving north in Deven's blessedly heated Range Rover, stopping at the wool factory, the sheep farms and the Riverhead distillery, staying at quaint bed-and-breakfasts along the way.

"The weather and the highlands are so strange and yet so fascinating. We'd be driving in the pouring rain and within five minutes the sun would be beating down on us in the valley. Then we'd drive up the mountain and it would be freezing again."

And once we'd arrived at Riverhead, I'd been blown away—literally because of the wind and bitter cold blowing in from the Beauly Firth. It was freezing now too, and dark, so dark I could barely make out my own hand in front of my face, but I was sufficiently bundled up. Luckily, it didn't rain in these parts as much as it did in other parts of Scotland. But who cared about the weather when everything was so magical?

Minnie Auntie and Niall Uncle were sweethearts, and so were Helen and Shyam and their three munchkins—Oliver, Tasha and Niall, who was obviously named after his grandfather and uncle. Flora seemed to keep to herself, but she was friendly enough, and she and Paris were exceedingly fond of each other. I'd met Uncle Liam at the Hogmanay feast at the manor house this evening, and I felt so much better staying at his place now that I'd thanked him in person. We'd clasped hands when we'd all tumbled out of the house into the courtyard, sometime before midnight, to make a circle around a bonfire and sing "Auld Lang Syne" when the new year swept in while the bells tolled and fireworks lit the sky. It was a custom, like the lavish Hogmanay feast that the whole family pitched in and cooked themselves. I'd happily helped. The Frasers had taken me into their bosom with open arms. They were a lovely close-knit family just like my— No. I wasn't going to think about them tonight.

They hadn't even called me. No one had called me to wish me a Happy New Year. *Stop thinking about them!*

Come midnight, the Frasers had joined in another amazing tradition of first footing, in which a tall dark-haired man was selected to enter the house for the first time in the new year. He had to enter the hoose bearing gifts of food, drink and silver thereby ensuring good luck and prosperity to the home-dwellers. As most of the Fraser men were tall and dark-haired, they usually chose the man standing closest to the main doors as that year's first foot.

It had been Deven this year who— No! I didn't want to think about him, either. Not in that way. Not in any way. Five days with him had turned my mind and moralities into Jell-O.

"Everything is splendid here. The people. The culture. The Frasers," I reiterated, huddling into Paris to block the cold.

We'd already been first footing for hours and it seemed it was going to go on for a while. There were lots of hooses in this part of the village and only four first footers in our group—Neal, Deven and two other lads. It seemed first foot-ers were sort of a precious commodity on Hogmanay as their services were required all over the highlands.

"Try marrying into the clan, then tell me how *splendid* they are."

I looked at Paris sideways. I hadn't imagined it. She *was* upset. She hadn't been speaking to Neal properly. They'd only pecked each other on the lips to wish each other a Happy New Year and not smooched or cuddled or anything—not at all since I got here.

"They didn't take it well?" It had to be the surrogacy.

Paris harrumphed. "I don't care what they think. It's my life. My choice."

"What does Neal think?"

"He can go jump off a cliff and into the frigid firth."

Oh-kay. "Give them time, girlfriend. It's not a conventional path. You have to allow them room to digest it."

"I'm not pissed at Minnie… Okay, I am a little pissed. But I'm more pissed at Neal. He won't do this unless they agree now."

I took in a deep, deep breath. The air was rich with the scent of the earth and water, of cinnamon and cloves, and sweet vanilla. I put my nose against the woolly lapel of my coat, then did the same to Paris's. It wasn't the air. Our coats were soaked in the scents of the manor house.

"It wouldn't hurt to think this through. Properly," I said, licking my lips.

Her head whipped toward me. "Are you having second thoughts too?"

I shook my head. Then nodded. Then I told her about London.

"It's my father-in-law. His health—mental health—is deteriorating rapidly. My mother-in-law can't handle him alone anymore and Sonam—you remember Kaivan's sister? She's helping all she can, but between her own family…she has a preschooler…and her work, it's just not enough. I've hired a round-the-clock companion for them, but they want…expect me to move to London. Soon." Bitterness welled up in my throat. When had my life become a runaway train?

"How soon? Are you going to?"

"I don't know." I didn't want to, but how could I not? I'd feel terrible if I dumped them on Sonam. I'd feel so guilty. "I may not have a choice," I admitted softly.

"What about Fraser Bespoke?"

"That won't change. Deven sees no issues about where I work from. I'll just be traveling a hell of a lot more."

Paris went rigid. At first I thought it was because of what I'd said, what it might mean for our plans, but I soon realized it wasn't me. Neal had come out of a house at the bottom of the lane. He'd whistled at us, a summons.

"And the surrogacy?" Paris turned her head to frown at me.

"I don't need to move immediately. We have a year or so." But I couldn't give her more. I couldn't give her what she wanted after. She'd be on her own once the bairn was born— *if* a bairn was born.

"Oh."

I could feel her processing what I hadn't said as we walked, arm in arm, toward Neal.

The lane ended in a roundabout leading to three other streets lined with houses. My life had become a roundabout. And even though I'd chosen the lane I wished to walk on, I kept getting sucked into spinning around in circles.

After much debate, it was decided that the first footers would split up and tackle one street each. Our group had to split up too, as first footers never arrived at doorsteps alone. They needed help carrying the gifts and bottles from house to house.

"I'll take care of the hooses on Dumfries Street, but then I'm done, lads. I've reserved the rest of the night for my wife," Neal declared to a cacophony of bawdy jokes. He yanked Paris to him—I got inadvertently yanked too, until Paris and I untangled our arms—and before she could react or retreat, he dipped her back and kissed her noisily on the lips, and kept on kissing her until she stopped pushing him away, and twined her arms about him and kissed him back.

The jokes got cruder. The worst of them were from Deven, who was more than a wee bit sozzled from all the Hogmanay toasts.

I seemed incapable of looking at him without blushing. I couldn't believe he'd seen me practically naked, or that he'd kissed me on the mouth at midnight. Only a quick peck. And he'd pecked everyone like that—man, woman and child—so I shouldn't read anything special into it. But I couldn't help myself. He'd been flirting with me, nonaggressively, since the towel episode. Or was it just the way he was with everyone?

Clearly, I'd lost my mind. We were going to be working together. We couldn't—shouldn't complicate or jeopardize our business relationship.

But the crazy thing was that I wanted to.

★ ★ ★

Deven's first footing went on until six in the morning, and I stayed with him until the end, tempting fate. Paris had been with Neal and everyone else was probably asleep at the house. I hadn't wanted to be alone. Didn't want to feel alone and pathetic even now.

Ever the gentleman, he came to drop me to my door. I'd been put up in the Blue Room on the second floor of the annex behind the main house. It was a lovely room, blue in color—obviously—with views of the well-maintained estate with its manicured gardens, thick wild woods and fields that promised to erupt into flowers when winter ended.

I switched on the lights and the first thing I saw as I entered the room was the olive green Briggs & Riley suitcase on the ottoman at the foot of the bed. Kaivan and I had purchased that luggage set together on our last holiday. The longing and yearning that I'd been trying to suppress, to harness, exploded inside me like firecrackers. It wasn't that I didn't think of Kaivan daily or miss him with every breath, but since London it had become unbearable, uncontainable. His parents had talked about him day and night, filling my ears with his stories and their grief. I couldn't—hadn't had the heart to tell them to stop. To just stop. I wanted everything to stop. I wanted time to move backward.

"Naira, let me say good-night."

His voice was scotch-soaked and so deliciously rough. It walked up my spine like the slow-moving fingers of a skilled masseuse.

I turned to face him. His right hand was gripping the door-jamb as if he wasn't sure he'd be able to stand on his own. Or, as if he was stopping himself from entering the room. He was beautiful, like his brother. But not as fair and certainly not as sweet. I felt far safer with Neal than I did with Deven. God. I had to stop comparing them. It wasn't right. And comparing him to Kaivan was a whole other level of insanity.

"Would you like to come in?" My blood raced beneath multiple layers of clothes and skin, heating everything up. I was still ridiculously bundled up and it was hot. So freaking hot.

Still, he hesitated, his black-as-night eyes never leaving mine, never wavering, searching for something on my face. He only let go of the jamb and stepped inside my room when I said, "I want you to come in."

Holy God! What was I doing? But I needed this release. I needed someone to get Kaivan out of my mind. I needed someone to show me that all was not lost, and there was light at the end of the tunnel. But only if one had the guts to walk into the darkness first.

But what about the surrogacy? I couldn't start something with him and then get pregnant with his brother's child. That was just too weird. But I didn't want a relationship. I couldn't have one. I had a million problems that wouldn't let me have a normal life.

He was still lounging by the door, his eyes soaking me in as I walked to him. I was crossing that tunnel. Maybe it was all just pent-up nothing between us. Maybe he'd turn into a frog when I kissed him.

And so I did, startling us both. And…oh, God, he was so not a frog at all.

I stopped to take a breath but I'd forgotten how to breathe. I panted while he stared at my lips, now wet because of him. I took a deep, stuttering breath and opened my mouth beneath his as his head bent to mine this time.

We kissed for a long time, tasting the whisky on our tongues, trying not to make any sudden moves and break the spell. He had me propped against the doorjamb when I pushed him off me, just a wee bit. I had to breathe. Somehow. I was sweating. His fingers traced my face. I pulled my hat and gloves off, stuffed them in my jacket pocket.

"I'd like for us to do this—" I pointed at the bed "—one time. But it can only be one time." I tried to sound worldly, like some hard-core connoisseur ticking off the terms of a clandestine affair.

His fingers stopped on my brow. He blinked a few times until the whisky haze on his face cleared a bit. His hand floated to his side, and he opened his mouth to say something.

I didn't want him to see sense or refuse, so I said in a rush, "It can't be more than that because of Fraser Bespoke, and many other things that I…don't want to think about right now." I bit my lower lip. I should just shut up. But my conscience, like my fate, wasn't on my side. "I'm still in love with my husband," I told him honestly. Oh, but I didn't want to be. What I wouldn't give for someone to cut out my heart and set it on fire.

Deven gave me a thorough appraisal, like he'd given one of the sheep at his farm. He stepped back, half pivoting toward the door, and my heart cried out. I clenched my fists so I wouldn't reach out and grab him. Why couldn't I have lied? I'd become so good at it, after all.

Then my stomach dropped because he didn't leave. Instead, he closed the door, locked it and turned to face me again.

"My heart belongs to someone else too. She's…unavailable." He offered me his own confession, his own albatross, and soothed my soul. "One time is fine with me, lass."

It wasn't one time though. By the time the sun rose—not that we could tell it had risen since it was predictably gloomy outside—we'd made lo— had sex multiple times.

"That was amazing. Thank you!" I exclaimed, flipping onto

my back, all loose-limbed and vibrating with gratitude and aftershocks. It was exactly what I'd needed. He'd blasted my pathos right out of me. Several times. I felt wonderfully de-stressed. And desired. God, when had I last felt desire myself?

"Entirely my pleasure, doll." Deven chuckled, and unbeliev-ably, his nose and ears glowed pinker, like some blushing bride.

I laughed too. I wanted to keep laughing. Delirious with pleasure, I watched Deven get up and make his way to the bathroom to dispose of the condom, which he'd had to run down and get from his bedroom in the main house after we'd used up the one he carried in his wallet. He'd brought back two foils—the entirety of his stock—and we'd used every single one.

He looked good naked. Taller, buffer than—*do not think about Kaivan*, I told myself sternly. I sat up, pulling the blanket up to my chin. I looked for my phone out of habit. I should call my in-laws and wish them a Happy New Year. My par-ents too, no matter if my father wanted to or not. Maybe even Sarika—no, not until she acknowledged that her hus-band was a villain.

My phone was programmed for a Do Not Disturb from midnight to 7:00 a.m. Since the screen was lit up by new no-tifications, I guessed it was after seven. There were dozens of messages from Vinay, I noted with a grimace. I deleted those without reading even one.

Nothing ever changed, no matter what I did, or what magic moments I snatched out of thin air. Every morning, the same screen greeted me, flashing dozens of messages and calls. I couldn't ignore the one from my in-laws. They'd left four voice messages and several texts. I closed my eyes and wished for it to be midnight again.

"Problem?" Deven walked back to the bed, his hips wrapped

in a kilt made of festive red-and-green tartan. He frowned at the phone I was trying to squeeze to death.

Deliberately, I placed the phone back on the nightstand.

I couldn't move to London. I wouldn't survive it.

Deven sat down on the bed. "Tell me," he said—commanded—taking my hand.

I shook my head. I was not his problem.

"I know most of it anyway," he said more gently.

"What do you know?" I was surprised by how unruffled I felt. No, not unruffled. I felt nothing. No fear, no embarrassment, not even the usual powerlessness. Maybe I should keep having one-night stands if this was the result. I didn't feel the urge to laugh, either.

Of course, Deven had run a background check on me before signing me up to represent Fraser Bespoke. But how deeply? And would any deep probe reveal the whole truth? Kaivan had been positive it wouldn't.

Deven knew about the financial problems, the creditors that kept crawling out of the woodwork to threaten and sue me. He knew about the lawsuits—that was public knowledge. He knew about the issues I was having with my family, why I'd run away from Mumbai.

I'll take everything from you, even the clothes off your back. Only then will I consider our account settled, Vinay had said when I'd refused to hand over the trust money and my body to him. Sarika hadn't believed me when I'd told her that her husband had implied I become his mistress in lieu of my bad debts. Or had she believed it and had still found a way to blame me for her husband's assholery? Was that what her rant about my fit figure against her symbol of motherhood had been all about? The whole incident had become a he-said-she-said battle that he'd clearly won.

"Do ye want me to take care of it? Make it go away—the lawsuits, the thugs, the debt?"

"Steep price for three fucks, don't you think?" Even as I said it, I flinched. Then tears began to spill down my cheeks. I wasn't a poor thing. I wasn't! And how bloody dare that bastard Vinay Singhal proposition me and get away with it? I wanted him dead.

"Lass…" Deven began, but broke off on a sigh. He hugged me to him, forcing me to rest my head on his big, warm shoulder, and I was tempted, so tempted to let him rescue me.

But I didn't deserve to be rescued. I didn't deserve to be cheapened, either. I couldn't let him rescue me because we'd slept together.

"No. Thank you, but no. Please don't do anything like that. And it's not… That's not it." I raised my head, determined to face him. He was strong and scary as hell when he was angry. But also gallant…like his brother. They both deserved to know what kind of a person they'd brought into the Fraser clan–force. I had to tell Deven what I could never tell Paris.

"Kaivan struggled to sort it out but too many things went wrong for him that year. It broke him, the arrest, being treated like a common criminal. I think… I'm pretty sure my brother-in-law, Vinay Singhal, arranged it so Kaivan didn't receive anticipatory bail or any bail and stayed in jail for months. My… I had a miscarriage while he was in jail, and it…broke him. By the time he was released on bail, he was half his size, and he'd been lanky to begin with. He was depressed. I told him it would pass, that it was part of life, the ups and downs. I told him he could build it all up again like he'd done before. And we'd make lots of babies and we'd get our respect back. The rumors, the gossip would die. But nothing helped. He got it in his head that if he was dead…"

I shuddered then, as fire ants crawled all over my calm. "He thought death was his only way out. And mine. That I'd be able to salvage my life with his life insurance money. I didn't know he was thinking this. I swear. He never told me!" I gripped Deven's hand hard.

"I believe ye. Take a slow breath, lass. Good. Now another one. Good. Now, tell me the rest." His words were calm, not shocked. Not threaded with revulsion. His touch was hypnotizing. He began to pet me, long steady strokes down my back.

Frankly, even if he'd been repulsed, I'd have spilled my guts. I'd kept this secret for two years and it was eroding my insides. I'd needed to confess to someone. Someone like him. Someone with the same code of ethics as Kaivan. Someone who'd understand.

"He added policies to his life insurance portfolio, increased the benefits, and put everything in a trust overnight. And through it all, he was poisoning himself while I believed he was trying to get us out of the mess." I'd been so stupid, so blind. I should've realized his weight loss wasn't about depression. He'd lost so much hair in the last month that I should have known. "He told me of his plan just days before, but I didn't stop it. I...let it happen."

"How would ye have stopped him?" Deven scrubbed a hand over his face as if to wake himself up. He wasn't hugging me anymore or petting me or touching me. But he hadn't moved away. Yet.

"I could have taken him to the hospital." I wanted to crawl out of my skin and die.

"So why didn't ye?"

"He said that the poison had spread to his organs and even if I took him to the hospital, I'd just delay the inevitable by a few weeks. And the tests would show the poison, and there would be a case filed against both of us. And our problems would worsen. So, I let him go."

Could I have saved him? I didn't know. I just didn't know.

If I were examining my motives, Kaivan's death was the main reason I wanted to be Paris's surrogate. I owed this world a life. I owed my soul a good deed.

Deven stood up and began pulling on the rest of his clothes—shirt, leather jacket, a fancy large-buckled belt, a sporran. All the while, he stared at me. I refused to flinch.

"Yer worried that someone will find out if they dig deep enough?"

"My brother-in-law may know. I'm not sure. He keeps insinuating things…threatening me."

"Ye don't trust him."

I barked out an ugly laugh. "Not a bit. Neither did Kaivan. No, Vinay knows…or maybe he's just guessing, but I couldn't take a chance. I gave him control of everything, and now I have nothing left except for the trust that I didn't want to touch in the first place." I'd inherited the money by murdering my husband—how could Kaivan think I'd use it without guilt? Without dying every single day?

"He's blackmailing ye?"

"Not overtly, but yes." In front of the world he'd become a saint because he was taking care of his helpless, widowed *saali*, his wife's sister.

I asked Deven not to tell Neal because he'd tell Paris. "She'll never understand. She'll never forgive me for my compliance before and after. Please, I have no one else left in this world."

He promised to keep my secret safe. And he told me not to worry as he doubted anyone would come for me in New York. Then he gave me a quick peck on my cheek and left the room. And just like that our one time was up.

PART TWO

The Tri-Mess-ters

CHAPTER FIFTEEN

Paris

I was glad the surrogacy was out in the open. But, if I'd hoped that the collective negativity generated by our decision would dissipate over distance and time, I'd been sorely mistaken.

When we landed back in New York, Lily took over the baton from Minnie, and called every day, several times a day, to kvetch over my Big Idea.

"Don't poke a sleeping tiger. Don't complicate your life," Lily said in dire tones when I divulged the name of our surrogate.

I rolled my eyes, took a sip of morning coffee. "Is that from today's horror-scope? I thought you liked Naira. You definitely liked her more than you cared for me ten years ago."

Lily had no comeback for the truth.

In cahoots, the mothers only wished to talk some sense into us—at least they were fair and distributed their badgering equally between Neal and me. But the more they made a nuisance of themselves, the more adamant I became.

"I don't get it. What's so unconventional about our decision? How is it any different than the crazy combinations of extended families populating society these days? For God's sake, the world at large worships the Lannisters and the Targaryens! How is that normal? A show both our moms watch, by the way. After *GoT*, no one should be weirded out about surrogacy," I railed one evening in mid-January.

"There's no harm in waiting a wee bit," said the family panderer.

I threw down an ultimatum. "I'm already injecting myself with hormones, and Naira may move to London. It's now or never. You decide whether you want to make Mommy happy or your wife."

I hated myself for saying it, for making him choose between Minnie and me. If he'd said something like that to me, I'd have walked out the door. I was making this into a competition when it wasn't, when it didn't need to be. But then, so were they.

Neal did walk out the door the next morning, and spent an entire week in Japan. I drowned my sorrows in Girlfriend Cocktails with my girlfriend.

"He hasn't called. It's been three days." I sipped my drink glumly. "Why do I always put my foot in my mouth?"

Naira hummed in response. Her eyes were closed and her head rested against the back of the booth. We were at Liam's Bar again. We'd come here every night this week. I'd head over to Naira's after work, she'd cook for us, and we'd head down for a drink.

"You haven't called him, either," she pointed out, eyes still closed.

"Will it seem too needy if I do?" Ugh. That would be mortifying. Neal adored my strength, my nonclinginess. He'd broken things off with his ex because she'd been needy and flighty, and because she'd repeatedly caused conflict between him and his family. And I'd recently compared his mother to one of the three witches in *Macbeth*. My mother being the second and Helen the third.

Again, Naira only hummed in answer. She was falling asleep on me. Her days had become as busy as mine. Possibly busier. She juggled interviews, business meetings, Skype calls all day. Sometimes until late into the night if the clients or associates were from the dark side of the world. She'd even started dressing in business suits, looking all businesslike. She'd been different since Scotland. Less weepy. I narrowed my eyes, looking at her closely. She *was* different, less waiflike. Her cheeks were rounder, and the shadows under her eyes had disappeared. Of course, she was wearing makeup so that didn't prove anything.

"What's up with you?" I was intrigued enough to be diverted from my own woes.

"Hmm?"

Her posture was better—shoulders straight, back gracefully arched like a dancer's and not hunched like a heap of soiled clothes. The grieving widow had taken a back seat and the old Naira was back in the driver's seat. Almost.

I backpedaled my recent memories of her, wondering when the restoration had happened. Then I remembered what Neal had said at Thanksgiving.

"Are you…having a *thing* with Dev?"

Naira didn't hum this time. Her eyes popped open and she went red in the face.

"Ack!" I screamed, scaring her and several of the patrons at the bar. "You are!"

"I can't have a thing with him, he signs my paychecks," she denied quickly. Then made puppy eyes at me. "Please, don't make a big deal."

"But, it is a big deal if you are or want to. I think it's great, honey." I meant it sincerely. It didn't look like I'd need a surrogate anytime soon, if ever, so why shouldn't Naira have fun? Move on with her life.

I flinched as I finished the thought. *Move on with her life?* Meaning I was keeping her from doing so?

"No, really. It's not like that. It was one time. Just once on New Year's."

"You had a one-night stand? Why you hussy," I teased in delight.

Her lips curved into an odd combination of shyness and pride and excitement. "It was amazing. And fun! I used to wonder what you got out of hopping into beds so casually. Now I know. And, Paris, it's so liberating."

"Better late than never, kid," I said, feeling as proud as a dame whose ingenue had finally learned the correct way to shtup.

Once upon a time, I'd been just that liberated. But I was a one-man receptacle now. Neal had spoiled me for good.

I let go of my pride and called my husband that night. When he came back to me, we were both a little less mad. He brought up the surrogacy this time, not me. I'd like to believe I would've backed off if he'd still been reluctant to proceed without his mother's approval. Thankfully, I wasn't put to the test.

"All right. Let's go make ourselves a family," he said as I jumped into his arms as soon as he walked in the door.

I had to underscore. "Let's go make *you* a daddy."

★ ★ ★

In vitro fertilization was approximately a six-week process from start to finish, during which I was pumped full of hormone stimulants that I had to inject into my body daily. That was the good part.

The bad part was that I was highly and intensely hormonally stimulated not just in body but in mind too. I felt completely, out-of-my-head crazy. Every sensation, every feeling was enhanced, and it was unnerving.

I wanted sex all the time—which, okay, wasn't all that abnormal for me and Neal. Until, one night, after about ten days of morning, night and weekend sex-a-thons, Neal gripped my wandering hand by the wrist and firmly pulled it away from his dick.

"It needs a rest, hen. I'm chaffed." Then he proceeded to make love to me with his hands and mouth, and I didn't even care that he hadn't come or that he didn't want to. That was how out of my head I was.

We decided to go with a boutique IVF clinic in Manhattan that came highly recommended by the Wilsons' doctor. I was at the Angels of Mary every other day after the first two weeks for various tests that monitored my hormones and ovaries until they were ready to be harvested. Naira also liked Dr. Stanley, our fertility specialist, but she still needed to choose an ob-gyn for the term of the pregnancy and the delivery. Naira was way less picky than I was and happily agreed to see my gynecologist who was also an obstetrician.

Once the doctors were sorted, we went through the finer points of New York's surrogacy laws more for Naira's sake than Neal's or mine. "We can't draw up a surrogacy contract. Well, we can, but it's void and unenforceable in New York State and therefore moot."

Our options were a preconception agreement or a coparenting agreement in which we could map out every single event in the bairn's life we could think of from conception to adulthood, and allocate the adult responsible for that event.

"And a default parent, or set of parents who'd get custody of the child in case something goes wrong." I ignored Neal's thunderous expression and Naira's stricken one. They might think I was a heartless bitch now, but when shit came raining down, they'd thank me. "It's just covering bases, people. Things happen, accidents, death. If it's all neatly written down and spelled out, less chance of misunderstandings and broken hearts."

I was in my element during this weeklong phase, being naturally pedantic about lists and laws and fine print. I refined every detail of our agreement. I also encouraged Neal to have his lawyer look over everything on Naira's and his behalf, or hire a surrogacy lawyer to do the same. He didn't care for it, but he did it—more for Naira's sake. All of Naira's medical bills and expenses accrued during the pregnancy, and some after, would be our responsibility as the intended parents— well, Neal's responsibility. Naira protested when I added taxi rides to and from the doctor's office, if she ended up going by herself if or when Neal or I were unavailable to take her.

"It's hardly an expense. Get rid of the stipend for clothes and groceries too," she argued, her cheeks red in embarrassment.

But, I held firm. "Anything you do for the baby will be listed here and will be paid by us. You'll need a pregnancy wardrobe and shoes when your feet swell up. And we've decided to go organic through the gestation. Organic groceries are expensive."

"Have you decided on your lactation options?" I asked after noting down the expenses.

Dr. Stanley had strongly suggested we consider breastfeeding, if Naira was receptive to it. Studies showed it benefited the baby's immunity and well-being. Minnie, who was now resigned that this was happening, had also requested we consider it.

I'd completely understand if Naira didn't want to breastfeed. Seriously, who'd want to be a cow for however many months it took a child to build his or her immunity? Dr. Stanley had also intimated that it was possible to stimulate my mammary glands into lactating, if I wanted to breastfeed the child myself. Ick. I hadn't said it out loud—my crazy stopped there. But I think my expression had been sufficiently eloquent.

Neal had flared his nose up—a look I found both irritating and unhelpful. Besides, how dare he judge me? All he was doing was sitting on his throne like a sultan while his harem scrambled to fulfill his wishes.

"It's perfectly fine if you don't want to," I reiterated, wondering if it was possible to stimulate a man's breasts into lactating. I made a mental note to email Dr. Stanley. Let's see how Neal liked that as a tit for tat.

"I...would like to," Naira said hesitantly, as if she'd agreed to do something illicit and unscrupulous, even villainous.

"Great. Let's add that in." I jotted it down, deliberately ignoring the censure wafting off my husband. It was best if we kept our focus on the details of the process and not our subjective feelings and opinions of the process. We were never fully going to be on the same page on anything.

"Next question is how?"

Would she prefer pumping the milk and refrigerating it, so anyone could feed the bairn—that way she'd be free to get back to work and travel if she needed to—or, would she rather do it in the more traditional way?

While Neal's disapproval came off him like a heat signature, Naira's awkwardness drowned us in a deluge. Was I the only sane one here?

"*Um.* I…need to think about that."

"Fine," I said briskly to save us all from unnecessary mortification. "If you do decide the traditional way, then I figure it'll be best if you stay with us after the baby is born. Perhaps even consider moving in before?"

"I'll think about it," Naira said reluctantly.

"Will we require a baby nanny? Or can you and Naira manage everything?" I turned to Neal who'd been drumming his fingers on our dining table for the past fifteen minutes.

"And what will ye do when we're doing all of this?" he growled instead of answering.

Was he kidding me? *He* was pissed at the way this was playing out? The sultan with his harem?

I flicked him a coy look. "Why, my love, I have pumped myself full of bat-shit crazy hormones to make *your* dreams come true. Technically, my work here is done."

The shocked silence in our high-rise aerie was deafening. More so because it was snowing outside and the dense atmosphere cocooned us from all the usual sounds of helicopters and birds and the rare low-flying planes.

"Chill, people. Learn to take a joke."

Only, it wasn't a joke. Not really.

My egg retrieval was a resounding success except for one annoying glitch. I reacted badly to the epidural and was left with a blocked nerve or two in my back, which shot spasms of pain through my lower back, upper back and sometimes all along my spine. I wasn't in pain all the time, but when it came, it was acute. The damage might be temporary or not so temporary. The anesthesiologist couldn't give me a more definitive answer since medicine wasn't an exact science and different people reacted differently to anesthetics. The risks had been written in bold on the medical waiver, so I couldn't even threaten to sue the doctor.

I'd been prescribed painkillers to take as needed, and had been advised to rest, which wasn't possible. I'd taken more than enough half days and late days and holidays since December, with more half days coming up this week for Naira's insemination. I couldn't take any more days off work. I was falling woefully behind on all my cases except the task force. I could actually imagine my nemesis dancing around the corpse of my case files in glee.

I'd scheduled my egg retrieval for a Friday afternoon, thinking I'd have the weekend to recover and would be able to bounce back into work on Monday. Well, it was Monday and even if I couldn't exactly bounce, I'd still popped a cup full of pills and dragged myself to work.

I'd hauled my tuches home only an hour early— seriously, I deserved a commendation from the mayor for my fortitude— to find Lily waiting for me in my living room.

"How are you feeling?" she asked as soon as I closed the door behind me.

I was in too much pain to physically or mentally register surprise at her presence or object to it. I registered one thing though. Her pale fine-boned face briefly contorted into an expression I'd seen on it a million times before when confronted by my latest shenanigans.

Must you always cause trouble, you silly, stubborn child? Tsk-tsk.

I. Could. Not. Deal. Not today.

I dumped my winter coat, bag, shoes on the bench in the foyer and tried not to crawl into my bedroom, where I lay down on my side as unjerkily as I could and moaned. I heard Lily *tsk-tsking* away in the hall. The closet opened and closed, followed by other shuffling sounds before silence reigned. It was too optimistic to think Lily had left the apartment, now that she'd seen me and knew I was alive, though hardly kicking. I'd have to rejoice in the fact that at least she was leaving me alone. Just her presence was a trigger. I resented the fact that she was cleaning up after me like I was a child. I could never do anything right in her eyes.

I nodded off, my brain and body simply shut down. When I came to, Lily was beside me, brushing my hair off my face.

"Sit up a bit. You have to eat something." She rose, picked up a tray from the foot of the bed and placed it close to me. It was laden with hot tomato soup, a couple of slices of toast and a cup of pills—all fancily arranged on flowery china. Naira's doing, I guessed. There was a single purple orchid in a small flowerpot in one corner of the tray. The purple matched the drapes in my room.

"Your doting man has left instructions that you finish all the soup and take your pills. Come on, honey. Up you go."

Lily helped me sit, stuffing pillows between my back and the padded mauve-colored headboard. I was hungry, so I dug in. Lily sat on one of the armchairs by the windows. The day was dreary and sunless, so there was no need to draw the curtains. I ate the soup and the avocado toasts, relishing whatever magic Naira had concocted in the kitchen. I wondered how her tests were going.

Lily fidgeted with the South Sea pearls around her neck, the ones Neal had given her for her birthday. She looked nice in them, and in her suede pants and knit pullover. Was she meeting Charlie after or had she met him before? She kept fidgeting in her chair, waiting for me to finish so we could talk.

I. Could. Not. Deal. If she read out our horoscopes and segued into strange cautionary tales and metaphors, I'd strangle her. Or myself. Or Neal. I got that he didn't want me to be alone since he was with Naira at the Angels of Mary, but couldn't he have found someone other than one of the witches of *Macbeth* to babysit me?

Naira's uterus was being examined, and depending on the thickness of her endometrium, Dr. Stanley would schedule the insemination sometime over the next five days. Neal was with her because I was in no shape to be. He also meant to check on the status of the embryos and whether or not they were chromosomally perfect. He hadn't texted me yet.

I finished the soup and felt so much better, but I still took the painkillers. I needed to sleep tonight, all night.

"No one said motherhood would be pain free. But it can be rewarding."

Seriously? That's what she thought I needed to hear right now?

I took a bigger sip of water than I'd meant to and my throat hurt when I swallowed the last big pill.

"You can go now. I feel fine."

"Neal asked me to stay until he gets back. He doesn't want you to be alone. That man takes such good care of you. But if you want to sleep, I can go back into the living room and watch my show."

I should've let her go, but something hot and nasty bubbled up inside me and spilled over. I was sick of her and Minnie's dire warnings and threats and condescension that they'd been filling my ears with since Scotland.

A woman's function is to generate life.

A wife's duty is to build a family.

What do you think that child will feel?

A man has a special bond with the woman who bears his child.

That one had poked a hole in my armor and cut me, even though it was hogwash. Fathers hurt the mothers of their children all the time. Husbands hurt their wives. I wasn't claiming women were saints. But there was no such thing as a special bond.

Why wasn't Neal home yet? He and Naira should be home by now. Why hadn't he texted me? What was wrong? Or should I take no news as good news?

I hadn't had the energy to remove my phone from my jacket pocket before crawling into bed, so I took it out now.

Be nice!

It was the only text Neal had sent, over half an hour ago, approximately when I'd entered the house. My mouth soured as I shrugged out of the jacket, my movements clumsy though not painful. I winced, more in reflex, when my back twanged. I waved off Lily's concern and switched on the TV.

"What were you watching? We can watch it together." *There!* That was nice enough, wasn't it? Bonus, we didn't have to talk if we were watching… *The Gilmore Girls.* Holy God, kill me now. We watched for about five minutes when Lily fiddled with her pearls again.

"Neal said something about checking the blastocysts? What does that mean?" she asked anxiously.

Ah, now we were getting to the heart of her visit. I explained the IVF process as best I could.

"Fertilization happens after the sperm is injected into the egg and forms a single-celled zygote. Within hours the zygote splits and multiplies into multicelled blastocysts. At this stage, generally at days three and five, the blastocysts are tested for abnormalities and the healthiest ones are set aside. Then comes the preimplantation genetic screening and diagnosis, which will pretty much tell us if the embryos are carrying any number of a thousand genetic diseases, so we can determine if we want to go ahead with the implantation or not."

Lily's biggest issue with me had been the mystery of my birth and genetics.

We don't know anything about her medical history. We don't know what we might be dealing with. I can't do this, Samuel. You can't expect me to. I'd eavesdropped on them arguing when the Judge had decided to adopt me. I'd already been fostering with them.

I didn't blame her for imagining the worst about me. I did it too.

"Don't worry, Lily. We won't be saddled with a diseased child," I said.

"They can do that?"

I'd been expecting to hear the usual displeasure in her question, not wonder. It made me sit up straighter. What the hell was that expression on her face?

"Yes."

"I didn't know." She gave me a tremulous smile. "We never told you," she whispered, and for a minute my heart pounded so loudly that I wouldn't have heard her anyway. What hadn't they told me?

"We had a daughter called Jessica. My little Jessie was beautiful, an angel. She had Samuel's smile and eyes and my delicate bone structure."

I wanted her to stop talking. I wanted her to leave.

They'd had a daughter.

I hadn't been the only claimant of the Judge's affections.

"When she turned two, she was diagnosed with spinal muscular atrophy, a neurodegenerative disorder we'd passed on to her through our flawed genes. While other toddlers ran about and jumped around the playground, Jessie had trouble even standing for long and her legs would cave from under her if she tried to run. They told me not to worry. She was a late bloomer, they said. Then she stopped walking and running altogether. She stopped trying to stand up. She suffered from a particularly aggressive form of the disease, and because she was so young, she couldn't fight it. We couldn't fight it. She died, slowly and in pain, two months after her ninth birthday."

Every part of my body froze as Lily spoke about her angel. Why hadn't they ever told me? Had I meant so little to them? Or had she meant so much?

I flinched when Lily reached for my tightly curled fist and rubbed it.

"It's good you can know about such things from before… and decide. It's good there are so many choices now. A sick child takes a toll on everything. You blame yourself for not foreseeing it, for not doing enough. You accuse your partner of being callous, of putting his work before his family. You wonder and curse and wish for the impossible. Then you lose faith in everything. Even your marriage."

I woke up gasping in the middle of the night. I'd dreamed of misshapen embryos, of screaming children with blood running out of their eyes and noses, of a whole school full of zombie children coming to attack me.

I started shaking. I squeezed my eyes shut when I felt them burn with tears.

"Hey. Hey! What's the matter?" Neal's arms came around me and I clung to him. "Hush. What's this now? What's happened?"

It came pouring out—the story Lily had told me, my nightmare, my fears.

"What if the genetic testing isn't enough? What if the child gets sick after? What if she falls off a slide and injures her head and becomes a paraplegic? What happens then, Neal?" I pressed a hand to my stomach. I was not equipped for this. I could not be responsible for a sick child. I could not. "What if my eggs are rotten? You should've used Naira's eggs. I cannot do this. Let's call it off. Please, let's just stop this now."

He held me as I spewed all the vile, ugly things that kept me up at night. He hugged me, rocking me until I calmed down. I didn't. I simply ran out of breath. The pain in my back shifted into my chest. What had I done?

My husband promised that nothing bad was going to happen. That I should have faith, if not in God, then in Dr. Stanley who knew what he was about. He asked me to have faith in him—in us. We could deal with anything, the two of us together.

"I'm terrified of motherhood, Neal. Even with you and Naira around, I'm going to be terrible at it. I've had three mothers—what a fucking joke! And between them, all they've taught me is how not to be one."

"Well, there ye are, then. Ye know what not to do, so ye just don't do it, aye? You will be a fine mother. I know ye will."

Was he being deliberately obtuse? He just didn't get it, did he? He didn't understand my terror, my…flaw. How could he?

"And what if I can't help but be just like them? What if that's all I can be?" I kept shaking my head as if I'd lost control of my muscles. "I can't risk it. I can't."

His tone hardened then. "You set this in motion, hen. We're invested, emotionally, physically. I'm invested, Paris. I want our family and I will no' allow ye to change yer mind now."

But it was too late. I'd already changed my mind. And Neal, it seemed, had made up his. We were deadlocked like a hung jury, exactly as I'd expected us to be. Only, our stances had reversed.

Naira would be our tiebreaker and I had no doubt which side of the scale her vote would tip. And so, the only recourse left, the only viable option for me, was to step back from it all and let it happen.

As I'd said before, my work here was done.

CHAPTER SIXTEEN

Naira

I became pregnant on the first try, which was both surprising and not.

I'd already felt the change even before Dr. Stanley confirmed the news with a quantitative blood test two weeks after the embryo transfer. An awareness had manifested inside me at the time of the insemination itself. Paris thought I was being fanciful, but I wasn't.

She'd been there in the room with me for the transfer, and Dr. Stanley and I had explained every step, described every feeling for her in great detail, so she could envision it. I planned to share every aspect of the pregnancy with her whether she liked it or not. I refused to accept she wanted to be completely removed from it.

We'd arrived at the clinic with my bladder full to the level of uncomfortable as required. Paris had filled out all necessary paperwork, then a nurse had taken us into a room that had been prepared for the insemination. There had been soft music playing in the background and the lights in the room had been dimmed so that it wouldn't hurt my eyes.

"Great. You get the salon treatment, and I got an operating table," Paris grumbled, comparing her egg extraction procedure to mine. Her snark actually calmed my nerves.

"You want to exchange places?" I grinned, though with sympathy. She'd been suffering back pain since her epidural, the poor dear.

It had been a quick procedure. Dr. Stanley had come in and explained what would happen in his matter-of-fact way, and then he'd shown us a grainy photo of the embryos under a microscope. They'd looked like eight-petaled flowers.

"These are what we call high-quality embryos. Do you see there is no fragmentation, and the cells are all similar in size and shape? We'll be inserting a couple of these perfect little guys into you," he'd said, smiling at both of us.

Paris had been staring at the embryo picture as if it was a thing under a microscope, which of course it was when the picture was taken, but we'd both exhaled our anxiety when Dr. Stanley said the embryos were high-quality and perfect.

"I feel a tug...on my heart," I said a little dreamily when he inserted the catheter into me and released the embryos. Up on the wall in front of me, there were screens showing everything that was going on inside my womb. A thin white line or tube entered me, and I'd swear there was a glowing ball at the end of it. The line inched deeper and deeper and then, suddenly, the glowing balls were floating inside me.

At that moment, I felt completely and utterly connected to the enormity of life. To the collective consciousness of the universe. I was life itself.

I told Paris and Neal a story my grandmother had told me a million times while growing up. A story about Mahaveer, the twenty-fourth, and last, Jina. A Jina was an enlightened soul who by example and through preaching guided other souls to liberation. A Jina was to Jainism sort of like what Buddha was to Buddhism, or Christ to Christianity.

"The reason I'm telling you this is that Mahaveer was also an embryo transfer," I said as I stretched out on their living room sofa.

I had to take it easy for the day, and had been advised not to climb stairs, if possible. So, going back to Liam's was out of the question, and I'd come back with Paris to her apartment. She was having a quick bite to eat and then would be heading to work—she'd taken the morning off for me—and Neal would keep me company for the rest of the day.

"In his final human birth before his enlightenment, Mahaveer, whose name means the Bravest One of All, took the form of an embryo in the womb of a Brahmin woman called Devananda. The king of the gods, Indra, didn't think it fitting for the next Jina to be born in the priestly Brahmin caste as they weren't the caste of great kings and mighty warriors. So, the Great Embryo was transplanted into the womb of Queen Trisala, who then gave birth to Prince Vardhamana Mahaveer."

"Good to know," said Paris. She didn't roll her eyes, but she complimented me on my imagination and left for work.

Ah, what did Paris know about spirituality, I thought, feeling utterly wonderful about life.

My grandmother had told me that for Prince Vardhamana to become a Mahaveer, he'd needed both the wisdom of a priest and the courage and strength of a warrior. Hence, he'd been an embryo conceived in one caste and birthed in another. I'd asked her if such fantastical stories like divine births could really be true? *If the mind can imagine it, the soul can manifest it,* she'd been fond of saying.

I wondered what it meant for our baby. Would she understand how special she was?

Neal wanted to know more about Jainism, so we chatted about it and Sikhism and Catholicism. I asked him about his beliefs, or if he believed in any religious doctrine at all.

"Well, I was baptized and I go to the *gurudwara* when needed. As ye know, my family celebrates both Christmas and Diwali. It's more about having faith, any faith, in my family. We weren't raised to put one over the other or discount any of the hundreds of other faiths in the world."

I liked what he'd said. A lot. My family wasn't so open. I'd never had a choice in my faith. It had always been Jainism above every other faith.

"I used to love listening to my grandmother's stories—the religious ones. They almost seemed like fairy tales." Neal was sprawled on the sofa opposite me, and was looking at me encouragingly. "I'm wondering if you—and I hope Paris won't mind because we didn't talk about this before—but I'm wondering if it's okay if I tell the little one stories in the womb? They say that it...helps." I touched my belly, and Neal's eyes dropped to my hand. Deep slashes of red appeared on his cheeks, and I felt my own face ignite into flames.

It was hard not to be embarrassed about it. I was more embarrassed that I was carrying his child than I was about carrying Paris's—which was just silly because it was one and the same. I didn't even know why I'd asked him this. We weren't at that stage yet. It was only a transfer. Dr. Stanley had said there was a possibility that it may not work and we'd have to try again. We had enough high-quality blastocysts frozen for several tries. I was trying hard not to get my hopes up and was obviously failing.

We'd decided not to congratulate each other yet, not until the blood test. And we were trying not to show our excitement by playing it cool—at least Neal and I were. And maybe I shouldn't make plans yet, but God, I wanted this so much.

I'd been right about being pregnant. And from the day of the blood test—no, even from before, the day of the transfer, the rightness only kept multiplying like the cells in my womb.

When my blood report confirmed my pregnancy, Neal broke into the biggest smile I'd ever seen on anyone. His face showed every vibrant emotion I was too scared to feel. He'd waltzed around the room with Paris until she'd laughed too.

This pregnancy was so different from my other one. It had all the joy and none of the worry. Sarika, helicopter mother of two adorable boys (whom I prayed for every day when I prayed for this baby, that they didn't turn into their father or their mother) had told me that every pregnancy was unique, and the child's temperament usually matched the ordeal. If I believed her theory, then my first pregnancy had been doomed from the beginning. It had taken Kaivan and me six months to get pregnant. Six months during which our hopes had dwindled into worry, and our excitement to desperation. Only I hadn't known the true reason for Kaivan's odd behavior, and had chalked it up to pregnancy disappointment. Had our baby known its fate and so had tried hard not to be born? Why hadn't Kaivan told me what was going on? Why had he hidden his financial worries from me? I wouldn't have gotten pregnant if I'd known. And I wouldn't have been hurt by his forced joy and lack of enthusiasm when we finally did.

Of course, it's good news, baby. But the timing could've been better, he'd said when I broke the news. I'd gone to the doctor with my mother because he'd been in Delhi, meeting with some minister. Too late he'd told me why.

This time the news of the pregnancy was music to three

sets of ears. Neal's enthusiasm was such a joy to behold. Even the morning sickness was tolerable and not violent like the last time. And while I was stressed about navigating the first trimester without mishap, Fraser Bespoke kept my mind off it. Best of all, I wasn't facing any of it alone.

I joined a prenatal yoga class as Lamaze classes wouldn't start until the third trimester. Dr. Kapoor, Paris's ob-gyn and now mine, had suggested yoga during pregnancy was a great way to stay in shape. It would calm the mind and prepare the body for the rigors of labor.

"I see no reason for you not to exercise as before," she said at my first ultrasound two weeks after the blood test. It was only to confirm what the blood test had already implied. My next ultrasound would be between six to eight weeks to check development, heartbeat and due date that we roughly knew would be in mid-November.

I loved the energy of the class where the master yogi took us through sequences of Vinyasa and Iyengar yoga to Buddha Bar music. Paris came with me on weekends, and sometimes Neal too. We'd just finished a class, and were meeting Lavinia and Juan at Sarabeth's Tribeca for brunch.

It wasn't time to put away our winter coats at all, but the weather was being kind to the Northeast this weekend in March. It was balmy enough for us to walk.

Sarabeth's was busy and noisy as usual. It was a forty-minute wait time without reservations. Luckily, we had them. Half the tables in the family-friendly restaurant were bursting with kids either crying or screaming for attention. I didn't blame Paris for complaining. "There should be a rule against allowing kids under the age of five into a restaurant."

Lavinia and Juan were already waiting for us. The newly married glow hadn't waned from either of their faces. It looked good on them. We got to talking about college, as we always ended up doing when our girl gang met. The men wanted to know how we'd met each other.

With Lavinia and me, it had been our common South Asian heritage. We both joined the Indian club and the Indian dance group and hit it off. Eventually, I'd persuaded Paris to join the clubs so she could experience the Indian culture firsthand, which had been a feat on my part. But before that, we'd met first in our freshman dorm on move-in day.

"I'd been expecting to room with an Indian American girl from Florida whose lifestyle and—" I paused, drew imaginary quotation marks in the air "—'values' were deemed appropriate by my father. He chose my roommate for me."

If I "had to be stubborn about studying in the culturally bankrupt West" and living with vetted extended family in New Jersey wasn't an option for freshman students, my roommate would have to pass muster, he'd said.

"Then, out of nowhere, there's Paris, throwing clothes inside her closet—her idea of unpacking—when my mother and I lumber into the dorm room, dragging three large suitcases and an assortment of storage boxes in our wake."

We'd gaped at Paris for a full five minutes before I could speak. She'd been wearing rumpled, shabby chic clothes, defiance beaming out of her every pore. She'd had badly cut bangs—a home job—and thick black eyeliner around her eyes. Her black razor-sharp lips had slanted into a genuine, welcoming smile that had quickly turned chilly when my mother turned her back to her and began bombarding me with questions in Marwari. It had been obvious we were discussing her. Paris had sneered at us, her nose ring quivering in disdain. It had taken me a whole month to win her trust back.

My mother and I had thanked God that my father had decided against joining us in New York, or things would've turned ugly pretty fast. My mother had extended her trip for an extra month just to make sure Paris didn't murder me in my sleep. Although, how she could've prevented it from her hotel room, I had no clue.

Paris told her side of the story. "I persuaded the floor RAs and Naira's would-have-been roomie to exchange rooms with me on move-in day. I'd gotten it into my head to learn about India and wanted someone fresh off the boat to teach me." She grinned, remembering the shenanigans we'd gotten up to. "I think we were both surprised that we hit it off. Perhaps we'd bonded over our aesthetically different, yet conceptually similar, nose rings."

I laughed, touching my nose where the hole for my diamond nose stud had long since closed. Paris hadn't pierced her nose at all. She'd worn a fake black metal ring for show.

Nothing else about her had been fake. Paris had achieved every goal she'd set for herself. Be it making the dean's list every semester, or finagling a date with a guy she'd crushed on but who hadn't given her a second look, or convincing my father—my staunch and overprotective father—that the trip to Cancún during our junior year spring break was for a research paper on the Mayan civilization. Never mind that neither of us had even one history credit between us all through college.

If Paris had learned about the Indian culture from me, she'd opened the door to a daring non-Indian world for me. Comparing our lives, I began to understand myself, my boundaries, my privileges and my shortcomings. I became more than the timid younger daughter of Baldev and Anjum Manral. More than a spoiled little princess who'd thrown a tantrum one day and gotten her father to grant her wish to study abroad. I realized I didn't have to toe every line, and that no lines were set in stone. That I could juggle a career *and* be a hostess with the mostess. In fact, I could be whatever I wanted to be. I could and should choose my own husband—if I was crazy enough to marry, that is—albeit from the list my parents had provided. I wasn't *that* daring, I'd realized too. I'd often wondered since then, if Paris hadn't unlocked those changes in me, would I ever have caught Kaivan's interest?

I'd envied Paris in every possible way in college. Now, watching her laugh at our college stories while leaning against her husband—a man I was coming to adore—I realized I still envied her.

The conversation took a surprising turn as my dessert arrived. I shouldn't give in to my sweet tooth, especially because of the baby, but I hadn't been able to resist ordering the strawberry shortcake listed on the menu.

"We have news." Lavinia's eyeballs ping-ponged between Paris and me. Her smile was so magnificent that I feared her jaw would dislocate.

Then I knew. I just *knew*. I jumped up and hugged her, squeeing. "Oh, my God, congratulations. When?"

"October," she answered gleefully and there were more congratulations, some backslapping between the guys, and a tiny bit of grumbling from Paris about overpopulation and the Human Agenda.

"We're expecting too in November. So, woo-hoo!" said Paris.

I was startled that she'd told when I'd expressly told her not to tell anyone until we crossed the first trimester. I wasn't being superstitious, but things happened. Until we heard the heartbeat or Dr. Kapoor said everything looked perfect, I didn't want anyone to know. I hadn't even told my parents—but that was for another reason altogether.

It was Lavinia's turn to scream and jump up and hug Paris until Paris set her straight by pointing at my belly. "The kid's not in here. It's in there."

I wanted to bury my face in my hands. Oh, Paris. When would she *not* shock the world? I raised my shoulders and hands in a "Surprise" sort of gesture and waited for Lavinia and Juan to school their expressions of shock and for the questions to pour out.

Paris didn't even wait for the questions. "You know my views on procreation. But Neal has a different philosophy, so does Naira. So, woo-hoo. Everyone's happy."

I kicked her under the table, telling her to shut up. She'd done the same thing at one of our surrogate-intended mother group meetings. She'd been exactly this flippant and it had not gone down well. Many of the intended mothers in the group had gone through hell, literally, before taking the surrogacy path. Some had tried to get pregnant for years, miscarried multiple times, had battled health issues or issues that no doctor could figure out. The point was that most heterosexual couples chose surrogacy when all other doors had been shut to them. Unless they were quirky celebrities and did it for quirky celebrity reasons. So, it was in exceedingly bad taste when Paris said she'd chosen this path even though she was perfectly capable of bearing children, and had gloated about it.

That wasn't true. She hadn't gloated, but when she talked about pregnancy and motherhood with all her eye-rolling, it sounded awful.

I accepted Lavinia's congratulations. She didn't seem as shocked by the news as the group women or Juan, and no wonder. Lavinia knew and understood Paris as well as I did. Excitedly, we began to exchange notes about weeks and stages and sonograms and morning sickness.

"Baby showers!" Lavinia exclaimed at one point.

Paris groaned on cue. "No. Oh, my God. No one's spending money on baby showers. Not when there are children—"

"Starving in the world," we chorused along with her.

Yes, Paris was idealistic and a *draamebaaz* and she worked hard to make the world a balanced place, but her candidness hurt sometimes. Couldn't she be happy and show excitement even for a minute? Did she have to bring up everything that was wrong in the world and compare it to our situation?

I caught Neal's eye and he winked at me, and I realized he and I were excited enough for all three of us. I didn't need Paris's endorsement.

Neither did Lavinia. "It's not up to you, darling," she told Paris and then turned to me. "You throw me a shower and I'll throw you one. Or wait! Let's plan one huge bash together."

"Um, okay," I said over Paris's louder groans.

"Let's lock in a date. Does early September work?"

Okay, this was running away from me. I wanted to do this. I wanted to celebrate the baby. I was in a mostly positive frame of mind. I'd even bought a dozen socks with the slogan Think Positive on them and planned to wear them throughout the pregnancy. But I didn't want to tempt fate.

"Can we decide that after I cross into the second trimester?" I crossed my fingers for it to be so. I'd only just completed five weeks.

Paris mumbled something like *kinahara*, and I shot her a steely glance. That better not have been a curse word. I was not happy with her today.

"Awesome! And we'll send out the invitations naming Paris as our host," Lavinia added cheekily.

I burst out laughing. "Deal."

I went home to Liam's alone, declaring I wanted to nap. I needed some space from Paris and Neal and they from me. I set my gym bag on the floor of the bedroom and took off my hoodie. Then I stripped off all my clothes and stood in front of the mirror. There was no change in my body, not yet. Nothing to indicate that I had a life growing inside me.

Please, God, let it be so. I was so afraid. *Let me just survive the next couple of weeks.* I'd miscarried between my tenth and eleventh weeks. *Just get me through it, please.*

When I was twelve, a woodpecker had nested in a copse that bordered my building complex. For three whole weeks it had plagued my existence, pecking at the trunk day and night until I'd called the building manager and demanded that he do something about the incessant rat-a-tatting. He'd hopped to it because no one dared to question orders from the Manrals, not even from junior Manrals. The manager had not only gotten rid of the nest, he'd chopped the whole copse down. Never again would a woodpecker dare to make his home next to our building.

When my grandmother heard about it, she'd taken me to task, explaining the tenets of karma to me. "You caused harm to a life or several lives, *choti*, little one. That was not a nice thing to do."

I'd argued that the manager had promised to shoo the family of woodpeckers away before taking down the nest. She said that it made no difference.

"Your intent was to cause harm to their home and, even if inadvertently, to their lives. In karma, intent is as bad as action, *choti*. Ahimsa means we do not harm in any form or any being, not even the lowest of life-forms."

Once an ant colony had sprung up in our holiday estate in our ancestral village in Rajasthan. My grandmother had fought and won against my father who'd wanted to call exterminators to get rid of the eyesores right in the front lawn. My grandparents, all four were gone now, wouldn't even drink milk because it came from an animal, and on certain days of

268 • THE OBJECT OF YOUR AFFECTIONS

the year, they wouldn't eat fresh fruits or vegetables either because even those had life in them.

After the talk with my grandmother, I'd been mired in guilt. I'd done such an awful thing and for what? So I could chat with my friends in peace? I was an avian mass murderer, I'd sobbed in my grandmother's lap. She'd prayed with me for the woodpecker and his babies as atonement, and I'd done community service at her temple for a year.

But karma didn't work like that, I realized as I grew older and understood it better. What goes around, comes around. I'd destroyed a woodpecker's home and family, and so karma had taken mine in return.

I didn't know how many baby woodpeckers had lost their home or lives because of my thoughtless action. I'd wondered when I miscarried if my long-ago actions had come back to haunt me.

I got down on my knees by the bed and prayed that karma was finished with me now.

CHAPTER SEVENTEEN

Paris

"Ms. Fraser! Paris!"

Taking my finger off the elevator button, I looked back to see—with some surprise—the acting US Attorney for the Southern District of New York striding toward me purposefully.

Jeff Chang was bald, short—for a man, though he was my height—and had the best poker face a lawyer could have. You'd never be able to tell what he was thinking, which was fantastic in a courtroom or negotiation. It was awful in my case, as my mind scrambled about trying to figure out what he could want with me. We weren't exactly friendly enough to exchange pleasantries every day, though we had been working closely on the factory workers case for several months now, but on different aspects of it.

"Thank you for waiting," he said politely as he came to stand in front of me as if I'd been waiting for him and not in fact for the elevator. "I wanted to thank you also for the work you've done here. I saw the deposition tapes from December with the female workers. You were great with them. And I understand you've been preparing them for court this whole week?"

I shrugged off his thanks. "Yes. They're ready."

Or, as ready as anyone in their positions could be. I didn't need to clarify. Jeff would know. The six women who'd been selected from a pool of three hundred to give grand jury testimonies had been working in the clothes factory since the beginning and had witnessed the most ugliness. They'd suffered the most too.

Jeff nodded. "I don't wish to hold you up, or beat around the bush. So, would you consider applying for a job here at the USAO? We could use more attorneys like you."

"Huh?" was my scintillating reply.

That had come flying out of left field. Apply for a position as assistant US Attorney? Well, sure. It was my goal for…after a couple of years. I'd thought I needed more experience, both in and out of the courtroom, for it.

"Think about it," he said when the doors to the elevator slid open. He held them open for me as I scraped my jaw off the floor and tried to give him a better, more dignified answer.

"Um, well…uh…hmm." That was about as intelligent as I could manage to sound, apparently. What I wanted to do was kick up my heels and scream.

He chuckled. "I asked Lance about you. He thinks it's a good move for you too."

What the what? He'd asked my boss, the DA of Manhattan, about me? Shit. This was serious. I cleared my throat. "I see.

Um, I'll definitely sleep on it. Thanks for the vote of confidence, Mr. Chang, I..."

"Jeff."

"Right. Jeff. Thank you."

Then he let go of the elevator doors, and I was on my way down with a moronic smile on my face.

"Sorry, sorry, sorry!" I burst into the ultrasound room at Dr. Kapoor's clinic.

While I'd been getting headhunted by the freaking USAO, Neal and Naira had been heading over to the doc's for the six-week ultrasound. Today, we'd hear the bairn's heartbeat for the first time.

Naira was sitting on the bed, which meant the doc hadn't come in yet or...

"Is it done?" I quickly peeked at the wall clock to check just how late I'd been. Barely twenty minutes. Dr. Kapoor was never on time.

"Not yet." Naira gave me a wobbly smile.

Neal, however, pointedly looked at the clock, his jaw muscles ticking. Guess he was pissed. He'd sent me three messages: first, when he'd left the house; second, when he'd picked up Naira; and the third one had been fifteen minutes ago from the clinic: Where the fuck are you?

Damn it. I had a job. A damn freaking important job serving this city. I couldn't keep hopping all over town for ultrasounds on my lunch break. The two of them could have handled the appointment, but no, Naira had insisted I come. So here I was.

I set my office bag on a chair and went to stand by Naira. She wore an elastic-waist skirt and a loose top so she wouldn't have to change into a hospital gown for the belly ultrasound.

I was dying to tell them about the potential job offer, but I'd wait until everyone was happier. It was too tense in here just now, and I didn't want to fight again or sound self-absorbed.

Naira had turned into a worrywart over the past few weeks and I hoped the *mishegas* would stop today. She was driving me bananas. I kept telling her this was not like her previous pregnancy. That Dr. Kapoor also seemed happy with the way everything was progressing, and we'd taken a million steps to ensure the baby was perfect, hadn't we? Frankly, I was getting a little sick of Naira's doomsday moods that switched at a drop of a hat into effervescent joy. Couldn't she pick a mood and stick to it? Or just be normal about the pregnancy?

"It's going to be fine. Chill." I hoped I sounded reassuring and not as exasperated as I felt.

Then Dr. Kapoor came in, all smiles and hugs for all of us. She'd been my gynecologist for a long time now, and knew us well. She asked Naira to lie back. The ultrasound machines were already humming. Dr. Kapoor did her thing, moved the transducer all over Naira's gel-smeared lower belly, explaining everything we were seeing on the ultrasound screen. Then she stopped talking. Moved the wand this way and that, making Naira wince since her bladder was burgeoning as that was how the best pictures came out.

"What's wrong?" I asked. Neal sucked in a breath behind me. He moved closer, placing his hand on my shoulder and squeezing hard. I guess *wrong* was the wrong word to use.

Naira's eyes squeezed shut, but tears were already leaking out the sides.

Shit. Fuck. *Fuuck!*

Don't react, I told myself. *Don't fucking react.* It does not help for everyone to freak out. *Keep it technical. Clinical. Light. No big deal.*

"What's going on, Doc?" I swallowed hard. The thing was

that I couldn't not react, at least inside. My heart was beating like a jackhammer.

"Nothing. Sometimes six weeks is too early to detect the heartbeat," Dr. Kapoor reassured.

I let out the breath I'd been holding. There, simple explanation. But Naira wouldn't quit looking terrified, and it undid all my good intentions. I started asking questions. I needed better answers. Explanations.

"Are we seeing what we expect to see? The C-shaped embryo? The arms and legs beginning to sprout? What's the length of it?"

Before addressing my queries, Dr. Kapoor asked Neal to step out and had Naira remove her skirt and underwear. "Let me try a vaginal scan. It gives a clearer image and…"

"Why didn't we do that in the first place?" I slapped my hands on my pencil-skirt-clad hips.

"Because your husband would want to hear the heartbeat too," said the doc.

Oh, brother. "Forget him. Let's not even consider him from now on and let's just do what's best for Naira and the kid, okay?" I said. Naira opened her eyes then, and even more tears spilled out. "Stop that. Do you want to give birth to a crybaby?" I said, intending to make her laugh.

The vaginal ultrasound didn't fare any better. We didn't hear a heartbeat, but the embryo was C-shaped and about an inch long as expected. Dr. Kapoor asked us to come back in a week to do another ultrasound. Then she patted Naira's hand and left the room, leaving us to deal with the riot brewing inside our minds.

This was not cool, I thought, as our solemn procession headed home. This was so not cool, Big Man Up There. I was doing this for them. This was not a selfish act. *You cannot do this to us.*

★ ★ ★

These days, I met with my therapist no more than three or four times a year, which meant I had a lot of ground to cover, and as such our sessions usually leaked past their prescribed hour.

I'd begun seeing Dr. Louis Barr when I was thirteen years old, after I'd been caught several times—sometimes red-handed, sometimes after the fact—executing various delinquent acts, the mildest of which had been shoplifting. Mostly, the Judge had managed to pay off the victims of my mischief or convince them not to report me to the authorities, and I'd walked away every time. He'd eventually sought outside help to sort me out.

Therapy had worked in that I understood myself better. Not that my issues had magically disappeared. My destructive need to self-annihilate, to disregard and mistrust every opinion except my own had been diluted to the point where I no longer felt that all of humanity was against me, or that I was better off as an island unto myself, rigid and unfeeling as stone. The Judge had been my stalwart champion. He'd believed in me, and for an orphan and a reject, that unshakable belief had been enormous. It had been everything. From then on, I'd never let him down by being anything less than what he'd expected—an upstanding citizen, a civil servant and a sensible individual.

While the Judge had built up my self-worth, Dr. Barr had helped me understand my nature, my triggers, my motivations. He'd already been an old man when I first started seeing him, now he looked ancient. His skin was like creamy paper that had been balled up and smoothed out. His posture was bent, his knobby shoulders poking up to his ears, probably from years of sitting in his high-backed chair, raptly listening to the troubled minds of his patients. But his mind, which was the only thing that mattered to a psychiatrist, was still as keen and sharp as a brand-new shiv. He was a man of few words—well, I supposed he had to be, at least with a patient—but when he did speak, his words usually hit their mark.

"Have you thought about why you're doing this?"

"I haven't thought of anything else in months." I was sprawled on a recliner angled away from him, facing a large picture window that showcased a row of prewar brownstones across the street. I loved this recliner. I'd bought one just like it for the apartment. I loved lounging in my recliner, reading, wondering or simply watching the clouds change shape high up in the sky. Sometimes giants fought battles up there, or horses grazed in meadows or raced across them. Sometimes Neal and I would share the recliner and imagine a whole world up there, our own Elysium.

And sometimes the clouds felt like prison walls I couldn't escape from. Dr. Barr had taught me a meditative technique to calm myself down when I felt like that.

But today I wasn't agitated. I was happy, despite the craziness at work and everything else.

"We were in LA over the weekend to attend a fund-raiser benefiting an orphanage in Nepal. Neal's friends, the Wilsons, were on the committee," I said abruptly.

My sessions usually went like that. He'd ask a question and I'd answer in my own time, or take the conversation in another direction. Eventually, he'd nudge me back to where he wanted me to go.

I told him about the gala, which I assumed had been a resounding success judging from the sheer number of people I'd seen there. Neal had wanted all of us to go, to take our mind off the disastrous ultrasound. Naira refused to come. She hadn't wanted to fly until after the next ultrasound.

It had been good for Neal and me to get away. Be alone.

"I didn't overreact this time when I saw the children."

I hated it when organizers of such events put the orphans on display to garner sympathy and larger donations. Even RiM made trauma victims turn their guts inside out for the audience. If they had a meltdown on the podium, even better. It was simply how it was done. I used to think it was the most brutal form of exploitation—I still did—but now I also knew that it was the only way to get the funds. Even altruism was all show and not just tell.

"Hmm," Dr. Barr hummed noncommittally since I hadn't really answered his question.

I grinned. I would get there, but I had so much else to tell him. "Guess who got offered a job at the US Attorney's Office?" Then I disgorged everything that had happened since Naira came to town.

"Even Lily thinks I've poked a tiger. Can you explain to me what that means? Does she mean Neal? Is he the tiger or is it fate? Oh, and she and I didn't spend either Thanksgiving or Hanukkah together. How did that even happen?"

I told him about the witches of Macbeth, and their reactions to the surrogacy. "Minnie has grudgingly bestowed her blessing. She's no longer badgering us. Thank God as we're seeing the clan in Courchevel in two weeks for the annual ski trip. Seriously, how much bonding time do the Frasers need? Also, they take way too many vacations—just saying. Good thing my boss is so understanding." Would I get the same freedom at the USAO?

I hashed out the pros and cons of a potential job transfer, including my toe-to-toe competition for the spot with my nemesis. It turned out that Jeff Chang hadn't exclusively approached me for the position: he'd also asked Jimmy Anderson to consider applying.

"I'm sure Anderson is going to play some nasty games and ingratiate himself with Jeff Chang." The rat bastard.

"What happens if he gets picked over you?" asked Dr. Barr.

A year ago, the very thought of it would have made me lose my shit. I'd have done everything in my power to come out on top. I wouldn't have left any stone unturned to leave my competitor in the dust. Now, if I got it, great. And if I didn't get the job—I shrugged—I loved being an ADA anyway.

"I won't kill myself to get it," I said, shocking even myself that such words had come out of my mouth. I wanted to slurp them back immediately. But I didn't. I left them there, floating in the air, letting them bounce about like the phantom shapes of clouds.

"I'm not giving up. I'm still going to be in the race." I couldn't seem to help justifying it. "I'm just not going to get hassled about it."

Dr. Barr smiled. "You seem content." He didn't say "finally," but I heard it anyway.

Was this contentment that I felt? Whatever it was, I liked it. I decided I liked doing things for other people for a change, giving them what they wanted, with or without an ulterior motive. I was making my husband happy. I was helping my best friend recover.

Please, God, we couldn't fail at this. We just couldn't.

"And there's nothing in it for you?"

I hated when he did that. When he wouldn't let me leave it simple.

"Of course there is." I let out a frustrated growl when he continued to peer at me under his bushy eyebrows. I could see him from the corner of my eye.

"Fine! I want to be in control of the situation. In control of my marriage, my life." I'd felt it spiraling out of control, with Neal traveling more and more, going farther and farther away from me. And there had been that frisson between us about children, which would have grown into a chasm eventually. So, I'd found a way to bridge the gap and make us airtight again.

There were things in life you couldn't control like your birth and your death, like falling in love. But there were things you could control, like the direction your marriage should take, or your career, or the genetics of your baby. And by God, I'd control the shit out of whatever I could control.

"What if it's me? What if it's my genes that caused the heartbeat defect? If it's a defect. I can't stop thinking about why it would go wrong. I planned everything so carefully. The best blastocysts were used. What more could I have done? I cannot fail in this. I simply cannot."

My body tightened in preparation for one of Dr. Barr's flinch-worthy but sage observations that would poke holes in my claims of having control over anything whatsoever. But, all he did was smile at me and wish me, "Happy Holidays."

That's right. Easter and Passover were upon us. Where had the months flown?

It was a miracle I survived the week without killing Neal, whose mood had gone all Darth Vader after LA. Naira wasn't handling the wait between the ultrasounds any better. She holed up in her apartment and prayed the whole time.

I still hadn't told them my "good news" about the potential job upgrade. Except Lily, who'd been over the moon because her daughter as an assistant US Attorney was a feather in her cap too. Lily was good friends with the state attorney general—they were patrons of the same Scrabble club and now Lily could gloat about me even more.

Would Neal consider it good news? The new position

would certainly increase my work hours if not my caseload. It might also mean that I'd have to travel for work at times.

How had I put myself in a position where my goals were suddenly inconvenient to my life? This was not what I'd envisioned when I'd endorsed the Big Idea. I'd thought my responsibility would end there. But there were doctor's appointments and prenatal yoga and discussions with midwives and reading up on trimesters and—a whole *fakakta* of things I had no interest in.

And then there was Naira describing every minute change in her body. Her breasts were bigger and sore. She had morning sickness—which was a good thing because it meant that the pregnancy hormones were elevated. But when I said as much to Naira and Lavinia, I got dirty looks for my trouble. Fine, then, if they wanted to take everything I said negatively, I wouldn't say anything at all. Let them worry themselves sick. Let them be consumed by guilt and thoughts of failure.

Naira gave me a long hug. "It's okay to talk about your feelings, Paris. Not just the biology of it."

I disengaged from the hug in a huff. "Feeling what? I'm not worried. The literature on baby heartbeats says it's normal not to hear one at six weeks." So, nothing to worry about.

The day of the follow-up ultrasound, Neal and Naira picked me up from work in the Tesla. I was back at One Hogan Place as my work with the task force was complete. It was up to the chief prosecutors to battle it out in court now.

I got into the car and nearly had a bout of teatime sickness myself. Gasping, I quickly lowered the tropical temperature inside the car to temperate. How bloody hot was it in here?

"Leave it on seventy-five," said Neal. "It's cold outside."

I shot him a gimlet-eyed stare, taking in his checkered shirt and dark jeans. No coat. Since when did he feel cold? He was usually a chugging furnace. I was the one who shivered because he liked the bedroom and car temps to rival Siberia.

"It's okay. I'm not cold now," said Naira, and it all fell into place. The pregnant lady was the priority. He was only following my directive.

I raised the temperature again, turned up the chanting music and shrugged out of my peacoat.

This time, the fetus passed the heartbeat test with flying colors. Hadn't I said not to worry? The clinic's exam room resounded with the sounds of heavy furniture being tossed— that was what a fetal heartbeat sounded like. *Ba-dum-ba-dum, ba-dum-ba-dum.*

We were all rejoicing in the symphony, and Neal had bent his head to kiss me, when Dr. Kapoor exclaimed, "Hang on. What's this? Oh, marvelous. Congratulations, Mommy and Daddy, it seems you're having twins. We have two hearts beating here."

Twins were a normal result of an IVF pregnancy since typically multiple embryos were inserted into the womb— with the gestational mother's permission, of course. Even so, when Dr. Kapoor gave us the news, I'd felt as if a stun gun had hit my spine.

I could. Not. Deal.

I couldn't go home and listen to Naira cry happy, stunned tears. Neal had teared up at the doctor's office and continued to shoot me sappy, exultant looks. I didn't have to go back to work, it was nearly five in the evening. I'd left the office with the understanding that I'd take the rest of the day off. Still, I asked Neal to drop me back to work, and told them not to wait for me for dinner. I'd be very late coming home.

I went into my office and got cracking on three of the cases that the chief ADA had dumped on my desk that morning. I'd argued about it being one too many then, but now I relished swimming in felonies and the bad apples of New York. This was normal. This was what humans were like naturally—greedy, filthy and savage. I understood these humans. I did not understand Neal and Naira or happy tears.

They were both the opposite of me. They were optimistic and courageous and shared their silver spoons so generously. They were clean—and I wasn't talking about their OCD, but the purity of their hearts. They didn't have ulterior motives. How had I even become friends with such people? Married one? What was it about me that they liked and admired?

I only hoped they never realized what a complete fraud I was.

CHAPTER EIGHTEEN

Naira

I deliberately kept my pregnancy from my family—even my mother—until I crossed over into the second trimester over Memorial Day weekend. I did that because, one, the first trimester was always chancy and anything could happen as I'd previously experienced. And two, I didn't want to get agitated by my family's agitation as it could've led to point number one. Of course, the second I told my mother, she was on the next flight out with my father.

I surprised even myself by how cool and collected I was when they showed up unannounced at my doorstep. I hadn't seen my mother in nearly eight months and wasn't prepared for the explosion of need I felt inside me. I wanted her to take me in her arms, take me back inside the fortress of her womb and keep me and my babies safe.

Other than that, I was as serene as I could be with my father. My calm was another gift from Neal. I didn't have words to express how wonderful he'd been since…well, since the beginning, even before the pregnancy. If he wasn't traveling, he was present at every checkup along with Paris. But unlike her, he was curious and cheerful about the whole process and not obsessed with ticking off all the boxes on the pregnancy chart. He called me several times a day, and of late had been working out of his studio so I wouldn't be alone in Liam's flat for any length of time, where I was also working hard to put together a trial pop-up show for Fraser Bespoke. His simple support was a nice counterbalance for his wife's policing and, of late, aloofness—which worried me, I admit—and I was coming to crave Neal's attention like the strawberry short-cakes I'd started to crave with every meal. If Paris found out I was sneaking and lapping up nonorganic dessert, she was going to jail me for the rest of my confinement.

I'd been expecting the third degree from my parents and they didn't disappoint, once they were done displaying suffi-cient horror at my increased waistline.

"What have you done, you stupid girl?"

Unbelievably, I didn't quake or cry or look away from my father's enraged eyes. That was how Zen I'd become. I told them the same story I'd told Neal and Paris months ago about the Great Embryo, the one my father's mother had told me a million times. I couldn't have explained my reasons to be a surrogate any more clearly, not without opening a can of worms I couldn't—no, I refused to even go near, forget open.

"It's done," I said to close the argument before it even began. "I'm pregnant with twins and there's nothing anyone can do about it now but to accept it."

"You have ruined yourself and us by this *harkat*," my father spat out. He was probably ruing the day he'd agreed to let me come to NYU. Or, even the day I was born.

I didn't care to please him. Not anymore.

"No more than before." I thanked my stars I'd fought him when I was eighteen, and fought him eight months ago.

Wasn't that something? I'd fought my father twice now, and won both times.

"Who will marry you after this?" my mother lamented, still on her trip to find me a husband.

"A good man," I answered quietly, thinking of Neal and Deven and Juan and all the good men I'd met in my life. My nasty brother-in-law, who my father favored now, didn't hold a candle to any of them. "A redundant question anyway, Mummy, since I've told you I don't plan to remarry ever."

I had everything I'd ever wanted in life. Except Kaivan. But, I'd decided I wasn't going to grieve for him anymore. I wouldn't do anything that could upset the bairns. No more crying. No despondency or worry. I'd only allow myself to feel all kinds of great and bold things.

My father washed his hands of me—I'd expected nothing else—and flew home to the daughter who made him proud, and the son-in-law whose character he failed to recognize. But my mother stayed back to make sure I was fine and was keeping good health. She defied my father too, when she wanted to, I thought with a smile.

She wanted to meet Dr. Kapoor, and with her permission, began feeding me a special diet for pregnant women, consisting mostly of fatty, delicious foods. Organic, of course.

"It'll prepare your body for the trauma of birth. Your bones, your muscles need to be strengthened," she said as she cooked for me in Liam's kitchen.

This was what I missed the most about Mumbai—my mother pampering me.

She made enough fenugreek *laddoos*, and edible gum-based *peth* and *raab* to last me for a month. "I'll keep sending you more every month. Make sure you eat one *laddoo* every day. The *peth* and *raab* you can alternate as you like. The *goond* in it will strengthen your bones."

I kissed my mother's soft, fleshy cheek. People said I looked like her, small and dainty, deceptively frail. She spoke to Minnie Singh too, about observing certain Indian rituals and customs meant for the protection of the pregnant mother and the unborn child. Those happened in the third trimester. There was still time, but the moms hashed it out in a couple of phone calls.

To my shock, Minnie Auntie also came to New York while my mother was there, to meet and talk to her face-to-face. She promised my mother that I would be well looked after, and she kept her word. Ridiculously, I began receiving two boxes of pregnancy food every month, which I gladly shared with the women in my surrogate support group.

With so many people taking care of me, I was free to worry about Paris. I wondered what she was thinking and feeling. She wasn't talking about it, no matter how nicely I asked. Neither of the moms had paid her any attention, not that she demanded it of them or even wanted it.

"I don't want you to feel left out of the process. You're truly missing out on one of the best experiences of being a woman."

Paris had sighed long and deep when I said that. "For you, it is. How many times do I have to tell you, I'm not you."

Still, she came with me for doctor's visits, and continued to ask scary questions—things I'd never have even thought of, much less researched—demanding answers regarding my reports, about the blobs on the sonogram, about the fetuses' development, the risk of having twins. Natural birth versus a cesarean section. Amniocentesis.

There, we had our first battle. As soon as the doctor mentioned the risk of a miscarriage, albeit a low one, that went with the procedure, I balked.

"I am not doing that test," I said flatly, wrapping my hands about my stomach as if Dr. Kapoor meant to do it right this minute. "The Down syndrome blood test was negative, wasn't it, Dr. Kapoor? So there's no need do it, right?"

"It was. And no, there's no reason to think that the babies aren't perfectly healthy at this point," she confirmed.

But Paris was vehement. "You agreed to do all the required tests, Naira. The blood screening isn't as foolproof as the amnio. We need to know of any fetal abnormalities and prepare."

"I agreed to do all the *necessary* tests. This one clearly isn't. Think positively, Paris. Why do we need to know? And prepare for what?" Then it dawned on me what she was about. I was horror-struck. "No. Absolutely not. No." I couldn't even put into words what she meant for us to do if...*if.* "How can you even think such a thing?" God. She was heartless.

"It's better to be prepared for any eventuality," she said grimly as I got dressed in jerky movements. The babies were biggish like their father. And their mother. I was small, and my stomach was already swelling.

"There's no preparation for something like that. Or for motherhood. You chose me, asked me to do this. To help you be a mother. Now let me help you. Let go of your worries, Paris. Please," I begged her.

"I'm not trying to upset you, Naira. But this is not your decision. Neal and I will make this decision. We need to know, and we'll decide what action to take accordingly."

Paris marched straight into Neal's office when we went home and asked him to be the tiebreaker.

"She's the one pregnant, aye? It's her body. It should be her choice," he said, siding with me.

He broke her heart that day. After that, Paris refocused on the tangible. So, I focused on the intangible. I drank in the color videos of the two hearts beating during a 3-D ultrasound. I hadn't reached that stage in my pregnancy before. I wanted Paris to feel the same wonder and amazement, and was dismayed because she stared at the screen with something akin to abhorrence. I preferred her blank looks.

I didn't know how to help her overcome her fear—and it was fear she felt. Not revulsion or apathy or disinterest, no matter how she spun it. She was so scared of these two bairns, of what they would mean to her, to Neal, that she refused to give an inch.

And while I tried to get her to feel for her children, I had to counsel myself not to feel too much. Paris was right. These babies were not mine, I could not get attached. I could not fight with her for them. But their health and their birth was my responsibility and I took that seriously.

I'd told my parents. I needed to tell Kaivan's parents, even though they already knew I planned to be a surrogate. They were angry with me, had been since my London trip. Sonam had understood though.

"I didn't think you'd go through with it. You decided to rebel at the worst possible time," she said when I broke the news. "Have you considered how this will impact your life?"

I'd thought of little else. And I couldn't drum up even one ounce of regret. I felt only joy for these babies. A lifetime's worth of it.

I'd become so carefree living in New York that I stopped looking over my shoulder. My mistake.

I'd expected Vinay Singhal to make an appearance in the Big Apple and harass me since I'd landed, and I'd wondered at odd moments why he hadn't.

About a month after my parents' visit, I walked home from Whole Foods, carrying two bags of groceries that would last me three days, unless I ended up cooking for Neal. Usually Neal or Ian helped me carry the bags up to the apartment—they sometimes even helped me carry them home from the store—but, the bar was shut on Mondays, so Ian wasn't around. And Neal was at the Diamond District today looking for twelve carats of yellow single-cut melee diamonds for a new design.

Later, I'd wonder if Vinay had known I'd be alone.

I let myself into the building and dragged myself up the two flights of stairs slowly, carefully. On the landing outside Liam's flat, I transferred the grocery bags to one hand—they weren't heavy—and pulled the keys out of my crossbody bag. I was in a hurry to get inside and use the loo. I always seemed to want to pee these days. Maybe that was why I didn't notice that someone had stepped up behind me. I pushed the heavy wooden door open with my shoulder as I fumbled to remove the key—not an easy task one-handed—and before I knew it, someone had reached out and unburdened me of both the grocery bags.

"Oh, thanks!" I said absently, busy grappling with the key, which always seemed to stick while I tried to pull it out of the keyhole. I didn't bother to look over my shoulder. It didn't occur to me to worry or wonder about the person standing behind me. I was so used to Neal and any number of men doing gentlemanly things for me since I got pregnant that I'd started to take it as my due. By the time I looked back and saw Vinay, it was too late. My gut had warned me too late.

"What...what are you doing here?" I stammered out, my

smile dying. Before I could even think to slam the door in his face and bolt it, he stuck his foot in the jamb.

"Some fellow with purple hair let me in downstairs when I told him I knew you," Vinay replied, his smile oily and fake.

That would be Kirk, one of the tenants on the first floor. Kirk was a successful musician but a space cadet most of the time. He lived inside his tunes.

"So why weren't you waiting in front of my door? Why sneak up behind me like this?" I refused to step back and let him into the house.

He shrugged, smirking.

I knew very well why he'd lurked in the shadows on one of the floors below me. Vinay loved to play mind games. I thought about kneeing him in the balls and running down the stairs and out of the building, but that was just stupid. What if I fell down the stairs and hurt the bairns? Besides, he wasn't going to murder me right here and now.

Oh, for God's sake. He wasn't going to murder me anywhere. If he killed me, the trust money would automatically go to Kaivan's family and that wasn't his goal.

I needed to pee. *Shit*.

He ran his disgusting eyes up and down my body. I was wearing a knee-length waistless summer dress in lime green, and I felt completely creeped out.

He was loathsome. How had my sister tolerated him for fifteen years?

I wondered if it would be better if I went into the bathroom and peed, and came out wearing body armor.

As I mentally debated my next words or move, Vinay began to squeeze his arm through the door gap, as if to hand the grocery bags to me. I had half a mind of telling him to leave the bags on the landing, but I'd have to deal with him sometime, so why not now?

"Thank you," I said, taking the bags from him and setting them on the foyer bench. Of course, as soon as I turned my back to him, he slipped inside the door. He left it ajar though. Thank God for small mercies.

Vinay was not a bad-looking man, really, his ugliness came from his character. Though, he was short and had developed the paunch most Marwari men sprouted sooner or later. My father had one, and so had Kaivan once he'd crossed thirty. Though, his paunch had disappeared after his arrest and incarceration. Thanks to the man standing in front of me now.

Vinay's nasty black eyes flickered disdainfully over Liam's living room. "This is where Fraser puts you up? In this hole?" He gave another one of his oily smiles. "I would've treated you like a queen. You should have told me you desired a child. I would have given you one. With relish."

"Get out." I wanted to shove him out but I'd have to touch him for that. I felt an unholy rage bubble up at what he insinuated. Ugly, asshole, paunchy bastard.

"Believe me, I don't want to stay any more than you want me to. As soon as you give me the money, I'll go."

"I can't break the trust. I've told you this over and over. *You* spoke to Mr. Weinberg. You know it's irrevocable," I lied. I'd already broken it, taken half the funds and invested them in Fraser Bespoke.

He sighed long and noisily as if irritated by my answer. As if he knew it was a lie.

I stiffened. *He knew.* How? This wasn't India. People weren't so easily bribed here. How had he gotten the information out of whoever it was at the Weinberg Law Firm, or had it been the insurance agent?

Still, I said, "I'm not going to dance to your tune anymore."

His bushy eyebrows shot up to his forehead. I'd never stood

up to him like this. I'd always been respectful or cowering be-fore. "If you don't, I'm afraid I'll have to tell people the truth."

I was so sick of his threats. If he wanted to tell, he'd have done so already. "So tell."

"Are you sure you want to go to jail?" He dropped his nasty eyes to my stomach.

I stared at his round, thick face, trying to glean if he was bluffing.

Suddenly, he rubbed a hand over his face. "Look. I'm tired of this game and so are you. I tried to do this gently, but you won't listen. Let me be blunt then. I need the money. There, I'm telling you the truth. I need it or I'll lose everything too, and your sister and your nephews will be out on the street. I know you don't want that. Just give me the money and I'll leave you alone. If you don't, I'll make sure everyone knows what you and Kaivan did—the police, the insurance compa-nies, even the Frasers. You won't seem so innocent then, will you? And your friend? The prosecutor? What do you think she'll say, huh?"

I was shaking hard by then. He knew everything. *Dear God.*

And…and was he lying about his business? He had to be lying. I hadn't heard anything about the Singhals being in trouble.

"You will hand over the money to me. Right, *choti*?" He used my pet name as if he had a right to call me what my family did. "Once you do, you'll be free of me." He waved a hand in front of my face when I didn't answer. "Understood? I'm here for a couple of days. Let's sort this out."

Vinay walked out of Liam's apartment, shooting a trium-phant smirk over his shoulder as if he'd won. As if I'd cave.

That did it. I rushed out to the landing, unleashing my fury.

"Go to hell, Vinay! I am done being afraid of you," I yelled down the stairs without thought to the consequence.

My sister called in less than half an hour. Vinay hadn't wasted any time calling his wife to bitch about me. And rudely woken from her sleep or no, Sarika had immediately hopped to do her husband's bidding.

"We are your family, *choti*. You seem to have forgotten that."

I couldn't help but laugh at her. "Did I forget or did you? Does family bully and scare and slander and steal?"

No, family had nothing to do with blood and everything to do with love and support.

I told her about her husband's deeds without mincing words, without sparing any detail. We fought again, as always two opposing poles on earth.

"Vinay would never say that. You're lying," Sarika shrieked when I told her about his crack about "keeping me in luxury."

"Believe what you want. Be a fool. Just tell him to back the hell off or…" I cast about for a threat big enough to make Vinay Singhal quake in his boots. Ah. "Or I'll sic Deven Singh Fraser on him."

I wouldn't. I had to fight my own battles. But Sarika and Vinay didn't know that.

The threat backfired spectacularly.

Whether it was Vinay's unhinged vindictiveness or the thirst gossipmongers had for fake stories, within a week, most of the gutter rags in India were running these headlines: "Gemstone baron has love child with criminal Dalmia's widow."

That was one of the nicest ones.

I'd never been so ashamed of my family. Or so afraid.

CHAPTER NINETEEN

Paris

"It's the price of celebrity," said Neal, as if that explained the vile things that were being written and televised about us in India.

At first when the rumors started, I'd been both stunned and amused, equally, as I often was when Neal and, by default, I were mentioned in Indian media, or in Scotland, and sometimes in other parts of the world. Those stories didn't concern me because they had no bearing on our life in New York. Neal kept me updated about all the key events, past and present. I had the testimony from the horse's mouth—why did I need to look beyond it? It was a fact that the same piece of evidence could tell two different stories depending on who told it—the prosecution or the defense. And what the jury made of it was another matter altogether.

This was different. Weeks of disgusting rumors, morbid speculations and photoshopped tableaus ran the gamut from whether I was a "barren baroness" or if Naira was hiring out her womb to pay off her husband's substantial debts with Singh Fraser money, or whether Paris Fraser was in fact a transgender woman and therefore incapable of bearing children and... more shit like that. Most of it was too ridiculous to be taken seriously, but I was hooked. I couldn't stop watching the coverage, couldn't stop reading the headlines.

Then yesterday, a photograph of Neal and Naira entering Liam's building went viral. She was smiling up at him as he opened the door for her. She looked well and truly pregnant now, her belly protruding under her maternity jeans and sweatshirt. She'd put on weight. It looked good on her. And the bairns were growing in as healthy a fashion as possible for twins inside her. She'd been trying to get me to feel their movements, but I was resisting. I didn't want to touch her belly because then I'd be expected to gush and coo and pretend fascination. So, I didn't touch it. I had to listen to her describe the feeling—apparently it felt like passing gas—and that was gross enough.

Back to the photograph. Neal had his hand on Naira's back. He may or may not have been touching her, but it looked as if he was. And he looked so happy as he looked down at her. They both looked happy and contented. Like a couple who were expecting a child together.

And weren't they? No wonder the tabloids were having a field day.

"This one is not Photoshopped. And it's pretty damn clear it's from New York," I said, turning my computer to show Neal. We were in bed. I was itching for a fight and some angry sex.

"So they sent a paparazzo here. I dinna care." Neal flicked

the screen a glance and had the gall to look amused. "Ah, this was two days ago. I was telling the lass a joke Fiona sent about Scots and Sikhs. Do ye want to hear it?"

"I dinna care." I crossed my arms over my chest. "How are you okay with this?"

He laughed, giving a very Gallic shrug. "Ye cannot stop them from printing rubbish unless ye pay them off."

And of course paying off gossip rags to keep you out of their columns wasn't cheap. Did I want to waste money slamming down rumors that would die a natural death soon enough just so I could stop the burning in my *kishkes*?

"Try to keep your distance in public then," I said, then winced because—ugh—it made me sound fishwifey and jealous.

"Don't be ridiculous, hen. We work together."

"No, you don't. You—" I started to say, but he cut me off.

"Aye, we do. There are things she needs to run by me. We need to find office space. Store space. There's a million things to do until the launch. Until we have at least the core team in place, Naira and I *are* the core team. We're not traipsing all over town without reason, Paris." He sounded annoyed now.

Well, I was annoyed too but I didn't want to sound like a bitch so I let it go even though the photo did not look like they were working.

The witches of Macbeth didn't show any sympathy, either.

"You chose to tread an unconventional path, people are going to speculate. People always speculate about the Singh Frasers." Minnie seemed very proud of the fact. She and Deven were of the opinion that any publicity was good publicity.

It was useless to chastise Naira because she was in equal parts stricken about it, abjectly humiliated and severely apologetic.

"I didn't think Vinay would take it this far. Or, involve you and Neal."

I couldn't understand it, either. "Why would your own brother-in-law start such rumors? First he takes those paintings. Now this. This family feud is getting a little out of hand."

"A little?" Naira laughed unpleasantly.

"I think," I said, watching her rub her belly around and around and around. She'd developed acid reflux of late. Apparently, it was a common pregnant woman ailment. "You need to tell me everything. No holding back. No protecting your family or getting embarrassed. We need to figure out if there's any legal action we can take to stop him."

"We can't sue. It just doesn't work like that in India," she echoed Neal's sentiments after she'd spilled the whole tale, and cried buckets while telling it. "Also, Vinay and his cronies have already filed cases against me. If I sue him, it'll just turn into a he-said-she-said disaster that will go on for years." She sighed tiredly. "I don't know if he's really in trouble like he claims, or if it's just a ruse to gain control of my money. But irrespective of it, I can't give it to him. I won't."

"Of course, you can't give in to blackmail. Like ever." In that, we were in sync. Which meant I'd just have to go blind, deaf and dumb about the rumors.

Naira nodded, dabbing her eyes with a tissue. "Paris, there are things Kaivan has done, that I endorsed...some knowingly and some unknowingly...that you won't approve of. I can't tell you about it, but just trust me on it, okay? It's what Vinay is holding over my head. I'm sorry. It's my fault. It's all my fault."

Well, shit. What was I supposed to say to that? Not for the first time it crossed my mind that I may have made a huge mistake with the Big Idea. In more ways than one.

A few days later, the gossip rags suddenly ceased their nasty speculations and overnight we became old news. Neal had obviously seen the light after our conversation and shut the rumors down. I took it as a sign that we both were on the same page and the same side again, until he dropped another bomb between us. During Sunday brunch of all days!

Lily and Rachel arrived wearing the frozen smiles of the recently Botoxed. Naira cooked while we showed them the most recent 3-D ultrasound pictures of the twins. The Merry Widows of White Plains were beside themselves that the family would be blessed with another set of twins. There was much hugging and tearing up, and rolling of my eyes heavenward. Then there was gushing over Naira's cooking. She had Lily and Rachel eating out of her hands both literally and figuratively.

"This is delicious. What's it called again? And you made it from scratch? No, really?"

"It isn't that great," I mumbled around a mouthful of *pav bhaji*, which was nothing but mashed vegetables on toast. All right. The dish wasn't that simplistic, but it wasn't fancy, either.

Overjoyed that she'd found two more foodies at the table, Naira bounced around serving seconds—and in Neal's case third helpings—to everyone.

"Be careful with the masala food," I warned the old ladies. "You don't want heartburn." But who listened to me anymore?

The conversation at the table leaped from bairns to brunch menus at baby showers to Fraser Bespoke. Naira and Neal babbled on and on about what was going on with the stores. They'd narrowed down retail spaces, vendors, collaborating brands…*blah blah blah*.

Naira and Lavinia had decided to have their combined baby shower at my apartment—they had gone over my head and asked Neal, and he'd agreed it was a good idea since I was the one who wanted to conserve costs. Drat it all. So now, I was officially the baby shower host. However, I'd made it clear I didn't want anything to do with the planning and/or prepping. And it was their demise if they asked me to choose between Bun-in-the-Oven burgers and Who-Baked-My-Potato jackets.

Are you getting the picture? Suddenly, being the crusader of justice wasn't as big of a deal as being a domestic *balabusta* who cooked and sanctioned rabid consumerism while baking twins in her tummy, altruistically for her best friend, and still found time to plan and execute her own baby shower. I felt so inadequate all of a sudden that I decided right then that I'd increase my caseload and volunteer at RiM every single evening for the rest of my life. At least that way I'd be spared the aggravations of coming home to domestic scenes such as this.

Abject inadequacy was not a good look on me.

And that was when my husband did his shifty-eye business where he was sort of looking at me and yet was not, setting off a red alert in my gut. *Danger, danger. You will not like what he says next so shut your ears!*

"I'm thinking we should start house hunting, aye? Somewhere within easy commute of the city, so ye can get to work without trouble. Perhaps one of those quaint little towns in Westchester County? Ye'd like that too, won't ye, Lily? If we moved a bit closer?"

Lily would *loooove* that. Me? I was about to blow a gasket.

At first, I thought he was being funny. Then he spoke about how bairns needed space to run amok like he and his siblings had on the Riverhead Estate.

"To be honest, I wouldn't mind tromping through the heather myself. My creativity is getting stifled in the city. There's no room to breathe here. We can get some dogs." He paused to wink at me roguishly. "Some sheep."

What? Since when did he feel stifled?

"Can you imagine me on a farm in the boondocks? Ha, ha, ha!" I fake-laughed, praying damned hard that Neal was kidding.

Naira seemed as dumbstruck as I was. I was gratified by her reaction. She knew me. She knew that planting a hard-core city girl like me in the middle of nowhere was nothing short of a disaster of epic proportions. But Lily, who'd known me for twenty-odd years and had dealt with many of my issues firsthand, didn't think much of my bucolic woes.

"Thirty minutes out of the city is hardly a farm in Montana, Pari. Oh, I have an idea! What if you join the US Attorney's Office in White Plains instead of the Southern District of New York? Speak to Rina Wesley, *bubbala*. She's the state attorney general and my good friend," Lily explained, sotto voce, to the table at large. "I'm sure she knows if there's a position available for an assistant US Attorney. It would save you a long commute and allow you more time at home with your family," she finished happily, her Botoxed face shimmering.

Neal's eyebrows had shot up at the beginning of Lily's speech, but now he frowned at me accusingly. Oops. I still hadn't told him of the job offer. And when was I supposed to have told him? In between tabloid drama and baby shower madness? We waited until everyone had left before having a full-blown fight.

"Why didn't ye tell me about the new job?"

"I've just applied. I may not get it. And when should I have told you? When you're flying all over the world? Or when you're running amok deciding our future? Deciding where we will live? How many dogs we'll have? You better have been joking about the sheep."

"Ye had to know this was coming. This place was temporary, to wet our feet. I need more space. I can't have my office here and a studio somewhere else. It doesna work like that for me." He stalked into the kitchen after clearing the dining table and took the sponge I was using to wipe the countertop from my hand and threw it in the sink.

He was in a temper, was he? Well, so was I.

I washed my hands under the single handle faucet. "So get a bigger apartment in the city. It's not like you can't afford it."

"Paris, we're having twins. We need space." He threw his arms out like Jesus Christ on a cross. "Lots of bloody outdoor space."

"At least, let them be born before disrupting our entire lives. Naira could just as easily…" I bit my tongue before saying what I'd been about to.

But Neal heard my unspoken words anyway. He took a step back from me, his eyes wild. Shocked. Afraid.

"Ye want her to lose the…?" He broke off too, unable to voice the horror.

Did I want that? I knew only that I'd started something and now I wasn't sure I wanted it anymore.

"No. Never. I don't want her to miscarry. God, I'm not cruel. But I've been thinking…a lot since I was approached for the AUSA position. I've been thinking that if I do apply, and I do get it, it would mean longer working hours. Some travel. Plus, I want to commit to this project with Right is Might. And bloody hell, domestic situations should not be the reason I either choose or not choose a job. I have goals, Neal. Just as you do. Why am I expected to give mine up when I don't even want children?"

"I'm not asking ye to give up anything," he said gruffly. He was looking at me as if he'd never seen me before.

I sniffed. "Really? Let's say we move to this wonderful fairy-tale castle in Westchester. You travel all the freaking time. Some months, you're gone for two to three weeks because you have events and shows back-to-back. Who will have to take care of that castle when its master is rubbing shoulders with celebrities? Me. Who will be taking care of your bairns when they have colic and…and chicken pox? Me. Who will have to set her job aside to do all of that? Me." I poked a finger into my chest to emphasize every point I made.

Oh, he did not like my tone at all. Neal drew himself up to his full six-foot-two-inch height and looked down his nose at me.

"No, lass. Ye willna have to change anything in yer life. If I'm not around, Naira will be. If she's not around, then the baby nurse will be there, as ye so thoughtfully jotted down in the agreements. And if neither of them are around, I'll hire a goddamn au pair…five of them…but yer schedule will no' get disrupted." His Scots always got broad when he was angry.

He stalked off into his office, and I was left standing alone in the kitchen, wondering what I'd just done. By three in the morning, when Neal hadn't come to bed, I realized he wasn't going to apologize this time. And we weren't going to have out of this world makeup sex. And that freaked me out almost as badly as being saddled with a goddamned castle in Westchester.

CHAPTER TWENTY

Naira

Lavinia and I began to spend a lot of time together. The baby shower loomed just a little over three weeks away, and we had plenty of details to finesse, from final menu to favors to shopping for decorations and paper goods. It all went quickly and without arguments as we were mostly on the same page about things. Karen came along sometimes. She'd stepped into the role of a semi-doula for us as she'd been through all of it so recently, and all her recommendations had been on point so far. An added bonus was her five-month-old baby, Thomas, who was simply a joy to be around.

The outings were such a marked difference from the time I spent with Paris, who seemed to have forgotten how to smile. Still, I felt it was my duty to ask her—even force her to come with us whenever possible. I was the one pregnant with whacked-out hormones. I was the one who was supposed to have highs and lows, but for some reason, I was experiencing all the highs since my second trimester, and Paris all the lows. I was getting very tired of her constant grouchiness.

That evening was the same. She came into the party goods shop with a frown and it hadn't lifted from her face even once. Clearly, I was a masochist for trying so hard.

We didn't know the twins' sexes, and neither did Lavinia—by choice—so the shower had to have a neutral color palette by default. We were debating between dotted or striped ribbon for the favors when I felt a distinct quickening in my belly. My babies were waking up. I laughed because the whole experience was just so wonderful, so amazing every time they somersaulted inside me.

I rubbed my belly in soothing circles. "Hello, my little dancers. Do you have a preference between dotted or striped?"

I'd begun talking to them. So had Neal. But not Paris.

"They're dancing, huh?" Lavinia smiled the smile of a Madonna.

She was a little over twenty-four weeks pregnant, while I was exactly halfway through my gestation at twenty weeks. She'd been feeling movements for a lot longer than me.

I nodded happily. Then I looked at Paris, felt a flash of irritation. She stood away from us in a section of the baby store where dozens of baby mobiles were on display. But was she looking at them? No. She was tapping away into her phone. Here and not here at all. I wanted to shake her. I wanted to take her hand and place it on my belly. But I knew she wouldn't like it.

I pushed back from the ribbon-strewn table and stalked—erm, waddled to her. I was determined to break through her nonsensical kid-repellent theory. She wasn't even making an effort to change. I grabbed her hand and pressed it against my belly. Of course, she snatched it back as if she'd been burned.

"They're playing inside. Feel how amazing it is." I reached for her hand again.

"What the hell, Naira?" she growled, hiding her hands behind her back like a naughty little girl.

I snapped. "What is the matter with you? You can't be as disinterested as you're pretending to be. You are going to be a mother whether you like it or not. You have to get past your issues, Paris. We... You have two beautiful babies on the way. Your life is no longer your own."

Karen and Lavinia rushed up to us. They'd been doing a lot of refereeing.

"Calm down, you two," Lavinia ordered.

"I am calm. She's the one who's got a bee in her bonnet." Paris stared daggers at me.

I was breathing hard. My stomach felt tight. Upset.

"Naira, take a deep, deep breath in. And a long, long breath out. Modulate your breath like Linda showed us. *Reeelax*." Linda was our prenatal yoga and Lamaze coach.

I did my deep and long yoga breathing, wondering why I was trying so hard when Paris just didn't care a whit. And why should I feel guilty for caring too much? Enjoying the pregnancy too much?

It was good I was there for our babies, and that Neal was so insanely excited about them. It would have to be enough.

In the taxi on the way home, Paris turned to me. "You told me once that you'd rather do something you didn't like and bitch about it, than not do it at all and drown in guilt and regret forever. Do you remember?"

I frowned, remembering. It was when my father had forced me to go all the way to Queens to attend a religious function hosted by some person he barely knew at the Hindu temple. It had been on an evening before a major test. *Nothing is more important than our standing in the community. Certainly, not your silly tests or degree.*

I'd gone to keep the peace. Paris hadn't understood why I wouldn't defy my father. Why I gave in to him so much. To me, my father had fulfilled my ultimate dream by allowing me to come to New York to study. The rest I could and would deal with. "Garnished with a pinch of bitching," I'd added cheekily.

"This is me bitching," Paris said now.

I couldn't believe she believed the two situations were similar.

But, she'd been right about the kid-repellent theory. Twice I forced her to touch my belly when the twins performed womb acrobatics and both times as soon as she did, they would go quiet.

I needn't have worried about any external pressures from Vinay Singhal or the media affecting my health. My own body became a threat to the babies.

I was already big by the time my sixth month rolled in. I was carrying twins who seemed intent on emulating their tall father and curvy mother in terms of size and weight. Moving about was getting a wee bit difficult, and I'd been restricted to climbing the two flights up to Liam's flat to just once a day. So, I began to spend my afternoons at Paris and Neal's.

That day, I had an urge to eat *moong daal shira*, a sweet dish that took a long time to cook as you had to slowly roast and stir the split green grains in a skillet until it smelled just right. My craving for sweet hadn't abated at all despite the *laddoos* I was eating. Halfway through the cooking, I felt a twinge in my abdomen. I didn't brush it off as gas because I'd felt something like it when I'd miscarried. The next spasm, which came ten minutes later while I was on the phone with the doctor, was worse. Far worse.

Dr. Kapoor told me to stay calm and that it was probably the Braxton Hicks contractions, but I should drop by the clinic just in case. I called Paris but she didn't pick up. She was in court. Neal wasn't at home, either. He was in midtown, meeting a client who wanted an engagement ring designed, but he picked up the phone on the first ring. I told him not to come back to pick me up as he was already in the vicinity of Dr. Kapoor's clinic.

He met me below the building as I got out of the taxi, his lips white, his blue eyes awash in panic. I burst into tears then. I'd been holding it together only because I'd been alone, and the babies were depending on me to be sensible.

"I'm sorry. I'm sorry," I kept apologizing, but I didn't know to whom. To Neal or the babies or to the universe in general for the many bad things I'd done? But I was trying to atone. How could karma punish the babies for my mistakes?

I gasped when the pain intensified as Dr. Kapoor pressed my belly with one hand while running an ultrasound probe over it with another. I closed my eyes and practiced the Lamaze breathing. Deep breath in. Long breath out. It did not bloody work! I began to pant.

Linda and my yoga master in Mumbai were going to be so mad that I'd forgotten how to breathe.

"One of the baby's feet is pressing against your kidney. Room is getting tight in there, and the munchkins are fighting for space. See there? They can move their legs now. Stretch out. Kick around. They're a little bigger and heavier than a good-sized cauliflower right now. Perfect," she continued to give us a breakdown, sounding extremely pleased, and not worried at all.

I let out a long groan with the breath I'd been holding.

"If you have trouble going to the bathroom, let me know immediately. We might have to coax the foot away. Other than that, just rest. Try to stay off your feet until the pressure eases off. Then you can resume your regular exercise and activities. Sometimes, getting on all fours in a cat or camel pose, or lying down on your side, will ease the pressure. Sit on a chair or a balance ball and gently rotate your hips in figure eights. Also, massaging her lower back will help." She said that to Neal.

With those instructions tucked into his head, Neal took me home. To his and Paris's home. "Yer not sleeping at Liam's anymore. Yer moving in with us. And no more cooking or anything. We'll get someone to come in and cook Indian food for you. No more eating out."

I was in no state to argue because right that minute the pressure on my kidney was making me light-headed. And too right, I wanted to be pampered. I wanted my mother. I wanted not to remember my own baby. I wanted not to cry.

Ignoring my wants, tears dropped down my cheeks as my whole body became one giant ball of hurt.

"I'm sorry." I'd conned this lovely man into trusting me when I had bad karma. Bad mojo. I couldn't carry one baby to term, how would I manage two?

He made me sit on the foyer bench, hunkering down in front of me to take off my slip-on sneakers. "Quiet, now. Nothing is wrong. Dr. Kapoor said so, aye?"

I wiped my face, but the tears wouldn't stop. I wasn't even crying anymore. "I'm sorry."

He brought me water, and I drank half a glass like Dr. Kapoor had instructed, so I'd pee. Then Neal helped me up and into his bedroom.

"Here?" I asked, shocked as he flipped the covers and helped me lie down on my side. Shudders racked my body as if I had the flu.

"There's more room in here and the bathroom is closer. And—" he waggled the remote, smiling "—there's no TV in the guest room."

Good point. Still, it was weird sleeping on their bed. It felt too intimate.

Then I promptly forgot my discomfort and worry when he switched on a Bollywood comedy for me. I loved *bhankas* movies. They cracked me up, and within minutes I was smiling if not laughing outright. Neal got into bed next to me, his knuckles kneading my back. It felt so good. I was pretty sure he was trying to hypnotize me through my spinal cord.

The combination of slapstick humor and a soothing massage began to work its magic. And the babies loved my reaction to the antics of Varun Dhawan and Shah Rukh Khan on the screen. My stomach went taut like a drum under the blanket. Then it heaved and settled, heaved and settled, as my two starlings began to perform their own item song.

Neal was fascinated. "What does it feel like? Does it hurt?"

"No. It feels peculiar. Surprising. Miraculous," I said, breathing exactly as Linda wanted me to. Relaxation breaths.

"May I?" he asked, and when I nodded, he placed his hands on me, gently, so reverently. He always, always asked for permission before touching my stomach. And he always, always wanted to touch. Unlike Paris.

Tears pearled in the corners of my eyes again, but I welcomed them this time. I wasn't ashamed of them this time. They were happy tears.

"They're safe," I promised. Or they would be once I did what I had to. I'd been selfish and foolish about so many things of late, and I couldn't afford to ignore it anymore.

The twins seemed to like the direction of my thoughts as they began to perform gymnastics in my womb. Perhaps to show off for their father. "They're dancing. Can you feel it?"

"Aye. Aye, they are." Neal smiled at me in wonder and gratitude.

Paris was truly crazy to be missing out on this, I thought, as I closed my eyes and gave in to pure joy.

CHAPTER TWENTY-ONE

Paris

I sprang out of the taxi even before it screeched to a halt in front of Liam's Bar. I ran into the building, clattered up the stairs, cursing myself for ignoring my messages all afternoon.

Phones had to be switched off in court. But court had ended at four, and then I'd simply forgotten to switch on my personal cell as I headed to RiM.

No, not forgotten. I'd purposely left it switched off because I didn't want to see cutesy baby memes, or messages from Naira about the joys of pregnancy and all that rubbish. Stupid, so stupid of me.

When I finally got around to checking messages, the fear that had choked me—God, I never wanted to feel like that again. Three messages from Naira about twinges in her lower back, then pain and contractions, and a dozen from Neal. The last one from him was brutal. And unfair.

In case you begin to care. She's all right. I'm taking her home.

Of course, I cared. I wasn't heartless. How dare he suggest otherwise, the absolute jackass. Just because I wasn't good at emoting or blabbing nonstop about whatever, didn't mean I didn't feel things. I felt everything—the pain, the apprehension. It was a constant knot between my breasts these days. I was scared stiff for Naira and the bairns. How could he not know that? When had he stopped reading my mind?

I pressed the buzzer on Naira's apartment, fighting to catch my breath. I'd stopped thinking of it as Liam's for a while now, though Naira insisted on calling it Liam's flat. Her reluctance to get attached to the flat was the same thing I was doing with the bairns. There was no guarantee that they'd like me or I'd like them. What if I repelled them? They didn't like it when I touched Naira's belly, did they?

God, it was complicated what I felt. What I didn't feel. What I didn't wish to feel. That was why I wasn't saying anything, doing anything. I didn't want to say the wrong bloody thing.

Were they fine? All three of them? I pressed the buzzer again and beat my fist on the door when no one came to open it. No movement inside, either. I called my husband again. He wouldn't have left her alone. He'd be inside. He didn't pick up the phone. Neither did Naira.

They were punishing me. I was sure of it. They were teaching me a lesson—one I was in no mood to appreciate. I finally concluded that Neal "taking her home" meant our home. So, there I went, hating that instead of reducing, my panic increased. He'd only take her to our place if she wasn't okay. I didn't want to think of the worst, but I couldn't seem to help myself. This was why I didn't want to feel or invest my heart. Not yet. My mind raced from one tragic scenario to the next as another taxi took me home.

I raced inside the apartment, noticing that the living room was dark as I kicked off my shoes. I rushed into the guest bedroom and stopped short. It was dark and empty too. I looked around in confusion. Checked my messages again, wondering if they'd detoured to a hospital.

Had she gone into premature labor? *Oh, God.* It wouldn't be ideal for the bairns to come at twenty-three weeks, but it wasn't hopeless. Six-month preemies had a 76 percent survival rate. Apparently, those were good statistics to work with—if that was the case. But Dr. Kapoor had assured me that wasn't the case when I'd spoken to her a half hour ago. She'd said Naira had experienced what she called some "baby kicks," that was all.

I poked my head inside Neal's office. They weren't working.

By then, my gut had worked out where my husband and best friend were, but my brain refused to consider it. So, I stalled. I went into the kitchen, drank some water. I cleaned the mess Naira had left in the kitchen from the cooking. She was always cooking. I put away pots and pans in the cabinets, hoping Neal would hear the clatter and come out. But he didn't.

He was angry. I got that. He'd been angry with me for a while. I knew that too. But I didn't know how to make him understand. How to make it right between us again. And I was angry too. Angry that loving him was turning me into a crazy person.

After I'd given him plenty of time to come to me, I squared my shoulders and walked into my room. If the Indian paparazzo saw them now, forget the gutter-rags, even the *Times of India* would make them into a headline.

They were both asleep on my bed, spooning. My husband had his arm curved around my best friend, his hand on her stomach that moved up and down as if it were alive. It was, wasn't it? I stared in fascination and terror.

I refused to acknowledge how much it hurt to see them like that on my bed.

I switched off the TV, which was playing a stupid Bollywood movie that I'd never understand or ever watch. They had that in common too, a perverse attraction to senseless comedies. They were like two peas in a pod.

Dr. Barr said it was natural to feel jealous in a situation like ours, and frankly it would be impossible not to. I wasn't jealous of Naira, I told him. There was nothing to be jealous about because nothing was going on or ever would go on between her and Neal. I trusted them both in that. Dr. Barr had given me a long, quiet look. "I didn't mean her. I meant the babies."

As usual, he was right.

Was I competing for my husband's affections with the babies? I was, wasn't I? His love for them was unconditional. Unlike his love for me.

I sank down on the bed next to Neal. I had to touch him. I needed reassurance, and I hated myself for it. I flattened my hand over his heart—my heart. *Mine.*

He rolled onto his back, mumbling an endearment in Gaelic in his sleep. Was it for me? For the bairns? Or for Naira, the mother of his precious bairns?

Ugh. What was I thinking? Why was I so abnormal? Seriously, who in their right minds would trust me with kids? I couldn't even be trusted with adults.

Blue-blue eyes blinked owlishly at me as his lips kicked up in a slow, sexy, utterly heart-stopping smile.

"Yer home," he mumbled sleepily. Then he curved his body into me and buried his face in my lap.

"Yes. I'm home." I sighed helplessly, kissing the whorls of dark hair on top of his head.

The foot-in-the-kidney incident triggered several changes in our daily life.

Naira moved in with us. I started coming straight home from work, putting a pause on my volunteer nights at RiM. I only went in if it was urgent, and if I was the only human rights consultant they could tag. The days I had to stay till late at work—sometimes until midnight for the task force—I checked my messages without fail, and stepped out periodically to call home, and I didn't care who or what I interrupted or pissed off while doing it. I hadn't withdrawn my application for the assistant US Attorney position, but if they gave me trouble about not putting work first, I would. I'd lost interest in any cutthroat competitions anyway.

Things with Lily were better in a way and weirder too since her revelation about her daughter. Every time we spoke, she told me a little more about Jessica Kahn. It was a new low for me, being jealous of a dead girl.

Jealousy covered most aspects of my life these days. I resented Neal for lavishing attention on Naira, and through her the bairns. I couldn't take it when he hopped about taking care of her, granting her every wish and whim, so I made jokes. Not that Naira demanded anything an enormously pregnant woman wouldn't. At least, I didn't think so. But what did I know of the needs of pregnant women? As Minnie was fond of pointing out.

Minnie and Anjum Manral had come to New York after the Braxton Hicks scare. We'd canceled the baby shower—Naira's half of it because she had become superstitious about it. We moved Lavinia's shower to Karen's apartment, and I gave her a big-ass baby gift for all the ruckus and upheaval we'd caused.

The moms had planned a low-key seventh-month baby blessing ceremony, which was more or less a baby shower but with cultural context. That both Naira and I were considered the mothers-to-be had thrown the moms for a loop for about half a day. They'd regrouped and decided that the main blessing would be done on Naira as the ritual was mainly for the protection of the mother and child during gestation and for a safe labor. Clearly, I wasn't at any risk, having played my part of the hen laying the egg, so I was asked to step aside.

I did so gladly. Wasn't a ritual blessing just a placebo like a horoscope? It was highly doubtful that some red-and-orange threads tied around Naira's right wrist would protect her and the baby in some mystical way.

"What about protection for after? Once they've popped out," I asked, genuinely curious. "It's equally hazardous raising children. At least, in there, they're protected by a mother's body and antigens. In the outside world, any number of things could go wrong, healthwise and otherwise."

I was told to shush and not mock age-old customs.

Neal winked at me from across the room. He'd been ordered to stand behind Naira as her guardian angel. He looked the part too, decked out in traditional Indian finery. Everyone was wearing glittery clothes—the moms had insisted the function was as important as a wedding. Even the apartment smelled like a flower shop with garlands of white jasmine tumbling down from the walls and adorning the tops of doors.

Helen and I were asked to pour fistfuls of rice into the sari-clad hollow of Naira's lap as she sat without back support on a low silver stool, facing some random auspicious direction in the middle of the living room. Dev was made to soak his palms in sandalwood paste and press them against Naira's cheeks.

He'd done the same thing to me at one of the ceremonies at my wedding, leaving a yellowish imprint of his hands on my face. He'd looked infinitely happier doing it to me.

I'd parked my tush on a bar stool after I'd done my bit to watch and comment on the goings-on from a distance. Dev came into the kitchen to wash the sandalwood paste off his hands.

"Inquiring minds want to know if you're going to pursue my bestie on a personal level, once she's done with..." I waved a hand, indicating the pregnancy madness going on in my living room.

It was sad Naira and Dev had become a tad awkward around each other of late. But I had high hopes for them.

"And how is it anyone's business?" Dev wiped his hands on a towel.

Then their love life—or lack of one—took a back seat because the moms had arranged Neal and Naira to sit side by side while they performed more ritualistic crap around them.

"This custom celebrates the mother and father together— the giver of life and the sustainer of life," Anjum explained to Lily.

I did not like it. Not one bit. Naira kept shooting me flustered looks as if she too was uncomfortable with the whole thing. She even patted her side, inviting me to sit next to her so that we were all part of the ceremony. But I refused. It was all a bunch of hocus-pocus anyway.

As Helen explained, usually, the ceremony was on a much larger scale where dozens if not hundreds of women were invited to bear witness and give their blessings to the pregnant woman, who symbolized the goddess of fertility. Due to our outlandish circumstances, the moms had decided this one should be a private affair, just for the immediate family. Lily had been invited though, and she was in her element, dancing from one side of the room to another taking pictures and asking questions and exclaiming, *"Mazel tov!"* like a broken record.

Finally, it was done. Neal rose to his feet and beckoned me over. From behind the coffee table, he brought out two identical velvet jewelry boxes tied in a profusion of curly ribbons and bows. The one in gold ribbons he handed to me with a peck on my lips. Then, with a mischievous flourish that made the moms beam, he handed the silver-ribbon box to Naira, bussing a kiss on her head for luck. If his lips lingered a beat too long on her forehead, I told myself I'd imagined it.

I put a stone over my heart and opened my box. He'd fashioned a custom case for my phone using a kind of metal and plastic alloy. On the back was a textured golden basket full of eggs—yes, the symbolism did not escape me. The belly was engraved with the date of my egg retrieval and an *I Love You* woven into a Celtic infinity knot. Affection flooded my veins as I caressed his thoughtful and beautiful gift. I'd been looking for a new case for my phone. My husband hadn't forgotten how to read my mind or fulfill my desires. I turned to him, to hug him and kiss him, but I was a split second too late.

"I can't accept this!" Naira squealed like a cheerleader, tears ever ready to spill from her eyes.

She thrust the box back to Neal. She'd become big enough that she couldn't stand without help. She couldn't even sit without a struggle on a sofa, much less on a stool that barely supported her tush. She teetered on her seat, and Neal immediately knelt in front of her, closing his hands over hers.

"Ye can and ye will." He took out two diamond-studded bangles from the box, and slowly, carefully he slid one over her wrist, like he'd done for me a hundred times.

He'd made her matching bangles for the rose pendant, which she wore today with a traditional red-and-gold sari and a halter-neck blouse that seemed obscenely snug around her boobs. They'd ballooned like her ass. Dozens of stylized petals made of rose gold and diamonds had been bunched together to form a bangle and arranged to look as if they were strewn across her still dainty wrist.

The bangles were possibly worth a hundred thousand dollars each, at least, as they were a Neal Singh Fraser custom design. That was a lot of starving stomachs we could have fed. But for once I didn't get snarky. I couldn't look away from the tableau they made even though I wanted to, even though I should have. They looked so happy; weepy pregnant lady and an over-the-moon dad. They looked so *right* together.

"It's too much. They're beautiful. But I can't accept them." Naira looked at me a little desperately. Did she expect me to rescue her from my husband's largesse? Hadn't she realized that in this—the surrogacy, his fatherhood—I had no say left?

Neal took her other hand and slipped the second bangle up her wrist. I flinched when he bent his head and kissed the back of her hands, one by one.

"For the bairns," he said as if making her a promise of some kind.

The moms rained the appropriate accolades and cheers on the expectant couple.

"Naira, dear. You can't refuse a gift from the father. It would be *upshukan*—unlucky."

I rolled my eyes. "Guys, just quit all the drama. *Sheesh*. If I'd known surrogacy came with rituals and crap, I'd have gone for adoption," I joked, triggering looks of abject disapproval from everyone in the room, including chill-as-fuck Deven.

That stone over my heart turned into a stake, and I hammered it in deep until there was nothing left inside me that could bleed or hurt.

The moms stayed for another week, so I stayed at the office until late with impunity. I left all the bassinet versus crib decisions to whomever wanted to make them. I didn't care where they set them up, either—Naira's room, the living room or Neal's office, which was in the process of being remodeled into a nursery. As long as it wasn't my bedroom, I was good. Neal was right: we needed a bigger place.

Besides, I seemed to be making all the wrong decisions lately, so I decided to spare everyone more grief. I'd be where I was needed the most and where my skills mattered, where I could effect positive change in the world.

A couple of days after the baby blessing, Naira called just as I was wrapping up work.

"'Sup?" I said, putting my phone on speaker as I shrugged on my faux fur–lined raincoat. It had been pouring cats and dogs since morning, and the air had turned again. Summer was coming to an end.

"I need a favor. Can you stop by Liam's and get some of my clothes?"

"Sure. Text me what you need." I picked up my umbrella and handbag.

"Will do. And call me once you're there so I can tell you where everything is so you don't waste time."

Grinning, I clicked the phone off. Pregnancy hadn't affected Naira's OCD at all.

I set off for Liam's on foot. This time of the evening, walking was faster than hailing a cab and dodging through traffic. It was usually a nine-minute walk, which took me fifteen minutes in the rain. I left the wet umbrella in the bucket placed for such purposes in the building lobby, and began to climb the stairs up to the third floor. My mood lifted as I crossed the second-floor landing and my ears picked up what I'd come to think of as Fraser-speak—a combination of Gaelic, Hindi and

English that Neal and his siblings spoke—spilling down the stairs. Neal had moved his office to the studio in its entirety.

Why hadn't Naira tagged them to bring her clothes and spared me the wet schlep? I checked her text. Ah, Ms. Prude wanted underwear. That explained it. She would've died before asking the men to touch her panties.

"Did ye know she was related to Singhal?"

This had to be Deven. Sometimes, especially over the phone, I couldn't tell the brothers apart. They both had deep, gravelly voices and the same Scots accent. Which magically changed when they spoke in Punjabi. It was so weird.

"I didn't," was my husband's clipped reply. A sigh. "Thank ye for shutting down the gossip. I don't want her upset. Not in her condition."

I froze halfway between the second and third floors. He didn't want *her* upset? When I'd asked him to shut down the gossip, he'd refused. Clearly, he didn't care about my state of mind.

I lowered my right foot to the next step, careful not to make a sound.

"She's more trouble than either of us bargained for, aye?" Again Deven. And what exactly did he mean by that?

"Dinna draw banshees in the air," said my husband colorfully, sounding irritated now. Well, join the party!

Eavesdropping was never a good idea, it was tantamount to hearsay. I'd learned that the hard way from Jared and Sandy. And as recently illustrated, from the Judge and Lily, when I'd heard only the part about Lily being against my adoption and had drawn the wrong conclusion. And yet, knowing all that, I still did it.

"Am I? Ye know how ye are with damsels in distress. Ye cannot resist them. Dinna get involved." Deven again.

"And yer not *involved*?"

This was madness. I couldn't just stand here hyperventilating, trying to guess the meaning of that cryptic exchange. Either I went up and confronted them or I should leave.

I left, tiptoeing down the stairs as silently as possible. My heart was in my throat by the time I fetched my umbrella and scampered outside. Three streets away, I realized I'd run away without fetching Naira's clothes. I was a bloody fool.

I didn't ask Neal about the conversation. How could I without admitting I'd eavesdropped and then run away? Besides, I didn't want an explanation. I'd become that much of a coward.

In law, the more we knew the better it was. I didn't believe the same principle worked as well in life.

The moms left, promising a return closer to the due date in mid-November. Deven was also leaving soon. Good riddance. I hadn't been myself after overhearing the brothers, and I found myself trying to read between the lines of every conversation Neal and Deven had, or Neal and I had, or Naira and them or me, or any combination of the four of us.

I began to observe Neal and Naira surreptitiously, trying to catch them doing or saying anything untoward. I didn't doubt them—not in the way that they were cheating behind my back. That wasn't my concern no matter what those stupid articles claimed about men—especially domesticated men like Neal who thrived in familial situations—being attracted to pregnant women. Something to do with the pregnant female fulfilling their ultimate dream of carrying and continuing their bloodline. There was also some hypothesis about fertile women throwing off pheromones that inflamed the male protective instincts. Plus, most pregnant women, despite their rotund figures or because of it, became more attractive—rosy cheeked, healthier and bustier—everything a man wanted in his mate. Apparently.

Neal's protectiveness toward Naira was natural. But, more

and more, I noticed how much more suited they were as a couple than he and I were. From tastes to backgrounds to the way they'd been raised. They were on the same page about most core values like how to raise kids. They were the definition of square peg, square hole. They had so much in common. So many things clicked between them. And the only thing clicking between Neal and me was an intense physical attraction. Was it enough for a lifetime?

It had to be enough. It must be enough because even though they had everything in common, Neal did not look at her the way he looked at me with his sexy blue eyes. He did not laugh with her the way he laughed with me, intimately, huskily, or pull her into his lap for a sometimes desperate, sometimes honey-sweet kiss. He didn't flick her nose teasingly or lace his fingers through hers or do any of the heart-meltingly romantic things he did with me, for me. He loved me, enormously. I couldn't—wouldn't doubt it.

But the thing was, he liked her enormously too. The affection between them was pretty obvious. And how far down was the fall from like to love? From personal experience, I didn't think it was all that far at all.

So, short of banishing the mother of our children from my husband's presence, I did the only thing I could in such a situation. I protected my heart.

CHAPTER TWENTY-TWO

Naira

I hadn't forgotten the woodpeckers. How could I while they perched on my shoulders, pecking away at my conscience?

Vinay Singhal's visit had pushed me into making a decision I'd been putting off for sentimental reasons. I'd always known how to stop him. I just hadn't been ready to let go of my old life. Not completely.

James Weinberg hadn't been too excited about my plan, but it wasn't his decision in the end. The only thing left to do was to convince Deven to agree to the terms.

Deven and I spoke on the phone every day about Fraser Bespoke, but this was...personal. I tagged him a few days before he was booked to fly out. He was staying at 11 Howard, a boutique hotel close to Liam's place where our moms had stayed the past two weeks, since I occupied the guest room at the Spruce Street apartment. I invited him over for tea after making sure that Neal wouldn't be around all afternoon. Neal didn't need to be part of this conversation. Or Paris. Not unless Deven said no.

As we sat across from each other, it struck me that it was the first time since our ultrafabulous night on New Year's Eve that we were completely alone.

He studied my face with his piercing dark blue eyes for long enough that I had to fight not to squirm. God, he was always so intense.

I brushed off the crumbs of embarrassment I felt on top of feeling ungainly and clumsy about my increasing size. "I need another favor."

"What do you need?"

My heart ached just a little bit then. It was such a typical Kaivan question. *What do you need, baby? Ask and it shall be done.*

The only thing Deven didn't do was snap his fingers. Otherwise, he could've been Kaivan's twin in temperament.

I shook off the thought and concentrated on what needed to be done to secure my peace of mind. I'd also promised my mother I'd try to mend the rift in our family.

"Forgive them, *choti*. Be the bigger person," she'd beseeched me every day that she'd been here.

"But I haven't done anything wrong. Shouldn't Papa and Sarika apologize to me?" I'd half groaned, half whined as her fingers pressed into my scalp while she massaged olive oil into my hair—to nourish my roots and cool my head. Not that my roots needed any more nourishment. My hair had become extra thick and shiny because of the prescribed doses of pregnancy vitamins and minerals.

"Because you are sweet and smart and you'll never be happy if you don't."

But it wasn't so simple. Before forgiving anyone else, I had to first forgive myself and Kaivan.

I handed Deven a sheaf of papers that James Weinberg had drawn up for me, and asked him to go over them as I explained what I wished to do with my trust fund—the whole trust fund, including the half I'd used to buy my stake in Fraser Bespoke.

"I'm going to dissolve the trust. I've asked James to set up a college fund for Sarika's boys for half a million dollars." Just in case Vinay had been telling the truth about his business being in trouble. My mother hadn't been able to shed light on whether it was true or not.

"Do you see what I want to do?" I asked after Deven had gone over everything. "I'm sorry for changing my mind, but I'll be withdrawing my stake in your company. Except for the money set aside for my nephews, I want the entirety of my trust fund divided into two parts. One third will go into another trust for Kaivan's parents for any medical eventuality. It will have to be set up in the UK. James has referred a barrister to me, but I'd rather go with someone you know and trust. The remaining two-thirds I wish to donate to a few different organizations that support women and children in need. And I want you to be the executive trustee for all of it."

"You want to give away all your money?" He blinked twice, the only indication that he was surprised.

"Honestly, it'll be a relief. I don't want to be hassled anymore. Vinay—" I shrugged, letting out a huge sigh. "He'll leave me alone once he knows I don't have it. And I doubt he has the balls to go up against you to break the new trusts. That is, if you agree to become the trustee."

I prayed my plan was sound. That Vinay wasn't that desperate or stupid to fight Deven. But either way, I didn't want the insurance money. I should have given it away long ago, but I'd felt duty-bound to hold on to Kaivan's legacy. But my husband hadn't felt any such need to hold on to me, had he? He'd chosen to die rather than live with me penniless.

I could never forget him. I would always love him. But I couldn't be tied to Kaivan anymore.

"I understand I'm asking a lot from you."

"You want to give *all* of it away?" Deven asked again, his normally stoic face cracked with incredulity.

I'd shocked him. Well, well.

I grinned. "Yes. I have a job that pays very well. An executive expense account you have given me carte blanche on. I'm set, unless I get fired." Which, considering I was soon going to give birth to the next generation of Frasers, didn't seem likely.

I was doing this for the twins most of all, to keep them safe. I wanted a clean slate of karma for them. And this was the only way I knew how to atone for the woodpeckers, and for what my part had been in my husband's death. I didn't want to benefit from such an awful event.

"I want to be free, Deven. I came to New York to be free."

I didn't have to explain further. Deven understood, and agreed to oversee the disbursement of my funds as an executive trustee. The next day, we both went to the Weinberg Law Firm to make it official. And while we signed the stacks of papers James Weinberg pushed at us, I privately indulged in a wee B-town fantasy where I stormed into Sarika's house, clothes flapping, hair flying, and threw the papers in Vinay's face with a dramatic "Up yours" with matching hand gestures.

Clearly, I wasn't as sweet as my mother believed I was.

The peace inside my soul was everything. I felt so much love for my babies—yes, they were mine, and I was going to love them enormously because their biological mother was too pigheaded and stuck in her delusions to be sensible.

We fought again at our penultimate Lamaze class because

Paris refused to give even an inch, forget meeting me in the middle. Linda was showing us what to expect during contractions. Dr. Kapoor had discussed the various birthing methods with us, and I wanted it to be a natural birth unless there were complications. This class was important.

"With twins, it can mean a longer labor," said Linda kindly. "Breath is the way through it. Breathing in patterns will help control the discomfort and reduce stress." She sat down cross-legged on a yoga mat and demonstrated. "Place your hands on your abdomen, middle fingers touching over your belly button. Now inhale to the count of ten. Push your breath into your belly, let it expand. Hold your breath. Now exhale to the count of ten. Breathe in waves. Let your chest and shoulders be motionless. Engage only your breath and your belly. As you exhale, relax your lower abdomen muscles. Feel them go soft."

I followed Linda's instructions, felt my body go lax with every exhalation. After a couple of rounds of wave breathing, she made the birthing partners kneel behind the pregnant women to show them what they could do to alleviate anxiety during labor. Back rubs, shoulder rubs, acupressure points to lessen the pain.

"Put your arms around your partner and place your hands on their stomachs. Middle fingers meet over the belly button."

Of course, Paris balked.

I shot her an aggravated look over my shoulder, where she crouched on the yoga mat, supporting my back. "Enough. Either step up to the plate, or let someone else be my birthing partner. You know what? I don't need a birthing partner. My mom will be there, and she'll be enough."

I turned back to face the class, envying all the women leaning solidly against their spouses and partners.

She had everything magical in life. Why did she insist on holding on to the negative?

I twisted around to face Paris again, suddenly furious. "Just what are you afraid of? I get that life hasn't been kind to you. But name one person who hasn't suffered something."

No, I would not think of Kaivan. I would not miss him. I would not feel guilty because I was having fun or was moving on without him.

Did I wish for a different life? Did I imagine that the babies I carried were mine and his, and not Paris and Neal's?

A million, trillion times a day.

"Life isn't kind to anyone, Paris. But it will be for these babies. I'll accept nothing less for them. Okay?"

Damn it. If she didn't drop her cyborg act soon, I…simply wouldn't allow her near the babies.

Paris made a frustrated sound inside her throat, but instead of snarling back, she crawled closer and brought her hands around me to rest them on my stomach. I was surprised at her capitulation. Thrilled.

I began to breathe and relax, following Linda's instructions and letting my stomach tighten and soften, simulating labor. With every exhalation, I began to lean farther and farther back against Paris. She began to relax too, our breaths synchronizing. Suddenly, my stomach heaved on its own, and Paris sucked in a shocked gasp. I tensed, expecting her to cringe or snatch her hands away. She didn't.

"No," she breathed into my ear. "Don't tense up. It's… They're moving. They are moving in there. I can feel them."

The wonder, the absolute awe in her words melted my angst. It was going to be okay. We were all going to be okay.

I cried then. She did too, when no one was looking.

I was wrong about us being okay.

On the following Saturday afternoon, Neal and I vegetated in front of the living room TV while Paris worked on something for RiM at the dining table. She had noise-canceling headphones on because we were being too loud for her to think. I challenged anyone to watch *Three's Company*—the original version with Jack, Janet and Chrissy—and not ROLF like crazy every other minute.

I wanted to spend all my weekends like this for the rest of my life—chilling at home with the family we'd created. I imagined two fat toddlers running around us in circles, adding to the hilarity and happiness.

Neal poked my waist. Normally, I was ticklish and would have jumped at his touch. But my expanded waistline kept sudden movements in check. When I looked at him, he jerked his square chin toward Paris, whose head was buried inside her computer. Her back was hunched and she really, truly looked miserable.

"I think she's been at it long enough. Let's go bother her," he mock-whispered in my ear as though Paris could hear us through her headphones.

I adored him the most when he was playful. I loved how he teased his wife, and I loved being his sidekick on such missions.

He hauled me up from the sofa, steadying me until my feet found their balance beneath my whalelike stomach. He switched off the TV and turned on the music dock, shuffling his party playlist, the volume high enough that my heart began dancing in reflex. My hips jiggled side to side gently, like I'd been taught in Lamaze. Catching the jungle rhythm himself, Neal began to bebop toward Paris. I waddled behind him, jerking my face and hands forward and back "like an Egyptian."

We circled the table once before she glanced up, her expression droll. "You both look insane."

But I could tell she was trying hard not to smile.

I raised my arms in the air and twerked—well, tried to.

Neal was vigorously thrusting his arms, hips, chest, just a wee bit offbeat. He really had no sense of rhythm. I giggled, watching him. These days I giggled with my whole body.

Paris removed the headphones, threw them on the table. But she didn't get up. She picked up her wineglass and nodded. "All right. Dance for me."

So, we danced around her chair, around the table. After a song or two, Neal yanked her up and tugged her into the living room, wineglass and all. He refilled her glass, refilled my mug of ginger tea and his tumbler of scotch. Then he sat in the middle of the sofa and stretched his muscular legs out on the coffee table in front of him. Rihanna's "Diamonds" came on.

"Now *you* dance for *me*," he ordered, wiggling his eyebrows.

"Oh, you are such a sultan wannabe. I should be repulsed." Paris wrinkled her nose at him, but her lips were twitching and so were her hips.

And so we danced for him. And we laughed at ourselves. And we had the best time ever.

Paris gave Neal a comical version of a lap dance, which scandalized me only a wee bit. I stopped caring that I resembled a whale as I merengued in place. Whales weren't clumsy. They were graceful creatures. They swanned out of the ocean and twirled in the air, water spinning around them like tutus. They always made a splash. And dolphins. I loved dolphins. I could be a dolphin, I thought. I could make a splash.

Neal joined us again. We rolled through a rumba, a salsa and a tango. He knew how to twirl Paris and I knew how to twirl around him. Group dances were my thing, after all.

A few dances later, Paris excused herself to go to the bathroom, and so for a bit I had Neal all to myself. I liked it. No, I loved it. Group dances were always boisterous and fun. But dancing with a partner, a man, was sublime. Kaivan had been a good dancer. He and I had done a mean bachata.

"Let's do the bachata." Though how we'd manage with my football stomach, I had no clue. "It's like the merengue. Or no, like a tango. You know how to tango, right?"

Neal nodded, shimmying toward me.

"Hold me like you would for a tango but less formal. Closer." I put my left hand on the nape of his neck, and he took my right in his. But he was too tall, or I was too short for our positions to feel comfortable. And the belly wasn't helping.

I laughed when my belly bumped into his hips. "Okay. Not as close. Maybe we should try this at an angle. Oooh, feel that music?" The song—oh, the song was singing through my veins. I walked him through the steps, nothing fancy. And every movement was slow, sensual.

"It's like *Dirty Dancing*," he murmured, smiling slowly.

"Exactly, my lad." I twirled away from him and sashayed back. The bachata was all about attitude. There were no complicated steps or fixed routines, it was just whatever you were in the mood for, and what the music made you do. And right now, the music was dirty.

I had to look ridiculous dancing, but I didn't care, and by the end of the song, Neal and I were in splits. He shuffled the playlist to another Latin song, encouraging me to continue teaching him. The next number went a little smoother—he was getting the hang of it, getting confident. We were moving in sync, and he'd stopped thinking about the steps and was simply holding me, letting me dance as I wished, stopping me when my momentum would've spun me off the floor. He even dipped me, as far as I could bend my back—which wasn't far right now—and then pulled me up again as the song ended.

Our hearts had been racing already with all the dancing we'd done, and it showed in the way our chests moved up and down. His T-shirt had wet patches in the middle of his chest and armpits. His face was red from exertion, mine was too. Probably. He was still holding me as I dropped my hands. I was sweating—dancing did that to you—and a drop of it rolled off my forehead down my nose to hang there, shivering, at the tip. He flicked it off sweetly, his other hand squeezing my waist. Then his lips twisted into a slow, lopsided grin of thanks. Somehow, I knew he was thanking me for more than this dance.

I smiled in mute thanks in return. But the moment called for a hug, so I hugged him. His arms came around me slowly, squeezed me in affection. I sighed, feeling beyond contented right then, radiantly happy. When I stepped back, I saw Paris watching us from the hallway, a funny expression on her face.

"What's the matter, hen? Are you feeling okay?" Neal asked before I could.

She didn't answer. She didn't move. She just stood there staring at us with a face leached of color.

A ghost crawled up my spine. She could not think... I couldn't even put the horrible thought into words.

"Paris. No." I moved toward her. But she didn't spare me a glance. Her focus was on Neal. I couldn't tell if her eyes glittered from anger or tears. She shook my hand off when I touched her.

"You gave her my smile."

What? I looked at Neal in fright, wondering if he knew what she was talking about. But, I may as well have been invisible because he wasn't looking at me, either. He was frozen in a staring contest with his wife. Then slowly, like in a time-lapse video of an artist working on a watercolor, strokes of remorse colored his face.

Oh, God. *Oh, my God.*

He reached for her, but she threw her hands up in a Do Not Touch gesture.

"You protect her. Okay. You tease her, laugh with her… fine. But you *cannot* look at her the way you look at me."

I backed away from them. Whatever was happening here was not good, not at all good. Not for any of us. And yet…a bad, bad desire took root inside me. A desire I'd made a conscious effort not to address. It made me not feel good about myself. I put both my hands on my belly where our bairns—*their* bairns were coming awake. They knew I was upset. Their parents were upset.

"Paris." It was a plea. He was begging her to let it go.

I willed her to let it go.

"I can't do this anymore."

Neal stilled. And I pressed my lips together to stop the moan that wanted to spill out.

"Do what?" he asked, his tone harsh.

Would she destroy the family we'd created—hoped to create—because of a look? A smile?

I pressed my back against a wall as Paris began to systematically list the things she'd been thinking about for a while, that she'd been feeling but hadn't voiced. She didn't look angry or upset. She didn't sound it, either. She just stood in front of us, ramrod straight and admitted to feeling jealousy and revulsion and anger and hurt.

"I wanted you to have everything you've ever wanted, so you don't regret loving me." Her gaze flickered in my direction, then sprang back to Neal as if she couldn't bear to see me. "I didn't foresee the complications."

"Didn't ye? And ye call yerself smart?"

I turned to Neal in shock. His face was already shiny and pink from the dancing, now slashes of angry red marked his cheekbones. What was he doing? Had they both gone mad? I wanted to yell at them for being stupid, for even having this stupid, meaningless fight. But it wasn't my place. It had never been my intention to come between them. And it wasn't me Paris was upset with. It was him. And he was equally angry with her.

"I did the best I could. I think it's time to cut my losses." Her voice would have frozen the Hudson. And the colder Paris got, the angrier Neal seemed to grow.

And me? I didn't know what was happening to me. I only knew that if I moved away from the wall, I'd fall. And everything would be finished.

"Coward." The accusation rang across the room like a whip.

It ticked her off. "If I'm a coward, then you are a bloody, filthy liar. You never should have agreed to it...to any of it. You..." Her voice cracked then, and like an iceberg splitting into two, so did her facade. Oh, God, she'd bottled-up so much hurt.

"You betrayed me. I knew better than to trust my heart to you."

"Me? Ye brought this on us," Neal roared.

I flinched. I didn't want them to fight. I didn't want them to regret anything we'd done because this whole journey had been beautiful. We'd each given the best of ourselves to this cause, didn't either of them see that?

But if they did...split up... Where should my loyalties fall?

I wanted to scream at them to stop it. Couldn't they just put the babies first?

"I know what I did," Paris cried. "I'm trying to fix it."

Neal's hands curled into fists by his thighs. "What the fuck does that mean? There's nothing to fix."

"I wanted to give you a family and I have. Don't you see? I'm the redundant clause in this agreement. I'm the one who doesn't fit. And moreover, I don't want to fit. This is not what I want. I don't want a family. I've never wanted it. I don't want a house. I don't want family holidays and rituals and dogs and…bairns." Her voice wobbled on the last word. Abruptly, she walked into the kitchen and poured herself a glass of water with shaking hands.

"What are ye saying?" He wasn't shouting anymore, wasn't angry. It was as if Paris had thrown a glass of icy water on his face and snuffed it out.

"I'm saying this is not my scene. Not even a little bit. But it's yours. And hers. And you both deserve it. I mean that in the best possible way."

She said it so sincerely like she meant every word. She stopped next to me, tried to smile, failed.

"I should have chosen adoption," she whispered, and bruised my soul worse than my husband ever had. Then she walked out of the house.

And still, I stood where I was, afraid that if I moved, if I took my hands off my stomach, Neal would know what was wrong. He couldn't know. I didn't want him to get focused on me. He needed to run after his wife.

But instead of storming off after her, he sank down on the sofa and buried his face in his hands. I rubbed my belly, round and round, trying to calm the babies.

"She didn't mean it," I said softly. "You know that."

He looked up, his face hard. "She meant it."

I shook my head. "You know how she gets when she's afraid. She lashes out. Or builds a wall around herself. She's done all of this…" I looked down at my belly. "She put herself through this for you. Only for you. You have to know that."

A dull throbbing had started in my lower back. I didn't know if it was because I'd been standing for so long or the stupid dancing or if it was part of labor. For a second, I entertained the thought of telling Neal that I was most likely in labor and handing the reins over. But only for a second. He wasn't my knight in shining armor. He wasn't my anything at all.

"Go after her. Woo her back. Be the man she needs you to be."

He stood up and I thought he was going to go, but he started pacing up and down in front of me. The desire to lean on him was so strong. To let him sweep me off my swollen feet and carry me to the hospital so I could push our babies out. But I'd been selfish long enough, hogging all his attention, his goodness. I didn't blame Paris for thinking badly of me.

"And what if she makes me choose between her and the bairns? What then?"

God. What a thought. No wonder he looked as if he wanted to rip his head off.

"Just go. You'll figure it out."

What else could I say? I couldn't speak for Paris or make promises on her behalf. All I could do was hope it wouldn't come to that.

But, I could control my own actions. I had to step away. Neal wasn't my husband. These babies weren't mine. Oh, but how I wished both those things were true, if only for a second.

"Please go, Neal. Before it's too late." He had to leave before either one of us did or said something irrevocable.

I called Paris as soon as Neal left but it went to voice mail. I left her a message, a pithy one telling her to stop being an idiot and to call her husband, who was roaming the streets of New York like a madman, yelling out her name. I also told her that I forgave her for what she'd said to me and the twins. I told her I was sorry for making her feel…all the awful things she'd been feeling. I promised her I'd leave New York, move away after the babies were born. That she need never feel redundant. Because she wasn't. I was.

Then I called Dr. Kapoor and told her about the backache and the baby gymnastics, which were still going on but were restricted to a very small area of my belly.

"Did I induce an early labor by dancing?"

"I doubt it." She chuckled. "It's coincidence. We discussed that it was unlikely that you'd carry the twins to full term. A month early is not bad at all. You say you've been having mild back pain for a couple of days? And some nausea? That was probably the start of your early labor. Some labors are slow. So, don't panic. Just gather your things for a hospital stay, and go there. I will see you there. Good luck."

I couldn't believe I wasn't panicking at the thought of doing this alone.

But I wasn't alone, was I? I rubbed my belly. My babies were with me and would be with me through all of it. Maybe they'd be with me forever if Paris didn't want them.

Stop it. Stop thinking psycho baby-snatcher thoughts.

I waddled into my room and added extra sweaters and socks into my half-packed hospital bag. The weather had been seesawing between hot and cold since the beginning of October.

Whoa. Had it already been a year since I'd come to New York? I couldn't believe it. So much had happened since then.

I changed out of my yoga pants and tank into a maternity dress. Then I called a taxi and took the elevator down.

I forced myself not to think about what would happen after. I only wanted joyous and positive thoughts while bringing these two beautiful babies into the world.

The doorman rushed to help me with my bag when I waddled out of the elevator and into the lobby. He pressed the steel button with a blue wheelchair embossed on it, and an automatic door opened for me to shuffle through. I stopped short when I saw Neal striding back toward the building, head down and frowning at his phone.

No sign of Paris. Oh, God.

He looked up, noticed me and shook his head helplessly. "Were ye off to look for her too? Dinna bother. She's not answering her phone, is she? Where in fuck are we supposed to look for her on a Saturday? She's not at work…" He trailed off as he watched the doorman roll my olive green Briggs & Riley cabin bag out of the building and place it by my sneakered feet.

Neal's eyes went from my frozen face to my belly, now covered in a long winter coat even though it wasn't that cold yet. Slowly, his hand floated up and settled on my head to shake it hard. "Ye wee fool. Ye were going to suffer this alone?"

I was undone by his kindness, again.

"What about Paris?" I asked once we were on our way to the hospital, and I'd stopped wetting his chest in a deluge of gratitude.

He didn't answer immediately. He was staring out of the window. "I'll leave a message. She'll come or she won't." Then he looked at me. His blue eyes were bleak and stark when they should've been sparkling with joy. "That'll be my answer, aye?"

Why did people like Paris and Kaivan make life so complicated? Why did they bulldoze their decisions on everyone as if only they knew best?

CHAPTER TWENTY-THREE

Paris

I ran all the way to Lily's house in White Plains.

Well, not literally. I took the Metro-North and then ran along Hamilton Avenue to the small white cottage just off Church Street. I was crying and shivering when I walked into the house because I'd rushed out of my apartment without a coat or my handbag and in my house slippers.

I'd realized my folly as soon as I stepped out of the building, but I would've died before going back to the apartment and facing them. I borrowed money from the doorman and… Yeah, so here I was.

I headed straight into the hall bathroom. I simply had to pull myself together. What was the use of crying now? It was done. I'd broken us. In trying to control my life, I'd lost control of it completely.

"Here's a sweater for you, dearie." Rachel knocked at the door gently.

"Dank you," I croaked, opening the door. I barely recognized my voice. I sounded like a frog with a clogged nose.

I took the sweater from Rachel and pulled it over my old NYU sweatshirt, my at-home garb. I felt a bit more composed now, less shivery and growing angrier by the minute.

Why hadn't he stopped me from leaving? He could've run after me. I'd waited by the elevators, letting three of them go before taking the fourth one down. But he hadn't come, hadn't even poked his head out the door. He'd chosen them—his bairns over me. Maybe even Naira.

Fuck. I'd literally put the idea of the two of them as a couple into their heads. I was so stupid.

While I'd been in the bathroom, Lily had made a pot of tea. She was arranging a plate of cookies, and urged me to sit at the kitchen table when I hovered by the stove.

"Where's Rachel?" I asked, taking a seat.

"She's in her room." To give us privacy, I supposed.

Lily poured the tea into matching daisy-yellow cups, adding a healthy dose of brandy in mine. I wrapped my hands around the hot cup. "I didn't know I could hurt so much."

"Oh, honey." Lily placed her hand on my cheek. She was so warm.

Pressing my cheek to my shoulder, I trapped her hand in the crook of my neck. Just for a moment. Then, I let her go.

I had to let them all go.

I wiped my nose with the back of my hand, trying—desperately—to stop the tears. I took a healthy swallow of the brandied tea even though I wasn't thirsty. Maybe if I was drunk enough I'd stop this caterwauling.

"You were right all along. About marriage and rules and

society. About the consequences of flouting convention. About poking the damn sleeping tiger."

"Hmm." Lily sounded uncannily like Dr. Barr just then.

"I should never have married. I sure as hell shouldn't have started the baby madness. God, I'm such a schmo." What had I thought? That Neal would prostrate himself at my feet for all eternity because I'd given him his dream?

"Hush. You're not a stupid girl. And you meant well."

"He… They…" The scene at the apartment replayed in my head like a Lifetime movie. He'd had her in his arms. They'd been dancing, joking, laughing together. Then the music had stopped, but they didn't let go of each other. They stood there staring into each other's eyes, blushing. Or had they been—flushed from exertion? And then—*oh, God*—then his finger had skimmed her nose like he did mine. Tenderly. Sweetly. And he'd smiled at her, his sexy half-lidded smile that meant…that *meant* something.

"They've become good friends. I get that. But it hurts to see them be close. So in sync. They laugh at the same things, and finish each other's sentences. No matter what I do, I'm always looking in from the outside." Tears started dripping down my face again.

It was never enough, no matter what I did. I was never enough.

Lily shoved a bunch of tissues in my hand. "That's not true, *bubbala*."

But we both knew the truth. I'd always felt different, removed from Lily and even the Judge sometimes. To feel like that again in my own home, in my marriage, had killed me.

Neal had fallen for my feminism, my uncompromising attitude toward social change, justice, way of life. He'd accepted me with all my flaws. But as soon as I'd dangled the carrot of family in front of him, a normal family, he'd flipped. It had validated all my fears about us. Hadn't I always known deep in my heart that we would end?

"I need to renegotiate the coparenting and preconception agreements. Obviously, I can't be part of the family dynamic anymore. I…" I choked, took a large gulp of the tea. "I'll relinquish all rights to the twins. Naira's name can go on the birth certificate as the mother." I got to my feet, nausea rising in my throat. "I need to figure out my domestic arrangements."

Lily looked disappointed. "Speak to your husband first."

"Why? So he can humiliate me again? Call me a coward and a liar?" I rounded on Lily, suddenly incensed. "I told him I didn't want to go through with the surrogacy, that I wanted to stop it, stop everything. He refused. At Christmas, I asked if we could shorten our holiday because I was swamped with work. He refused. But he canceled our ski trip because Naira had morning sickness and he didn't want her to be alone. He takes her side in everything." Ugh. I sounded like a petulant, spoiled child. "And don't say he's only humoring a pregnant woman. He…he has feelings for her. Beyond that of what he'd have toward a surrogate gestating his bairns. He looked at her the way he looks at me and I couldn't… I cannot bear it." I broke into sobs again. I wanted to die.

"Oh, honey." Lily's arms came around me and I wept until I had no more tears left.

"I won't forgive him for that," I croaked.

Lily patted my back. "You will, once you calm down."

"No, I won't. I *can't*." I felt miserable.

"You can and you will. Now sit down and tell me what this is really about."

I was too taken aback by Lily's brusque tone to argue. Or maybe I needed to confess it all to someone. Either way, the words gushed out of me like blood from a fresh wound.

"I'm prickly and uncompromising. Unlikable. Neal was

bound to open his eyes one day. He's beginning to. He has to be comparing us, maybe without meaning to, but he must be. She's how a woman is supposed to be, how a mother is supposed to feel. And I know the twins will love her and... hate me. How could they not? I just want to spare us all the heartache and finish it now."

"Oh, Pari. Samuel was prickly and stubborn as a mule. You get that from him, honey. But did that stop us from loving him? Oh, my dear, I'm so sorry you have all these doubts about yourself. It's my fault—mine and Samuel's that you feel this way." She patted my cheek when I would've spoken, protested. "I knew what you went through before you came to live with us and yet I didn't...couldn't risk opening my heart to another child. You needed me, needed my support and unconditional love and I failed you."

"That's not true," I protested weakly.

"Oh, it's true. And Samuel didn't help by being who he was—a judge first and a father second. I know you loved him and worshipped the ground he walked on, and you pleased him so much. You were the light of his life. But he should not have let me wallow in my grief for our Jessie. He should not have taught you to be belligerent and tough, and to put your head above your heart. He didn't handle either of us well."

Lily talked about the past until both of us were drained. I was so confused. And stunned. What she'd said... But I didn't have the strength to deal with any of it just then.

"Can I nap in your room for a bit?" Tomorrow. I'd resolve it tomorrow.

Did I really mean to walk away from my marriage? Did I mean to reject the twins just like I'd been rejected—not once but thrice? If I walked away from them, and from Neal, that was the legacy I'd bequeath them. That they'd been unwanted by their biological mother.

But, how could I stay? If Neal stopped loving me I'd…

I'd just have to get over it. I'd survived a broken heart before, hadn't I? And he'd clearly chosen his future. He hadn't come after me. I had to prepare.

As Lily led me into her bedroom, I determined not to think about it anymore. I'd deal with it all tomorrow.

For all her personality mutations, Lily's room was exactly the way it had been when we'd lived on the Upper East Side. Heavy wooden furniture; a monochromatic color scheme; the throw that smelled of patchouli. It comforted me so much. I lay down, pulling a thick quilt over me.

When I'd been a teenager, I couldn't wait to grow up and take charge of my life. But now? I'd happily regress to childhood and let Lily and the Judge take care of me.

Lily switched off the lights. "Sleep. I'll wake you in a bit."

"Thank you." I'd been about to shut my eyes when Rachel burst into the room.

"Naira's in labor. Neal left a message on my phone. He's been looking for you everywhere. Lily, dear, he's been calling you too. Have you misplaced your phone again?"

"What? But she's not due for another five weeks!" I bolted out of the bed. Twins rarely gestated full-term, and three weeks ago, Naira had crossed into the safe delivery zone. Still.

Then I remembered everything else. Guilt roared through me, and drilled a hole in my gut. Fuck. Had I triggered Naira's early labor? Had I put the babies in jeopardy because of my insecurities and abandonment issues?

"I can't go to the hospital. This is my fault. Don't you see? I'll only make it worse." Oh, God. I'd told her I'd rather have adopted. What kind of a monster was I?

Lily tsk-tsked. "This isn't how we raised you, young lady. You will hop yourself down to that hospital right now and take charge of your family."

344 • THE OBJECT OF YOUR AFFECTIONS

I burst into tears again. I supposed I'd accumulated enough of them over the years, when I'd have died but not cried, to fill the Great Lakes.

And it was just what I needed to hear. *My family.*

I hugged Lily…this little woman who I refused to call my mother. "Thank you. I love you," I said, kissing her papery Audrey Hepburn cheek. "Mom."

Of course, that set her off. But as Lily had pointed out, blubbering would have to wait.

I rushed inside the hospital as Lily and Rachel drove off in their cute red Mazda. I'd sent them home to bring back my handbag and phone and shoes and some clothes and the food Anjum had said Naira needed to eat after the babies were born.

All the way into the city, I'd cursed myself for forgetting my phone at home, conjuring up worst-case scenarios about what was happening at the hospital. Clearly, something had gone wrong. Had they taken her straight into the operating room? It was safer to deliver twins in an OR, even naturally, in case they needed to perform an emergency C-section.

How could I have been so stupid? became a litany in my head.

I was Naira's designated birthing coach. Not Neal. She'd be panicking without me.

I skidded to a stop at the reception, got Naira Dalmia's information and felt slightly better when they told me she was still in the birthing suite. Okay. Not an emergency…yet.

Briskly, I made my way to the maternity care unit on the fifth floor. There was a family and visitor area just outside the ward teeming with people and balloons and bears and happiness. But as I crossed over to the labor and birthing section, my feet began to drag. Then they turned to lead.

Suddenly, it was impossible for me to take another step or

breath. This was happening. Right now. My life was changing in scary, irreversible ways. Right now.

Was this what I wanted?

I whipped about and dashed down the corridors to the elevators. They were fine. It was okay. I didn't need to be here. I didn't want to be here. They had a whole hospital at their disposal. I would just be in the way. A grumpy annoyance.

I sank down on the floor by the elevators, wrapped my arms around my stomach and moaned. People rushed to me, asking me if I was sick and whether I needed a doctor. I growled at them until they backed the hell off.

God. Humans and their nosiness. Could a woman not have a panic attack in peace?

I crawled out of the way of major foot traffic and sat with my back pressed against a wall, my legs up to my chest, and began to inhale and exhale like Linda, the Lamaze instructor, had shown us. Five minutes of deep breathing and I felt reasonably sane. I sprang up and marched down the hallway again. It took me another five minutes to get up the nerve to knock on the door of the birthing suite. I kept thinking about Neal smiling at Naira, holding her close. If they hadn't noticed me, would they have kissed?

Could we ever go back to the way things used to be?

Determined to face whatever I had to, I pushed open the birthing suite to Naira's helpless whimpers. She was sitting up in bed, pillows stacked behind her. Her legs were spread, slightly bent at the knees, and covered with a light blue blanket. She was clutching the sidebars of the hospital bed so hard that they were shaking.

Neal wasn't kissing her. He was nowhere near her. Rather, he was standing in one corner of the room like a naughty boy who'd been punished by his elementary schoolteacher. In his hand was a remote—*oh, shit*. He hadn't listened. I shook my head. I'd told him the stupid electrode machine wouldn't help with the pain. Only an epidural would, which Naira had chosen not to get because of the mishap I'd suffered after my egg retrieval. And also because we'd been told that sometimes, with the epidural, the woman in labor may not be able to push as hard, and if that were the case the chances of a C-section increased, or the doctor might need to pull the bairns out with a suction cup.

The minute Neal's agitated eyes met mine, his whole posture changed, went slack with relief.

I ignored him, went straight to Naira.

"Good. Long and deep breaths in counts of twenty-two." I touched her hand, felt tears well up in my eyes to match those that spilled down her cheeks. Neal was right. I was a coward. I'd been so stupid, so selfish. "I'm sorry. I'm so sorry for freaking out."

When her contraction passed, she stopped gritting her teeth long enough to glare murderously at Neal. "Be sorry later. Get your husband and that damned remote out of here before I kill them both." Right then, Naira looked exactly as she sounded—one pissed-off Valkyrie.

"Done." And I burst out laughing.

Events unfolded quickly from there with no medical complications. Both babies were in the vertex/vertex position and stayed that way even during late labor and the transition. They moved Naira into the OR, where, besides Dr. Kapoor and our midwife, two pediatricians, two pediatric nurses and an anesthesiologist were also present—just in case.

But my waiflike best friend was no weakling, and despite the moaning, babbling, praying and panting—did anyone truly expect a woman giving birth to maintain any sort of breathing pattern or verbal etiquette?—delivered our twins like a trouper.

I wasn't quite so sanguine. But as long as I was useful—holding Naira's hand or massaging her back or timing her contractions or wiping sweat from her face—I was okay. I had a perfect view of what was going on from behind Naira's shoulder, and the whole time Naira pushed and pushed and screamed and pushed, I shook. How the fuck did women do this? And survive?

My heart started pounding in terror. What would we do if…

"Congratulations! It's a girl!" sang Dr. Kapoor through a hospital mask, holding up a tiny little human, already wailing and pumping her arms and legs. She was mostly bald.

"A *girl*. A sweet, sweet girl." Naira smiled through her tears.

The world tilted—or was it just me?—as I watched the doctor clamp and cut the umbilical cord. Someone else wiped fluids from tiny human orifices before she was swaddled in a blanket and brought forth for inspection.

The girl was covered in vernix, a white substance with loads of antibacterial properties. That was good. Her Apgar score was six. Which was acceptable, but not great.

"Here you go, Mommy," said the nurse, holding the squirming bundle out like a pagan sacrifice.

I clasped my hands behind my back, while Naira reached for the baby, crying, laughing, still in labor. We all froze when it became clear that the nurse was offering the squealing bundle to me and not Naira. I was the intended mommy, after all.

I took a step back from the bed. There was no way I was holding a human that tiny on my own.

"Give the baby to her." I pointed at Naira, who began to shake her head and wipe her eyes with the backs of her hands.

"You should hold her first, Paris. You're her mother." She

gasped suddenly as if she was in the most god-awful pain—which she was.

I came around the bed so she could see my face clearly. "So are you. I'm not sure…"

"Paris, just hold your daughter! *Gaaah!*" Naira yelled, then fell back against the pillows, grunting and groaning.

Not even I would argue with a woman in labor.

That Great Lake inside me? It spilled over and just wouldn't quit when little miss Samyra Naira Fraser was placed in my trembling arms for the first time. Thank God the nurse didn't let go until I was sure I wouldn't drop her.

I gaped at the wee creature Neal and I had made. That Naira had helped bring into this world.

Was it weird and icky to hold a wrinkly, blood-covered mini human in your arms? You'd better believe it. Would I do it again? I did, slightly more confidently, when Liam Neal Fraser shot out of his birth mother and howled his displeasure at the world—just like his biological mother often did—as soon as he was cleaned up.

Their father had slipped inside the steel-forged walls of my heart like a stealth missile. Our babies smashed through the remaining debris like battering rams and staked their claims on me forever.

So, there it was. Motherhood was as painful as I'd imagined it to be. As scary and immense. I worried the twins would hate me for not carrying them, laboring for them, breastfeeding them. I worried they'd love Naira more for all those reasons. But what if, despite it all, my babies loved me just like their father did? Like I was afraid I was beginning to love them. Because as Lily said, being prickly and uncompromising and unlikable didn't mean you couldn't be loved.

After Naira had cooed and gushed and showered kisses on our precious cargo, I brought the twins out to where their father waited with Lily and Rachel and friends and family. Neal rushed forward. Of course, he cried when he saw our babies for the first time. He'd cried reciting the vows at our wedding too. I hadn't.

"*Mazel tov*, Daddy," I said softly, watching him fall in love with our babies. I didn't even get jealous. Okay, I did. Slightly.

He gathered us into the strong circle of his arms, just holding us. Adoring us. He kissed us one by one. I was the last to get his attention, but his lips lingered on mine the longest.

"Are we good?" he asked, his blue-blue eyes solemn and forgiving.

I sighed, letting love fill the pockets of doubt inside my damaged heart. There was nothing I wouldn't do for this man. Or for the precious sweeties we'd made. If that meant I'd have to risk heartbreak from time to time, so be it.

"We're perfect."

CHAPTER TWENTY-FOUR

Naira

I woke in semidarkness to the beeps and hums of hospital machines, and the scent of antiseptic and antibacterial cleaning agents. It was weird, but I loved the sanitized smell of a hospital.

Groggily, I rolled to the left, my favored sleeping position, and came instantly awake as a burning pain shot between my legs because I'd jostled my episiotomy stitches. I sucked in a painful breath as sweat popped up on my forehead and along my lip.

I'd thought I'd known what childbirth would be like. I'd read dozens of birthing books, listened to firsthand anecdotes from surrogates and mothers. I'd devoured every single horrible story plastered on the internet about labor pains and birthing twins. I'd thought I was prepared in mind and body for a natural birth. I was wrong.

Let me set one thing straight: *nothing* prepared you for actual childbirth. It was an event one had to experience to fully appreciate.

I remembered cursing at myself during the pushing phase for refusing an epidural and a C-section. I remembered screaming for drugs. *"NOW! Please. Oh, please, take the pain away!"* But the utterly magnificent, most handsome anesthesiologist had explained it was too late to administer an epidural. Instead, he fed me oxygen through a mask and let me squeeze all the bones of his hand into pulp. He was my hero.

I shifted again, slowly, carefully this time, to a more comfortable position. I'd been instructed not to sit upright until the stitches healed, or didn't feel as tender. I had to either stand or lie down, even while breastfeeding. Which was fine with me. I didn't think I had the energy to move yet. My bones were soup, my muscles like spaghetti. Oh, I was a mishmash of emotions and aches from scalp to toe. But the worst, the deepest pain was in my soul.

What was I supposed to do now?

I touched my belly where the babies had lived for eight-and-a-half months. It was no longer round like a drum under the hospital gown, but sore and as squishy as freshly kneaded dough. I wanted to go to the babies. To see them again. Hold them.

My beautiful babies. So precious and sweet. They already displayed distinct personalities. Samyra had had to be coaxed into taking her first meal, the power-packed colostrum from my breasts in the OR. She was a light and fussy eater. I'd bawled, beyond honored and humbled that she had my name, and the Judge's—Samyra Naira. I'd bawled when I fed Baby Liam too. The greedy little guy had stolen my heart as soon as he'd been placed in my arms. He'd latched onto my nipple and not let go until he'd had his fill. I'd have happily let him drain every ounce of nutrients from my body, but I'd been fighting to stay awake by then, and the OR staff had been in the process of shifting me into a regular maternity room, and the twins to the neonatal intensive care unit.

"We'd like to keep them under observation in NICU for twenty-four hours since they were born at thirty-four weeks. There's nothing to worry about. They're both in good health. The girl is nearly six pounds, and the boy is a solid six and a half. It's strictly a precaution," the pediatricians had explained.

All night, Paris and Neal had taken turns to peek in on the babies while I rested. I hadn't seen the little ones since their second feeding just after midnight, when they'd been brought to me. I hadn't been alone with them even once. Paris hadn't left my side except to go to the bathroom or the NICU. Her commitment was wonderful in a way, but I was desperate for a few minutes alone with my babies.

But they weren't *my* babies, were they? They were hers.

All of a sudden, sobs hacked my upper body and I had to bite my lip hard to keep from crying. I turned my face into the pillow to muffle the sounds of my weeping. Paris was sound asleep on the pullout sofa beside me and I didn't want to wake her up. Didn't want her sympathy or hugs or her apologies or reassurances. I couldn't get yesterday out of my head. The awful stab in my soul when she'd said she should have adopted.

My tears burned away as a rush of anger blasted through me toward her *and* Neal. Why had she done it? Why had she said those things? Why had he smiled at me?

But she'd rallied in the end, hadn't she? my conscience reasoned.

So what? Did it make it all okay? And what about the next time she got scared or offended or objected to something?

What then? Had I really thought coparenting would work? And if it couldn't work, what in hell was I supposed to do now?

I cried for a long time. I felt gutted. And yet, when the door opened and brought with it a profusion of sunshine, I forced a smile on my face and opened my heart to love. I'd been expecting the lactation nurse to roll in Samyra and Liam for their breakfast, and so was utterly dumbfounded when my sister walked in instead, carrying an Ernie and an Elmo soft toy and about a dozen pink and blue balloons.

"Surprise! And congratulations!" Grinning madly, Sarika bounced into the room in metallic Stella McCartney sneakers and a velour pink travel tracksuit.

My sister was a plumper, broader version of our mother, but was several inches taller than either of us. Of the three Manral women, Sarika had the best skin and hair—a peaches-and-cream complexion, and thick, lush tresses that fell to her waist in stylized waves. It swished about her shoulders as she looked around the room, trying to find a free spot for the soft toys and the balloons. Finally, she placed them in the corner by the windows and turned to me.

"What…are you doing here?" I couldn't stop gaping at her.

"I couldn't let Mummy come alone. Besides, postnatal care for one child is harrowing enough in the first few weeks, and you have twins. You need all the help you can get if you want to get any sleep," she said as if it explained anything.

I'd called my mother when I'd gone into labor, and she'd meant to take the first flight out of Mumbai to New York. I wanted my mother by my side when I felt so vulnerable. I needed her help to do the right thing.

Neal was supposed to pick her up at the airport at 8:30 a.m. and bring her straight to me. Which meant it was later than I'd thought. With the curtains closed, the light was falsely diffused inside the room, making it seem like it was barely dawn.

Sarika bent down to kiss my forehead and give me a brief hug, her gaze softening when she saw my face up close. My eyes had to be red and swollen and devastated.

"Oh, *choti*. The pain and haywire hormones are going to make you crazy. Be happy at least the pain fades in a couple of days."

Sarika had gone through natural childbirth twice and her boys had been nine and ten pound babies each. I guess she knew what she was talking about.

"I sent Mummy home with Neal. They'll be back once she's prepared the fattening food she'll start feeding you for milk production and whatnot. Don't eat everything she gives you or you'll end up round like me, and there's no getting rid of pregnancy weight. Trust me, *choti*."

My mouth dropped open at her unsolicited advice. This whole scene was just...bizarre. "But...what about *jiju*? Our problems?"

That was when Paris woke up. We'd been whispering, not softly enough though. She blinked at Sarika in confusion for a few seconds before her eyes cut to mine and her eyebrows touched her hairline. *Want me to boot her out of here?* her expression read.

I sighed tiredly. "Paris, can you give us a few minutes? I want to talk to my sister."

"Sure, honey. I'll check on the bairns." She rolled out of bed, stretching to wake herself more fully, and frowned. "Hey! Did the kiddos finish nursing already?"

"No. The nurse hasn't brought them to me yet. Find out what's going on?"

"Absolutely," she said, marching out of the room.

The first thing Paris had thought of were the babies. She was going to be a fantastic mother whether she realized it or not. She didn't need me at all.

Feeling pathetic tears prick my eyes, I looked at my sister again. "Why are you really here, *didi*?"

Her smile fell from her face. "It's come to this, huh? You don't trust me even a little?"

Was she kidding me? I closed my eyes briefly and counted to ten. "Why are you here? What do you want from me?" What new pound of flesh did she and her husband want?

"I don't want anything. Mummy told me what you want to do for Arhan and Sidh. Their college fund. I… Thank you," she said, sitting down on the bed next to me and taking my hand in hers.

I squeezed her hand. "It's nothing. I adore your boys."

"I know." She brushed my hair from my forehead with a manicured finger, her eyes glittering with regret and shame. "He's my husband, Naira. I have to believe him, don't you see? Our marriage won't survive if I don't."

I flinched at her flawed reasoning because that was exactly what I'd told myself when Kaivan got in trouble, and the media crucified him. Had I been as big of a fool as Sarika?

"And I'm your sister. Your younger sister. You were supposed to take care of me, help me." No, Sarika's and my situations were nothing alike. Kaivan had protected me. I should not doubt it.

"You don't need my help, *choti*. You always land on your feet. You get away with everything," she said, her mouth twisting. And there. Jealous Sarika was back.

"You're kidding, right? Get away with what? Sarika, you're the one who has everything. I have lost everything, remember? My husband, my business. My whole life is gone. I've just given birth to two beautiful little souls…and I have to give them up too. They are not mine. They… I am not their mother. I'm… I'm…"

Nobody. Oh, God. My chest hurt as badly as if I'd cracked a rib. I squeezed my eyes shut, willing myself not to cry again.

"You are their birth mother."

I froze. That…had not been my sister. My eyes flew open, met Sarika's, who seemed to have gone still as a statue too. She looked over her shoulder and quickly stood up.

Paris stalked into the room, a pink-swaddled baby in her arms. She looked cross. Paris, not the baby. Little Samyra was sleeping, the sweetheart. My breasts started leaking of their own volition as soon as Paris set her down, ever so gently, beside me. My eyes drank in the sight of Samyra's sweet face and rosebud mouth, like her mother's, which was sucking on an imaginary nipple.

Paris straightened up and slapped her hands on her hips, her own pout out in full disapproving force. "Now then, are you going to stop doubting that we're in this together, or shall I sue you for breach of a coparenting contract?"

I started laughing even as my tears slid out from my eyes, wetting the pillow. "Are you sure?" I asked. "I don't want you to feel bad because of me."

Paris lost some of her fierceness then. She took the spot Sarika had vacated and cupped my cheek in her hand. "I am sorry, Naira. For yesterday. For the last few months. Shit, for the last few years. Please forgive me, honey. Don't you know you are my family?"

I nodded, sniffling. "As you are mine."

Eleven months and three weeks later…

A scary sort of excitement gripped me as a private taxi pulled up in front of a grand mansion in the suburbs of New York City. A promenade of red and yellow leaves covered the driveway like a welcome mat. Fall had crackled into place here too, as it had in London.

I got out of the car while the driver took out my luggage—three of my trusted Briggs & Riley suitcases. My trip had extended longer than expected, but had been super successful. Fraser Bespoke was now officially launched in four countries around the world, and Deven had finally agreed we could, potentially, slow down the launch madness. Just a tad.

"Look who's in time for the birthday party!"

I spun around, squealing as Neal came toward me, carrying a piece of my heart in his arms. Oh, the little lamb had had a growth spurt in the six weeks I'd been gone. His face was shaping up like his father's, the promise of the broad Singh Fraser bone structure beneath the chub. Minus the blue eyes. The twins both had dark brown eyes from their mother or perhaps their grandmother, Minnie Auntie.

I kissed little Liam on his lollipop cheek, breathing in his syrupy baby smell. God, I'd missed them. Would they remember me after six weeks? Would they know me, know my smell since I was no longer nursing them?

"Welcome home." Neal kissed both my cheeks. He looked as tired as I felt. The shadows under his eyes hadn't lessened a bit. Our angels kept completely separate sleep schedules.

"Can I hold him?" I asked, afraid to simply pluck the babe out of Neal's arms like I would've done a mere six weeks ago. I was petrified Liam would cringe away from me as if I were a stranger. The twins were turning one next week. They recognized faces, knew who was family and displayed clear preferences.

Neal quirked an eyebrow at my coyness, then he simply deposited the baby in my arms.

"Oh, be still my heart. I missed you, my little bunny rabbit," I cooed as the weight and warmth of my godson, whom I'd brought into this world and nourished with my milk, settled in my arms.

And when he giggled at me, snuggling his head in the crook of my neck, everything disappeared—stress, anxiety, backache, my homicidal intentions towards Liam's ruthless whip-master of an uncle, Deven. Everything vanished into the clear blue autumn sky, leaving only love and hope behind.

Neal took my bags inside, and I bounced Liam into the house. I crossed the threshold, and removing my shoes in the bright, sky-lit foyer, I quickstepped my way into the family room that had been converted into a playroom. It made Liam laugh so I twirled him some more, coming to a dizzy stop.

The playroom had already been colorfully chaotic when I'd left on my business trip, and it was even more so now. Princess Samyra was fast asleep on the *Blue's Clues* floor mat, her cuddly giraffe by her side. I wondered if she still loved playing peekaboo, and would shyly hide her face in her mother's long hair until I coaxed her out with silly faces and love. I blew her a kiss, then quickstepped over to the kitchen.

I found Paris there, hands on her hips—not cooking as usual. She was supervising the sanitizing of baby bottles and nipples and standing on the cook's head as the poor woman stirred an organic breakfast broth for the little still-toothless wonders.

"You're home. Finally." She gave me a hug, looking harried. Then, she gestured to the charming mess of her domicile, which included her husband, son and sleeping baby daughter. "Your turn. I'm going to shower and head to work."

"Hear that, my peach? It's just you and me on this play-date," I said, smooshing another wet, noisy kiss on Liam's chubby cheek.

We walked out of the kitchen and crossed the playroom together.

"How's the family?"

I gave Paris the classic Indian head nod, a weird side-to-side movement that denoted both *yes* and *no* and *so-so*.

My father-in-law was slowly moving toward oblivion. My mother-in-law was learning to cope. My father was still miffed with me. My mother was still trying to marry me off, and had roped my sister in on the mission. My nephews were getting snarky. And Vinay...was no longer my problem.

Paris paused on the first step of the stairs that led up to the bedrooms. Mine was on the far right of the landing.

"I heard you went on a date?"

I blushed, thinking of Vikram Cooper's thick beard and teasing wit, and Deven's outright rudeness when Vik had come to pick me up at Fraser Bespoke and I'd introduced them. "Not exactly a date, but kind of. And I didn't figure Deven for a gossip. Anyway, long story. Come back early and I'll share, especially as I think you'll want to meet Vik too for RiM. Big philanthropist."

"Ah. And will do," she said, dashing up the stairs. "Or, meet me in the city and we can gossip over Girlfriend Cocktails," she yelled down from the top of the stairs.

"That sounds even better," I hollered back, making Liam giggle again. Clan Fraser did not startle easily. "And we'll round up Auntie Lavinia and Auntie Karen too!"

I went back into the playroom. Neal had woken his daughter up from a nap, and was trying to jiggle her into a good mood. He was semi-succeeding.

Princess Samyra hated having to suffer one of the most senseless rituals of the world—breakfast, early in the morning—and she was letting her opinion be known.

Oh, but it was good to be home.

★ ★ ★ ★ ★

ACKNOWLEDGMENTS

Let me begin by thanking Niyati V Reddy, who shared her surrogacy journey with me and answered all my questions with candidness and generosity.

Thanks also to Regina Kyle for opening up the daring world of US prosecutors to me. Although I'm bummed that law and order IRL doesn't really play out like *Law & Order*.

To Stacey Agdern and KK Hendin, thank you for helping me distinguish *kvell* from *kvetch*.

My forever gratitude to Lisa Wexler, friend, artist and sounding board, for her uncanny ability to see past the first nonsensical draft of a story to the gem within.

It is every writer's dream to work with an editor who not only champions her work but gets the heart of the work. Allison Carroll is my dream editor and I am truly privileged to work with her. Thank you, Allison. None of this would be possible without you.

Thanks to the entire Graydon House Books/Harlequin team for their kind, enthusiastic and timely support. Tahra Seplowin for your boundless cheer; Linette Kim and Shara Alexander for showing me an amazing time at PLA; Pamela Osti for answering all my silly questions. And Lisa Wray, there are no words to express my awe for what you do. Thank you so much!

HarperCollins India for the gorgeous covers and support.

Many thanks to my agent, Andrea Somberg, for tirelessly opening doors for me to waltz through.

Kathleen Carter, thank you for expanding my world of "possibles."

Kate Tilton, thank you for taking care of all the tedious minutiae of a writer's life for me.

A special thanks to my writer friends from RWA and WFWA, all my ladies from Fiction From the Heart, my tribe from India—S, RT, Sue and AB. All of you are as inspiring and multifaceted as you are talented and I am so fortunate to know you.

To my family and closest friends, your patience with me is mind-boggling. Never lose it.

And lastly, to all my readers, thank you for your invaluable support.

THE
OBJECT OF YOUR
AFFECTIONS

FALGUNI KOTHARI

Reader's Guide

GRAYDON
HOUSE

1. What did you think of the title of the novel? What does the phrase *Object of Affection* mean? To whom and what does the title apply to?

2. Which of the two main characters (Paris and Naira) do you most relate to and why? Do you relate to any other characters in the novel?

3. What are some of the themes the novel touched on?

4. Discuss the special friendship Paris and Naira share. Do you share such a friendship with anyone? What are the pros and cons of such a friendship?

5. Discuss what parenthood means to Paris, Naira and Neal. Or, any of the other characters. What does it mean to you?

6. One of the themes explored in the novel is modern women in modern relationships. What do you think about surrogacy and unconventional lifestyle choices? How relevant are they to our times and to you?

7. Do you think Paris was being selfish or selfless about her choices? What about Naira and Neal? What would you have done in their positions?

8. Family is an important theme in the novel. Discuss the various family dynamics shown between Paris, Naira and Neal with each other and with their various families.

9. All the characters changed over the course of the novel. Discuss how and why. Who do you think underwent the biggest change?

10. Did the novel surprise you or change you? If so, why?

11. Paris, Naira and Neal come from diverse backgrounds. What did you learn from them? How are their lifestyles similar to yours or different from yours?

12. Discuss setting. How did it enhance the plot and/or the themes of the novel?

13. Have you read other books by this author? How did they compare with this one?

14. Share a favorite quote. Why is it your favorite?

15. Who would you recommend *The Object of Your Affections* to? And why?